Book Two of the Trilogy:
The Last Scroll

The Return of the Ka
&
the Mending of the Su

Patricia S. Christy

ISBN: 978-1629671222
Library of Congress Control Number: 2018938995

PRAISE FOR THE TRILOGY

"This story is contemplative, moody, and cleverly subversive... (Temple's) spiritual journey is engrossing...and many other characters are written with delightful complexity... It's nice to keep this in mind—that these characters feel alive and true...Christy's imaginative scope is daunting, thrilling, and just plain fun."

~ **Kelsey Vetter / Blogger/Pagegirl**

★ ★ ★

"Although this reader generally shies away from publications of a spiritual nature, I was pleasantly surprised by Patricia S. Christy's first tome in the Last Scroll Trilogy. "The Education of Temple Fox" contains all the elements of a terrific adventure novel (a genre I heartily embrace), comparing favorably with works by Douglas Preston, Lincoln Child and Clive Cussler. When Fox's biplane, a de Havilland Moth, is struck by lightning, he's forced to parachute into the sea. Rescued by denizens of a nearby island, the mythical and mysterious Makol, Temple is received by the inhabitants as a long awaited god. Populated with such memorable characters as mountainous Queen Palomei, High Shaman Mefakani and the gauguinesque Losha, Christy expertly weaves a sublime and fascinating plot, which I believe will appeal to a diverse audience. The pleasures of "Temple Fox" are not ephemeral, but like any good work of art, remain with the reader, encouraging thought and instilling wonder. I look forward to obtaining a bound copy upon publication, destined to occupy an honored niche in my home library."

~ **J. Michael Modlin**

★ ★ ★

"Probably the most ingeniously skillful and creative writer I have ever read... An amazing wordsmith... Very captivating, alluring, suspense filled and funny!"

~ **Marisol Cervantes**

★ ★ ★

"Christy is a genius. This powerful story is delicious...rich, hopeful, insightful and spiritually expansive."

~ **Mimi Kates, Songwriter/Musician**

"I gobbled up the pages and fell in love with the characters. It was like taking a thrill ride through an expanded version of reality that included the presence of past-lives, ghosts, primitive creator gods, a power lusty shaman, and even aliens! As Temple Fox expands his own consciousness through the story, you find that his awakening process is not so unlike our own. Wonderful!!"

~ Stacie Coller, Author of Awake in Angelscape

★　　★　　★

"Phenomenal! Great read. Couldn't put it down."

~ Bobbe Allender

★　　★　　★

"I'm writing to tell you how riveting The Education of Temple Fox was for me, and how I needed THIS story, this MOMENT. Although remembering one's divinity is an ongoing necessity, your book's adventures and character epiphanies have been a very helpful reminder of that for me right now. The voice of your writing, so clear and lyrical, was a pleasure in itself. So thanks for all the work of all the years that went into your book and for the persistence of putting it out there."

~ Susa Silvermarie, Poet/Author

★　　★　　★

"I could not put this book down. I wanted to keep reading to the end. No housework got done while reading this book. So many life lessons imbedded within. So many interesting characters. What a wonderful imagination and talent this author has and I look forward to more of her books."

~ Carol A. Taylor

★　　★　　★

"Welcome to the magic. Christy takes her readers by the hand and sweeps us into a strange land. The rules of life are as different as the characters who live here. The joys, the love, the tragedies and the hate, however, sound a familiar chord. This books brings both fantasy at its best and reality at its most poignant. A spellbinding read and a great first book of Christy's long-awaited trilogy."

~ Bob O'Connor, Author of Unholy Ground & Unholy Seed - A Max Steele Thriller

FOR

Kit,

My Beloved,

&

For The Spirit Which Moves In All Things

ACKNOWLEDGEMENTS

I am most grateful to my partner, Kit Moorehead, for understanding my need to write, and for allowing me the time to express myself. I couldn't have written this book without her love and continual support. Thank you. I love you.

My gratitude goes to Myra Schoen for her generous spirit, her editing expertise, her sound advice for improving the manuscript, and for her friendship. Thank you for mentoring me and making me a better writer. In addition, I would like to thank Suzanne Hinton Kahn, who made her husband jealous by falling in love with Temple Fox. She helped to edit the beginning of the second manuscript with great humor, and encouraged my writing efforts.

Acknowledgement goes to my Publishing Consultant, Brian Schwartz, past President of the Colorado Independent Publisher's Association, and Veronica Yager for their expertise in turning my manuscript into reality.

Appreciation goes to Barbara Lakshmi Kahn's brilliant graphic design for the book. You rock!

Thank you to my old friend, Barbara Jones-Smith and Richard Brown, for their financial assistance to keep me afloat. Your friendship has been invaluable.

A big thank you goes to my next door neighbor, Sandra Schmidt, who bolstered my spirits by giving me gifts of homemade creams and herbal potions honoring my character, Elder Tani. It kept my spirits up, and made the writing of this all the more real.

It is best, perhaps, to list some of the people who contributed to my thinking and parts of my writing. I acknowledge Luke Easter for her quote about the strength of women. I thank my friend, Stacie Coller, for her wise affirmations so brilliantly expressed in her book: 'Awake in Angelscape', and to Diane Wolkstein and Samuel Noah Kramer whose book, 'Inanna, Queen of Heaven and Earth' helped me to form the song in the second to last chapter. Thanks go to Jaes Seis, as well as other shamans who taught me about soul retrievals, and other shamanic healing concepts. I am also beholding to 'A Course in Miracles' published by the Foundation for Inner Peace for its inspiring thought provoking wisdom. Bless you all.

THE LAST SCROLL

BOOK II: THE RETURN OF THE KA AND THE MENDING OF THE SU

TABLE OF CONTENTS

MAKOLESE GLOSSARY OF TERMS

Adiwan A'geed: Ancient male Makolese prophet

Agaluga: Spirit of the Tornado

Ahglehsh'kahlah: Spirit of the Lizard

banalak: A bitter plant used to thicken sauces.

Beata: Ancient female Makolese prophet

'bi kana' or 'bi kana lo': Slang for "Help me Gods!" or "Oh my soul!" Sometimes meaning, "Eat someone else!" or "Eat me raw!" which is a coarse, lesser used archaic term, referencing Makolese history when the Royals of the Si Te Cah Clan engaged in cannibalism.

Boddaloto: A man-god from the Makolese ancient past

brahmatic codes: The template of subtle light energies in genetic codes

bu-dahl: Ritual dagger

bunya: 'Boss man' in Swahili

Cabiria: Ancient female Makolese prophet

channak: A ritual bowl made of tortoise shell

Chokahpeiyape: *(pronounced: Cho'-ka-pay'-ya-pee')* A derogatory word aimed at a woman, meaning: 'One who no one wants' or 'One who cannot bear children'.

Chumban Mati: "Kissing Sun" when the Sun touches its reflection in the water. Also known as the "Twin Sun" *(Judavaan Mati)* or the "Vain Sun" *(Sia-Sia Mati).*

Dakini: Ancient female Makolese prophet

Fuzail: A male Moslem name meaning "an accomplished person".

Gadji: An old man and the lone survivor on Makol Island after it was destroyed in ancient times. Consort to the Goddess Hianna worshipped by the Makolese.

gris: Specially designed Makolese dagger denoting the status of the one who carries it.

Henakaga: The Spirit of the Owl

Hianna: Principle Deity or Goddess who replenished life on Makol Island after it had been destroyed. She is said to have turned into a coconut tree, and then the First Woman. After turning herself into a young woman, and Gadji into a young man, she married Gadji, the lone survivor of Makol Island, and returned the island to fertility.

Judavaan Mati: "Twin Sun" when the Sun touches its reflection in water. Sometimes known as the "Kissing Sun" *(Chumban Mati)* or "Vain Sun" *(Sia-Sia Mati)*

jamalac: Fruit similar to breadfruit

juk: A flower blossom that is used in a concoction that can help loosen a spirit from its physical body.

Jushinjunshi: An Elder or Chief who is the recipient of an important message, which they vow to follow, or accept death.

Ka: Lifeforce in all things. Prana.

kaca: *(pronounced kay-kau)* A colorful Makolese parrot

Kintsuke waabee-saabe: Viewing things from the Gods's perspective. Accepting the imperfect beauty of an object or a person's life that has been broken and mended, even though the thing, or life, has not been restored to its former beauty. It is the understanding that the thing, or life mended, is even more beautiful for having been broken.

kumbab: A potent medicinal potion or poultice.

kamukamu: Bush grown near rivers. Its fruit has anti-viral and anti-depressant properties. Also, good for gums, eyes, skin and immune system.

Kikuyu: Tribe in East Africa

Krishram: A man-god from the Makolese ancient past

Likeze: Ancient male Makolese prophet

Lord Issa: A man-god from the Makolese ancient past

Maasai: Nomadic Tribe in East Africa

Mao-Atua: Shark God the size of a whale known to us today as Megalodon.

Mal-Sudaik Ritual: A dark secret ritual between a High Shaman and his supplicant that involves conjuring the Spirit of Lord Tagheetu.

Mata Mati: "Eye Sun" is when the Sun and its reflection merge on a horizon of water. The "Kissing Sun" hangs over the sea and merges with its own reflection becoming eye-shaped or vesica pisces shaped. The vesica pisces is when the two circles' center line lies on the circumference of the other.

Maut Mati: "Dying Sun" as it sinks close to the horizon at dawn.

Ma-zutu: Sacred covenant to the Mother Stone.

Mimi-ishi: "Stone ear". Fossilized ear bone from the inner ear of an ancient whale.

Mizu Mati: "Water Sun" or when the Sun is reflected in water.

Mother Stone: An ancient holy oracle stone in the shape of a woman that lies deep inside an immense cavern. This natural translucent white onyx formation stands fifteen feet tall, and sits on a narrow plinth of vertical clear quartz crystal surrounded by a deep chasm. Islanders journeyed to her, seeking her guidance and prophecies.

Naji: A male Moslem name meaning "close friend".

pujo: Medicine

sa-kun: Makolese breadfruit

Sang-Wehtu' Spring: Makol's most sacred spring.

sha: A warm fermented brew that is a cross between beer and wine

Shomei: Authentic witness to a person's innocence.

Shuntshu Junshi: Principal leader and Elder authority, who is bound by spiritual law to follow an important message, or accept death.

Sai-Sai Mati: "Vain Sun" or when the Sun is reflected in the water and merges together. It is said the "Kissing Sun" is kissing itself.

Si Te Cah: Ancient race of giants

Sin-Ni: The Northwestern land said to be the land where the Goddess Hianna had flown from to Makol Island.

Su: Meaning the 'good seed'. Also a mating ritual where islanders make love to strangers who have come to their shores. The ritual was designed to extend the Makolese notion of family and to mix the gene pool.

Su Shapa: The bad seed. Known culturally as the children of rape

Tagheetu: The Spirit of the Swamps known as Lord Tagheetu, the Makolese principle Crocodile God, Guardian of the island, Eater of Men's Fears, and former companion to the ancient hero Gadji.

Tahnah-henah: The Spirit of the Hummingbird

Tahneyah: The Spirit of Air

tai: yes

truklum: The Makolese equivalent of American poison ivy.

tit-wee: Tiny nocturnal bird whose tongue is eaten as a delicacy. Meant as a means to stop the bird from chattering through the night.

uruku: Roots used for bedding with moss to keep bugs away.

Wakazoontei: Spirit of the Black Widow Spider.

Wambli Galeshka: Ancient Makolese prophet

yage: A sacred herbal medicine that helps one see beyond the veil of ordinary reality.

Zoozaycha: The Spirit of the Snake, and ally to the Lord Tagheetu

ZoonZoona-ikitan: A large poisonous hairy Makolese cave spider

PROLOGUE

THE LAST SCROLL

From the end of Book I: THE EDUCATION OF TEMPLE FOX

The ambitious Shaman Mefakani has tricked Unbelievers into thinking he is the True Teacher foretold in an ancient prophecy scroll. He captures Temple, the True Teacher, but his efforts to permanently alter Temple's lifeforce, or Ka, has failed. What the rebellious Unbelievers don't know is that Mefakani has now been transformed into a new man by Temple Fox's awesome power.

In a surprising twist of fate, Losha, the Queen's Interpreter, has also fulfilled the prophecy along with her lover, Temple Fox. Flying into the Shaman's secret chamber as a great white Swan, Losha rescues Temple by interrupting Mefakani's dark magic, and by aborting an assassination attempt on Temple's life by Senior Elder Sahdon. Sahdon, the head of the Rebel faction, is now dead.

Elder Tani, who had been kidnapped by Mefakani, and had died in his captivity, has been brought back to life. The old Healer is pleased that her protégée, Losha, bears the sacred mark.

Mefakani, Temple Fox, Losha, and Elder Tani are not alone. They are joined by the Shaman's young apprentice Jabal, the mute servant boy Tiv, and Mefakani's former lover, Winyon, the Exile. Trapped in a shaman's cavern filled with the smoke of dark magic, Temple Fox must find the strength and courage to fulfill his spiritual obligations as one of the True Teachers. His beloved, Losha, finds her own power ripens as she takes center stage helping Temple and their friends devise a plan to escape. But danger lies behind a megalithic stone door – the only exit – where a band of armed Rebels believe Shaman Mefakani to be the True Teacher. The Rebels expect Mefakani to leave his chambers with the head of Temple Fox, proclaiming victory over the white Wizard. But the Shaman is a changed man now.

Bitter emotions toward Mefakani runs high. Can Temple and his friends trust him to help everyone escape unscathed? Can they prevent a civil war between Believers and Unbelievers? Will all the Kas, Mefakani had stolen from the Makolese people, be returned? Most importantly, will the lifeforce on the island ever be restored?

THE RETURN OF THE KA AND THE MENDING OF THE SU follows each character's personal journey into wholeness. A spiritual, fantasy adventure about the web of beliefs we weave and how reality bends to those beliefs. A novel about beauty amidst brokeness, soul healing, and the true meaning of peace.

CHAPTER ONE

SECRETS

SECRETS
What would it mean
if all the world's secrets
were melded into one
and you found it gleaming
by a stream?
Would you pick it up
and tuck it in your pocket
for good luck?
Share it with the world?
Sell it?

I am guessing
you will skip it
over the surface of the water
and count the times
it bounces
before settling to the bottom.
I am guessing
you will find
meaning in the numbers.

And you will find your star
in that smooth roll of ripples
where it last fell,
where the Sun above
hinted at Home
as it glinted in that stream

you know as Life
and the Dream-stone
you know as Love.

The Elders say
withholding secrets is the last challenge
for an Initiate of the Great Mysteries.

Elo Tivluk, popular Makolese poet
The Makolese Scroll on
the Return of the Ka and the Mending of the Su #1

A distant tapping sound roused Maśon from deep sleep into the twilight world of half wakefulness.

Tap, tap, tap…tap, tap, tap.

Thinking he was dreaming, he rolled over on the blanketed ground, this time facing the woodstove. His senses began to thaw.

Tap, tap, tap…tap, tap, tap.

Any dreams he might have had melted away and were now forgotten, and the sound stirred him awake. With eyes still shut and ears more alert now, he focused on the sound. There was a soft hush behind the sharp noise.

Snow? Wind? Branches tapping against the window?

The sound grew louder, more insistent.

Tap! Tap! Tap! Tap! Tap! Tap!

Maśon threw off the bed covers and searched for the source of annoyance. A pale shadow slipped past the window and Maśon groaned as he rose and hobbled over to the window as fast as his pain would allow him. He flung back the curtain.

Nothing there but a bounty of fresh snow bowing the branches.

Maśon limped back to the center of the room to toss a log into the woodstove, when the sound rang out again.

TAP! TAP! TAP!

He wheeled around to the opposite window and caught the movement of a light shadow. Stumbling over to the window, he ripped back the curtain.

Huge, dark, round eyes drilled a hole in his auric field with nothing separating him from the great horned Owl but a quarter of an inch of glass.

Maśon lurched back with a start and found himself shouting. "Temple!"

The penetrating stare ran through Maśon's soul like a dagger that flayed him open and reamed him out until he felt naked – raw – exposed. The Owl blinked and all at once the spell was broken and Maśon, his heart still racing, recovered from the initial shock. He saw the bird flutter its great wings and Maśon was left with a view of the forest cloaked in white. And beyond his small hut he scanned the soft blue hues of the Carolina mountains in the distance, their white tops peeking through curtains of rising mists like islands, their colors layered from soft whites to muted grays, to cyan.

Maśon thought he saw a flash of light that blurred all the white snow together. He wasn't sure, but seconds later he heard a duller rapping sound at his door.

The Scribe staggered to the door, his soul still charged from having been energetically impaled. He flung the door open and a flurry of snow rushed in. Temple was standing in the doorway, his green wool cape swirling in the wind, his head covered in a fur cap encrusted with snow.

"Are you going to let me in or not?" he asked.

Maśon bowed and stepped aside and let the centenarian step through. He closed the door and watched in silence as the old man ambled over to the welcoming woodstove.

Temple whisked his cap off and beat the snow off against his pant's leg. "Sorry, I'm a bit early."

"By…two weeks," Maśon said.

Temple turned to face him and winced. "Am I that early?"

Maśon gave a slow, but distinctive nod.

"I see the community gave you a cabin and a woodstove. That's quite an improvement from the tent you were camping in. You sure it's not too much technology for you to handle?" he said, smirking.

Maśon returned the smirk with a grin. "It's still better than that tiny round hut you stay in when you visit here."

Temple looked around the simple room. In the corner lay a pile of colorful blankets and a rumpled sleeping bag. To the side sat a washstand and ceramic bowl. Two sawhorses supported a meager table made from wide wooden planks. A hole cut into it held an old stained iron porcelain sink with an open drain pipe that emptied into a bucket beneath it.

Temple smiled. "Next thing you know you'll have insulation, a real bed, and your own outhouse."

"I am grateful," is all Maśon said.

"I brought you something." Temple burrowed inside his cloak and pulled out what looked like a rectangular piece of plexiglass about a quarter of an inch in thickness and the size of an average sheet of paper.

"A window pane?" Maśon said, his tone sardonic. He took the gift from Temple and turned it over in his hands. It was transparent and lightweight.

"Kind of," Temple said. "It's a device I thought you might like to try out."

The Scribe started to hand the tablet back. "You know I don't like technology. And besides, this community forbids it."

"Oh bullocks. Rules are designed to be broken."

"The RF energy interferes with brain function. You know that."

"Yes, but this kind of device is totally safe and isn't linked to the drag net or anything from the outside. I think you'll find it helpful. Watch."

Temple waved his hand over the device. A luminous translucent image of Makol Island as seen from the sea appeared on the screen as a three-dimensional bas-relief raised above the slick surface by no more than eight inches.

He twirled his finger and the picture revolved to give Maśon his first view of his ancestral home as if he were watching it from a fast-moving boat. Temple flicked his finger and an aerial view appeared. The top of Hollow Mountain glided gently by. The hills and forests came crisply into view. And the contours of stone buildings, huts, and the island's coastline slipped past the viewer. Temple waved his hand again and the bas-relief collapsed inside the tablet and vanished.

"Where'd you get this?"

"On the outpost on Ganymede."

"From the little Mountain Gods on Makol who you said originated in another star system? Is Ganymede one of their outposts?"

"Oh no, no," Temple said. "By the way, I would prefer if you didn't call them 'Gods'. They are merely biological constructs repeatedly reprogrammed from another star culture.

"Actually, many of the extraterrestrials work together on many different outposts throughout our solar system and beyond. Ganymede is largely populated by more evolved Orions. The creatures inside Makol's mountain do have these devices, of course. They're busy like little ants right now. The Great Alliance has more than a dozen Brahmatic programs in the works for creating the new human. And the little creatures you mentioned will be presenting one of their programs very soon. Frankly, I'm hoping all of them create a new male with a frontal lobe developed earlier so young males don't act like such violent arseholes. But I digress."

He gestured to the device Mason still held in his hands. "This device is used on many of the outposts. Remember, Mason, technology isn't evil. It's how it's used. I know you. You'll use it as a tool and not an enslavement. Besides" – he grinned – "you'll find no naughty pictures of naked ladies on this. Believe me, I tried."

Mason let out a hardy laugh. "Thank you, Temple. This will help me learn about my ancestors I never knew. For now, I probably need to hide this from the others." He slid the tablet between a pile of blankets, then helped Temple off with his cloak and draped it on a chair by the fire.

Temple's eyes lit up. "Ah, I see you've procured an old, but interesting relic of a chair to sit on, which should make you more comfortable with that bad knee of yours than sitting on the ground."

"I got that chair for you," Mason pointed out. "Besides, my damaged knee is painful no matter how I sit. And I like sitting on the ground. It makes me feel connected to my Makolese heritage and to the Earth. Would you like some breakfast?"

"No thanks. I had two very plump mice for breakfast." He patted his stomach.

"You mind?" Mason said as he grabbed an iron skillet and placed it on top of the woodstove.

Temple shook his head. "Your ability to enter dreams and other altered states of consciousness is very advanced, you know. Your knee is curable. I know you can heal it yourself."

"It isn't healable," Mason snapped back a bit too quickly, his tone piqued by a sudden sharp pain.

Temple shrugged his shoulders. "So be it, then."

"So what brings you here so early?" Mason asked to change the subject. He broke two eggs into the skillet.

"The schedule has been pushed forward for the release of my biography."

Mason looked up in horror. "But I haven't even written it yet!"

"Then we need to get on with it," Temple said.

"Any reason why?" Mason asked. He grabbed a metal spatula off a rack of kitchen implements leaving a clacking chorus behind him.

"Relax. There's plenty of time. Which is why I brought the tablet. It will help to speed things along. And," he added pointedly, "it writes in Condensed Makolese OJ-Script."

Mason's eyes lit up. He tossed his spatula into the hot skillet and scampered awkwardly like a crab to the pile of blankets where he had hidden the device. He whipped it out, waved his hand over it, but nothing happened.

"Here, hand it to me. I will give you a quick lesson."

The Scribe handed the tablet to Temple. The proximity of Temple's unique energy signature activated the screen and it began to glow. His fingers danced over the screen. "The commands are given by thought, by voice, or with brisk abbreviated Condensed Makolese OJ-Script motions. Here, now you try it."

Maśon took the tablet. He eased himself down on the ground, his fingers racing over the glassy surface and his eyes aglow with scrolling text detailing the history of Makol Island. "I love it!" he said excitedly.

"Good," Temple said. "Your eggs are burning."

CHAPTER TWO

TRAPPED

*"Dissolving into death was bliss – ecstasy even –
like sex, only better."*

Elder Tani
The Makolese Scroll on
the Return of the Ka and the Mending of the Su #2

Temple Fox wrapped himself in a blanket of warmth by the creaking woodstove, the scent of cedar and wood smoke lingering in the morning air. He remembered the Makol Islands and its great swaths of fog that swirled around them. A longing stirred in his breast for the good things of the past, even for the cruel events that begged to be remembered for no other reason than so others would learn from his experiences.

Temple hummed to himself as he waited for Maśon to prepare his ink brushes.

"Don't ask," Maśon said. "You must believe me when I say I am quicker with the brush than the tablet. The tablet will be of great use to me later."

"Did I say anything?" Temple asked innocently.

"Remember, I can read your mind."

"Then you will know today is a day to remember some of the harsher things. What would a Scribe know about being strapped to a stone table and having their Ka wrenched out of their body, eh? By then we all were trapped – myself and Losha, the Shaman Mefakani, Elder Tani, Jabal, Winyon and Tiv."

Maśon closed his eyes in concentration. "I see the image in your mind of Mefakani's private cavern where he worked in secret."

"Good. We'll begin there."

★　　★　　★　　★　　★　　★

The cavern air was still smoky and weighted with the pungent smell of herbs and the dense energy of dark magic. Losha wrapped a piece of barkcloth around Tani to stem the chill and damp that had settled inside the old woman's bones.

The web of wrinkles that spilled from the corner of the Elder's eyes and ran the length of her face had softened in the brine she had floated in for a week, giving her a pearly translucence like a newborn babe. She glanced at Losha out of the corner of her eye sensing Losha could detect a shift in her energy field.

Tani had a deeper understanding of her limitless nature, and yet there was also an acceptance for the limitations of the flesh imposed on her by the physical plane she resided in. Spirit inhabited matter, divinity dwelled in flesh, and yet the physical body was really only a tool for learning. This was understood by Tani, even before her self-imposed coma and subsequent death. Still there was something odd that lay hidden beyond that ancient knowing, which Losha couldn't quite discern.

Tani is still Tani and yet there seems to be more of her present now, Losha felt.

Losha and Temple held her firmly yet gently as the old woman took a feeble step forward from the water-filled niche made of rock.

"Old bamboo does not bend," the old woman grumbled. Losha took hold of Tani's trembling hands to steady her. "I am like a newborn babe again," she whispered.

She leaned heavily on Losha as she took small wobbly steps over to a bench made of limestone, its natural form shaped like an immense throne. They lifted her up onto it, her diminutive figure dwarfed by the fantastic stone structures surrounding her.

"Oh, I am weak from floating in that foul soup without food for so long," she complained. "But I suppose one does not feed the dead too often."

The centenarian leaned back against the high fluted shafts of flowstone, and rested her arms on a cluster of stalagmites that had formed thin ledges on either side of her; a formidable chair for such a fragile wisp of a woman. But Tani was not just any woman. She was an old, wise Makolese woman, and the fringed canopy of translucent onyx that hung above the chair seemed to glow in her presence.

Tani rubbed her eyes with her gnarly knuckles and looked around her, trancelike, casting off the deep somnolence of death. "I am no longer in the world of brilliance. Or that tunnel filled with abalone light." In front of her sat the ponderous slab of stone where Mefakani performed his perverse magic. To her right there were vast rows of wooden shelves that held the tiny obsidian vials with all the islanders' essence, their Ka, which the Priest had stolen by consent. The images of the others slowly came crisply into focus.

"This world seems like a shadow land – a mirage – and yet you all are here before me."

She leaned forward slightly and arched a thin eyebrow when her eyes lit upon Winyon, the Chokahpeiyape, a woman in her prime whose hair had silvered prematurely. The old Healer stared at the woman who had once been unjustly accused of witchcraft and murder. Tani smiled at her kindly. "Such a lovely face. And one that I have not seen for many seasons," she said brightly. "Hopefully, you are here to stay with us for a time."

A tear escaped the Exile's eye and she smiled and gave the Healer a respectful bow. "Once I prove my innocence," she asserted.

"We will make certain of that," Tani declared, then slumped back against the cold, damp stone out of breath as if her declaration had taken all of her strength.

Tani breathed deeply and blinked back the smoke that stung her eyes. Winyon, Losha, Temple, the recently deposed High Shaman Mefakani, and his Apprentice, Jabal, even the mute boy, Tiv, waited quietly, patiently as the Healer took account of her surroundings. She peered through the twilight of the smoky cavern. On the floor beside the tablet of stone, that once held her captive, laid a figure of a man. She squinted harder in the firelight. The man's face was hidden in deep shadows, but his grotesquely scarred and withered leg spoke of his identity.

Losha answered the unasked question. "Elder Sahdon," she whispered.

"Dead?" Tani asked.

"Poisoned by no one's hand, but his own... and that of Mefakani's snake."

The old woman gave an acquiescent nod, almost of approval, Losha thought, then smiled broadly when Jabal, the Apprentice, appeared by her side with a cup of coconut milk.

"A drink for a High Shaman," he said, his eyes smiling back.

Tani winked at him and nodded with a kind of regal solemnity.

"A cup of warm palm wine would be more to my wanting," she said, "but a cup of the Mother's sacred milk is what I need."

She took the cup from his hands and gulped noisily until the milk rolled down the faded spiral tattoo on her chin. She held out the empty cup for more, which Jabal quickly refilled.

"Were it not for my ability to breathe like a dolphin, I would not be having this conversation with you all right now. I lost my sense of time, but I must have spent days floating in that watery vat. Then this potent, dark energy came over me and pushed me under until I finally drowned."

"That must've been the whirlpool of energy Mefakani conjured when he had me strapped to that stone slab," Temple conjectured.

"Ahh." She nodded with understanding. "Then I got lured into a pearly tunnel. I spent only a flicker of time in the Great Light." Her translucent skin buckled into a frown. "Returning leaves me heavy," she said sadly. "If it were not for seeing the miracles before me now I would say returning was a punishment." She grinned at Losha and took her hand. "Losha, child, you, by far, are the best miracle. You have found your true identity and your power. And you have saved Temple. I am so proud of you." Her toothless grin widened and though her eyes were still gummy they sparkled from within.

"And then there is you." Her smile dropped when her gaze set upon the Priest who had tried to take her power and enslave her soul. "What are we to do with you?" she huffed.

In a superficial sense Mefakani outwardly appeared no different than before. The jagged tattoos still marked his cheeks. His head was still clean-shaven, except for the long length of graying hair gathered at the base of his skull. But Tani drew him deeper into her consciousness through the gateway of her eyes.

Something in him has... She searched for the right word. *...Softened.*

Around his dark, puffy eyes there was a moist sadness, a childlike look of remorse – the look of a haunted man. When Tani peered deeper into his soul, allowing what she had perceived to stir her, she spoke again. "My heart aches for you, Mefakani, for now you have seen the Light as I have." She fell suddenly silent. She lowered her head and stared down at her tiny feet as they dangled over the bench of stone. A hint of guilt dulled the luster of her pruny face.

"I know the Divine Light loves you equally as It loves us. It does not judge," she said. "We are all perfect by Divine design, innocent and pure." And then with a tone edged with frustration, she shook her head and said. "But what do we do now? What a mess we all have before us."

Winyon stepped further into the torchlight. She folded her arms in front of her, pulling her shawl around herself tightly. "He is to blame," she said, tilting her head in Mefakani's direction, avoiding direct eye contact with him.

Temple looked into the face of the Wounded Hummingbird, the Exile shunned by her own people. "It may take some time, but perhaps you'll forgive Mefakani and give him a chance to prove himself again."

"Not I," she replied coldly. "He is a murderer and thief of souls."

Mefakani looked guiltily at the tall, thin woman with the long silver hair. She had been the Hummingbird, the beautiful woman he had obsessed over in his youth, thinking it was love. *What have I known of love? What have I known of love just an hour before?* he thought.

Her face was etched with such sorrow and bitterness he thought his heart would burst. "I have surely put my mark upon her all these many years. Who can blame her for how she feels now?" he said.

Winyon could no longer tolerate the weight of Mefakani's silent, sorrowful gaze and turned her back on him. "Look at poor Tiv," she started again. "Look at what the Priest has done to him," she said as if Mefakani was absent from the chamber.

Mefakani lowered his head, but spoke directly to Winyon. "I am fully aware of what I have done to him, Winyon...and what I have done to you...to everyone. I vow from this day on that I will never use my magic again, unless it is to heal."

Winyon sneered bitterly. "And can you mend a broken heart? Or bring back a soul long dead? Or heal this boy whose soul is lost and mind is scrambled by your dark magic and fine speeches?"

"Mefakani," Losha interrupted, "from now on you are forbidden from performing any magic again, whether it is even to heal," she stated flatly. "You will teach us, however, how to reattach the Kas of all the people. It is the least you can do."

Mefakani stood silent, the weight of judgment falling heavy on him.

Losha could feel Winyon's torment and the growing tension in the chamber. She was a widow the same as Winyon and understood the depth of loss. She looked from Winyon to the others and then to Temple with sadness for things past and for the anger that she too held toward the evil Priest.

How can I ever forgive Mefakani, especially knowing what he had done to my precious Tani and to Temple? He is an aberration of nature.

Still, there were hints of understanding flickering at the corner of Losha's newly expanded consciousness as to who Mefakani was and the role he chose to play out in this lifetime.

When Losha's heart reached out to find peace within her, she broke the tense silence. Although she was not the creator of the words, these words tumbled from her lips. "The Divine Light, which Tani speaks of, and which Mefakani has experienced, makes new its promises and miracles every day. Tani has returned from the dead, but Mefakani is a new man reborn in spirit as well. And both he and Tani have returned because they have work to do. All of us have work to do."

"She's right," Temple said. "Mefakani should've died, but returned to complete himself. He's here for a reason. So, in spite of the damage done in the past, and what you personally feel about one another, we're all going to have to put our trust in the Divine so we can solve the problems before us now...and do so while trying to prevent civil war."

Winyon pointed at the Priest accusingly. "He is responsible! Make him get us out of this!"

Temple shook his head. "Right now the Unbelievers behind that door believe Mefakani is the True Teacher and expect him to show them my dead body. And Queen Palomei and the Believers think Mefakani is negotiating a peace treaty right now. All of us are needed to get out of here and do so without getting killed."

"Bi kana, I should have stayed in the spirit world," Tani grumbled to herself. "There is little I can do now," she stated louder.

Temple moved closer and engaged her ancient eyes. "But your will is strong and your wisdom is needed. Will you at least trust the Divine to guide us in getting us out of here?" he asked.

"Who else is there to hand this over to? Who else is there to trust?" she answered. "We must all band together now."

Mefakani nodded in silent agreement.

"I will do what I can," Jabal called out with enthusiasm.

The mute boy, Tiv, moved forward and pointed to himself, signaling his eagerness to help.

Winyon looked to Temple and then to Losha sheepishly, feeling suddenly alone. "Tai, tai, I will help as well," she said in defeat, "as long as I do not have to work with him." She jabbed a finger in Mefakani's direction.

"That's a start," Temple said. "But you must realize, Winyon, that whatever we do here will depend a great deal on Mefakani and how people react to him." He looked to the Priest, giving him his full attention. "First we must learn what the others outside are expecting from you. What exactly were your plans?"

The Priest stood before the five of them and spoke candidly of what he had originally plotted. As hard as it was for him to speak, he pressed on as if the Priest he spoke of was someone else who had lived a lifetime ago.

"I drugged you, Temple. After sealing you with the Mal-Sudiak ritual I would have commanded you to lie still and be silent." Mefakani stopped for a moment. It was the memory of the ancient Mal-Sudaik ritual that made his stomach and his heart collide and he began to tremble. He pushed passed the nausea and self-loathing, knowing he was needed now. He sucked in a deep breath and let it out slowly to compose himself. "The Unbelievers would have thought you were merely a corpse. After being imbued with your power, I had planned to take Sahdon's Ka first, then Cranik's and the other Unbelievers. One by one I would have made them all compliant. The Unbelievers would have ended up as my army elite.

"After I had taken their Kas it would not have mattered if they saw you were still alive. They would have done anything I commanded without question."

"So you were simply going to use me to placate the Queen and all the others?" Temple asked. "Making it appear as if we both had fulfilled the prophecy?"

"Yes. I believe it would have ended the bloodshed between the Rebels and the Queen's army, and order would have been restored. But at a tremendous cost." He paused, a look of shame darkening his face. "I had planned to steal the Kas of the Queen's army, even the Queen herself, eventually. Together, the combined forces would have taken on the armada you predicted would invade our shores."

Mefakani paced a couple of steps, then stopped. His eyes spoke of deep regret. "You know I would have taken everyone's Ka – everyone's life essence on the entire island," he confessed. "I would not have merely altered their Kas as before, but taken them completely as I have Tiv and the new Commander Boran, Gabu, and the two Rebel soldiers – just as I tried to do to you, Temple Fox."

The others waited in silence and Temple nodded briefly. "Go on," he insisted.

"After our victory against the armada I would have imposed a draft on all males and females age twelve to sixty, then..." His eyes met the gaze of each of his six confessors. "Then I would have taken our army elite outside the Barik Limits to cleanse the Outside World."

The others stood in stark silence at hearing the Priest explain his own insanely ghastly scheme.

Tani squinted at Mefakani, a swarm of thoughts swirling inside her brain. "And how would you break through the Barik Limits?" Tani questioned. "The Gods have not permitted us to leave. There is no way through them."

"I…I would have found a way. I needed someone to stop me – someone powerful," he said with a quiver in his voice.

Jabal stepped forward into the lighted space. He gazed at the man whom had once been his Master, then stood before the white man whom he had once plotted against. He spoke to Temple uneasily. "The Believers know you are the True Teacher, as do I. But with the Rebels thinking Mefakani is the true Teacher now, I do not see how we can avoid a civil war."

"We may not," Temple said. "Still, we must seek the most peaceful solution first, as I've done with your Master."

"Tai, but I have made a knot of things," Mefakani whispered hoarsely.

"Why not tell them the truth?" Winyon said from the half-light.

Mefakani held a look of horror. "Temple cannot just walk out of here," he explained. "The Unbelievers will think he defeated me. They would kill us both...kill us all!"

"You're both right," Temple exclaimed. "We all can't just walk out of here. But in the end, we owe them the truth."

"Tai," Tani said. "But you cannot give a baby a piece of meat."

Losha spoke. "I agree. We must tell them the truth by spooning the truth to them in a way that is palatable to both sides and their way of thinking. We must do so carefully and then sit back and watch the wind blow the way it wants to."

"But how?" Jabal asked.

Temple scratched his ragged beard in thought. "The only thing to be done is for all of us to ask the Divine for guidance. Let's all gather together and see what information we can get with the focused intent on how to get out of here first, and then on how to deal with the Unbelievers."

CHAPTER THREE

KINTSUKE WAABEE-SAABE

"It is how the Gods see. It is the grace that comes with accepting the imperfect beauty of a life or a thing that has broken and is now mended, but has not been restored to its former beauty. Kintsuke waabee-saabe is understanding that the life or thing is more beautiful for having been broken."

Elder Tani
The Makolese Scroll on
the Return of the Ka and the Mending of the Su #3

Tani closed her eyes again and folded her legs under her in the huge stone chair while the others circled together on the hard cold ground. Temple rested his aching back against the tablet of stone where he was once held captive. Losha was by his side. Winyon made certain she was not sitting next to the Priest and not directly opposite him, for her bitterness was still simmering. Everyone grew silent as Temple and Losha led the others in meditation. Even Tiv closed his eyes and breathed the way one does when they go into deep meditation, three deep breaths through the nose and three long breaths out through the mouth.

Temple noticed that the profound peace he had felt when he was out of his body only minutes before was fading fast and replaced with a sensation of light-headedness and nausea.

Temple kept his thoughts private and fought back the nausea. *I'm still under the influence of Mefakani's poison and dark magic*, he worried. *And I've had no food or rest for days.*

Although his eyes were closed they began to twitch uncontrollably. The memory of his being bound by iron, the taste of something sticky and sweet being forced into his mouth – all the images and sensations came alive all at once causing his head to spin like a toy top. The stench of ozone filled his nostrils again and he grabbed his temples where his hair was singed as he relived the dreaded electric pulse that had collided inside his brain. He held his head tighter as an excruciating lance of pain pierced his skull and his vision was blotted out by multicolored streaks of lightning.

He let go for only a moment and a sudden fatigue overtook him. His backbone leaned heavily against the rough stone that still pulsated with dark magic, and his thoughts became increasingly ungrounded. Any cohesive thoughts scattered and swam between past memories of who he used to be and who he was now.

Who am I now, he thought. *What've I become? And how have I gotten here? What's led me to this cold, smoky cavern on the Misty Isles on the edge of the known world? Where's the old me? Is the old me lost forever?*

He slumped into random memories that ricocheted off the limestone walls, firing back into his distant past to the sounds of a young America.

The grind of car engines, jingle of horse harnesses, and ringing hooves echoed on the cobblestone streets of Baltimore. The six-year-old darted between his parents' parked Damlier and an A-rab wagon so quickly that neither parent had a chance to react. The black A-rab didn't see the boy and wailed out a long, melodious, "Fish Maaan!" drowning out his mother's panicked cry.

The young Temple raced down Fellspoint Avenue to the harbor, past the aroma of baked bread and baklava to where the air carried the scent of the bay and salt and sweaty men. He jumped onto the closest pier and paused for a moment, feeling the sun on his face and the weathered boards beneath his feet leaning against the current. The boats tied to the docks bobbed up and down, and the thick, heavy mooring ropes pulled taut, making the pier groan in a way only wet wood can groan.

Temple sat and listened to the rhythm of the water as it slapped against the boat bottoms. And he watched the sun skip over the smooth surface of the bay, making the sun's reflections appear like Chinese script brushed fast with light. The music of the waves and the blinding, flashing sun pulled him deep into daydream and a longing for something far away that he couldn't yet identify, until a stern voice yelled out, bringing him to the surface of a harsher world and out of the magic he had escaped into.

Temple felt the boards beneath him vibrate to the rhythm of a heavy clipped footfall. He stood still in his smooth silence, mesmerized by the cry of gulls above him, and a distant place he knew he had never been to, but yearned for.

A large hand grabbed him firmly by the shoulders and shook him.

"You don't run off like that, lad! You understand?"

Temple shifted on the cold, stone floor, unaware that he was only half back from the memories of his life in Baltimore, back into the world of blood ritual and resurrection, when he found Losha shaking his shoulders sharply.

"Temple, you are uncentered. Your thoughts are wandering," she whispered. "Perhaps the drug is still affecting you."

The clean edges of Temple's memory faded into the dreamlike reality of the present. The cold numbness of his buttocks stirred him out of his watery state of mind and he felt the confines of the cavern closing in around him. Still, the marooned pilot, stranger among strangers, pivoted on the apex of knowing and not knowing.

Losha placed her hands over Temple's solar plexus and allowed the Divine Energy to run through her like a conduit to bring him back into balance. But with her loving touch came the rough edges of his present reality and the knowledge that a civil war in an alien land loomed before him. He didn't want to know the feeling and tried to push it away so he could drift to a peaceful place – a soft place. He was feeling too ragged to want anything else. And yet he longed not for Losha's warm touch, but his Mother's bosom, the taste of ginger bread and lemon sticks and oranges wrapped in gold foil. He ached to see the sun glide over Maryland's bay once more in the deep heat of summer.

Losha's hands were burning with the power of healing and Temple pulled his arms around him to capture the warmth. His mind skipped a season and he remembered brisk winters at the hearths of his parents' London estate. He recalled the trips into the bustling downtown.

If only I could have one more bite from a savory black pudding, he thought. *Or something else, like a...*

He could see that blood sausage hanging high, waiting for him in the butcher's shop, where the black-and-white marble floor was covered in sawdust. The stout butcher, Mr. Pruit, wiped his bloody hands on his blue-and-white striped apron and tipped his straw boater back onto his bald head. Mr. Pruit wiped his brow.

"And what does young Master Temple want today?" he asked. "A slice of liver? A kidney or two?"

A heart! A slice of tender heart is what I really long for. He pressed his face against the glass case and stared at the slabs of meat, watching his breath fog the glass. One fly, then two, landed on the heart he wanted and he tried to shoo them away with his breath.

The lost Edens of Temple's childhood vanished when the sound of flies filled the chamber and Losha called to him from a distant place. She shook his shoulders again, harder this time.

"Temple, hold this. It will ground you," he heard her say.

Losha handed him a small green stone. No sooner was it in his palm then Temple felt the drifty part of him pull downwards inside himself, until he was surrounded by the cold reality of the present. When he came to full consciousness his eyes landed on Elder Sahdon's body covered with flies, and the stench of death lodged in his nostrils.

"I apologize," he finally said. He glanced up into their faces to see if anyone could have possibly sensed what had just happened to him. Both Winyon and Mefakani seemed too preoccupied with their own thoughts. Old Tani appeared weary and frail, while Tiv had fallen asleep with a pile a rags under his head. Jabal was still deep in meditation.

He balanced his forearms against his thighs, but his dizziness returned and he thought he might pass out. When he opened his eyes again, he saw that everyone else's were closed except for Losha, who was staring at him wide-eyed with concern. He leaned over to Losha and whispered for her to follow him to the far reaches of the cavern, swaying uneasily as he rose.

Temple's ungainly stride caught the attention of Elder Tani as he crossed the enclosure and dragged himself behind the barkcloth curtain. His legs felt leaden and he nearly fell to the floor. Hundreds upon hundreds of obsidian jars resting on wooden shelves encompassed his field of vision as he rolled over onto his back.

Losha followed him behind the curtain and sat beside him, her face flushed with worry.

Not bothering to hide his pain and fatigue from Losha any longer, he visibly winced, but suppressed an audible groan so he would not alert the others to his condition.

Tani slid off the flowstone chair and shuffled over to the barkcloth curtain. She squatted on the floor and hid behind the curtain to listen to the two Great Teachers. Temple was obviously in agony.

Temple stared at the stalactites hanging high above him as if they were pointing an accusing finger. "I'm done," he began, defeated. "I fulfilled my obligation to stop the Priest. I'm sorry. There's nothing more I can do."

Losha leaned over him, blotting out the needled stones from Temple's vision. "Whatever do you mean?" she asked, desperate.

"That's all I reincarnated for. Remember? I stopped the Priest and did so without violence. I've fulfilled my purpose in this lifetime and now it's time I go back to the Heavens for a respite and to return to true peace."

Losha gritted her teeth to hold her temper back. "You will leave us NOW?" she whispered harshly. "Nothing has been completed. Where is your courage? Where is your trust? You must follow through with this commitment, Temple!"

"But, Losha," he complained. "He took too much out of me. I can barely move or even think straight. I'm useless to everyone now."

Losha straightened her back and leaned into his flustered face. Her tone was biting. "Does our relationship mean nothing to you?" Her chin began to quiver. "Do you not..." She paused and bit her lip.

Temple sat up fast and grabbed her hands. "I do love you, Losha...purely and with all my heart. But the Shaman stole a piece of me. It's too much for me now. I don't think I can go on any longer. And I'm...I'm so afraid."

Tani sat quietly listening behind the curtain.

The Elder cast a wary eye over her shoulder at Mefakani, who wasn't meditating, but so thoroughly absorbed in his own misery that he paid no attention to anyone else's conversation. She cleared her throat to signal to Temple and Losha that she was present and pushed the curtain aside. Stepping into the enclosure, the old woman nodded, apologizing for the intrusion, then moved behind Temple. She swept her hands across his body until he felt some of the heaviness release.

"Please, you mustn't," he fussed. "You've been through too much yourself."

"No, no. Let her," Losha whispered. "She is pulling some of the dark magic out of you to create a void. Do not worry. When she releases some of the darkness then she will fill you with goodness. Remember, the healing runs through her and she will benefit from the energy as well."

A warm river of healing energy coursed through Temple's body. Slowly he relaxed and allowed his head to fall forward in trust. He began to quietly weep.

"Your body is still in shock," Losha said. "I am sorry for being so harsh." She rested her hand against his stubbled cheek, her own tears streaming down her face. She placed a gentle hand on the wound in his chest.

Temple raised his head, nodded and managed a weak smile.

He is not invincible, she thought. *How could I have been so callous?*

"Tai, I am sorry I did not do this sooner," Tani groaned as she sent one last pulse of soothing energy into his nervous system. "I should have known how traumatized you were."

"No apologies needed," Temple whispered. He grew quiet and closed his eyes.

"We will let you rest awhile," Tani said. She scooted back on her buttocks and flicked an eye of concern at Losha, gesturing with a tilt of her head for Losha to do the same to give Temple his own space. The two moved to the far end of the cavern next to the stone niche filled with brine where Tani had been held captive.

"How has Temple fallen into disharmony with Spirit?" Losha whispered frantically. "He has been far more unified than anyone else. He had already surrendered to the Divine days before Mefakani took him hostage. Is it true that a tiny portion of his soul somehow managed to break off from the wholeness of his Divine Self while escaping Mefakani's dark magic? Or was it simply a fragment of his physical body that was stolen from him that causes him to feel incomplete?" she rambled. "He should know that the consciousness of his physical body is different from his soul. He certainly knows he is not his body. Maybe he thinks he has severed ties with the Creator because he has fallen into the illusion of separation again."

Tani clasped Losha's hand and held it tenderly. "We are all like a sea sponge at the moment it is being pressed through a sieve, when it separates from the colony of cells that defines the whole creature, only to reconnect on the other side. Temple has lost sight of the wholeness of his greater being. And although it is true that he is still a powerful soul, and one of the rightful Teachers, it is that one small act of misperception that has splintered him now. He feels powerless to leave this cavern. Can you blame him?"

Losha squeezed Tani's hand. "I must do a healing on Temple…one designed specifically for him."

Tani grinned and tilted her head in Temple's direction.

Temple opened his eyes and blinked at the two women huddled in the far corner. Losha and Tani hurried over to him.

"I don't feel totally back yet," he said, "but I do feel far better. Thank you." He let out a deep sigh and thought for a minute. "There's something I saw while I was trying to meditate. It has to do with the piece of my heart that Mefakani stole. The piece of energy Mefakani stole from me served, in the end, to add a more open heart to the

Shaman's own distorted heart, mending it in ways I can barely comprehended. But the loss…?"

Temple fingered the raw wound in his chest and a flush of nausea rose again in his gut.

"He's been forever changed by having a piece of me. He has more heart now," Temple concluded. "And now we're rid of the darkest side of him…but I've lost a piece of my own heart in the process…and…."

"And we are trapped in a cave with Unbelievers behind that stone door," Losha reminded him.

Tani placed Temple's hand between her leathery palms. "Will you not stay to help, Temple Fox?"

The memory of deep peace resurfaced along with Temple's physical discomfort. It was a confusing mixture of sensations. Without the need to think any longer he nodded his head in agreement.

Losha gave a reassuring smile. "Tai, we will work together."

"But can we trust Mefakani?" Temple wondered.

Losha parted the curtain a slice to allow a narrow view of the Shaman resting against the far wall. He sat in silence. Her gaze became soft and unfocused and she grew quiet for a few moments. And as she did, the space just above and between her brows began to glow like a soft throbbing diamond.

Tani and Temple looked at one another in awe then back to Losha as the glow grew brighter.

"I see no malice in him," she said. "All I see is beauty. He is telling the truth. He wants to help us."

"*Kintsuke waabee-saabee,*" Tani whispered to Temple.

"What's that?" Temple asked.

"It is how the Gods see. It is the grace that comes with accepting the imperfect beauty of a life or a thing that has broken and is now mended, but has not been restored to its former beauty. *Kintsuke waabee-saabe* is understanding that the life or thing is more beautiful for having been broken."

Temple nodded. "Then we will trust him."

CHAPTER FOUR

THE PLAN

"A body in pain is a soul longing for communion with its spirit."

Elder Tani
The Makolese Scroll on
the Return of the Ka and the Mending of the Su #4

Temple, Losha, and Tani moved back to where the others were sitting quietly. Jabal gestured to the three with his eyes that he knew something and wished to speak. He looked sideways at the Priest and then to the other three with concern.

"You may speak," Tani coaxed. "We have nothing to hide."

The Apprentice gazed into Temple's sharp blue eyes. "I think what you saw at the end of your daydream is what is missing. Tai?" Jabal inquired with a quizzical look on his face.

"You saw it, too?" Temple asked.

Jabal nodded.

"Yes," Temple answered, "which is why you're so needed. Everyone must not look to me for answers anymore like I'm Makol's savior. We're a team now."

"I do not agree," Jabal began, but Temple cut him short.

"The sooner you accept your own Divine power, Jabal, the better we'll all be. We need you more than ever now."

The four were energetically synchronized. Without explaining to the others what they were doing, Temple, Losha, Elder Tani and Jabal sat in quiet meditation. When the four sensed a charged fullness in themselves, and a completeness in their task, they opened their eyes and compared their feelings and thoughts with one another until they had forged a coherent plan.

★　　★　　★　　★　　★　　★

"You call that a good plan?" Tani complained. "It is full of tangles and tears like an old fishing net."

"Yes, it's complex and quite risky," Temple confessed.

"But what else can we do?" Losha complained.

"These ideas feel stillborn to this old midwife," the Elder huffed. "And you…" The old woman pointed a bony finger at Temple, her eyes narrowed in mock scrutiny. "You are becoming a conjurer like Mefakani…and myself," she added with a sly gummy grin.

Temple looked to the others. "Well, it's only a general plan. Losha, Jabal and I still need ideas from the rest of you to flesh it out. But I warn you…we haven't much time."

"In what way do you need my help?" Mefakani asked.

Temple glanced over at the corpse on the floor. He spoke again. "The thing that we don't know is if Sahdon was being opportunistic when he hid here in this cavern to spy on you. If he wasn't and it was planned, then he may have told the others that he was going to hide in here."

"I did not know he was even here when I began the Mal-Sudaik ritual," Mefakani stated.

"Master Temple," Winyon spoke up. "When Losha, Jabal and myself were searching for you, the first thing I did was to fly inside the tunnels from outside this cavern where Elder Cranik and the Unbelievers were waiting behind that door." She pointed to the door made out of megalithic rock that separated them from the Rebels. "I overheard the Elder complain that he did not know the whereabouts of the Senior Elder. Some of the men thought that Sahdon had slipped in here to spy on Mefakani. Others thought he had gotten lost in the tunnels somewhere. Regardless, Elder Cranik refused to send a search party for him and ordered his men to stay to watch the door."

"That's valuable information," Temple said to Winyon and gave her a little smile.

"It is unlikely Cranik would rush to Sahdon's aid if he thought the Senior Elder was lost," Mefakani explained.

"Tai, that old dried up turtle would just love to be the head of the Rebel faction," Tani warned, "and the next Senior Elder of the Elders Council if he could."

"In that case," Temple said, "we can make certain the Rebels think Sahdon became hopelessly lost…"

"…and fell to his death somewhere inside the cavern complex," Jabal chimed in.

"Where," Winyon added, "he had been seeking guidance from the Mother Stone."

Temple cocked his head. "Mother Stone?"

"Tai. If one of us could place one of Sahdon's possessions there it would act as proof that Sahdon had been there on a private pilgrimage."

Temple looked lost. "What's a Mother Stone?" he asked.

The Exile answered. "Our people once made pilgrimages to the Mother Stone to seek guidance from the Spirit of the Earth. But Mefakani," she said, giving the Priest a hard, sideways glance, "forbade all but Initiates to journey there."

Mefakani stiffened. "There have been many cave-ins in that region. That was the real reason I forbid the pilgrimages," he said defensively.

Tani, who was back resting in Mefakani's chair of dripstone, shook her white disheveled head of hair. "That is not quite what happened," she said to Temple. "Years later our Priest declared it unsafe for even Initiates to go there, so they would not seek spiritual guidance on their own. That," she said, looking Mefakani straight in the eye, "was the real reason."

Jabal moved forward. "Still, a few of us have ventured back there on our own without our Master's knowledge." He looked at Mefakani and bowed his head apologetically.

The shamed Priest looked up at Tani, his eyes pleading for understanding. "But it is too dangerous to journey there now. Initiates could get buried alive!" he complained.

"Dangerous?" Tani asked, her voice rising a bit and echoing off the cavern walls. "This business of civil war now is dangerous! Life is always dangerous when there is something to be learned, and journeying to the Mother Stone was designed to be just that. But better to venture there than rest blindly in the numb security provided by an arrogant Priest, who enslaves his own people and treats his Elders like monkeys." The old woman jabbed a crooked finger in the air between her and the Priest then leaned sideways and spat on the floor. "What you do not realize Mefakani is that journeying to the Mother Stone became almost impossible because you angered the Spirit of the Mother Stone and Her Guardians. It was you who broke the sacred ritual, and you who caused harm to those who still dared to journey there. Tai, it will be dangerous for anyone to go there, but you have designed it so."

Mefakani rubbed the top of his bald head painfully. "Everything I have done has been to no good end," he said in exasperation, flushed with shame.

Tani leaned forward in her stone chair. "Tai, it is true. And you must own up to your mistakes, for now you have the chance to untie every knot you have ever made. Seldom do we get such a chance in the same body," she said, easing herself back against the chair.

He looked up at the old Healer whose eyes were fixed on him. Her penetrating eyes were not fiery with hate and judgment as he expected, but only spoke the hard truth. He noted the difference in her countenance and something stirred inside his breast. There was something in her eyes that spoke of the deeper understanding she had for the nature of humanity, their foibles, their passions – their crimes. Behind those black slits lay both the hard edge of truth and compassion, and Mefakani ached, knowing that her words were not meant to rub sea salt into his wounds, but cleanse the wounds of his guilt with truth so healing could take place.

"It is true," he said. "I have to own up to all I have done wrong and pray that it will not crush me."

A span of silence thickened the energy in the cavern and Mefakani diverted Tani's stare. But the glint of forgiveness in the old woman's eyes was recognized by Mefakani and he admitted to himself that were it not for that look he would have been swallowed by the heaviness of his own guilt.

He bowed his head respectfully before the Elder then cleared his throat. "Thank you," he sighed. "Still, I do not feel it wise to risk anyone's life should they journey to the Mother Stone to create this ruse you propose."

"I will go there in my lizard form," Jabal offered. "I can make it look as if Sahdon had been seeking an oracle. It would also offer an explanation for the Rebels as to where I have been for several days." He looked up at Mefakani with a quiet defiance.

"Be careful, Jabal," Mefakani warned. "If you are seen by the Queen's soldiers they will think you are a spy."

"They will?" Jabal asked, throwing the Shaman a disturbing look.

"I figured out that you were working with the Rebels long before you showed up here. I made a list of conspirators for the Queen and added your name."

Feeling like he had been trapped between the pinches of two crab claws Jabal glanced at the others with disgust.

Mefakani caught the look. "I am sorry, Jabal."

"I will go with him," Winyon suggested. "Lizards are slow and I can fly back to tell you whether Jabal has succeeded or not. And," she added, "I chose to do this to protect the others and try to prevent civil war."

To ease the tension further Temple put his hand on Jabal's shoulder to calm the boy. "You're very brave to do this, Jabal. We'll do everything else that has been planned until either you or Winyon return. But we must work fast. Cranik's patience must be wearing thin." Temple raised his arms out to encompass the group. "Does everyone feel ready?"

The others nodded their heads in agreement.

Losha worked out more of the details with both the Apprentice and the Exile. She purified the two with smoke then said a prayer of protection.

Temple took hold of Jabal's and Winyon's hand. Everyone in turn clasped each other's hand to make a circle and together they prayed for the Divine's continual guidance and protection.

CHAPTER FIVE

O'JUMA

"The less you know, the better."

Jabal, the Shaman's First Apprentice
The Makolese Scroll on
the Return of the Ka and the Mending of the Su #5

The evening sky was glazed in hues of deep amber. Birds swooped through churning clusters of insects in the hot, moist air to feast during the noisy business of roosting. The shrill shrieks of violet howlers settling in for the evening pierced the air.

The Hummingbird perched on a liana vine and waited for the Lizard to climb up through the hole from the cavern below, praying that his movements would not be detected by the hungry birds. Her tiny heart beat rapidly in anticipation as Jabal edged over the lip of rock, his skin changing from a mottled dun brown and gray to a malachite green to match the lichen he perched on. In quick jerky movements he buried himself beneath the shelter of leaf litter and frog moss. Winyon watched with fascination as the tiny heads of ground orchids shook, one by one, until a circle of quivering blossoms glowed an eerie green on the forest floor below her. She blinked in wonder as his man-form rose out of a pillar of smoke and garish green light.

Winyon flew down and hovered by his face, her wings thrumming wildly. He signaled for her to follow him.

The Hummingbird flew from tree to tree, with an occasional pause at a blossom or two to drink nectar, as Jabal made his way through the forest to a small hill at the edge of the Shaman's compound. He knelt beneath a benibaul bush and scanned the encampment below.

As Lesser Apprentices wandered to and fro, busy with their evening chores, Jabal could sense the cloud of anxiety that hung over them. The threat of civil war was pervasive, but he knew the Gods were guiding him, for sitting by the central fire was the one whose help he sought.

O'Juma was a muscular deep caramel-colored man three seasons older than Jabal. Being a Lesser Apprentice, and lower in rank and skill than Jabal, O'Juma didn't have the customary shaved head, but wore his hair long and loose with colorful feathers, and bone and shell beads as adornments.

The Initiate tightened the sinew on the drum he was finishing when Jabal twittered like a titwee in the secret code the two had devised. O'Juma stopped his work abruptly and lifted his head, scanning the depth of jungle.

The young Apprentice let out a sharp twitter again when O'Juma was faced in the right direction.

Hoping no one would notice, O'Juma abandoned his work and set out alone, casting a cautious eye all around him. He kept his footsteps slow and controlled as he walked toward the signal call.

When the call came keen and clear from atop the hill the young man began to walk faster, until he spotted the Apprentice crouched behind the bush. Knowing he couldn't be seen by the others below, O'Juma broke into a run until he fell upon Jabal and wrestled him to the ground.

"O'Juma, wait!" Jabal pleaded, but the Initiate pushed him onto his back and pinned him down by his arms.

"Where in Lord Tagheetu's name have you been?!" the man asked plaintively. "You just vanished! I thought you might have been in the battle at Hollow Mountain and were... "

"Dead... Not yet," he said, and he struggled to push O'Juma off of him.

When Winyon saw the two men wrestling on the ground below her the tiny bird took to the air in a flash and dived at O'Juma's head.

O'Juma felt a sharp thump on his back and a pecking at his head. He let Jabal go and waved his arms at the annoying blur above him. "Bi Kana! What is that?" he complained.

Jabal rolled O'Juma off of him and the two sat watching the bird fly in mad circles around their heads. "Do not harm her. She is a friend and my protector it seems." Jabal laughed out loud and the tiny bird calmed down and perched lightly on his finger.

"Your guardian is a Hummingbird? Just what in Lord Tagheetu's name is going on?" the Initiate asked.

The Apprentice tossed the Hummingbird into the air, and seeing that the men were really friends, she flew up onto the closest branch overhead.

Jabal sat for a moment struggling with what he should tell O'Juma. "Believe me," he said. "The less you know, the safer you will be."

The setting sun traced a thin line of deep gold round the rim of O'Juma's moist eyes. Jabal could see the caring and the worry there. He pushed his friend flat on the ground very gently, and drew himself up on top of him and held him there for a long while.

"I can take care of myself. Remember, I am the First Apprentice," he asserted.

O'Juma pushed Jabal away a little and looked around him to see if anyone saw them. "And a bold one to be demonstrating your affections so openly. If the Shaman finds out..."

"Someday you will be a full Apprentice like me and a High Shaman like I am destined to become. I have a strong feeling the religious laws about Shamans remaining celibate are about to be changed."

"Oh, so you are a prophet now, as well?" O'Juma asked.

"I will be a dead prophet if I do not make haste." He pulled himself out of the tenderness of O'Juma's arms, and got up and moved to the edge of the forest to study the compound below. "Any idea where the Queen's soldiers are?" he asked.

O'Juma moved close behind him. "There is the new Commander, Boran, and he is in Mefakani's private garden, guarding the new airboat. The others must still be in the foothills of Hollow Mountain, below where the Unbelievers are encamped."

Jabal turned to face his lover. "Boran is the new Commander?" he asked.

"Tai."

"And what happened to Commander Lobutu?"

O'Juma raised an eyebrow. "Queen Palomei..." He made a sweeping gesture with his hand across his neck. "I have heard rumors."

"It seems a lot has happened in my absence. Did you see our Master Mefakani fly the airboat?"

"Tai.

"That must have been a miracle to behold."

"Tai, and now he has proclaimed that he is the True Teacher and Prophet foretold long ago from one of the Prophecy scrolls."

"Tai, I know," Jabal replied. "But do not believe it. It is a great lie. Temple Fox is the great one."

"I thought you did not like Temple Fox. You said he was a White Devil."

"I have gained much wisdom, my friend. You must trust me on this one."

"I trust you with my life, my sweet one."

"Then you must also know that Losha, the Queen's Interpreter, has also fulfilled the prophecy. I can tell you as a personal witness that she too is the True Teacher and Prophet. They both are."

O'Juma grabbed his head. "I am confused. Who is the real Teacher?"

"Losha Ninti and Temple Fox."

O'Juma rubbed his head which set his shell beads rattling. "Both? Can that be so? And Mefakani is not?"

"I know it is hard to believe, but the prophecy scroll never said it was only one person. But for certain Mefakani is the impostor."

O'Juma blew out his breath. "I will have to trust you on this because I have nothing else to go on right now. But still, it is hard to believe."

"Are there any Unbelievers outside the caves?'

"Ah, tai, I forgot. There are two guarding the entrance to the cave that leads to Master Mefakani's private cavern. Why do you ask?"

"O'Juma, trust me. The less you know, the better."

"It is hard knowing you are up to your rump in something you chose not to share with me." His friend gave a sad smile. "Maybe I should get on with the business of making myself a widow's sash."

Jabal stood and stared, a sudden chill ran through the caring warmth O'Juma had wrapped him in. "May the spirits withhold from you the gift of prophecy," he said.

O'Juma drew closer and placed his hand on Jabal's cheek. "How can I help you?"

Jabal clasped his hand and held it to his breast. "Food," he declared. "If you can go down into the compound and bring me a bundle of dried purple algae and some fruit and nuts enough for six people, that would be the greatest help."

"That is all?" O'Juma complained.

"It is no small thing I ask. I cannot do it myself, for my life could be endangered if I am seen."

O'Juma shook his head with new worry. "Your life…endangered? Jabal!"

Jabal laughed it off. "Everything will be all right, my friend. Stop worrying." He squatted down and gestured for O'Juma to do the same and leaned closer. "There is a more important reason why I called for you. I need for you to create a bit of a rumor."

"A rumor?"

"Tai, about Senior Elder Sahdon and myself."

O'Juma's eyes grew wide. "You have been in league with the head of the Unbelievers!?"

"Shhhh! Just listen. Before you gather food for us, gather a lot of food, water and some sha in another large basket. Tell the guards in front of the cave entrance that you wish to bring food and drink to those below in the caves. Slip into the conversation that you would have brought more, but that you knew the Senior Elder Sahdon was not down there because you saw him with me above the cave to the northwest."

The muscles in O'Juma's face tensed and he gave his face a vigorous rub setting his hair beads into a clattering chorus again. "How do I go about saying these things?"

"You are clever. You will think of something. Tell them we were praying together."

O'Juma huffed in frustration.

"The guards will never let you pass. They will insist that some other guard take the food to the Rebel Elders below. When the guard takes the food, bring the other sack of food back here to us quickly, but make sure no one sees you."

"And how will this start a rumor?"

"Remember," Jabal said with an upright finger held to his lips.

"Tai, the less I know…" O'Juma grunted.

The Initiate mumbled over his shoulder as he lumbered down the hill toward the compound, complaining his worry would be the death of him someday. And Jabal and his tiny companion hid behind the bushes and waited patiently for O'Juma's return.

In the twilight of the camp no one noticed the Initiate when he loaded a large basket with the requested food, water and a bit of sha gathered in several pipes of bamboo. He lifted the heavy load onto his back and made his way over to the cave entrance where only one of the Rebel guards was standing alone at his watch with two torches by his side. He scanned the compound searching for the other guard. A prone figure close by snored under a cedar, a spear still clasped in his hand.

In front of the cave entrance stood Tundaas, one of the Queen's Warriors turned renegade. He was the same height as O'Juma, but lacking the young Initiate's muscle mass. He wore the customary garb of a warrior – a pair of crocodile buskins, a diagonal chest band made of the same hide, and a crocodile wraparound, instead of the common barkcloth skirt. He tensed when the stranger approached and blocked O'Juma with his spear.

O'Juma approached the guard cautiously with his head held down in supplication and respect. "I thought perhaps you and the others would enjoy a basket of food and fresh water. I have brought some sha as well." He lifted the caddy of food up for the guard's inspection. "I would have brought Senior Elder Sahdon some food too, but I know he is with the First Apprentice above the caves. I pray this is enough."

The guard looked up and down the Initiate with spiteful shrewdness, amazed at the boy's strength and alert to his message about the Sahdon. "You say you saw the Senior Elder…with Jabal, the Apprentice?"

"Tai. I saw the two of them above the cave to the northwest soon after all of you gathered in the tunnels."

Tundaas grunted. "You are a Believer who has come to poison the Elders," the guard stated flatly.

"I am neither a Believer or Unbeliever," O'Juma explained as he put his heavy load down. "I am only a humble servant to Lord Tagheetu, to all the Spirits and to the Ancestors."

O'Juma gazed directly into Tundaas's eyes, a silent plea for mercy and reason. "All men must eat and drink," he finally said.

The guardsman squinted in the torchlight and eyed O'Juma's clan and status tattoos and his long curly hair adorned with shells, bone beads and colorful feathers. "You have the markings of a Shaman's Lesser Apprentice. Is that not true?"

"It is true."

"You say you are neither a Believer or Unbeliever? Do you not also serve your Master, Mefakani? And do you know that your own Master is the True Teacher?"

"Tai, I serve my Master. And I have heard he has fulfilled the prophecy."

"And yet you do not believe or disbelieve? Did you not see your own Master ride in the heavens? He also carries the sacred mark upon his brow."

"Tai, I saw the airboat, but I do not know who is the Prophet," O'Juma confessed, feeling he had suddenly been caught off balance. "When Master Mefakani is not ignoring me, he is putting me through rigorous tests which always result in harsh reprimands for my failings. If he is the True Teacher then he is a hard taskmaster. I respect the discipline, but…"

"Maybe you are trying to trick our leaders into eating tainted food."

"But there is a truce. And negotiations are going on. Why would I want to poison anyone?"

The guard examined the contents of the basket and picked up a ripe plum. "Eat one of those," he demanded, tossing him the plum.

O'Juma caught the plum, let out a deep sigh and took a huge bite out of it.

"Swallow it," the guard insisted.

O'Juma made sloppy, joyful noises and an exaggerated face like he was enjoying it. He swallowed and took another bite. "Ummm," he moaned as he let the purple juice roll between his fingers.

"If you have poisoned this food how do I know you do not hold an antidote for the poison? You are a shamanic Initiate after all."

O'Juma raised an eyebrow. "If the food was poisoned would I not be poisoning everyone indiscriminately?" He let out a snort of pleasure and licked his fingers. "Should I eat another?" he asked mumbling with his mouthful.

"No," said the guard. He scrutinized O'Juma's well-built body. "Do you have any weapons?"

"Only my good looks." O'Juma grinned, revealing a row of perfect white teeth now stained purple.

The guard let out a hearty laugh and tugged on the front of O'Juma's waistband. He ran his fingers around the inside to search for weapons. "Turn around," he ordered.

The Lesser Apprentice spun around with the lightness of a dancer then gave the guard a challenging smirk. "Satisfied. Or do you expect more from me?"

"Ahh, you are a pretty one – a chicken in a rooster body," the guard chuckled mockingly. "I see you have no weapons. Go and give the food and water to the Elders yourself. And tell them what you told me about seeing Elder Sahdon and the Apprentice."

O'Juma's grin suddenly faded.

"Go on!" Tundaas said and pointed his spear at O'Juma's crotch.

O'Juma heaved the heavy basket over his shoulder and ducked his head through the low rocky archway. He walked slowly into the dark tunnel until he came to a fork in the passageway and stopped abruptly.

"Do you not know the way, girlie-man? Your Shaman's chamber is to the right."

O'Juma groaned in response. "I know where it is. Will you give me no torch?"

"So you may set one of our leaders on fire? Not likely. Find your way in the dark."

O'Juma inched his way into the darkness with his promises to Jabal weighing heavy on him. The familiar smell of burning torches alerted him to which direction he should go, but he was offended by the trace of urine in the cramped suffocating air.

He walked cautiously down the right passageway with his left shoulder glancing the rough wall as a guide while he crept along with his load. The strong smell of sweaty men and urine grew bolder and he could hear the sound of the old men's voices reverberate off the stony walls.

They were arguing with one another when he suddenly appeared in the torchlight and all conversation came to an abrupt halt.

A tall guard, who had to crouch so his head didn't hit the rough ceiling, held him back with the point of his spear. "Stop right there!" the guard called out, towering over O'Juma.

O'Juma bowed steeply and kept his head down. "I am just a courier," he croaked out, suddenly taken back by the sharp weapon held inches from his chest.

Cranik came up to inspect the intruder in the half-light. "Who are you and why are you here?" he snapped.

O'Juma raised his head to look the ugly Elder in the eye. "My name is O'Juma-Jay. I thought you all might be hungry and thirsty. We still have a truce, do we not?" He pursed his lips together.

Kulo rolled onto his side with difficulty then drew himself up on one arthritic knee, then the other. He had to grab the hand of one of the guards to pull himself to his feet. When he straightened up to his full height everyone heard his back crack into place. "Agh!" he grunted then hobbled over to the others. "Thank you, boy," he said.

"I…I am sorry I did not bring more sha," he stuttered. "I know the Senior Elder enjoys sha a great deal, but since he is not here…"

The two Elders looked at one another then back at the boy.

"How do you know he is not here?" Cranik asked, a stabbing stare aimed at the boy.

"I saw him above the compound…shortly after you all arrived. And I did not see him return." O'Juma didn't elaborate.

Cranik looked up at Kulo. "I told you he was not inside the Shaman's chamber." He turned back to the Lesser Apprentice. "Exactly where did you see him last?"

O'Juma improvised as he went along, steering the Rebels clear of where Jabal and his Hummingbird companion sat in wait. "I saw him on top of the northwestern hills…behind some bushes. There are smaller caves above this vast cavern complex. I saw him near a shallow cave…where the Ancestral shrines are…with the Apprentice, Jabal."

"With Jabal?" Cranik asked.

"Tai. It seems both share in the dislike of the White man, Temple Fox."

Kulo leaned over and cupped his mouth over Cranik's ear. "The secret Informer?"

Cranik nodded without taking his eyes off the boy. "Our Guards have already searched for Sahdon. No one reported seeing him there. What in Tagheetu's name would our Senior Elder be doing there? And what were you doing there, boy?"

"I just happened upon him…but he did not see me. I was simply gathering some roots. I…I think he did not want anyone to see him. At least that is the impression I got."

It was enough of a distraction to create confusion. The Elders gathered and started gabbling to one another in unison.

"What is he up to?" Cranik wondered out loud.

"I do not wish to be ill mannered," O'Juma began politely, but a bit too boldly, "but before Jabal arrived, our respected Senior Elder was emptying his bowels when I came upon him, which I must say is a more respectful way of relieving oneself than what you all have done in this sacred cave."

Kulo held a look of guilt, but the comment stung Cranik.

"How dare you speak to your Elders in such a manner!" Cranik growled. "We do as we must! We are not leaving these tunnels no matter what our needs are!"

Feeling he had gone too far, O'Juma flushed with regret and sudden shame. He bowed his head quickly.

"Sahdon did not tell us he was leaving. Why has he not returned by now? Speak!" he shouted at the boy.

O'Juma had to think quickly. He raised his head, but averted Cranik's gaze. "I do not know. I did not disturb them. I gathered my roots and left."

"And you heard nothing?" Cranik pressed.

"Well…I think I heard them say they were going to…to pray…together," O'Juma announced not knowing what in heavens he would say next.

"Praying?" Cranik snarled back at the boy. "Shitting then praying? When he should be here!"

"Tai, it is best to empty ones bowels before praying. It is less of a body distraction and frees the mind," O'Juma offered. "There are numerous shallow caves and overhangs in that area. Shrines have been built in them for Initiates to quietly pray and meditate. I think they went in there to do ceremony. But I am only guessing."

Cranik retreated a few paces in thought with Kulo pressed behind him.

Kulo bent down to whisper to Cranik. "This ceremony the boy speaks of, perhaps Sahdon and the Apprentice were conjuring together to affect the outcome to Temple Fox."

"But why did he not tell us he was leaving?" Cranik whispered over his shoulder.

Kulo shrugged. "The Senior Elder often acts without our consent. But for certain he is planning something with Jabal, who we now know is the Informer."

Cranik glanced up at Kulo. "Trust no one," he whispered and walked back to where O'Juma stood.

O'Juma kept his eyes downcast, his heart pounding. He bowed slightly. "May I leave the food now and go?"

"Poison!" Cranik spat on the ground. "This is just a trick! And that stupid guard let him pass through!"

O'Juma was wide-eyed.

"If this fruit is not poisoned then eat one and drink some of that water."

"If you wish," O'Juma said. He took another piece of fruit, a calamansi this time. "I have no knife."

"Bite into it!" Crank demanded, showing his own large yellowed teeth.

The Lesser Apprentice dug his teeth into the outer skin of a calamansi and peeled the thin skin back until he could pry a piece of it with his teeth. He chewed, swallowed, chewed another piece and swallowed.

"And those?" Cranik pulled out his dagger and pointed it at the lengths of bamboo pipes.

O'Juma started to reach for a pipe of bamboo containing the water until Cranik's dagger stopped his hand. "You must take a sip out of each one," the old man ordered. He pulled out a pipe of bamboo filled with sha, sniffed it and handed it the boy.

"I...I cannot drink sha," O'Juma protested. "I would be breaking my shamanic vows."

"I will break more than your vows for you if you do not," Cranik pressed.

O'Juma whispered a prayer for forgiveness for his transgression and took a little sip from the bamboo pipe.

"More!" Cranik insisted.

The young man drew a deep breath then a deep drag from the brew. He burped and wiped his mouth with the back of his hand.

The others all laughed.

"Now we wait," Cranik said.

"Wait!?" O'Juma asked.

"To see if you die from your own poison," Cranik grinned.

CHAPTER SIX

CHANGES

*"One does not change the course of a river too
quickly without drowning."*

Elder Tani
The Makolese Scroll on
the Return of the Ka and the Mending of the Su #6

Mefakani held the knife up to the back of Temple's head and with one stroke made his cut. "There. That should be enough." He held the thick shock of hair up for Temple's inspection.

"You really think this is necessary?" Temple asked.

"You do not know Cranik like I do. Now, for the curtain." Mefakani ordered his servant boy, Tiv, to pull down the barkcloth curtain that had divided his chamber and cut it up into wide strips. The mute ran obediently over to the curtain and yanked on it until it collapsed on the floor in a great heap.

"One does not change the course of a river too quickly without drowning," Tani grumbled.

Mefakan's eyes fell on the old woman and he held his arms out as if to ask, "What have I done wrong now?"

"We do not have time to teach you to be human, Mefakani, but I will tell you this. If you order that boy around like your personal slave one more time, I am going to bite off the end of your nose!"

The Priest gave Tani a shallow bow and turned to his young helper. "I am sorry, boy. Better that I had asked you first." He gestured to the heavy cloth that was now lying on the floor. "Would you like to help us cut this up?"

Tiv nodded and the others knelt on the floor with the boy to cut sections of the broad cloth with Tani instructing them from time to time, spitting occasionally and mumbling quiet prayers to herself.

"Temple and Sahdon are the same height, but what about the weight difference?" Tani pointed out.

Everyone but Tiv stopped their work and looked up at the small, shriveled woman.

"Well, Sahdon is lighter than Temple by at least fifteen stones. Do you not think so?" she asked.

Temple got up and walked over to where Sahdon's body lay and examined the Elder's exact size and shape. "You're right. And then there's the matter of his withered leg. It won't look right unless we add something to it. Maybe that's where we can make up some of the weight."

He scanned the cavern, measuring each and every stalactite and stalagmite with a keen eye. "Here," he said. "That shape is perfect." He pointed above him to a tall, thin pinnacle of white dripstone.

Mefakani moved quickly to assist Temple. "Here," he said and handed him a long metal rod he had stashed in the corner. "Use this to break it off."

"Wait!" Losha said, rushing to Temple's side. She paused beneath the stone and poured an offering of coconut milk on the ground. Then Temple hoisted her up onto his shoulders. He handed her the metal rod.

She sat on top of his shoulders without making any movements for several long moments.

"Well?" Temple asked, annoyed.

"I am asking its permission," she explained. "I do not wish to break the spirit of the stone."

Temple started to wobble under Losha's weight. "I can't hold you up like this all day."

Losha stroked the stone lovingly and gave it a gentle tug until the stone cracked and dropped off into her hands. She passed the precious sword of stone down to Mefakani.

Temple eased her down to the ground. She handed the rod back to Temple and smirked at him impishly.

"Thank you, but I did not need this after all," she said.

"I think I know why I love you so much." He smiled.

Temple made quick work of lifting and rolling Sahdon's body so Losha could wrap it in strips of barkcloth. When they came to the Elder's withered leg, Temple placed the long horn of stone snuggly against it and bound it tightly.

Losha looped the last strip of cloth under Sahdon's foot and tied the end back up around the ankle, then leaned back to examine her work.

"How does he look?" she asked Temple.

"Like me, only dead," he answered. "The flies are a nice touch."

Losha looked around her and, seeing no one was watching, she leaned forward toward Temple. "I am so relieved this is not your body I am wrapping up."

Temple's face drew close to hers and he placed a gentle kiss on her waiting mouth. "I owe my life to you," he whispered.

Losha lingered close to him, sharing his moist breath. She stole a quick glance behind her and seeing that Tani's eyes were closed she whispered softly. "What are we going to do with Tani? She must not be found here when the Unbelievers come to take the body."

Temple whispered back. "We can hide her back inside that rock trough and cover her up."

"You think I am still dead and cannot hear you?" Tani called out. "If you think you are going to hide me inside that moldy pit again, you can forget it!"

Temple looked back at the old Healer. "But Tani, you can't be found here when the Unbelievers come inside this chamber. It won't be safe. Why not spin into a dolphin? We could fill that niche with fresh water. Then we can lift you up and place you inside it. You'd be more comfortable there in your dolphin form. Besides, they would never know it was really you."

Tani groaned. "Now all I need to do is have enough strength to spin again."

Temple squinted at her through the torchlight. "You can't spin?"

Tani held her bony arms out, her shriveled skin hanging from them loosely like wet laundry. "I am a hundred and ten seasons or a hundred and twenty season old. I forget. I have just spent five suns underwater in a stone trough, and you ask me, can I spin? I am lucky if I can walk from here to there without tripping over my breasts."

"Well, I guess I never thought about it," Temple said, somewhat disappointed.

"Temple, I have not spun for years…not after everyone lost their Kas," she confessed. "Losing their lifeforce affected me profoundly. Believe me, if I had been able to spin I would have been able to visit Winyon without rousing suspicion. I might have been able to break the spell on her before Jabal did. But the Gods have their timing," she sighed, "and the children of the blue Earth grow old."

"Temple," Mefakani interrupted, "I have been pondering what to do with Elder Tani as well."

Tani crossed her arms over her breasts. "I refuse to leave until Temple is completely well. He has been through too much trauma," the old woman said with a stubborn huff to punctuate her point.

"Now Tani," Losha spoke boldly. "You must leave this cavern. I will take care of Temple myself."

Tani saw the fire and power inside the beautiful Swan and a joyful tear came to her eye.

Her time has ripened.

"As you wish," she said and bowed her head toward Losha.

"I have an idea," Mefakani said. The Priest explained his simple plan.

Even though she appeared small and fragile, and more than a little wrinkled from having soaked so long in the chemical brine, Tani sat on the throne of flowstone alert and authoritative. She nodded in approval.

"I look forward to the fresh air," she said.

"Good. We're set," Temple replied, "but we must wait for either Winyon or Jabal to return first."

CHAPTER SEVEN

THE ALLY

"If I do not return, please help my friends."

Jabal, the Shaman's First Apprentice
The Makolese Scroll on
the Return of the Ka and the Mending of the Su #7

"Bi Kana! What took you so long?" Jabal said admonishing his friend as O'Juma marched up the hill carrying a basket.

O'Juma shoved the basket at Jabal. "Here! Mind your birdbrain friend does not try to peck me to death."

"I do not know why you are so angry," Jabal said. "You would think you would be happy to see me alive."

"I am happy to see you at all!" O'Juma said. "And would very much like to know if and when I will see you again…alive that is."

"Dearest friend, I do not know. But please try to not worry about me."

"Worry? Why in the starry heavens would I worry about the Shaman's principal Apprentice who is up to his ass in some sort of political and religious whale dung? Which reminds me," O'Juma said. "I was delayed by a mean-looking guard and a tunnel full of dirty, sweaty Rebels who fouled the tunnels with their own personal filth."

"I am so sorry," Jabal said.

"First they got me drunk. Then they made me clean up their latrine and bring in new sand for them to defecate in since they will not leave the door to the Priest's cavern – even to relieve themselves. Just so you know, I made them believe that you and Senior Elder Sahdon were above and beyond the cavern to the northwest to pray in one of the shrines."

Jabal glanced at the Hummingbird with a smile. "That fits well into our plans." He turned back to his lover. "Great work my sweet friend. Was there anything else you could glean from their conversation while you were there?" he asked.

"Tai, they talked freely in front of me as if I were nothing but a common bug." He grabbed Jabal by the forearm. "Have you somehow become a spy for the Unbelievers? You told me before I left that you believed Temple Fox was the True Prophet and Teacher - along with the Interpreter."

"It is complicated. Please believe me when I say Temple Fox and Losha Ninti are the true Teachers. Come. I have one more thing you can do for me." And with those last words O'Juma, Jabal and the Hummingbird moved swiftly through the forest back to the air vent from which they had escaped.

Jabal came to a small clearing circled by trees. He showed O'Juma the air vent above Mefakani's private chamber. He lowered the basket of food on a vine through the small hole, then informed the others below where the Believers and the Unbelievers were positioned. He told them about O'Juma's success with the rumor he had planted.

"If I do not return, please help my friends," he said to O'Juma. Then, saying goodbye, he took off into the forest with Winyon flying above him.

O'Juma stood still brooding over the course of events. He turned slowly, lost in thought, and ambled back to the hillside of bushes above the Shaman's compound. And from there he lumbered back down to the compound with bewilderment and worry crowding his thoughts.

CHAPTER EIGHT

ZOONZOONA-IKITAN

"The Spirits can be such misers."

Elder Tani
The Makolese Scroll on
the Return of the Ka and the Mending of the Su #8

The Apprentice climbed atop a small, stony hill above and well beyond the sight of the Shaman's compound. He pushed aside curtains of hanging moss, struggling in the fading light to scour the jungle for the area Losha had described to him. On the other side of the hill he slid down into a grove of mother banyans thickly carpeted in moss. It was here where he'd find what he was searching for. Gnarled roots curled up out of the thin soil, twisting themselves into thick-knotted snake like shapes. The Apprentice leaped over them hurriedly until he came to an embankment where a recently toppled banyan had a death grip on a tumble of jagged green boulders. Jabal peered into the large gap the rocks made in the upturned soil. Through this craggy crevice Losha said he'd find the small cave that had once been her prison. That cave would take him into the complex of tunnels below.

He whistled like a titwee and within seconds Winyon soared down from a strangler fig and hovered in front of his face.

"I think I found it." He pointed to the fissure between the boulders and watched as Winyon flew inside. While he waited for her return he took Sahdon's leather sandal, which he had taken off of Sahdon's body, and tucked it in the back of his waistband. Then he took the bejeweled silver gris, which was Sahdon's personal dagger noting his office as Senior Elder, and rolled it tightly inside the back of his waistband along with the sandal. He secured them both with a strand of jute.

When Winyon reappeared she circled around Jabal excitedly.

"Good. It is the right one," Jabal declared with equal excitement. He stepped into a clear, level area to make his change.

"Too bad I do not have wings like you," he said. He closed his eyes and crossed his arms by placing each hand on opposite shoulders. And as he invoked the powers of the Spirit of Ahglehsh'kahlah he slowly pivoted in a circle, using his left foot as an anchor. And while he spun he sang his song of changing.

His spinning was so balanced and his intentions so clear that his man-form quickly spiraled down into a tiny cloud of luminous green light, until his reptilian body spun to a skidding halt. He waited for his dizziness to subside before he took a few steps to see if the sandal and dagger were still secured. Seeing that they were balanced well on top of his back, he scurried down through the crevice, using his tiny, sharp claws to clutch the pitted surface of the rock.

As Jabal crawled deeper into the hollow darkness he heard a loud buzzing and the air stir softly around him and knew that the Hummingbird was by his side. The Lizard jerked his head in her direction and an impulse was roused in him to flick his sticky tongue out to catch and eat her. He squelched the temptation through his half-human will and snatched a few flies and mosquitoes instead, satisfying both his instinct and hunger, until he could focus his intention on climbing down the rock again.

After his four feet found level ground he crept to where the timber door sat ajar. He slithered around it and waited on the other side until he heard the thrumming of Winyon's wings again.

This was a narrow tunnel that connected to a maze of corridors, which the Apprentice knew well enough. But at ground level without a torch to guide them he paused every so often to climb a dank wall or two to make certain he had taken the right route.

It was about a quarter of mile into their journey when the weight of Jabal's heavy burden shifted and caused him to lose his grip. He was pulled off a wall and fell with a thud onto his back, his legs kicking in the air. Winyon buzzed around him in a frenzied circle, until the tired lizard braced his legs against the wall, pushed and righted himself.

Better to stick to the ground, he thought.

Just when the journey was about to exhaust his patience he spotted a hint of torchlight coming from a tunnel that branched off sharply to his right. He stopped and peered around the corner. In the distance lazed more than a dozen men huddled together on the cold ground, some standing in relaxed stance. Guards stood alert at the entry to Mefakani's private cavern and the far passage that led to the outside.

All were armed including Elder Cranik who squatted on the ground talking with Elder Kulo in hushed whispers.

Jabal cocked his head upward with a jerky motion and rolled one eye up at Winyon and blinked, signaling he'd found the passageway where the Rebels waited, guarding the way to the Mother Stone deep within the labyrinth's interior.

The Lizard slithered around the opposite corner, slowly to the left, then dashed across the ground, hugging the wall and keeping in the shadows as he scurried.

Winyon hovered in the air at the junction for a fearful moment, then darted down the tunnel past Jabal until she was swallowed in the distant darkness.

"Damn bats!" someone yelled. A soldier stomped forward and threw a stone haphazardly at the fleeting shadow.

The Lizard froze in the shallow cleft of rough rock, his heart drumming faster. When the soldier retreated in disinterest Jabal scrambled to the next shadow, careful not to call attention to himself.

After the two rushed further into the obscurity of darkness for a hundred yards they slowed their pace. Jabal had to be sure he had the right passageway, especially from his vantage point on the ground.

I have only been to the Mother Stone once and that was with Tiv two years ago. Thank the gods he made me memorize the path in case something happened to him.

Jabal stopped to lick the dust from his eyes. *Two sharp turns to the left*, he remembered, *and then we will have to go two miles zigzagging back and forth until we reach five tunnels in a row. Then we take the third, which leads to a narrow opening that spirals downward to the right. At least, I hope I remembered that accurately.*

He felt each opening with his belly and his lizard senses, counting as he went, until he found the right one, then he would wait for the familiar humming above his head.

Jabal felt like he had been swallowed by a large beast and had been trapped inside its entrails. And the load he was carrying was awkward. Taking slavish, tiny steps blindly through the dark, serpentine tunnels in the stale air made him feel as if the journey would never end.

Jabal shifted his focus onto the bulky load tied to his back. His backbone was sore and his belly chaffed. But it was the knowledge that tons of stone pressed down on him from above that became the most oppressive weight on his mind and psyche. Still, he was an ancient species, at least in part, and also highly adaptable to all kinds of conditions. Knowing this eased him of his pain.

Time melded into a no-time delirium until a sound roused him to full alert. Ahead of him a series of high-pitched twitters cried out in panic and of warning.

It was Winyon!

Jabal followed the sound and found himself swiftly climbing the rugged walls, the sound growing louder and sharper. His eyes rolled around, searching the darkness until not his sight, but his ears caught the almost imperceptible sound familiar to all lizards. Beneath Winyon's frantic cries drummed the stacatto sound, *tick, tick, tick,* of eight fragile legs clambering over stone.

She is caught in a spider's web!

The Hummingbird hung in midair, her wings splayed out helplessly. The only thing holding her in place – a spiraled plane of webbing glued to an arched entry to yet another tunnel. She kicked her legs and beat her wings with madness, but the faster Winyon flapped her wings the more tangled she became in the sticky web. She tried to free herself by shuddering and then tossing her weight from side-to-side, but all attempts proved fruitless. Then she began pecking at the webbing one strand at a time until her tiny beak became ensnarled with the gluey filaments.

She sent out another muted shriek for help!

Jabal crept forward, stopped and listened. He moved again, stopped again and tested the air once more. The air around him was stirring madly. He charged forward full force scampering up the rough wall and cutting the silk using the dagger and sandal as a cutting ram as he ran. He started circling around where the filaments were attached, slicing through the webbing as he went until he heard a shrill cry and heard Winyon free fall and land on the stony ground with barely a thud!

The Lizard stood motionless to get his bearings. He heard the faint sound - *ticky-tacky-ticky-tacky*- of eight tiny legs walking backward, then a silence.

Larger than the length of a man's foot. Long-legged, he discerned with his keen lizard senses. *Probably a Zoonzoona-ikitan cave spider. Deadly.*

Knowing the spider viewed him as its next prey, Jabal took quick and careful aim where he had last heard the cave spider. With split second accuracy he flicked out his sticky tongue and captured one leg of the huge spider, snapped it back into his mouth and crunched down on the leg and half the torso of the hairy brittle creature.

The Zoonzoonza-ikitan's other seven legs folded up like a Swiss army knife.

Dazed, Winyon pumped her little legs in the air and let out a series of high-frequency tweets to let Jabal know where she had fallen.

Swallowing the last of the Zoonzoona-ikitan, Jabal raced down the wall to where Winyon had fallen. He gobbled up the sticky strands that still held her captive and used his tongue for the finer cleaning until the fragile bird was unbound and free to move.

The wet bird shivered, then once again rose into the air. She buzzed around Jabal's head, expressing her gratitude, then soared into the next tunnel past the tattered spider web.

The tunnel meandered on and on, slowly spiraling downward until Jabal fell into a kind of malaise. But slowly a sourness in his intestines vied for his attention.

Feeling the cold more keenly now, he longed to bask in the noonday sun. But daydreams were a luxury and he pressed on, small steps-by-step, another inch, another yard. The acid in his stomach grew increasingly vile and he paused to adjust his load, thinking the gris and the sandal might have been bound too tightly against his belly.

All at once stomach bile rose into his throat. He darted off the main tunnel to another passageway and regurgitated undigested fragments of the spider onto the stone ground.

"Yuk!" He let out a throaty groan and smacked his tongue, letting a string of drool fall from his chin to form a little puddle at his feet.

Winyon clung to the rough side of a stalactite to conserve her energy while Jabal sat for several minutes grooming himself until he felt some of the poison was out of his system. And while he crouched, sliding his tongue over his claws and feet, he suddenly realized he had lost his bearings. He took off a few yards in what he thought was the right direction when his feet scampered over something that felt out of place.

These are not rocks, he thought. He sent out a squeak to signal Winyon to wait until he investigated his surroundings.

Still unable to see, Jabal used his feet to trace the length of the long rounded object he was perched on. He stopped abruptly.

Bones! Human bones!

The tunnels were cramped with the bodies of Rebel Soldiers, old men and the stench of their bodies.

Cranik stood facing the monolithic stone that separated him from Mefakani. "What is taking so long?" he complained.

Kulo, who was sitting on the ground, flicked his thick fingers over his white curly hair. "Bi kana! I have spiders in my hair! You cannot hurry magic," he said wearily to Cranik.

Cranik turned to face the Elder. "Oh, how would you know?" he said.

Kulo narrowed his eyes on Cranik. His jaw tightened. "Then for Lord Tagheetu's sake, take a break. Go up and get some fresh air. It will do you good."

Cranik jutted his oversized jaw down into Kulo's face. "And leave this door? Never!" The old man worked himself into a lather and kicked the stone door with his sandal. "Ouch!"

Kulo guffawed. The soldiers repressed their laughter.

Cranik's face twisted in pain and fury. He hobbled backward. Unfinished with his rage, he swung around sharply and thrust the butt of his scimitar into the mammoth rock door with a forceful grunt.

"That was very effective," Kulo said dryly.

"Shut up!" Cranik snapped.

★　★　★　★　★　★

The sound of metal against rock reverberated inside the Shaman's chamber. Everyone stopped what they were doing and looked at each other candidly, afraid.

Tani gummed the last bit of food and swallowed. "Do not worry. There are a multitude of Spirits that assist us now." She tipped a length of bamboo upside down into her mouth. Only one drop of liquid fell on her tongue. She creased her leathery face. "No sha left. The Spirits can be such misers."

CHAPTER NINE

THE OFFERING

THE CAPTIVE
"The bee encased in amber
like a sweet jewel of surrendered death;
the desperate dance captured
before the liquid embryonic breath.
Smoldering heat of life,
you glow like magma
trapped beneath the Earth
like a quiet death
escaping
the noisy hammer of birth."

Fragment of a poem by
O'Juma-jay, the Lesser Apprentice
The Makolese Scroll on
the Return of the Ka and the Mending of the Su #9

Jabal patted the bone with his feet then rolled it over.
Ribs!
His tongue flickered over the old bone until he explored further and found a vertebra and then another. Feeling his way up the spine, he paused over the vertebra directly behind where the human heart would have been, but had long since turned into dust. Resting his chest against the bone, his own heart pounded softly to the slower rhythm of the human heart that had entrained its rhythm inside the vertebra, he divined the history of its owner.

This bone is from a woman – an old woman, he gathered from the vibration. *She was seeking the Mother Stone and got lost. But she was so close to finding Her!* he lamented. His heart wept as he sensed the old woman's overwhelming grief before she succumbed to hunger, cold, and despair.

"An oracle," he grunted. *She had sought counsel about her grandchildren's fate during the Great Massacre. She saw them chained and loaded onto a boat by the Slavers!*

Jabal's heart was about to break when the air above him stirred. The Hummingbird zipped back and forth through the tunnel, each time weaving a different pattern in the air to alert Jabal to something important she had discovered behind them.

Jabal ran a slippery tongue over his eyes. Casting a blind eye above him to where Winyon's wings thrummed, he said a silent prayer before leaving the remains of the old woman behind. The Lizard-boy scampered over the loose bones until his four feet touched the ground again and he faced in the direction Winyon now urged him to follow. And from there, Jabal set his intentions to press onward to the original tunnel from which he had veered.

Fifty feet further and the Apprentice discovered something familiar underfoot, something that broke through the sorrow he felt within his half-human heart. He paused to get his bearings then circled round a large, distinctive scallop housing a small pool of water in the stone floor. He knew where he was, stole a quick drink from the pool, then scurried a few yards forward excitedly, until the hilt of the dagger tied to his back collided with something striking a loud metallic clang.

A huge horn of smooth stone rose from the floor at a peculiar forty-degree angle. That was the landmark Jabal had been anticipating. *Twenty feet beyond this stone I should find the Northern passageway leading to the antechamber and then the cavern holding the Mother Stone!*

Gauging twenty feet with his tiny steps, Jabal found the passageway. "This is it!" he cried and scratched the stone ground with a deft claw to signal to Winyon that their journey's end was near.

The Apprentice and the Exile wound their way past several tusks of limestone until their pathway was once again blocked, this time by a huge pile of broken stone.

This must be where the cave-in happened, Jabal reasoned.

He scuttled over the sharp rock, searching for an opening that would lead to the antechamber, which would inevitably lead them to the chamber where the Mother Stone was enshrined. The Hummingbird found an opening first and flew in and out of it, whipping up a soft breeze to catch the Lizard's attention.

The opening through the rubble was small, not large enough for even a child to climb through. Jabal scrambled up, over, and down the other side where the enclosure opened into a wide antechamber and a larger chamber beyond where the Mother Stone would be found.

Winyon landed beside her companion and the two stood very still. This was sacred ground and the Spirit of the Cave had to be appeased. Winyon plucked a few iridescent feathers from her delicate frame and laid them out in front of her. Jabal bit through the jute that bound Sahdon's sandal and gris. They loosened and Sahdon's dagger fell clattering to the ground. He nosed his offering forward.

It is time to make a change, he thought.

Jabal raced in a circle, head to tail until a small cyclone of green sparks shot out, casting an eerie glow against the flowstone. The cyclone rose in height and, in a bright flash, Jabal returned to his man-form.

Now we need light so Winyon can make her change.

The Apprentice ran his hands haphazardly across the wall about waist high, patting the stone in the direction he had remembered. All at once one hand yielded to a deep niche in the stone. Jabal examined the perimeter of the carved niche, exploring its arched shape until he was satisfied. He reached down blindly. His hand came to rest on a familiar shape – a round-bellied oil jar. Beside it sat three torches, a piece of flint and a heavy chunk of iron pyrite.

"We are well supplied for light," he called out.

He opened the lid to the oil jar, took a quick approving sniff, then pulled out a torch. Dipping the torch head first, he let the excess oil drip back into the jar until he was certain the bark and cloth wrapped around the torch was soaked but not dripping to avoid catching himself on fire.

He rested the torch on the ground, then struck the pyrite and flint together over the torch. Striking the stone in furious succession created flashes of sparks that shattered the darkness, if only for split seconds. When one spark finally hit the oily bark, the torch came alive with a *whoosh* and a blinding flash. Jabal quickly grabbed the burning stick and held it out in front of him, a satisfied smile spreading across his face.

Jabal lit another torch from the first and stood back in wonderment as the darkness was driven back. He found a hole in the wall and secured the end of the torch therein. As his eyes adjusted to the flicker of flame and shifting shadows, the antechamber revealed its vaulted ceiling, hand-carved by an unknown race who came to Makol before the Giants of the Si Te Cah Clan, or so the legends said. Surrounding the wide perimeter sat thousands of years of treasures brought by seekers of the Mother's oracles.

Winyon flew down and perched on Jabal's shoulder. Together the two stood staring.

Gifts of long forgotten herb bundles, roots, and barkcloth stamped in colorful designs sat rotting on the dank ground. But the more durable treasures carved in bone and stone, and forged in the best metals, sat around the perimeter of the chamber on ledges and wide plinths formed from thick stalagmites. There were swords and daggers obtained from Javanese, African, Indian and Arab traders, fine jewelry made of Spanish gold, and a heap of precious iron nails with the wooden barrel, which had once contained them, also rotting, having fallen apart long ago in a radiating circle. Many of the offerings that had been obtained from the Outsiders during Su rituals and war were now covered in thick mold, dust, and cobwebs.

The Apprentice looked down at himself and eyed the abrasions on his chest. He attempted to dust himself off, but he was so filthy the act seemed futile.

Winyon flew off Jabal's shoulder to inspect something that caught her eye – a silver teapot of Indian design. She rubbed herself against its black belly, long since tarnished, and pecked at her shadowy reflection. When she darted into the air to escape her own image, her wings stirred up the dust into tiny eddies.

Jabal chuckled and coughed. "You better spin and change before you peck yourself to death."

Soon a mad humming filled the cave as Winyon, the Chokahpeiyape, flew to make her transformation.

The energy from Winyon's magic was so strong that Jabal backed his way over to a thick buttress of pink flowstone to ground himself. As she circled round, the buzzing grew louder and the cave glowed with a subtle rainbow light. The bird flew ever faster in the large enclosure, a thin luminous lavender-blue-green line being her signature now, but Jabal could tell it was taking too long.

"Come on," he whispered. "Do as I taught you! You can do it!"

He held his breath as he watched the streak of light suddenly bounce and wobble out of control, and the opalescence flicker then fade.

He prayed aloud quietly, diligently. "May the powers of the Mother Stone and the Hummingbird Spirit, Tahnah-henah, help Winyon make her change. May all who dwell in Divine awareness help. Please," he pleaded. "It is only the second time she has attempted this!"

Jabal felt the chamber suddenly grow crowded with the presence of spirits. He thought about what he and Winyon were attempting to do as a way of explaining his intentions to the unseen. His part and Winyon's part seemed so small, and yet there were numerous lives at stake should any of their plan fail. "We must succeed!" he insisted.

The Apprentice sighed with relief as Winyon's delicate thrumming wings filled his ears again. Suddenly thoughts of O'Juma came sharply into his awareness. O'Juma's warm and caring presence was so palatable Jabal was certain O'Juma was somewhere deep in meditation, sending him energy. The Apprentice let the back of his head rest gently against the smooth wall and relaxed in the fullness and power of O'Juma's love, his eyes filling with tears of gratitude.

"We are nothing without love," he whispered.

With that all-encompassing feeling suffusing his mind and open heart, Jabal extended love out toward the Hummingbird and prayed fervently for her.

Slowly, ever so slowly a luminous spark reappeared faintly at first, then grew into an unbroken line of fox-fire blue as Winyon regained her rhythm once more. Jabal whispered words of thanks to the Mother Stone and Her Guardians, to the Spirit of Tahnah-henah, and his dear O'Juma for the power they all sent, when the Hummingbird spiraled in ever smaller circles until she grazed the floor.

Winyon landed on the gritty stone ground in a storm of explosive color. Jabal shaded his eyes as a thin cyclone of incandescent light rose from the center of the floor, and out of the brilliance staggered Winyon. She tottered to the ground and was panting wildly.

Jabal rushed over to her.

Pearls of sweat glistened on the round of Winyon's cheek and forehead in the flickering torchlight. Her face contorted in pain. "My arm," she gasped. "I bruised my wing."

Jabal placed his hands on Winyon's arm and called forth his healing powers. "Losha hurt herself too when she first learned to spin. That is how she received the sacred mark upon her brow," he said.

"I did not think...I would make it," she said, her heart still beating out of control. "Then...all of a sudden...I felt this tremendous love pour through me." She looked up at Jabal from the cool stone floor. "It was exquisite."

Jabal smiled broadly. "I was beginning to think I had been a terrible teacher."

"Never." Her mouth was dry and she swallowed hard. "You just do not know, young man. You just do not know. Five seasons I have spent in exile with my husband. And two seasons after his murder...I have been in total isolation...with not another ear to hear me...not a soul to speak with. And then Temple Fox flies into my life." She raised her head off the ground and smiled. "And here I am spinning…and drinking nectar from flowers…and spinning back into myself again and having this conversation with you. Oh, you just do not know."

Noticing her pain had diminished, she eased herself into a sitting position. "I do not know why it took me so long to make the change," she said, still gasping for breath.

"It takes a lot of intense concentration and practice to raise your vibration. Considering you are new at this, you did extremely well." He smiled.

The woman lowered her head with respect. "To my teacher," she said in praise.

Jabal offered his hand and helped Winyon to her feet. She walked over to where she had left her tiny feather and repositioned it on top a plinth of flowstone with as much reverence as if she were offering gold.

Jabal knelt down and picked up Elder Sahdon's leather sandal and tucked it into his waistband. He walked over to the silver gris lying on the ground next to the altar and picked it up, too. The torchlight gleamed against its fine filigree, its gemstones of carnelian, jet, and the rare green and white eyeball jasper stared up at him.

"The eye that never blinks," he said, addressing the jasper. "You will serve a grander purpose today and be a witness." He turned to his companion. "Cranik and his men will think Elder Sahdon left this as his offering to the Spirit of the Cave."

"And what will you leave as an offering?" Winyon asked.

Jabal dug into his soiled and tattered sash and pulled out a smooth flat piece of something that flashed golden in the firelight. He held it up to the flames for her inspection then handed it to her.

Winyon stared at the piece of polished transparent amber, noting the tiny ancient honeybee encapsulated inside, traces of its death dance, where its legs had scrambled helplessly, having marred the interior. "It is magnificent…and so light!" She handed the specimen back to Jabal. "Where did you ever get such a prize?"

Jabal looked into Winyon's beautiful, but dirty face. "Tiv gave it to me."

Winyon's lips parted in surprise. "Tiv?"

"Tai, when he was Mefakani's First Apprentice. He gave me this as a gift when I had reached an advanced level in my healing skills. The High Shaman had given it to Tiv as a gift when he had first learned to spin. But, of course, that was before Mefakani experimented on him." He gazed down at the tiny bee imprisoned inside the ancient fossilized resin and lowered his head in humiliation and guilt. "I was not kind to him," he confessed. "I will leave it as an offering and pray not only for the salvation of our people, but particularly for Tiv's healing."

"It is the perfect gift for the Mother Stone," she whispered.

He nodded his head then quoted:

> "The bee encased in amber
> like a sweet jewel of surrendered death;
> the desperate dance captured
> before the liquid embryonic breath.
> Smoldering heat of life,
> you glow like magma
> trapped beneath the Earth
> like a quiet death
> escaping
> the noisy hammer of birth."

"Who wrote that poem?" Winyon asked.

"O'Juma," Jabal answered with quiet pride. "Those were his first impressions of the amber when I showed it to him."

Winyon smiled and watched as Jabal reverently placed the piece of amber onto a plinth of pink flowstone. He bowed reverently, then backed away. "Come," he said, "we must widen the opening at the cave-in so Cranik will believe we climbed through it."

Although Winyon only had one good arm to work with, which slowed their progress, the two worked side-by-side clearing the mass of rubble that blocked their exit.

"I will do whatever Temple, the Master Teacher, says. I owe it to him," Jabal grunted, heaving a large rock to the side.

Winyon looked up from her labor as if to ask why.

The Apprentice stopped his work and slung his head low. "I formed an agreement with Senior Elder Sahdon," he whispered in confession. "I am the one who arranged for Temple's assassination in the swamp."

"I had not heard of this," Winyon said.

Jabal's shoulders slumped forward, the weight of his guilt pressing down on him. He looked up at the slender woman. "I almost killed the True Teacher," he said, choking on the words.

"I do not think you could have killed him," Winyon said. "Do not be so hard on yourself. We all have been fooled at one time or another.

Think of how so many have been fooled by Mefakani? I once was in love with him, Jabal. Who is the bigger fool, you or me?"

"I did not know," he said in a breathy voice, astonished that Mefakani could have been the object of such love. Jabal looked away from the depth of her gaze and set to working again, his heart in a quandary about how feelings that speak the truth one moment, feel false the next.

When they had finished, an area large enough for a grown man to fit through had been cleared. To prove it was large enough, Jabal climbed through with ease and squeezed back again. He stood in front of Winyon, his face turning slightly in the shadows to hide a nervous twitch. Pointing to the Northern entrance where a deep archway laid in wait, he spoke again with hesitancy. "I think we are ready to meet with the Mother Stone," he said anxiously. "Then I will plant the Elder's sandal as planned."

"You have been here only once?" she asked.

"Tai," he replied.

"And did She speak to you?"

"It was a brief encounter, but She did speak to me. She told me that some day I would become a High Shaman, but that I had to pass an important test involving discernment. Naturally, I thought I had passed the test when Temple Fox fell from the sky and Mefakani claimed the White man was the True Teacher. I thought Temple was a Wizard and secretly aligned myself with the Unbelievers. Now I see it was more of a test than I ever imagined."

"And you? Have you ever been here before?" he asked Winyon.

"I came here when I was studying to be a Shaman's Apprentice, but that was long before Mefakani and I broke off our relationship. Mefakani led me here right after his Master forbid women to come. I thought his Master was being ridiculous! The Mother Stone, after all, is female."

"And did She speak to you as well?" Jabal asked.

"I never made it this far. We got caught. I was barred from making the pilgrimage and banned from all sacred teachings after that. And Mefakani was severely punished for encouraging me to come."

"Well, there is no one stopping us now, unless of course the Spirit of the Cave or the Four Guardians that guard the Mother Stone have not accepted our offerings. Here is our chance to find out. Are you ready to go now?" he asked again.

Winyon nodded her head and placed a sympathetic hand on Jabal's shoulder as if to say she was apprehensive as well. She turned to retrieve a torch.

"Believe me, you will not need that," Jabal whispered.

Winyon nodded and took a deep breath. Without further delay the two walked slowly toward the Northern passageway – a short arched tunnel leading to the larger chamber that held the sacred stone.

Once through the thick arched passageway they stepped inside the dark cavern and a barely distinguishable luminescence grew slowly and steadily brighter acknowledging their presence. High above them sparkling pink stalactites hung from the tall cavern. The domed ceiling was carved in the same pattern as the antechamber, with six radiating lines cascading down. Columns of stalactites and stalagmites, which had long since joined together, formed huge shawls of flowstone with narrow waists. They came alive in the growing light in earthy hues of reds, luminous pinks, whites, and warm browns. The walls, too, began to glisten with minuscule pinpoints sparkling brilliance.

Awe overtook the pilgrims as they walked deeper into the center of the cavern, the unfathomable beauty and the energy intensifying and sending a distinct exhilarating tingle through their flesh. And in the distance stood the glowing Mother Stone, a natural formation of white translucent onyx that rose two and a half men tall from a narrow plinth of quartz crystal. A deep chasm surrounded Her like a moat with a narrow bamboo bridge, the only thing physically connecting the Mother to Her pilgrims.

At such a distance her shape seemed amorphous. But as the two drew closer they could see that the white, translucent stalagmite held the vague shape of a woman – a holy woman draped in a flowing robe or cape of some kind. She had ample bosom and round hips, her arms stretched slightly outward. Her face remained elusive and ill defined as if veiled, and what looked like long white hair fell behind her shoulders in thick luminous strands. Her legs were indistinctive as well and grown together into a massive pillar that anchored her to the narrow platform of quartz.

A curious feeling washed over the pilgrims. Although the temperature of this place was cool, they felt their insides fill with a nourishing warm.

Both ventured further until they stood in front of the great oracle. They placed their heads against the ground. Before the two had a chance to thank the Spirits of the Cave and state their intentions with prayer, the glow from the Mother Stone started to flicker. Suddenly there came a short, deep rumble and the Earth shook beneath their feet, showering them with grit. Jabal clasped his arms around Winyon and doubled her over on the ground, using his body to shield her.

When the shaking stopped all that remained were dust particles choking the air and muting the light.

Jabal unfolded from a crouch and shook the grit from off his back. "We are fortunate that it was only a small tremor. Are you all right?" he asked.

Winyon worked the dust out of her throat in coughs. "Tai," she sputtered.

The dust had obscured her vision, but she could still see the arched stone entranceway that was their only passage back to the antechamber. It was still clear. She tightened her grip on Jabal's hand when she stood up.

"Your back is bleeding!" she said in alarm.

"I am only scratched. Besides it will look more convincing to the others if there is a little blood," he said, and laughed. "Consider it a flesh offering."

The Wounded Hummingbird looked at the blood on her own aching arm and then Jabal's dirty, blood streaked back and chest. "I would not laugh Jabal. The Mother Stone and the Guardian Spirits of this place are angry. And who can blame them." She scanned the vast ceiling of the chamber in the twilight, looking for loose dripstone that might fall on them. "Are you not frightened by all of this?" she asked.

Jabal hesitated slightly. "Tai, I am." He fell silent again and then spoke with a kind of melancholy. "I wish I had said more to O'Juma before we left."

"O'Juma is your beloved." It could have been a statement or a question.

The young man nodded his head and smiled. Suddenly the Mother Stone burned brighter, illuminating the cloud of dust all around them.

Winyon smiled back. "I had heard the Mother Stone glows at the mention of love. It does not judge. And I do not judge either, for I have been alone long enough to know that when you find love, no matter how it expresses itself, you must accept it and hold it to you dearly." Her voice diminished to a whisper. "You are blessed," she said.

"Thank you," he whispered back.

As the dust cleared they walked toward the edge of the chasm that separated them from the isle of rock holding the Mother Stone. They bowed again with deep respect and prayed aloud for the Makolese people and for the safe return of the captives in the High Priest's private cavern.

Jabal wiped his eyes with a dirty hand. "We beg of you to forgive us for the deaths that were caused through our spiritual ignorance, for the harm we caused the Earth and Her many kingdoms. We pray for the dead and ask their forgiveness." Jabal choked on his own words. "And we ask for a healing for Tiv."

The two sat in silence hoping their offerings and prayers would be accepted. Although their eyes were closed they felt the Stone glow brighter, and new warmth filled the cavern.

Winyon placed one hand over her heart, the other to her head from the dizzying energy. As she opened her eyes she exhaled in one long puff. "Whoa!" she exclaimed with a start.

Jabal opened his eyes and looked over at his companion. "What is it?"

"Can you feel that?" she asked. "Her energy is like a love potion – an elixir of true compassion. And did you hear Her?"

Jabal raised an eyebrow. "She spoke to you? I heard nothing."

"She acknowledged my suffering and said the second half of my life would bring me many blessings. She also said that because of my suffering I would help to heal someone special."

Jabal silently took in what she had said. "You are very lucky to have gotten such a message."

"Tai. So what do we do now?" she asked.

Jabal pointed to a narrow bamboo bridge that spanned the short distance to the pinnacle of rock. It was still swaying slightly from the quake. "I will place Sahdon's sandal on the bridge. You can tell Elder Cranik that the Senior Elder fell off it during one of the earlier quakes."

Winyon peered over the precipice into the darkness far below. She picked up a fist-sized stone and dropped it into the chasm. It took several long seconds before they heard a faint patter against stone below. "No one could survive that."

"Tai. And no one would risk their life to recover his body down there either. No one even knows how deep it is. As planned, I will stay here until Cranik's men come. Let them know I am the Informer, and let them see for themselves where I have been these past few suns. They will still think that I am loyal to them. Hopefully, the Mother's Guardians will not show their wrath again. You should go now."

Jabal stopped to gaze at the gracefulness of the older woman as she walked back toward the antechamber. In spite of her ragged appearance she was still a Makolese beauty.

Winyon turned to face Jabal.

"I apologize for saying this to you," Jabal started, "but you are an Exile, and in the eyes of those who can still remember you – you are a witch and murderer. We cannot afford having them recognize you.

The dirt has hidden your clan tattoos and personal markings well enough. But I think you should pull the shawl over your head. That way I am certain no one will know who you are in the dark."

Winyon drew her dirty shawl over her head, covering her long, silver hair.

"Think you can find your way back in the dark?"

"Tai. Hummingbirds have good memories for places." Winyon gave her young companion a motherly hug.

"I will pray for you," he whispered.

"And I for you."

CHAPTER TEN

THE MOTHER STONE

"Have mercy on me, Mother."

Jabal, the Shaman's First Apprentice
The Makolese Scroll on
the Return of the Ka and the Mending of the Su #10

They were a bedraggled mob crammed into the narrow corridor, the stench of their bodies hanging in the stagnant air. Few had slept, and when they had, it had been an uneasy sleep in shifts on the hard stone ground.

Elder Kulo groaned as he eased himself up on one knee and held his arm out for assistance. One of the Rebel guards lifted the Elder up and steadied him as the old man unfolded to his full height. His wooly white hair was matted and his face drawn in pain. In the harshness of heavy shadow and torchlight Elder Cranik looked no better. His cheeks were sunken and his eyes hollow as if they had been poked out.

Winyon waited for the right moment then staggered around the corner, wailing in desperation. "Help me! Please help me!" She dropped her burnt out torch and fell to the ground only after she was spotted and could see the movement of torchlight.

The echo of footsteps advanced and the flicker of torchlight against the rough walls grew brighter. Two Rebels with raised spears came into view. Each held a torch over Winyon.

"Please!" she pleaded. "You must help Elder Sahdon!"

They started to lift Winyon by both her arms when she cried out in pain, "Oh, my arm! Please, no!"

One guardsman saw the blood on Winyon's shawl and called out behind him to Elder Cranik.

Hurried footsteps echoed from the corridor walls. In no time more torches were gathered around the woman and Cranik was asking questions.

Cranik shaded his eyes in the firelight and squinted. "What is this about Sahdon?" he asked with suspicion.

"Elder Sahdon has fallen!" she said.

"Where?"

She pointed in the direction that led to the maze of tunnels in the innermost interior. "At the Mother Stone. There was a quake," she started to explain.

Cranik frowned with concentration. "Who are you?" he asked sharply.

"Please, I am only just a servant to the High Shaman."

Kulo sidled up behind Cranik and looked down at the woman. "What in Tagheetu's name was Sahdon doing there?"

"He had asked the Shaman's Apprentice to take him to the Mother Stone to ask for a miracle," she explained, with no hint of her lie betraying her.

Kulo shuffled closer, his eyes twitching nervously. "Jabal is with him?"

"Tai," she sniffled. "He is injured too. The Apprentice and I met Elder Sahdon near the shrines on the hill above the Shaman's compound. He asked us to take him to the Mother Stone. It was meant to be a quick journey, but Elder Sahdon has fallen and I fear he is dead."

"How on this good green earth could Sahdon have slipped past us without us noticing him?" Kulo inquired.

"Oh, there are other entranceways above us from the northwest that lead to the interior," Winyon said with such nonchalance she amazed herself.

Kulo ran his large arthritic hand through his wooly hair and looked over at Cranik in disgust. "Why, he just slipped passed us while we were here all along. And still he did not tell us where he was going."

"And now we know for certain who the Informer is," Cranik added with equal disgust. "Sahdon acts alone without us knowing anything or consulting us. If, indeed, he is dead then I am the next Senior Elder of the Elder Council."

Kulo looked away from Cranik with guarded eyes, then gazed down at the suffering woman. "Do you think you could lead us to the exact spot where you last saw him?"

"None of us are going anywhere," Cranik spat back. He began to mumble beneath his breath and sucked on his teeth noisily.

"But they need your help," Winyon pleaded, and cast a concerned eye up at Cranik.

The Elder gave an icy stare in return. He pulled out his scimitar and placed the double-pointed tip close to Winyon's eyes. "Now, why would you want us to leave this doorway? And why would you want to help Sahdon, if he is really where you say he is? You are a Believer, are you not? And this is a trick!"

Winyon drew a sharp breath, her heart beating rapidly. "I am just a servant. I know not who the real Teacher is. I came because the Shaman's Apprentice asked for my assistance. Please let me go," she begged. "I have marked the way for you with the soot of my torch, which has long since given up its flame, and yet I found the rest of the way in the dark. Take only a few men if you must. But please, go! And take water!" she added.

"Let her go," Kulo insisted.

Cranik lowered the sword and stared down at the frightened woman.

"The quakes?" Kulo asked more sympathetically. "Have they created much damage?"

Winyon pulled on her shawl nervously. "Tai. The way into the antechamber was blocked from a past quake. We had to remove many rocks to gain entrance. It will be dangerous to get there if there is another quake. The Mother Stone is angry," she cried wincing in mock pain again.

Elders Cranik and Kulo looked at each other nervously.

"I have marked the way for you, but I can draw you a map, if you like," she offered.

All looked to Cranik for leadership. His face hardened and he gestured with his sword. "Give her some barkcloth. Here!" he said cutting into the back of Kulo's wrap-around and ripping a piece from the bottom.

"Stop that!" Kulo complained. "Take a piece of your own clothing, you idiot!"

Cranik handed the frayed swatch of barkcloth to Winyon and watched with needle-sharp eyes as the woman sketched out a rough map with a charcoal splinter from her torch. When she had finished, she handed the map back to the Elder.

Satisfied, the Elder spoke again. "Go then and tend to your own needs," he said to her. "I will send three men."

Winyon was helped to her feet and then scampered off, her sandals echoing through the dark corridors that led to the outside world.

★　　★　　★　　★　　★　　★

Jabal rocked on his haunches until his nausea subsided enough to gather his senses. A puddle of undigested cave spider lay at his feet. He touched Sahdon's sandal wedged in his waistband, anxious now to place the sandal on the bamboo bridge. He eased himself up onto his feet and staggered to the bridge at the cliff edge, which spanned the chasm from where he stood tottering to the slim rise of clear crystal that held the Mother Stone.

Jabal held onto the upper ropes of the sway bridge and took a cautious step onto the first plank, which set the bridge bouncing and squeaking. He stopped for an anxious moment until the bridge was still then took another more confident step, bearing his full weight now. He crept midway across when he heard the sound of ropes creaking and a cacophony of bamboo snapping beneath his foot. A sharp second passed as he tightened his grip on the top guide ropes.

A loud crack sounded!

He caught sight of the midsection of bamboo give way, twisting his torso dangerously in midair. The sinews of rope stretched until he felt his body suddenly drop and he swung toward the cliff side. Wham! He hit the rock full force crushing the air out of him, bruising one arm and cracking some ribs.

He flailed and twisted on the ropes like a puppet on a string, suspended over the chasm, the sound of the debris still not finding bottom. Caught up short by the pain in his chest, Jabal struggled to hold on and breathe until his panicked panting had evened out. By using his good arm and his feet he climbed the ropes until he was able to throw one leg over the cliff side. He let out one loud grunt from the sharp pain and pulled himself up and over the lip of rock.

Resting at the cliff edge to catch his breath, he stared blindly at what remained of the bridge, each splittered half hanging limp from each cliff side. Unwilling to risk his life any longer, Jabal placed Sahdon's sandal at the cliff's edge and crawled away.

The young Apprentice looked up at the Mother Stone from across the chasm, then placed his head to the ground. Dark thoughts ricocheted in his mind like a fly trapped in an obsidian jar and he began to tremble. A shame overtook the boy and he sniffed back his tears.

"I guess I deserved that for all the harm I have done. But why does the Mother Stone not talk to me? Give me an oracle… guidance…anything. After all, I am a High Shaman's First Apprentice."

Jabal waited in the bowels of the Earth, but the Mother Stone remained still in her stony silence.

A new wave of nausea overtook him. Anguished and impatient, the Apprentice drew himself up into a painful crouch. He raised his head to address the Mother's Northern Guardian. "Great Guardian to the North, place where the Ancestors and the Ancient Ones dwell, please allow me to seek the Mother Stone's advice. I have left my flesh and blood here as an offering."

He waited for an answer or a sign, but heard nothing. Keeping his eyes to the towering white stone, he started to repeat his plea when coldness fell over him with increasing intensity.

The silence was dense – the cold inescapable. Knowing whether he'd make it out of the deep interior alive was uncertain. Were it not for the soft light glowing from the amorphous Mother Stone, the Apprentice would have been blind as well.

The boy shivered from the talons of damp chill that had clawed its way inside his bones. Like ice knives chipping away at his resolve, numbness spread over him, causing him to huddle into a knot with his knees pressed up against his broken ribs and his arms wrapped around his legs, cold gooseflesh against cold, clammy flesh. His breath appeared in soft white puffs as if his life was escaping from him moment by moment.

Jabal's teeth chattering was the only noticeable sound now, except for the drumming of his heart in his ears. He breathed into his hands and rubbed them together. It wasn't until the ice crystals clung to him that he noticed a slight breeze. From deep within the dark chasm that separated him from the Mother Stone came an outpouring of frigid air. It was as if a force far below was pumping the frigid air upward and pushing it out onto the cavern floor.

The breeze intensified into a strong stiff wind and pushed through a narrow gap in the flowstone, answering Jabal's darker thoughts with a shrill whistle.

"Guardian of the Mother Stone, I pray to you for mercy and understanding," he cried out. "I will not leave," he said, his courage warming him a moment.

The air grew thick and charged with an energy that made the hairs on the back of his neck stand up.

A sibilant echo reverberated throughout the stone chamber. "Lies!"

Jabal felt a palpable presence fill the chamber, a presence heavy with power and icy anger. The cold wind swirled around the sacred stone, gaining speed as it circled, then rushed into Jabal so violently he rocked on his heels until he lost his balance. He flattened himself onto the ground, thinking the wind might pass him overhead, but kept his head turned toward the sacred stone. Her warm light restored his hopes, in spite of Her Guardian's cold rage.

He addressed the Guardian directly. "True," he confessed nervously. "I…I had come for other reasons. Still, I have come with all respect. And I have come to tell you that the spiritual order will be renewed along with the honor of the Mother Stone. All the people will come to her once more."

The wind answered with a mournful cry, then stopped so abruptly Jabal thought the numbness from the cold had dulled his senses. He eased himself into a sitting position, his eyes still focused on the light of the Mother. All at once, he felt something light brush against his back. He stole a glimpse over his shoulder. Had a piece of debris from the ceiling fallen on him? No, he found nothing. He dismissed the sensation and turned his attention back to the Mother's light, letting the sight of her pulsating glow gently warm his spirit. Again, something elusive grazed against him. He turned around fully to examine his surroundings in the half-light, and, seeing nothing, he looked back to the Mother Stone again.

Then he flinched when what felt like a frigid hand touched his back, and the wind wailed again in his ears. He froze on the spot and covered his ears, quivering uncontrollably as the icy fingers pushed through his back and probed his heart as if his body were made of nothing more than mist. The invisible hand probed deeper still, and a shock wave spread through Jabal's spine and up inside his brain.

"Have mer…mer…mercy on me, Mother," he stammered, his lips turning blue, his tears hardened into ice. "It is true, I originally sought no oracle, no guidance. I will seek nothing from you now, but to deliver my gift and my message. High Shaman Mefakani's mad takeover of the souls of our people has been stopped by the prophesized prophets, Losha Ninti and Temple Fox. They have sent me here. The spiritual order will be restored soon. Have mercy," he murmured once more.

A sudden hush came over the cavern. A small cloud of vapor gathered just below the chamber ceiling and a rain of fine ice crystals fell.

Jabal looked up, his sense of wonder renewed. The snow caught in the soft glow of the Mother's light, creating points of crisp rainbow light that turned and flashed in the air all around him. He held his palm out to examine their fragile beauty, and his brown skin slowly turned pale. And the soft sound of dancing ice crystals filled the cavern like a chorus of whispers.

Jabal bore his mantle of white bravely, while his pain numbed and his breathing became shallow. When he took his last desperate breaths, like the ancient bee encased in his gift of amber, he gazed at the Mother Stone in sweet surrender. It was the last thing he remembered before falling into a nowhere place, before his mind was emptied, his heart slowed, and before he slipped into the waiting hands of cold, quiet death.

CHAPTER ELEVEN

TANI'S ESCAPE

*"Air! Thank the Spirit of Tahneyah. It is like my
first cup of palm wine. Like sex for the first time."*

Elder Tani
The Makolese Scroll on
The Return of the Ka and the Mending of the Su #11

The forest was washed with gentle rain and veiled by growing night. Losha brushed the few bits of white down off her arms then quickly bent down into the undergrowth to make certain no one had seen the flash of white light that marked her transformation. Winyon was on all fours doubled over on the ground.

Losha placed her hand on the older woman's back. "Are you ill?" she asked.

Winyon dry heaved. She steadied herself by clutching the earth and squeezing it between her fingers, grateful for the feel of damp earth.

"Tai. Tai," she panted.

Losha felt Winyon's head and pinched the back of the woman's hand. "You have a fever and are dehydrated." She peeled the woman's blood-spotted shawl off to examine her arm. She saw that the wound at one time had been larger and had healed quickly, all except one area. "This wound is small, but it has become infected. I will need water to clean it."

Winyon nodded.

Losha scanned the forest. She picked a bowl-shaped leaf that had collected rain and used it to gently wash Winyon's wound. She picked a dozen more of the same leaves, then tipped them to Winyon's parched lips. Then she broke the healthiest leaves off a nearby plant, thanking the plant spirit as she did, and rubbed the leaves until they were moist and pulpy.

"This will have to do for now until I can get you some stronger medicine," she said as she placed the pulp on Winyon's wound. "But before I do that, I must get Tani out from below."

Winyon wiped her mouth with her dirty shawl. "I can wait," she replied with a grim smile. "I can help. I will do whatever you ask of me."

Losha listened to the soft patter of rain for a moment and walked back over to the small hole she had escaped from as a Swan. Winyon stood up to help and wobbled a bit uneasily. Losha grasped the older woman by her good arm and sat her down again.

"You are not well enough. Just sit by the hole and guide me," she said.

★   ★   ★   ★   ★   ★

"Bi Kana, I should have stayed in the world of the dead!" Tani muttered as the vine around her thighs and hips tightened and she was raised a foot off the ground.

Losha gripped the hefty vine and pulled again, lifting Tani a little higher. "She is as light as a child," Losha whispered. A swifter tug followed and Tani swung dangerously close to a fringe of needled stalactites.

"Slower!" Winyon instructed. "She is beginning to sway!"

Tani's gravely voice echoed out into the forest above. "Great Tagheetu's ghost! If you go any faster I will look like an Apprentice doing his first Makolese piercing!"

Losha hauled in another foot of vine. "Tell her to hush."

"Hush yourself!" Tani retorted loudly. "It is not you suspended down here with stone teeth waiting for your withered rump. I trust you, Little One," she called out. "But should you drop me I swear by the Healers before me I will..."

Losha above and the two men below joined in unison. "Shhh!" they all said.

Tani's mumbles and grumbles echoed softly up through the crevice. "What if I do not fit?" she asked quietly.

Losha knew that if she could squeeze through as a swan that a tiny woman such as Tani would fit as well. Still, she couldn't resist. She winked at Winyon. "Tell her we have some whale grease," she whispered loud enough for the Elder to hear.

Losha grinned and Tani gave out a sour huff.

Losha gave a few more long, slow tugs and secured the vine around a cypress. She took hold of Tani's fragile arms and lifted her onto the mossy earth.

The old woman lay like a newborn babe onto the belly of the Mother, the vine twisted around her like an umbilical cord. Tani rolled onto her back and grunted softly. It was dark, but past the silhouette of leaves far above her hung the radiant moon, the stars and...

"Air!" Tani breathed. She inhaled deeply as if tasting air for the first time. She took another deep breath and filled her lungs to capacity. "Thank the Spirit of Tahneyah. It is like my first cup of palm wine," she reminisced. "Like sex for the first time. Like..."

"Shhh!" Losha rebuked and quickly untied the vine wrapped around the Elder. "Lie still for now and rest. Winyon will stay with you while I get her a more potent medicine."

The old woman fixed her eyes on Winyon. Suddenly realizing her companion was ill, she went about the business of doing what Tani did best.

CHAPTER TWELVE

UNFINISHED BUSINESS

"Allowing violence to oneself is no greater or noble a deed than committing violence against another. It's still violence."

Temple Fox
The Makolese Scroll on
The Return of the Ka and the Mending of the Su #12

There was an eerie stillness in the cavern after Losha and Tani had left. Tiv was still curled up in a dark corner on the hard, cold floor snoring softly, a pile of rags placed under his head by his Master. Temple sat quietly in the huge grotesquely shaped chair made from dripping limestone. The torches were growing dim and Mefakani moved around the cavern extinguishing all but one torch to ration the rest for later. He stared at Temple nervously when he had finished, watching the True Teacher deep in meditation.

Sensing Mefakani's unease, Temple opened his eyes. His voice broke the tense silence. "I could've killed you, you know. It would've been easier." His tone was as smooth as the words were jarring.

The Priest stood in the lone firelight, the shadow carving his eyes into deep hollows. "You can still kill me now if you want to," he said defeated. "That is why you stayed behind - to kill me?"

"I wanted to be certain the others were safe first. You and I have unfinished business."

Mefakani arched an eyebrow.

"I will talk to you in all frankness. I haven't completed what I came here to do."

"To teach the people, you mean. And to prophesize," Mefakani replied.

Temple shook his head in dismay. "All this talk about me being some sort of God or Master Teacher or Prophet. I don't buy into all of that like you do. No. What I came here to do is end your reign without violence and to gain my integrity."

"But..."

"It's true. I haven't taken your life and have committed no violence on you. But I've allowed the violence to be done to me and you still reign in a sense. What I did, Mefakani, was a supreme sacrifice on my part, and although you have gained wisdom in the process, I feel I have failed myself."

Mefakani held his arms out in surrender. "But, Temple, you have stopped me cold. You have ended my 'reign' as you call it and have gained your integrity. My appearing now as a Shaman-Priest, even a man-god to some, will only be an act to help bring a transition to peace."

"And yet you still have over one hundred followers who'll fall on your every word. It could be a temptation for you to return to power."

Temple paced the floor and kept a watchful eye on Mefakani. "I've allowed violence to be perpetrated upon me to protect Losha and in hopes of stopping you," Temple said. "Perhaps that sacrifice of self – that violence – was necessary in order to help your people. But it's unacceptable now. Allowing violence to oneself is no greater or noble a deed than committing violence against another. It's still violence."

Temple scratched his beard in thought. "And yet, having said all that, killing is not that black and white. Killing is a part of nature. We kill for food. We even kill the fruits we eat. Mother Nature is violent and kills so other life forms can thrive. But what I want you to know is – killing without respect has no rewards. Killing without respect has consequences."

"Then you could have killed me" – the Shaman paused – "once you had learned to respect me? A hard task," he said, with a twisted note of sarcasm.

Temple nodded. "It's true, I've forgiven you. And, yes, it's the hardest thing I've ever done. But along with forgiveness I had to learn to respect and love who you were first. I had to recognize your role here. You mirrored the one I hated – the one I judged within myself. Our souls may be different, but your spirit is exactly the same as mine. This spirit I speak of is the greater part of you. It was created in wholeness and is always flawless, innocent and pure. To hate you is to hate a part of myself. You know the greater part of both of us dwells in the oneness of the Holiest of Spirits. I never would've learned that had I not encountered the little creatures in the mountain and all that I experienced here. Without your challenge I would've never found that singularity of vision my sacred scar represents. I never would've been forced to understand and love so deeply.

"Right now it would truly be a benevolent act to kill you and send you back to Divine Peace. By my not killing you, it would be a lot harder for you to live out your life and try to correct the mistakes you've made, which largely are mistakes made by your perceptions. Still, like all matters, whether we see them as a consequence of the Light or the Darkness, your being here has been a part of the Divine Design."

"How is that so, Temple?" Mefakani asked.

"You've shattered just about every sacred trust and ritual originally given to your people by the Gods and the Spirits. These blatant acts functioned to bring me to where I am now. You see Mefakani, what we perceive as the spirit of Light has been created to perfection by the Divine. It's the Darkness that we all created together. I created you as much as you created me. We are stuck in the same play we wrote. You're my character. And I'm yours.

"And your people were developing their psychic abilities faster than their spiritual wisdom. There was an imbalance. That's why some misused their powers and sorcery broke out on the island. You tried to bring balance, only you misused your power as well and disempowered everyone by collecting a piece of their Ka. Now that will change. In the months and seasons ahead the Makolese will ripen as they should, and, having mastered heavy hardships, will become great teachers for the world as prophesized.

"Do all that you can while you're still in physical form, Mefakani. Your body is a vehicle for learning. Now that you've been to the Light and back you have a deeper understanding of how your actions affected others. Open your heart and let it lead you like never before. The longer you wait to learn forgiveness of self and love of self, the greater you will suffer."

Mefakani fidgeted uneasily at hearing this and withdrew from the brightness that swirled around Temple's form. Then the two were plunged into silence once more until Temple broke that silence again.

"I want you to know, Mefakani, that you've been my teacher in every sense of the word. And I thank you."

Mefakani could feel the love pour through Temple's eyes, which was the same energy he experienced when he had died and encountered the Light. "And now you are my teacher," Mefakani gasped. The power of understanding, of love and forgiveness, permeated his very soul and tears welled up in his eyes.

Temple squinted in the half-light and spoke again. "I want you to know I accomplished one very personal goal."

Mefakani's vision blurred. He was awed at Temple's candor.

"I didn't hate you when I surrendered to you willingly. I didn't hate you when you strapped me down on that table and drove that dagger into me with your magic. I simply understood who you were and who you really are in the Light of God where you reside in eternity. And I forgave you as I forgave myself for allowing your dark magic to be done to me. I forgave myself for creating this dark aspect of myself."

Mefakani's breathing became labored and a river of tears streaked down the jagged tattoos on his face.

"Nor did I curse you like I did with Nawaze KaSeipa millennia ago when he cut me and poured hot poison into my wounds."

The Priest took a step closer, his wet face shining in the light. The word escaped his lips in one blast of breath. "Gadji!" he said in astonishment.

"We are one," Temple replied. "And I've, at last, reconciled that lifetime from long, long ago."

"And so it seems you have destroyed the priesthood once again. History comes full circle."

"Destroyed the priesthood? Time will tell. But for certain I did not kill the priest," Temple said. "As Gadji I did end the priesthood, yes, but one surviving priest created a new religion that was more ghastly than the first. And he used my image to enslave the minds of others into thinking I was a god, the one and only god. I want you to know that I was not a god back then or before the challenge in the mountain in this lifetime. Nor am I now. You were under the impression I was some newly created god birthed out of thin air. I'm not. I've had many past lives as dark as your present life, and I still have far more to learn before I can claim godhood. And yet, I'm a part of god and am filled with spirit and with great power – a power," he added, "not to be reckoned with lightly."

Temple pointed his finger at the cloth wrapped around Mefakani's head. "There's more to tell you. If you take that off you'll see that your wound has healed and your scar has vanished."

Mefakani ripped off the cloth. He placed a finger to his brow and rubbed the smooth skin on his forehead. His head dropped.

"I know I have not fulfilled the prophecy," he said. "Losha and you were the ones spoken about in the prophecy all along."

"And yet, there'll be more," Temple said.

Mefakani's shiny head tilted slightly to one side. "What do you mean?"

"There'll be many that follow in our footsteps. All of us are potential gods disguised in flesh. All of us. And yet we're like unripened fruit."

"But surely not I. I have perverted the natural laws. I have offended the Spirits and the Ancestors. Corrupted the people and the land."

"You have one of three roads to follow," Temple said. "And I've seen them all. It's up to you which road you'll take."

Mefakani was still for several minutes until Temple shattered his thoughts again.

"As always, all paths lead back to the Divine."

Temple walked around the cavern as he spoke. "Now, there's the matter of the unfinished business we need to attend to. And knowing what I'm about to tell you will help you decide your path."

The Priest engaged Temple's eyes giving his full attention.

"You have something of mine...and without it I can't spin into an Owl to escape this place."

Mefakani was wide-eyed. "Then all the plans you made...the Divine guidance you spoke of...it can fail?"

"It all rides on you now, Mefakani. Even civil war."

"What is it that I have of yours?" he asked eagerly.

"A part of me. A part of my soul," Temple answered.

"Your soul?"

"You stole an essential part of my heart," Temple explained. "I don't understand how the dark magic works that you stole from those creatures in the mountain, but without that portion of my heart I haven't the power to spin into an Owl so I can escape this place. And I can't be here when Cranik comes to take Sahdon's body, thinking it's mine."

"So you mean...?"

"You have the power to kill me now, if you want to."

Temple looked into Mefakani's eyes to see what he could glean from them.

"I may not have been sealed by your perverted ritual, but I'm totally vulnerable now...to death and anything else you may want to do to me. You could continue with your original plans if you choose to. But I warn you, in spite of the part of me you stole, I'm still powerful and will defend myself."

The Shaman stood still, his head hung down in thought, causing the shadows to engulf him. He looked up at Temple slowly.

"Then you could kill me too...if you wanted to," the Shaman said. "A killing done out of self-defense...and done with honor and respect...even compassion."

Temple nodded. "But that's not what I want to do," he said.

Mefakani was so overcome he sat on the floor below the torch. Temple simply sat on the floor at the opposite wall, and waited silently for the Priest to decide.

CHAPTER THIRTEEN

LETTING GO

"Let my power go… It'll be just as much of a healing for you as me."

Temple Fox
The Makolese Scroll on
The Return of the Ka and the Mending of the Su #13

Mefakani looked at Temple from across the cavern. "Having seen the Light, that is the path I chose. Maybe you do not believe me, but I will not kill you, Temple Fox. You have twice spared my life and I do not want the second half of my life to be like the first. But..." He paused. "I do not know how to return the vital part of your Ka I have stolen. I ingested it!"

"You suggested before that I was your teacher now."

Mefakani nodded.

"Then let me teach you how," Temple said.

Temple took awhile to spell out the basic principles and techniques to retrieve the missing part of his soul, but Mefakani was an adept and he grasped the principles quickly.

"It will never work!" Mefakani protested. "It is too simplistic. Why my Master Tagon once said... "

"Forget what Tagon said," Temple exclaimed. "He's the dark soul who helped lead you into darkness. I've come as prophesized to teach the Makolese new ways. And this is a new way that is, in fact, a very ancient method of healing."

"I am not certain I can do it."

"I'm not asking you to do this on me, Mefakani. I've spoken to Losha already and she will do this for me once she sees that Winyon and Tani are safely on their way to the Queen's compound. I'm teaching you so you can do it on Ijebu, Mumbula, Boran, and Tiv later.

I know it would be hard for you to do this for me now. Your spirit remains intact and pure and always will be, but your soul is still greatly splintered."

"Then what is it that I am to do now?" Mefakani asked.

"Let my soul piece go. When you feel it being pulled out of you – let it go. It'll be just as much of a healing for you as me. All you must have is clear intent and trust. Trust the Divine and its Spirit Helpers to give you the power. But first you must let me go back to myself in peace."

"And me," Mefakani started to say. "Will I lose what I know; what I experienced after I release your Ka to you?"

"No, the experience you had was your own and the knowledge and the wisdom is in you now. I can't take that away from you. It's yours forever."

Mefakani stepped further into the light. "Then I will do it, Temple Fox. You have my word!"

CHAPTER FOURTEEN

LOSHA, WINYON, ELDER TANI, AND O'JUMA

"As the Gods will it, just when we ask for water we have a deluge."

Elder Tani
The Makolese Scroll on
The Return of the Ka and the Mending of the Su #14

Losha moved so swiftly through the black forest that one would have thought she had wings again. Slipping through the arms of a tangled liana vine, she bounded over fallen rosewood, praying as she went, until she caught a whiff of wood smoke. She stopped, her eyes breaking through the dense foliage to a hint of firelight beyond. She walked cautiously now, mindful of the noise she might make or animal she might startle. She crept on all fours through a field of dianella dotted with benibaul bushes, until the earth gently sloped downward and she saw clearly that she was on the hill overlooking the Shaman's compound. She hid behind the thickest bush and whistled in the signal call she had learned from Jabal.

One of the dark figures by the fire below rose and walked off in the opposite direction, leaving Losha wondering if Jabal's friend had already left for the night or if she had given the wrong signal call. She whistled several times and waited, but none of the figures stirred. She listened to her whistle fade and sat in the stillness as it began to rain. And there she remained, mesmerized by the quiet drumming of the rain against the leaves.

Her heart jumped in her breast when a voice close by called out softly.

"Name yourself," the voice demanded.

"Losha. Losha Ninti," she answered, her eyes straining in the dark. "And who are you?"

"O'Juma," the voice declared.

"O'Juma!" she called out in sudden relief. "Jabal said that I could trust you."

The voice spoke as it moved nearer. "I am sorry I frightened you. But I could tell it was not Jabal who called me."

The sky rumbled and the night became illuminated with a soft flash of lightning from behind heavy clouds. The figure of a man came into view. He bowed then knelt beside Losha. "Is he in more trouble?" he asked.

"No. I am certain he is fine. What I need is your help right now, but it could be dangerous for you. I need for you to take Elder Tani and a friend of mine to the Queen's compound under the cover of night."

"I thought Elder Tani was being held in Master Mefakani's private garden behind those stone walls." His eyes darted in the direction of the stone wall far into the distance. "This was done by the Queen's own decree."

"That is true, but please ask no more. The less you know, the..."

"...safer I will be. Tai, I know," he said. "If you and Jabal are co-conspirators, then I will join you. I need no further explanation."

Losha nodded her head. "Thank you, O'Juma. You are a loyal friend. Before we go I need some ginger and ipecacuanha root and some barberry and myrrh. Also a gourd so I can collect some water. Any food you might have would be greatly appreciated. Do you think you could bring those for me?"

"You are not only Jabal's friend that I am helping. He told me you are one of the Great Teachers." He bow his head with reverence. "I will raid the Shaman's personal supply if I have to."

"I will wait here," she whispered.

Losha sat for several minutes with the rain soaking her skin before the voice returned.

"It is I, O'Juma."

Losha felt a huge banana leaf plop down over her head.

"The rain is getting heavier. You will need that," he said, and held up two barkcloth bags and a gourd already filled with fresh water for her inspection.

"Thank you," she said, and the two marched up the hill of wet grass with the storm blowing in full force overhead.

★　　★　　★　　★　　★　　★

Losha and O'Juma ventured back into the wet forest where Elder Tani and Winyon waited under the cover of broad leaves. O'Juma bowed to both women, then handed the gourd of water and medicine to the Elder.

"As the Gods will it, just when we ask for water we have a deluge," Tani said. She passed the gourd to Winyon first.

Winyon took the gourd and looked up at the young man. "I believe we have met before," she said.

The rain beat down on O'Juma unmercifully as he stood staring at the woman in the dark. He shook his head. "I cannot recall," he said.

"You are Jabal's closest friend."

The young man squatted down in front of her and stared with curiosity. "Have you seen him? Is he all right?" he asked anxiously.

"I left him in the company of a beautiful woman. But you are not to worry," she said, smiling cryptically. "She is very old."

Losha asked O'Juma to collect some more fruit and more rainwater from the leaves while she replaced the herbal poultice on Winyon's wound. Not wishing to delay their journey any longer she bid the three good-bye.

Winyon looked up with surprise. "But where are you going?" she asked.

"I must go back inside the cavern," she said. "There is unfinished business to attend to."

Before Winyon could inquire further, O'Juma lifted Tani up into his arms and motioned for Winyon to follow.

Tani pressed her tiny palm against the center of O'Juma's broad, wet chest. "It has been ages since a handsome man has swooped me up into his arms like this." She cackled softly, and though the light of the moon had long since been veiled by the downpour, she saw his teeth and knew he was smiling at her.

CHAPTER FIFTEEN

THE RUNNER

*"They could be at war and I would
not even know it!"*

Queen Palomei
The Makolese Scroll on
The Return of the Ka and the Mending of the Su #15

There was a disquieting energy among the people in the Queen's compound and an even tenser foreboding force surrounding and clouding the Queen's Chamber. In spite of the great height and breadth of the pavilion it felt cramped with worry.

The weight of waiting had darkened the Matriarch's mood as she sat in her rattan throne, the base of her pearly scepter nervously rapping against one of the skulls that functioned as a footstool. There was a scowl upon her face.

"Why has there been no word from the Shaman?" Palomei asked.

Owane, her First Consort and First Advisor, shook his head, an equally dark countenance upon his face.

"Not one message in over two days! They could be at war and I would not even know it! Look at this!" she said, staring at the small paper scroll. She read it out loud yet again. "Temple Fox has returned from inside Hollow Mountain. He is safe. Together we formed a truce with the Unbelievers and are now negotiating a lasting peace.' That is all! No details on how this was done? Well, I will not be kept in the dark. Find me a Runner!" she barked.

Owane left the chamber in a hurry and returned just as quickly.

Palomei grabbed her writing table, placed it across her broad lap and slapped a length of barkcloth paper onto it. Sensing her mood, the bees churned in a mad little cloud above her head. Her brush moved quickly with an imperative hand, demanding that Mefakani tell her what was going on without further delay. She signed it with the triple spiral of her clan, her family symbol, her title, her name and, without knowing she had done so, a squashed honey bee. She allowed the ink to dry, then rolled up the scroll and bound it with twine. By the time the Runner was brought in she had slipped the scroll into a sharkskin sheath and placed the sack into a tube made of crocodile hide.

"You know where you are going?" she asked the Runner. "And who you are to give this to?" She handed the Runner the case and Tu'lusing slung it across his shoulder.

Tu'lusing was a tall thin boy, with a bony frame and enormous ears he hadn't grown into yet. He was also very pale. It was the first time he had met the Queen in person. He gave a stiff awkward bow from the waist. "Tai, my Most Beloved Queen," he said. "I am to go to the Shaman's compound and give this to him personally."

The Queen affirmed this with a nod. "You are pressed into service to me for we are short of staff. What I ask you to do has precedence over all your other responsibilities unless I tell you otherwise. Understand?"

The boy nodded.

"I also want you to be aware of things. Listen to what people say and what they do. Keep both your ears and eyes open." The boy nodded again. "Good. Now be gone and be swift!"

The boy gave his awkward bow again. He walked backward until he collided with the partition. He fumbled with the screen, slid it open, and stepped out of the Queen's private chamber.

"Well, he will certainly be able to keep his ears open," Owane said.

"Tai, I pray they do not slow him down," Palomei said.

CHAPTER SIXTEEN

THE CLIFF EDGE OF RECALL

"Did She speak to you?"

A Warrior
The Makolese Scroll on
The Return of the Ka and the Mending of the Su #16

When they found Jabal he was lying on his side curled up like a babe at the foot of the Mother Stone, the soft glow fluctuating in hues of white and gold against his nut-brown skin. A quiet hum filled the air.

Jabal's consciousness rose to some blurry place where voices were as dull and indistinct as a sky full of...

Snow?... How do I know what snow is?

He ran his mind around the vague parameters of a memory. Snow. Pure. White. Cold. He felt a hard, dry smoothness beneath him, but neither wetness nor cold: oddly, warmth beneath him.

Is it my imagination or are all traces of the snow gone?

His thoughts filled with the vision of his first snow again.

Snow. Silent. Sleep. Eternal sleep.

He fought the urge to fall back into unconsciousness until the voices of men roused him like distinct footprints in the snow. He opened one eye and in his mind reassembled the picture of three Rebel soldiers standing at a cautious distance. They each held ropes and were staring at him dumbfounded.

"Jabal!" one man called out.

The Apprentice blinked back the fogginess in which he wanted to drift.

Where is the snow? Where am I? He grew more alert.

One of the Rebels stood at the arched entranceway, a litter of stones surrounding him. The other two drew closer, but kept their distance. "Jabal, where is Elder Sahdon?" one asked.

Sahdon?

It was like another footprint emerging in the snow inside the cavern. When his memory started to clear, a series of marker events coalesced in his mind. He remembered Sahdon's sandal.

When Jabal didn't answer, one of the two renegades waved his companions back and moved to the edge of the cliff, across from the plinth of clear quartz where the Mother Stone towered over Jabal. The Mother's warmth and soft radiance suffused the air and cast a velvety light on the boy lying beneath her.

The Rebel Warrior prostrated himself before Jabal and the Mother Stone.

The Apprentice blinked in confusion. "Why do you honor me?" he asked.

"It is not you, Jabal, but Her." The man pointed past the Apprentice.

Jabal rolled onto his back and found himself staring up at the Mother Stone in all her glory, her smile still mysterious and ill defined, her outstretched arms looming above him now, her gaze distant as if her mind were focused on bigger things than the young Apprentice. Startled, he drew his knees up to his chin in one nimble move, which caused a lancing pain in his chest. Feeling embarrassed, he leaned over a bit to scrutinize the deep, dark chasm three feet from him and his head began to spin. He threw his arm out in a wild panic to grab hold of the long fluted skirt of the Mother Stone and found a firm handhold. He clutched on to her as if he were a frightened child, then turned to face the Warrior. Rising slowly, painfully onto his feet with his back pressed against the stone, a sudden sweat poured from him.

Jabal looked at the Rebel wide-eyed.

"Jabal," the man called out gently. "How did you get over there?"

Jabal clung tightly to the Mother's stony body as he rolled his head in the opposite direction. From his dangerous perch he spied a few broken planks, the only remains of the old bridge still hanging from the cliff edge like a flayed tongue of splintered bamboo.

"I…I have no memory," he said weakly.

"And Elder Sahdon?"

Jabal rubbed his head in bewilderment. But he remembered the scheme they had plotted to fool the Rebels into thinking Sahdon had fallen to his death.

"Dead," he stated flatly and pointed down at the chasm that divided them both. "He fell before he ever got to the Mother," he said convincingly. "You must know I did not kill him. I have been working with the Senior Elder as an informant. Please let the others know that."

"I will. I will. But, Jabal," the man whispered, hoping the others would not hear him, "did She speak to you?"

The boy rubbed his forehead again with a sweaty palm, then looked at his hand in disbelief, realizing how hot he felt.

"Well?" the Rebel whispered eagerly and cast an anxious glance behind him at the others.

The memory of a voice surfaced in his mind and ran along the pathway of his nerves, causing him to sweat even more.

"The heat?" Jabal asked. "Where has the heat come from?"

"What heat?" his rescuer called. "It is cool in here. You have fallen into a fever. Here, catch this and we will get you back over here safely."

The man threw one end of the rope to Jabal. And while the Apprentice tied it around the thick base of onyx, he thought about the message the Mother Stone had buried in his brain.

CHAPTER SEVENTEEN

THE TROUBLED HEART

*"Being in a state of unforgiveness is like trying to
carry the dead around."*

Elder Tani
The Makolese Scroll on
The Return of the Ka and the Mending of the Su #17

The maddening cacophony of rain against leaves made such a constant deafening white noise that the three were prevented from making conversation except for the occasional grunt of complaint or to argue where the overgrown trail led.

Winyon was left in her own bubble of isolation, her darker thoughts taking precedence. Her emotions rattled around like a crab in a trap, her mounting anxieties scuttling from one side of the cage to the other with no escape.

Should I have killed Mefakani when I had the chance? Strike him dead with his own dagger?

No sooner had Winyon regretted her inaction when her thoughts scampered to the other side of the crab trap.

There were others to consider, she thought more carefully. *And I am a part of something greater than myself now.*

She remembered her first meeting with Temple in her coral cave on that memorable night. She relived the confession she had made to Temple and his promise to return her to the mainland. She had barely made out his form in the obscurity of night as he spun his magic and lifted back into the black sky in his Owl form.

And then there was Jabal, who reminded her of Mefakani in his youth. She recalled how the young Apprentice had been carried to her island of exile with a pod of dolphins.

And who should follow after him? she recalled. *The Great White Swan appeared before me and transformed before my eyes into a woman I barely know – a woman who, like the white Stranger, also bore the sacred mark! Am I dreaming?*

It was only days before she had learned to use her Ka and spun the old Makolese magic. She remembered tasting nectar from a flower, her tiny heart thrumming wildly and the powerful sensation of flying. "Freedom," she caught herself saying out loud in the wet air.

But soon the feelings of joy melted into the rain and the hummingbird she had remembered becoming ceased flying, her heart becoming hardened again. Her thoughts sidestepped over to the center of the cage she had constructed in her mind and fed on the bait that had trapped her to begin with – Mefakani. How she hated him with every vital spark of energy that ran through her tender core behind the armored self. Her blood boiled and turned to venom at the thought of him. Even the rain couldn't cool the heat of her anger. It only served as a barrier to hide her thoughts from the others.

Tani sensed the turmoil swirling around the Exile. Her weak voice called out in the din of rain. "I feel I am drowning in the air," Tani called out. She tapped O'Juma on the chest. "Stop until the rain subsides."

Winyon peeked from beneath her rain hat made of banana leaves. "Do you need a rest, too?" she asked Tani.

"Tai," the old woman groaned. "And a little food."

Winyon pointed to an outcrop of rock that provided a slight overhang they could sit under. O'Juma placed Tani gently on the driest spot of moss there, then took his blade and started hacking palm leaves. He leaned these against the overhang to create more shelter.

Under the cover of branches and lava rock, the women took off their hats and shook the rain from them.

"You would think it was enough floating in that brine for five suns," Tani complained. "If I get any wetter I will turn to mush."

Winyon managed a weak smile and twisted her long silver hair to wring the water out.

The centenarian opened one of the barkcloth bags and pulled out some fruit. She cut a thin wedge of papaya and popped it into her mouth. She cut another piece then sliced slivers of wild ginger root on it for Winyon. She handed the slice to Winyon.

"Nausea better?" she asked, sucking on the fruit noisily.

"Tai," the Chokahpeiyape answered without further comment. Winyon diverted her eyes from the old woman's gaze.

"What troubles you, child?" Tani asked.

Winyon put her papaya aside and rubbed her sticky hands together nervously. "Elder Tani, before we make our way to the Queen's compound I need to speak with you...about what happened to you in the Shaman's cavern...before we arrived." There was a slight tremor in her voice.

"Speak."

The Wounded Hummingbird peered out at O'Juma through the latticework of fronds he was fashioning, concerned that so private a conversation would be overheard.

"There will be no more secrets," Tani said, prompting her along.

"Well," Winyon began uneasily. She could not look the Elder in the eye. "The Shaman did unspeakable things to you." A knot formed in her throat and she could not continue with words.

Tani stopped gumming her food and clasped the woman's hand, making Winyon's sad eyes meet hers. "You worry that he broke the Su with me. That he raped me in his foul ritual." She patted Winyon's hand. "He did not. Yet, in a sense, he raped everyone's spirit by convincing them to give up a bit of their Kas. And that very act, which I had fought hard against in the Elder Council, caused my own power to wane, even though I held my own Ka intact. My power dwindled for the simple reason that we are all connected and we nourish one another. We can move more easily together like a school of fish and the birds when they fly in a flock. But the current of energy on Makol had changed direction and I was fighting against it like a small boat moving against strong tides. I fought largely alone, except for the fact that I had Losha. Still, she was only one young person and, though I taught her well, she had yet to ripen into her full power."

Tani spit a melon seed onto the ground and wiped her mouth with the back of her hand. "That is where Temple Fox came in. It made sense that such a soul as he would come from outside the imbalance of our world, beyond the Barik Limits."

"But what about me?" Winyon asked. "I had my Ka intact all along."

"Tai, but Mefakani had violated you, too, in a different way," she said delicately. "Sweet woman, even though no physical act was thrust upon you, and even though a piece of your Ka had not been taken, the Priest did steal some of your power."

Winyon hung her head. "I know."

Tani took the woman's chin in hand and raised it so she and Winyon were eye to eye. "But now you are recovering your power and your confidence again. Is that not true? Jabal and Losha have helped you. And I will help you. Make certain you do not give your power away to anyone else again. Keep your power here." Tani placed her hand on Winyon's solar plexus. "That is where your sun is. To allow another to bleed you of your precious light, even out of what you feel is an act of compassion on your part, can cause that light to flicker and dim. Try to keep it inside you and keep it centered there."

"You say that and yet... Did you not also...well..." Winyon stumbled with her words.

Reading her thoughts, Tani felt moved to reveal her secrets. "You think I caused my own suicide in an attempt to keep Mefakani from stealing my entire Ka, my power and my knowledge? That is only partly true. Had he gained my power through his magic he would have known too much about what I knew about Losha and would have turned me into one of his mindless slaves." She spat another seed out. "He would have added my power to his own and corrupted it. But you should know, Winyon…I did not commit suicide."

Winyon looked at her with puzzlement.

The old woman leaned closer. "The Elders in the Spirit World feel deep compassion and pass no judgment on such an act, but still there is a bit of disappointment for those who take their own life. Life is precious, very precious, and we are to respect and honor and cherish each lifetime, no matter how hard our life has become. There are always other pathways to get us out of a tangle.

"Like the Elders of Old say, 'A strong woman knows she has strength enough to make the journey. But a woman of strength knows it is the journey that will make her strong.' Yet, the Great Elders understand that to end a painful life is sometimes kind and merciful," she said.

Tani leaned back a bit. "But I was not dying or in great pain. I was angry! So you see, I did not commit suicide. I only drank a potion to place me into the nether regions of the deep sleep world.

"I am an old Dolphin who knows how to breathe so slowly that not even a High Priest can tell whether I am alive or not." Tani pulled a wrinkled face. "But how was I to know he would put me inside a stone trough and cover me with concoctions so I would not petrify? That vat of herbs ruined the antidote I had hidden on me. I stayed alive for days. But in the end, in the last few minutes, I did drown. Still, it was no suicide. It was a choice I had made...to buy time for Temple and Losha. Everything is choice, and I have no regrets. And I am blessed by that experience, for things are different in the Light. You feel whole again."

Winyon stared at the old woman in wonderment. "Then why did you not choose to stay in the Light?"

"Oh, I have a couple more things to complete before I return to the Great Light," Tani said, then fell silent as she listened to the rain wash away the harshness of the world she returned to, blurring all boundaries.

Winyon looked into the black slits of the Tani's eyes. "Knowing all that Mefakani did, you said your heart ached for him," she said. "My own heart is hardened with anger and hatred...for what he did to my husband. For what he did to Temple, and Tiv and all the others." Her voice tightened with rage. "If I had been Temple I would have killed him! And you...with all the knowledge and power you have, why had you never moved to kill the Priest? You could have easily poisoned him!"

With a simple sweep of her hands Tani smoothed out the ripples of turbulence swirling around them. Remaining calm, she spoke softly. "It is a good question you asked, and one I have mulled over thousands of times." She leaned close to mark the significance of her words. "I have taken life before," she confessed. "And I did not take the decision to do so lightly." Tani let the words find their way deep into Winyon's consciousness. "As I said before, life is precious."

Winyon held her breath without realizing she had done so and a chill ran up her spine.

"Besides," Tani continued, "it was not time yet to stop the Priest."

"I do not understand," Winyon said.

Tani tugged on Winyon's shawl and Winyon allowed the old woman to take it from her. "The people needed to go through the darkness, like sprouts pushing up through the Mother's soil to the warmth of the Father's sun," the Healer said. Tani examined the wound on Winyon's arm. "The darkness the people are experiencing will help them to grow. Who am I to take that lesson away from them?"

Satisfied that the wound was mending, Tani wrung out the shawl. "If not Mefakani, there would have been someone else to draw the people deeper into darkness and forgetfulness. True, I kept my own light burning and held it until the people were ready to embrace their true essence again. This I knew because I am an Elder and older than dirt." Tani gave the shawl a shake and wrapped it around Winyon's shoulders.

Winyon pulled her damp shawl tightly around her. A frown twisted her face. "And you think the people are ready now? Unlike the others, I have my Ka. Yet my heart is full of bitterness," she admitted. "I cannot begin to find a place of peace, or what you call true compassion for this beast of a man. And I doubt if the people will either, having learned what the Priest did to them."

Tani nodded. "And yet to be in a state of unforgiveness is like carrying the dead around." Tani ran her bony hand over Winyon's shoulder to smooth the shawl and calm the Exile. "Tai, the people struggle with the darkness now more than ever, not realizing all is in Divine Order. Temple and Losha already know this, but if it were not for Mefakani, Losha and Temple would not have come into their true Divine power."

Winyon remained silent for a moment, then asked. "What do you feel will happen to everyone now?"

The Elder took a deep breath and let out a sigh. "I do not know the outcome," she said. "But I do know this. Makol is a testing ground for Spirit. What we do here reflects on what will happen in the future to the larger world."

"What do you mean?" Winyon asked.

"Our people, and all the peoples of the world, will someday drop their petty judgments. They will let their notions of what is right and wrong fall from them like tears. And they will see the absolute unity of all life...but not before," she added with a dark look, "they have their wars."

"Then the forces of Darkness and the forces of Light are destined to merge into oneness?"

"You are beginning to understand," Tani said with a glint in her eye. "They will see that war bears seeds of only more destruction. They will tire of the struggle and see that struggle is no longer necessary. Only then will they desire to move into their original state of wakefulness, where all awareness is unified and in harmony."

Winyon stared at the Elder, the air around them thick with the presence of Spirit. "Though I have not mastered such a teaching, I await the day of such an awakening," she said, with a bit more optimism.

Tani smiled knowingly. "Tai, so do I. But before that time arrives, know this." She looked into Winyon's eyes until the woman could not escape the intensity of Tani's gaze. "No problem is so great that it cannot be handed over to the Divine. Pull the Divine Light inside you and surrender to it. Try to see Mefakani in the Light as well, for Spirit is in every moment and looks from every face."

CHAPTER EIGHTEEN

THE GRIS

*"Have we not endured enough of the Mother
Stone's wrath?"*

Elder Cranik
The Makolese Scroll on
The Return of the Ka and the Mending of the Su #18

Mefakani was given his task and felt ready. Losha did as she was instructed. She waited until her trance had deepened, and when she felt the room filled with spirit she sank to the barkcloth laid out on the floor beside Temple. She took hold of his hand, making a complete circuit of energy between them, then repeated her intention clearly in her mind.

"Akhus, Spirits of the Ancestors. I am your daughter Losha Ninti, of Hianna's Clan. I ask your help in finding the lost soul parts of your beloved son, Temple Fox, so that I may retrieve them and bring Temple back to wholeness."

★   ★   ★   ★   ★   ★

Elder Cranik paced back and forth through the underground corridor sucking on his long yellow teeth in thought. When he reached the limits of the torchlight he stopped, grunted, then turned around again to walk past the massive stone door that blocked Mefakani's private chamber. He paused at the monolith, grumbled to himself, then set out a few more paces where he stepped mindlessly over Elder Kulo, who was massaging his own aching legs, and headed to the other end of the tunnel. When the Elder was swallowed by the darkness again he stopped, grunted then turned around again to resume his annoying tooth sucking and restless pacing.

"What is that incessant clacking noise?" he complained. "It is driving me crazy!"

Kulo addressed Cranik's legs as they stepped over him. "Must be part of the ritual to kill Temple Fox," he said.

Cranik beat his fist on the standing stone door. "Bi kano lo, how long does it take to kill him?"

"I imagine it may take quite a while to kill a Wizard," Kulo said quite coolly.

Cranik looked down at the Elder and sneered until his long yellow teeth showed. "Well, it is too long!"

"Like I said before, go outside awhile. Get some fresh air," Kulo offered.

"I will not move from here until I see Temple's head!"

"Well, my bones are aching," Kulo began. "Surely you do not expect me to wait with you. This hard, cold ground is beginning to feel like…"

"You will stay here with me!" Cranik snapped.

Kulo groaned loudly as he tried to make himself more comfortable on the ground. "Why Sahdon had me come here instead of Ikus, I will never know. He let Ikus stay by a warm fire on the mountain. But me, he makes stay on this hard, cold ground, which is beginning to feel like…"

"Stop complaining! Sahdon is probably dead!" Cranik barked back.

"I could go outside for a bit of food, a little air and to stretch my legs. Besides this hard, cold ground is beginning to feel like…"

"Shut up!" Cranik's voice echoed down the passageways, then faded, but the clacking noise inside the chamber persisted. Beneath the noise another sound drew closer, softly at first, bringing everyone to attention. Two Rebel guardsmen readied their spears, looking around for the direction the sound had originated. From a tunnel deep within the interior they heard sounds of sandals scuffing against stone and the labored breathing of men.

"Go!" Cranik ordered.

Several of the Rebel guards moved down the corridor to engage the source of the sound. A few tense seconds followed and a guard reported to the Elders. "The other guards have returned! And they have the Shaman's Apprentice! But Senior Elder Sahdon is not with them!"

From the tunnel's twilight three Rebel scouts emerged carrying Jabal. The four were covered in grime and sweat.

"Where is Sahdon?" Cranik demanded.

"He is dead," a scout answered, his breathing still labored. "He met his death…during the quake. The Apprentice said he fell off the cliff into the crevice that surrounds the Mother Stone. And he admitted to being the Informer for the Senior Elder."

"So it was Jabal all along," Kulo said. "What of the boy?" he asked, eyeing the limp figure draped in the arms of another guard.

"He will die if we do not get him to the Priest soon."

Cranik tilted his head in the direction of the door. "Mefakani is *still* inside," he said, biting into every word.

The mob listened to the strange sharp rhythmic sound echoing from behind the stone barrier.

The Rebel placed Jabal gently onto the ground. Kulo raised a gourd of water to Jabal's lips, but there appeared to be no life in the boy. The water rolled down Jabal's chin.

"It has been two days now," Kulo said, "and there has not been one word from our new Teacher." The Elder looked up at Cranik with concern. "Maybe we should take the boy to one of the Lesser Apprentices and see what they can do for him. Or find Elder Tani. She will help Jabal no matter if she is a Believer or not."

"Tai. Go then," Cranik ordered. "And when the boy regains consciousness find out more of what happened at the Mother Stone." The Rebel guard picked Jabal up again and marched to the passageway, leading to the outside.

"You go with him," Cranik ordered another of the guards who was bent over with fatigue. "And find replacements for you two."

The one remaining scout, who had found his way through the maze of tunnels to the Mother Stone and back, fell wearily onto the ground. He was given his own gourd of water. The scout pulled a leather sandal from his waistband and handed it to Cranik. "We found this…near where the Senior Elder fell," he said between gulps of water.

Cranik brushed his hand across the sandal's leatherwork, noting the familiar design.

"You are the leader of the Unbelievers now…and our Senior Elder," Kulo said sadly and without challenge.

"You forget we are at war. There are no councils now for us. But, of course, I will lead us."

"Forgive me," Kulo said. "I long for the things we once had and for the way things used to be."

"We also found this." The Scout rose to his feet and bowed to both Elders. He handed Cranik a sheath and dagger, hilt first.

"What is this?" Cranik asked, dusting off the gris.

"Jabal said it was Sahdon's offering to the Mother Stone."

Cranik's eyes flew open. "And you did not leave it behind? You idiot! If he meant it to be an offering you should have left it there! Have we not endured enough of the Mother Stone's wrath?"

The Scout bowed his head apologetically. "I had not thought of that. I...I am sorry."

Cranik pulled the dagger from its sheath and eyed the hilt's familiar filigree and jeweled inlay.

"Should I return it?" the Scout asked.

Cranik ran his eye along the thin edge of the obsidian blade. "No," he finally said. He shoved the ornate gris back into its sheath and tucked it into his waistband. "Go outside for a rest. And tell another to take your place down here," he said.

Then he walked a short distance down the corridor, reentering its shadows, to be alone with his thoughts.

CHAPTER NINETEEN

THE CAPE, THE CROWN, AND THE STAFF

*"Oh, Hianna! Mother of us all. Give courage to
your humble servant!"*

Losha Ninti
The Makolese Scroll on
The Return of the Ka and the Mending of the Su #19

The monotonous, clacking sound Mefakani made by tapping stone against stone faded into the background as Losha entered her trance. Her consciousness shifted into a deeper place and the rhythmic clacking grew dull and distant to her bionic ears. Her mind drifted into a dark featureless place until a familiar white smudge appeared in her vision. A great white Swan coalesced with clarity in her mind and flew over Losha's head, its wings creating an eddy of air and a force field that pulled her through a green forest to a narrow hole in the ground beneath the tangled roots of a Mother banyan.

Without hesitation Losha slid through the entrance to the Lower World headfirst and down the smooth passageway, slowing now and then as she coursed over inclines and curves until she fell onto a bank above a collar of beach.

Losha shook the sand from her bushy hair and looked around. A calm sea spread before her in the dusky light. But this was no ordinary sea. A vast interior waterway, whose distant edges were defined by the cavernous walls that contained it; walls that rose like the fluted columns of a mammoth cathedral to a height partially obscured by a fog so dense that sea and sky merged as one.

The water lapped gently at Losha's feet and both she and the sea breathed easily in unison, until she watched in wonder as the Swan soared up into the misty sky and vanished into the fog.

"Where are you going?" she asked. "Do not leave me now!"

She felt suddenly alone and lost until she detected a strong presence behind her. She turned around slowly. A luminous figure, its form slender and genderless, its face featureless except for softly radiant blue eyes, drew closer. The Being bowed to her.

Losha bowed in return.

Wishing to feel the experience more keenly, Losha closed her eyes and sensed a gentle energy graze her shoulders. It brushed lightly against her hair and back, and a loving force enveloped her. Although the experience was more felt then seen, Losha sensed that something of weight had been placed upon her head. Something of greater weight was placed onto her shoulders and a slender object was pressed into her right hand. She opened her eyes and saw that she held a long staff made from a hard branch of sleek rosewood. And on her shoulders sat a cape made from an animal she had never seen before. She ran her hand over the soft, yellow fur with black spots, sensing the power of the creature from which the garment had been made. She placed both hands on her head and fingered a crown made of precious gemstones.

"What are these gifts you have given me?" Losha asked. "And who are you?"

The Being conveyed its message within Losha's mind. *"I am Guardian of this sacred place. You will need more power to retrieve the fragment of Temple Fox's soul. We have given you a cape made from the hide of a leopard, a great cat, not unlike the lion Temple has told you about. Draw grace and power from it. The jeweled crown was designed to help you receive guidance more clearly and to amplify that energy. The staff is to help you focus your power, your will. These are all gifts befitting a great leader."*

Losha bowed again in thanksgiving.

"Come," the Being said.

Losha followed as the Being floated over the sand around a crop of rocks and beyond the curve of beach to where Losha could see further into the distance. Before them a great waterfall roared, driving itself into the inland sea and filling the air with mist. Playing on the crystalline rocks were tiny children, naked and free, some diving, some splashing, some sitting in quiet meditation behind a curtain of falling water.

"Children," Losha whispered. "Who are they? Where did they come from?"

"They are the future children who will be born awake and aware."

Losha engaged the luminous eyes.

"Come," the Being said.

Losha followed the Being to the shoreline. She moved to the water's edge where her footprint had made a deep impression in the sand. The lapping water filled the footprint, then withdrew. When the surface of the tiny puddle calmed, Losha used the depression as a mirror to gaze at her own reflection. On top of her bushy head sat the crown made of jade carved into vines, green tourmaline cut and expertly shaped into leaves, and orchids carved from starry rose quartz and ruby.

Not understanding the full measure of the gift, Losha asked another question. "What do I do now?"

The answer came at first in subtle ways as the waves rippled against the shore, then withdrew, then reached closer still, until the tide was breathing like a panting dog. When the waves splashed up onto Losha's feet she leaned her senses out into the distance. There was an almost imperceptible stirring in the waters, and a sheet of mist parted long enough to reveal the source of the sound.

Out of the cloudy obscurity came a small round boat woven from reeds with no boatman to steer the vessel. The boat glided to the shore.

An invitation?

"You will be taken to another place where you will meet a new teacher. Your new teacher will instruct you further on how to retrieve Temple's missing soul part." The Being bowed again, then vanished in a flash of bright light.

Losha stepped into surf and climbed into the boat. She sat down in the flimsy vessel, causing it to rock precariously. With a mysterious force, the boat pulled free from the shore and sailed back into the mists in the direction it had come.

Losha looked down at her feet and noticed how badly the boat leaked. "A great ship designed for a queen this is not," she mused, adjusting her crown. "Oh, Hianna! Mother of us all," she prayed. "Give courage to your humble servant!"

The clacking sound became the rhythm of the water slapping against the bobbing reed boat. Losha's trance deepened. The shore behind her was swallowed in fog as the tiny round boat coursed further into the blinding whiteness of the mist. Then, just as Losha thought she would refocus back onto the Shaman's private chamber where Temple lay beside her, the boat pushed through the fog, and the hazy light of some unknown interior sun lit a rise of land in the distance. Losha instinctively knew the lush, green island dead ahead was her destination - The Island of the Power Animals. The reeds scraped against the sand and the boat lurched to a halt. Losha stepped onto the sandy beach.

The tide rose swiftly and without a sound the boat lifted off the beach and drifted back into the mist.

Losha found herself alone on a stretch of beach edged by a dense jungle. She pulled the fur cape around her snuggly and stroked the smooth wood of her staff, bristling with new pride and confidence in the spiritual gifts she had been given. She strolled the empty beach, poking holes in the sand with her staff in her regal stride. She waited for her animal teacher to appear, wondering what it would be.

She mused that her Guides apparently felt the Swan wasn't suited for her next task. *It will most likely be a powerful predator,* she thought, *like Okon's Shark or Temple's Owl.* She ran her hand down the soft pelt she wore. *Or perhaps it will be something wholly awesome like the strange animal I wear, or as fierce as a Killer Whale!*

She came to a pond of still water that had been captured by a deep scallop of sand fringed with ferns. Losha bent to gaze at her reflection again, noting that her dark skin was smooth and flawless. When it came to admiring her large almond eyes, two small beady eyes stared back. Losha blinked back in horror. All at once her reflection quivered and a turtle's scaly head rose from the quiet pool and stretched its long, rough neck clear up to Losha's nose. Losha rocked back on her heels.

"I will be your mirror for you," the old Turtle said.

Losha responded with a coarse laugh. "That is pretty unlikely."

"Oh, is it now? And why is that?" the Turtle asked.

"Because you are old and scabby. Reptiles are...well...pretty ugly," she said a little too indelicately.

"Is that so?" the Turtle said. The Turtle drew its head back and climbed out of the pool. "And what else am I?" she asked.

"Well...being a turtle means being painfully slow."

"Is that a judgment or an observation?"

Losha looked sideways for a second in quiet thought, then back at the old Turtle with a squint. She winced. "You would not be my new teacher, would you?"

"I am," the Turtle said. The old reptile plodded slowly across the sand, the water rolling off its large, gnarly, patterned shell.

Losha gave a little bow to her teacher. "I am sorry," she said, grinning guiltily. "I suppose I was expecting someone else. Someone..."

"More powerful?" Turtle said, and Losha nodded sheepishly. "Oh, so you think I'm not powerful enough for you. In the affairs of spirit don't be surprised if you end up with a minnow for a power animal. We are all equally powerful." The Turtle stretched its neck out to match Losha's height again.

"As for turtles, we are older than the race of humans. We are millions of years old and live everywhere in all climates and circumstances. We have the uncanny ability of living on both land and sea. And," she added, "we live to a ripe old age." The old Turtle's eye met Losha's. "Still want me as your teacher?"

Losha nodded back, smiling.

"Good, then I must tell you this. I am sacred and the most ancient of all the animals. The fate of the world rides on my back. I wear this hard shell for protection because I'm delicate and tender inside. One has to treat me with utmost respect, for my wisdom comes directly from Mother Earth, from whom all life springs. I am, also, ally to the Goddess Hianna, the eternal Mother. My power is derived from my adaptability, my slow, plodding, preserving pace and my good nature. You must learn to be like me, especially today, for there's the business of you recovering a fragment of Temple Fox's soul."

"You will teach me how to do this?" Losha asked.

"Yes, but first you must put aside your cape, crown, and staff."

Losha remained silent for a long moment. "But I cannot do that. The Guardian of this place gave these to me as gifts - spiritual gifts."

"Yes, I know. And these gifts speak clearly of your great spirit. Still, you must hide them as I hide my tender inner self so you can accomplish the dangerous task before you."

Losha gathered herself together so she towered over her teacher. "Turtle, you do not understand. I was just given these gifts. I now hold the gifts of power. And power is what I will need to pry Temple's soul away from Mefakani."

"What you need," Turtle insisted, "is to be like me and keep your feet firmly on the earth. This is not the time to be preening like a peacock or rushing off to be a hero. We must plan our strategy first, then bury our ideas to allow them to incubate, as I would to protect my precious eggs in the heat of the hot sun and sand. Then when you are ready you must move slowly and patiently. Learn to protect yourself by being more inconspicuous. You are on a dangerous quest that could harm both you and Temple should you fail.

"Keep your head down. Tuck that power inside your protective shell for now. Be unassuming as you plod forward. When you need to move swiftly you will be able to snatch Temple's soul as fast as I catch prey," she said, and snapped her jaws in the air between them for emphasis.

Old Mother Turtle crawled past Losha as she spoke. "Now, I have a lesson for you so you will understand better. Climb onto my back, but do not fall off and do not speak until I tell you to. I have something to show you."

Losha threw her legs over the old Turtle's back, and the ancient reptile shuffled slowly through the sand into the island's dense interior.

Losha ducked below a twisted branch, but her hair got snagged and ripped from her scalp. And along with her disheveled hair, full of leaves and broken twigs, came the crown, which became entangled in the branches and was pulled from her head. She reached back to retrieve the crown, but brambles tore her flesh. She flattened herself against the Turtle's back and noticed her arms turning blue from bruising and crimson from blood. Try as she might to make herself small and balance on top of her Teacher's shell, the brush grew thicker, and the branches and thorns shred the pelt she wore until the sacred cape was a complete tatters.

She squelched the dam of complaints she had been concealing and rode on in angry silence, the sting of humiliation and pain building within her. Spying another wall of thick thorn bushes ahead she quickly moved into action by beating back the briars with her staff. But the staff, ensnared in the tangle of shrubbery, was pulled from her grasp. Losha left it hanging behind in the thicket, her heart heavy with the loss.

By the time Losha and Turtle made it to the other side of the torn bushes, Losha was stripped of any vestiges of power, dismembered from all notions of who she used to be just minutes before, patches of her fur pelt and her own flesh flayed and mangled together now.

Turtle came to a full stop when they had crawled past the last of the prickly barbs and goose grass and were back onto a span of empty beach again. Turtle called behind her. "You may get down now."

Losha slid off her teacher's back brooding in silence, her bejeweled crown and staff lost, her precious cloak shredded into rags, and her beautiful skin mutilated.

"Think you can keep your head low and your energy tucked inward from now on?" Turtle asked.

"I will have to if I want to survive," Losha said, pulling burrs out of her hair.

"Precisely," Turtle said. "Now don't fuss over your appearance. You look exactly as I need you to."

The pair sat on the beach and formed their strategy slowly, mindfully, until Losha heard a fluttering above. Two swans circled in the air, one carrying her staff, the other her crown. They landed beside her in the sand and dropped their precious loads at her feet.

Turtle spoke again. "You have your crown and staff again. Come now. I will take you to where Temple's soul is held captive."

Losha climbed onto the Turtle's back once more and together they slipped into the warm, silent sea.

CHAPTER TWENTY

SMOKE AND OBSIDIAN MIRRORS

"Showing compassion will betray me."

Losha Ninti
The Makolese Scroll on
The Return of the Ka and the Mending of the Su #20

Turtle crept out of the sea and onto a gray shoal with Losha clinging to her back. Beyond the empty expanse of dark sand rose the interior of the island like a mammoth bone from some forgotten carcass, its white, bleak hills and craggy cliffs devoid of tree or plant, its air reeking with the stench of death.

Turtle spoke in quiet tones. "I will wait here for you," she said.

Losha pulled her tattered cloak over her crown, allowing her face to fall into shadow, and hid her staff inside the cape. She crossed the barren sand to where the naked walls of rock formed a crooked pathway to the Caves of Lost Souls where Temple was held captive.

When she drew closer to her destination she found many people milling about aimlessly. They were fragments of lost souls, more than Losha ever imagined, people with heads lowered, ashen faces drawn in quiet pain or in perpetual numbness. Pieces of soul lost and bereft of their life force. Incomplete souls slumped over their own despondency.

The walking dead were plentiful.

Losha found the cave Turtle had described to her where guards waited at the entrance. She tucked her energy inward and walked even slower. It was easy to avert the guards' gaze since they stood thirteen feet high. Still, Losha couldn't help but notice their muscular physique and their mottled, reddish-brown, lizard-like skin as she passed them by. The scattered bones littering the pathway vied for her attention, but she shuffled along at the same slow pace as the others, also with eyes cast down and energy contained deep within so she could enter unnoticed.

She slipped passed the guards without mishap and coursed her way down cold, dark tunnels, deeper and deeper into the airless maze of passageways, until she heard cries echoing up from a darker depth. She gripped her staff tightly and followed the sound by running her fingers against the rough walls blindly, chilled by the sound that grew louder and the oppressive weight of energy engulfing her. She stopped when she came to a dimly lit chamber where the cries escaped in mournful tones, then stepped inside with a minimum of movement.

Huddled before her were hundreds of lost soul fragments, villagers she knew who had had their Kas altered. And all waited before her now with an almost mindless passivity for what looked like the moment of their annihilation. And preying upon them was none other than the Thief of Souls himself - the splintered identity of the High Priest Mefakani.

The Crocodile Priest crouched over one of his victims, sucking on his breastbone, until he was satisfied and another victim stepped silently, meekly, into place to be fed upon.

Losha was aghast at the lost souls' placid acceptance of Mefakani's madness. She drew her life force closer to her body. She bit back the ache that gripped her heart. *Showing compassion will betray me,* she warned herself. She walked slowly around the cave, using the gait her teacher had taught her as she searched for Temple in the crowd. But with each breath she drew she felt her own well of energy drain.

I must not fall into the same misperceptions as the others have. I must keep my power strong inside me and remember my connection to wholeness.

She took a deep breath to renew her strength, but Mefakani's dark power and the stifling air seemed to suck the life out of her. In spite of the wisdom that she held close to her heart, her head dizzied and she struggled to maintain her sense of balance, and the short, unobtrusive steps that caused the ethers to smooth around her and shroud her presence.

She was at the moment of collapse when she found Temple in a dark corner bound with chains and iron rings attached to the wall, his head slumped forward and his eyes closed. Seeing him this way made her tremble, but she pushed the torment of her lover from her mind so she could keep a clear head.

This is all smoke and obsidian mirrors, she told herself. *I cannot afford to fall into illusionary fear right now.*

Losha crept over to her lover. "Temple," she whispered softly. "It is Losha. I have come to take you back to yourself."

Temple lifted his head and a dull pair of blue eyes stared back – eyes that had seen too many storms.

"You have survived Mefakani's ritual. He reigns no more. And you have done this without committing any acts of violence against him." With her staff still concealed beneath her tattered cloak, she focused on her intent. She pointed her staff at Temple's chains. The chains fell from his wrists and her nimble reflexes caught them before they had a chance to clatter to the stony floor. She snatched a breath of relief, then took Temple by the hand. "Come. I will take you back."

Temple gave a silent nod, then paused and looked around him with a sudden alertness. His eyes flickered to his right and Losha followed his gaze. "It's Tiv," he muttered weakly.

Several feet away a slim figure slouched on the floor.

"We must take him with us," he insisted.

Losha stole a glance behind her to see if the fragment of Mefakani's former self was still occupied. "It is too risky," she whispered back. "I will come back and get him later."

Losha pulled Temple close and, making certain her jeweled crown was still concealed, she encircled her cloak around him. She led him to the entrance of the cave with small shuffling steps, past the horrible sight of Mefakani feeding with abandon.

"We will come back for Mefakani, too...later on," she said in hushed tones.

And once they moved into the lifeless corridors, she crept unhurriedly until they came to the entranceway where the reptilian guards stood in wait. She pulled Temple closer still, slumped her shoulders and dragged her feet past the guards for what felt like an eternity, until she made it to the safety of the distant shore where Turtle waited.

Turtle's bumpy head pushed out of its shell and looked up at the two when they fell to their knees in exhaustion. They were breathing hard.

"Congratulations," Turtle said.

Losha crawled to the shoreline and scooped up a handful of water so Temple could drink from her hands. Then she splashed some water over his face to revive him. She splashed her own face with water to wash the grit and the stink of death off of her, then drank.

"Now that you have done the hardest task, retrieving Temple's other lost soul part should seem easy," Turtle said with a reptilian kind of grin.

Losha felt as if someone had dumped a bucket of dirt over her. She drew the cloak back from her head and glared at her Teacher. Her nostrils flared. "You mean there is still more?" she asked, wide-eyed.

"Finding and reuniting soul parts is like putting together the layers from one of those foul onions you humans eat," Turtle said with a grinding chuckle.

Losha rolled onto her back and gazed up into the misty sky, the rhythmic knocking filling her ears once more. She skimmed the surface of normal consciousness briefly and felt Temple's hand in hers. But the echo of Turtle's voice drew her back into the nether world. When she opened her mind to where the voice came from she felt a hot, dry breeze tousle her hair and heard grasses rustling around her.

Losha squinted up at a bright yellow sun that rode in a rich cerulean sky. The wide savannas held the scent of sweet grass. Beside her Temple lay close to her side, and beyond him lay her Teacher waiting patiently.

"You will find the younger Temple here," Turtle said.

"The younger Temple?" Losha asked, raising herself up on both her elbows.

"It's unfinished business from his past," Turtle said.

Losha pushed herself erect, then pulled Temple to his feet. Her eyes skimmed atop the sea of wavy grasses and came full stop at an acacia tree that rose from a small rise of dirt. A large male Lion lay in the shade of the tree.

They approached slowly through the high meadow, and the Lion rose onto his powerful muscular legs, gazing in their direction. But there was nothing threatening in his demeanor.

Temple pointed up at the thorn tree near where the Lion waited. There, sitting shivering in fright on the uppermost branches, was Temple at fifteen years old.

Losha looked up at the boy, her heart aching for what she knew the boy had been through. She called to him. "Temple, I am a friend. There is no need to be frightened any longer. The Lion will not harm you. He is your ally and your friend."

The boy shielded his eyes from the sun and stared out across the plain as the strange black woman with bushy hair, a white man wearing a skirt and a giant Turtle slowly approached, leaving a path of bent grasses in their wake.

The three drew closer, then stopped several yards from the Lion and boy. "Temple Fox, you have been up there for ten years, and now is the time to come down," Losha called out. "You are a grown man now, a wonderful and courageous man."

"No, I'm not," the boy called back. "I'm a coward and everyone bloody well knows it!"

"Look," Losha said. "Here you are as your future self." She pointed to her companion.

The boy craned his neck for a sharper look. He started shaking even more and climbed a higher branch, which began to bow dangerously under his weight.

Bloody hell! That bloke looks like me! the boy thought.

"Go away!" he cried. "I don't want to know you! I'm a coward! Everyone knows I couldn't kill that Lion, so bugger off!"

Losha turned to shoot a castigating glare at her Turtle teacher. "I thought you said this would be easy?"

The old Turtle blinked her beaded eyes. "Have patience," she said.

Temple gave a tug on Losha's arm. "Let me try." He gazed up at the boy and spoke. "Temple, look at me. Don't you recognize me?"

The boy squinted in the bright sunlight.

"I am you ten years from now. Look, see my scar?" He pointed to where the Lion had ripped his side open and left distinct claw marks ten years before. "I have the same scar as you do. That's because I am you."

The boy scrutinized the man who looked like him, but was taller, more muscular and robust. "And what is that other scar you have on your forehead? I don't have a scar like that."

"Well, come down and I'll explain it to you," Temple said.

"Fat chance," the boy said. "I'm not coming down with that Lion there. I may be a coward, but I'm not bloody stupid."

"Temple, look," the older Temple said as he walked up to the Lion and let it lick his hand. "See, he won't harm you." Temple ran his hand over the Lion's dusty mane, relishing in the touch and the healing calm that encompassed him. "This Lion is your friend and your ally. What happened between you and I and Dad happened a long time ago. Everything's okay now. He doesn't think we are cowards anymore."

"Yeah, and who's my father? Do you know what he does for a living? Do you even know his name?"

"He's a big game hunter here in Kenya," the older Temple explained. "And this tree you are sitting in is what the Maasai call an anabole tree. Remember how Dad used to go out and shoot an antelope and then hang it up in a tree to bait leopards?"

"You're daft. Most people know he's a big game hunter around here, and everyone knows how to bait leopards," the boy said.

"Oh, really," Temple said. "And do most of them know Dad's birth name is Lincoln Stevenson Fox the Third, but everyone called him Linc? Remember Dad's father, Granddad John? He died of hiccups when he was fifty-one before you were born. And remember Dad's mom, Grandmother Beatrice? After Granddad John died she started dating another man whom Dad didn't like. Only you and I and Mom and Dad knew that the man who was courting Grandma was slowly poisoning her so he could get her money, until Dad, of course, figured things out and threw the guy out of the house. Remember? It was one of the skeletons in the Fox family closet.

"Our Mother's name was Marian, by the way. She was from London. Dad was from, Baltimore, Maryland. Remember the big ships at Fellspoint you loved so much?

"You might also like to know that I got this scar on my head from falling out of an airplane. We became a pilot, you know. Remember big old Blake who used to fly supply runs for Dad? He taught me how to fly. And later we became business partners flying supply runs all over East Africa. He and I bought a de Havilland Moth, but you wouldn't know that because they hadn't been built yet. And you might also like to know that there is this device you wear while flying called a parachute. It was invented about a year before I used one when I fell out of our airplane. It's made of silk and balloons and opens after you jump and catches the air…"

"I became an airplane pilot?" the boy asked excitedly. "God, I always wanted to fly."

"Well, you did and it took a lot of courage to fly."

The boy pointed to Losha who was standing next to Temple. She had shed her crown and ragged cape in the heat and was wearing only her skirt made from barkcoth. He had seen many of the bare-breasted Maasai, Kikuyu, and Luo woman, but this woman seemed different – special.

"Who's the bird?" he asked, pointing, making no attempt to avert his gaze from her beautiful breasts, but trying to hide the sudden thrill that coursed through his body.

"This is Losha. We're together." Temple smiled.

The fifteen-year-old let out an audible snort as he mulled over all that he just heard. "Have you gone all to pot? You're with a bloody Negro? That's a real cockup!"

"You'll find you change your mind about a lot of things in time. Come on down, lad. It's time you and I joined as one," Temple said, coaxing his younger self along.

"And that Lion?" the boy asked as he climbed a limb lower.

The ancient Turtle stretched out her neck and the Lion and the Turtle came nose to nose.

"He will not harm you," Losha called out. "He is your power animal and teacher just as Turtle here is mine."

Trusting himself now, but not knowing why, the boy wiggled his way down branch by branch until he was one branch from the ground, poised midway between escape or potential attack. "I will come down," the boy said, "if you promise to teach me to fly."

The older Temple turned to Losha and smirked. "I can't believe this. I'm being bribed by my younger self."

Temple looked up at the boy again. "I'll do more than teach you to fly, Temple. I'll teach you to fly without an airplane. We can travel together as an owl or even out of our body."

"You're very strange," the boy said as he dropped to the ground with a soft thud. He dusted himself off and looked up at his older self. The two locked eyes for a long silent moment. The older Temple made a move to embrace the boy, but before he could complete the gesture the boy took a step forward and leaned into Temple's embrace. As the two held each other, Losha sensed the love and merging of energies.

Both Temples wiped tears from their eyes and stood side by side staring at the calm Lion. The boy reached out to touch the Lion's muscled flanks and Losha gently clasped his hand. She looked into his blue eyes in wonderment and joy, knowing she'd fall in love with him in time. She held her other hand out to the older Temple. When he placed his hand in hers, Losha rested all of their hands on top of the Lion's head. They stroked the Lion's head together, and the boy felt a newly kindled fascination as well as trusted protection from his new friends.

"Go on!" Turtle called out encouragingly. "The three of you climb on top of the Lion!"

Losha climbed on first, inviting the younger and older Temples to sit in front of her. While they clung tightly to the Lion's mane, Losha wrapped her arms around the two and nodded to her Teacher.

"Thank you," the boy said, feeling the warm strength of the two behind him and the power of the Lion beneath him.

Losha came part way back to normal consciousness and blew the two soul fragments and the Power Animal into Temple's heart. Although she struggled to retain the memory of her otherworldly journey, Losha had enough awareness to grab Mefakani's rattle and shake it all around Temple clockwise four times to seal in the soul parts, the freewill and power she had just recovered for him.

And to end the healing, Losha sang a song of profound gratitude as her lover's vigor and color were restored to normal.

CHAPTER TWENTY-ONE

SANG-WEHTU' SPRING

LANTERN OF LOVE
"Your heart tonight glows pure white
like a paper lantern –
flamed source thinly veiled.
Down the river we slowly drift
like orchid blossoms
and the monkey's plaintive wail
carried on the night air.

"Our lovemaking makes the fish leap –
scales brightly flashing,
offering their last light
to the dying day.
The Moon rises higher
and when it crests,
the rushes at the lush banks sway.

"Oh, how your hands caress
and your tongue moves quick and smooth
like the finest calligraphy brush,
and at once I understand the invention of writing,
mystical signs
and the language of touch
in the lamplight –
in river time,
in the damp night.

"Another fish leaps.
The Moon quivers.
A soft rustle in the reeds.
And every pulse I slip over
becomes a carnelian bead,
a rosary,
a circle of prayers.

"We fall together wet and naked,
covered by the breath of night,
sweat thinning in the open air
as we ride the river of moments
to some inexplicable beginning."

An ancient Makolese poem
Author Unknown
The Makolese Scroll on
The Return of the Ka and the Mending of the Su #21

The three moved under the tangled canopy of liana vine, the fungi's pale green phosphorescence marking their trail in the dark, when they came to a fork in the trail. Tani patted O'Juma on the chest. "Put me down!" she said. "I will walk from here."

O'Juma placed the Elder's tiny feet gently to the earth. "Are you certain? We still have a ways to go," he said.

"How will it look if I am carried in to see the Queen?" she asked.

"How do you feel?" Winyon asked.

"Oh, I am 'weak from wear and worse from worry,' but otherwise I feel stronger," she said. She took a couple of wobbly steps forward to get her old balance back. Without another word she shuffled down the western trail with the others staring at her in bewilderment.

"Elder Tani!" Winyon called out. "That is the trail to the Sang-Wehtu' Spring. That is the long way. The other trail leads to the Queen's compound."

"Do I look like a worm-brain?" Tani grumbled without turning. "I have walked both these paths thousands of times. That is where we are going, to the sacred spring."

The two caught up with her. "I thought you were in a hurry to see the Queen," Winyon said.

"I am," Tani said. "But she is in a temper right now."

"You can feel that?" O'Juma asked, astonished.

"Like an earthquake," the old Healer said. She stood still. "There is something else that…"   She stopped mid-sentence, her senses reaching out like groping tendrils. The slits of her black eyes took on a vacant, faraway cast as if she were listening to something from an unfathomable distance away or from deep within. As suddenly as she had entered this trancelike state, she broke it off and continued down the trail.

Winyon and O'Juma glanced at each other, startled. "Are Temple and Losha all right?" Winyon asked.

"They are performing the miracles which they were born to do," she answered without turning.

"How about Jabal?" O'Juma asked.

Tani took short sideways steps down a small incline. "Come along now. Or do I have to carry *you*?"

★　　★　　★　　★　　★　　★

The sunlight filtered through the dense canopy overhead, and the heavy blackness of night turned a hundred shades of green. The three pushed through the last of the ferns on the overgrown path and crept down to the mossy banks of the round spring, listening to the frogs make little splashes. The breath of the sacred spring settled over the pond and down the length of its streambed in a soft blanket of morning mist.

Tani stopped to commune with a trailing orchid and to listen to the spring's delicate voice above the hum of insects. She moved to the water's edge and prostrated herself on the damp ground. The others placed their heads on the damp earth while the Elder invoked the Spirit of the Sang-Wehtu' Spring in ancient Makolese.

> "Oh, Spirit of the Sacred Spring,
> Sang-Wehtu'
> Bringer of Life,
> Holy is your name.
> Your veins
> are our veins.
> Your blood,
> is our blood.
> Your nectar,
> becomes our sweetness.
> Oh, Spirit of the Sacred Spring,
> Sang-Wehtu',

> We ask you to
> purify our bodies,
> purify our hearts,
> purify our minds,
> and purify our souls.
> All is in perfect moving peace,
> like the rain that becomes the spring,
> and the spring that becomes the river,
> and the river that becomes the ocean ,
> that becomes the rain once more.
> May your abundance flow forever.
> We thank you
> Sang-Wehtu'.
> We thank you."

When the prayer was over, the three sat upright, and the mists began to move. But only Tani's eyes perceived it fully. Though there was no breeze to stir the air, the fog pulled apart like strands of shredded silk. Cottony coils swirled in little eddies above the water, softly churning, curling, folding into itself. The wisps of vapor gathered at the center of the spring and began to spiral counter-clockwise. And, like a lump of clay rising from a potter's hand on a potter's wheel, it coalesced into a milky white column.

It was from the hollow of this mist that Tani listened to the Spirit of the Spring, the voice rising and falling as gently and as rhythmically as the old woman's breast. The Spirit spoke of renewal, a return to wholeness, a purifying and a deepening of energies. In the Spring's own watery language, which only Tani understood, it acknowledged the unspoken plans to return the Ka to the Makolese people, which was something it could sense from the trees and plants, the birds and the air itself.

Tani bowed and thanked Sang-Wehtu'. The hollow pillar of swirling mist uncoiled itself like a dying cyclone and spread itself back across the length of the spring like a thick carpet of white cotton. The three watched in reverence until the sun found its way through the foliage, and the mist slowly dissipated.

Tani turned to the others with the music of the magic spring babbling softly in the air, her wrinkled face mottled now with dappled light. She nodded to them and smiled.

Winyon spoke in hushed tones. "The mist moved into a swirling column. I could feel it, more than see it, but I did witness it."

"Tai," O'Juma whispered. "I felt something, too, but do not know what it was."

"It was the breath of Sang-Wehtu'," Tani said. "She spoke."

Winyon arched one thin eyebrow. "I did not hear anything," she said.

"I did not either," O'Juma said.

The old Healer pointed to the center of O'Juma's tattooed chest. "That is because you do not possess all of your Ka yet," she explained. "And you have your Ka," she said to Winyon, "but only know how to use a little bit of it."

O'Juma turned to Winyon. "You have all of your Ka?" he said with surprise.

"Mefakani did not alter it," she replied, "for he had planned for me to be his wife and join his priesthood. When I did not return his affections, he put a curse on me."

"Then you are the Chokahpeiyape?"

In a gesture that was done with as much modesty as grace, Winyon slipped her tattered shawl off her slender shoulders as if it were some finery and gave a slight nod to the younger man.

O'Juma read her tattoos, then looked into Winyon's face. "You were the Hummingbird who attacked me in the forest."

"I apologize," she said. "Now it seems you are our protector."

Tani cleared her throat. "If you two children are finished with your introductions, I wish to perform a rite of cleansing."

Tani turned toward the spring again. She closed her eyes and dipped her fingers into the cool waters. She touched her wet fingers to her brow first, then lips, then tapped her breastbone several times. After repeating this four times, she dipped her hands back into the water and drew her cupped hands to her mouth to drink. When she had had her fill, she gestured to O'Juma and dipped her fingers back into the spring. The young man closed his eyes. He let the Elder's wet fingertips touch his brow above and between his eyes, then his lips. Then she tapped him lightly on his muscular chest.

Tani whispered in prayer, "Ta, ta, ta. Ta, ta, ta. Ta, ta, ta. Sika, sika ta-jaloma."

Tani nodded and O'Juma dipped his hands into the water and raised his cupped hands to his lips. When he had finished drinking he opened his eyes again. He smiled and nodded, deferring his spot on the mossy banks to Winyon.

"I am not finished with you yet," Tani quipped and pointed for him to stay put.

The old woman dug into her waistband and pulled out two folded leaves. She opened the first and put it aside. When she unfolded the second a foul odor filled the air.

O'Juma jerked his head back from the stench. "What is that?" he asked, wrinkling his nose.

"Hush! It is potent women's medicine – moontime blood."

O'Juma couldn't suppress a smile. "Is this man before you now to be given a woman's medicine? And for what reason?"

Tani reached under her sash again and pulled out a vial carved of rainbow obsidian. She held it up to the sunlight and chuckled. "The Shaman must have thought you were quite special to be placing your Ka in such a colorful vial when you were born." She looked back at O'Juma and winked. She patted the ground in front of her. "Come lie down," she coaxed. "I will reattach your Ka that was taken from you in infancy."

O'Juma looked over at Winyon with surprise then lay down before the old Healer. "Where did you get that?" he asked.

"Jabal told us you were his dearest friend and that we could trust you to help us. I stole this from the Shaman's private cave before I left. I strongly feel you will need this before the sun sets."

When Tani had finished reattaching the piece of flesh with the sticky paste, she held her hand over O'Juma's heart and called forth her powers of healing. She mumbled a prayer that would renew his energies, then thanked her healing ancestors.

"There," she said. "Now rest while I attend to Winyon."

O'Juma sat upright. "But I am not tired." He raised a hand to touch the poultice Tani had placed over his breastbone.

Tani slapped his hand away. "Leave it alone! You must rest for awhile so you can readjust to having your full life force again. When the poultice dries, it will drop off on its own. But for now lie down! And REST!" she ordered.

Winyon knelt before the Elder and gave the Healer a gracious nod as the rite of cleansing was repeated for her.

"Ta, ta, ta," Tani chanted.

Winyon's breath became uneven.

"Ta, ta, ta," Tani repeated and Winyon's chin began to quiver.

"Ta, ta, ta," the Healer crooned softly, all the while tapping the Wounded Hummingbird's heart bone. "Sika, sika ta-jaloma. All is cleansed. All is purified. All is healed. Water is life and is ever changing." She dipped her fingers in the spring again, this time touching the top of Winyon's head, letting the water trickle down the younger woman's face. "Ta, ta, ta," she chanted over and over until

Winyon could not contain the tears any longer and fell into the old woman's arms, weeping.

"It is all right. It is all right, child," Tani said, rocking the woman gently in her arms.

"It is here," Winyon sobbed, "that the Captain…proposed marriage to me."

Tani whispered. "There is nothing but love in this place."

O'Juma's heart was moved. "So beautiful a woman punished unjustly by my own Master. It is unthinkable. I am sorry," he whispered, then fell silent.

When he was finally able to speak again his voice was barely audible above the babble of the spring. "You must have loved your husband very much, for this is where the Goddess Hianna and the God Gadji first made love. Do you remember the poem about it?" he asked.

Winyon gazed down at the young man, her moist eyes full of memories. "Tai," she sniffled. "It has been several seasons since I have heard it recited."

O'Juma smiled back from where he lay, his deep husky voice smooth and smoky.

"And the God Gadji said to his love, the Goddess Hianna," he recited.

> 'Your heart tonight glows pure white
> like a paper lantern –
> flamed source thinly veiled.
> Down the river we slowly drift
> like orchid blossoms
> and the monkey's plaintive wail
> carried on the night air.
>
> 'Our lovemaking makes the fish leap –
> scales brightly flashing,
> offering their last light
> to the dying day.
> The Moon rises higher
> and when it crests,
> the rushes at the lush banks sway.'

"And then Hianna said of Gadji:
> 'Oh, how your hands caress
> and your tongue moves quick and smooth
> like the finest calligraphy brush,

and at once I understand the invention of writing,
mystical signs
and the language of touch
in the lamplight –
in river time
in the damp night.

'Another fish leaps.
The Moon quivers.
A soft rustle in the reeds.
And every pulse I slip over
becomes a carnelian bead,
a rosary,
a circle of prayers.'

"And together they said:"
'We fall together wet and naked,
covered by the breath of night,
sweat thinning in the open air
as we ride the river of moments
to some inexplicable beginning.'"

Winyon pulled herself from Tani's nurturing arms and smiled at the prone figure on the ground. "That was lovely, so lovely. Thank you," she said, bowing from where she sat.

Tani fanned herself with her bony hand and screwed up her leathery face. "Any hotter and these waters will turn into a hot spring." She grinned.

Winyon was laughing now. She rose with a natural kind of grace and straightened her ragged skirt and shawl. "And I thank you, Elder Tani." She bowed respectfully, then turned toward the spring and bowed. "And I thank the Spirit of Sang-Wehtu'."

Winyon looked up at the little piece of sky she could see through the verdant leaves. "I am concerned that we have lost the cover of darkness. Should we continue now? Or is Queen Palomei still toppling buildings?"

O'Juma rose and helped the small Elder to her feet. Tani tilted her head slightly, focusing her senses far away. She closed her eyes and pursed her thin lips together in thought. "There is a bit of rumbling left," she said, nodding. "It comes in waves." The old centenarian opened her eyes and stared up at the handsome boy. "You will heal someone today who is close to death."

This sudden proclamation made O'Juma rock back on his heels. "Me? Heal?"

"Make two kumbabs…one to pull out poison, the other for fever and infection," she said. "It does not matter if it is made with only a few drops of water, for it will be potent enough. When you have done this sacred thing, leave here immediately. Understand?" She looked O'Juma squarely in the eye. "Make haste and return to the Shaman's compound. Winyon and I will go from here alone." Tani turned to leave.

"But I have failed in keeping my promise to get you safely to the Queen's compound," he complained.

"That is none of your concern now," Tani said. "Journeying to the Queen's compound means you will be detained too long and will miss an opportunity to help someone."

"Who?" he asked. "Who is it I am supposed to heal?"

Tani looked at the young man with full reproach. "Make haste!" she snapped. And with that declaration the two women left.

CHAPTER TWENTY-TWO

WINYON'S ESCAPE

"'Do not be a victim and the Gods will guide you. Like I told you before, remember to keep your sun centered here," she said, placing her hand on her own abdomen. "And do not let anyone bleed you of your light. Never! And never let anyone put you inside a water trough for several days or you will grow moldy and very hungry!'"

Elder Tani
The Makolese Scroll on
The Return of the Ka and the Mending of the Su #22

Elder Tani and Winyon made their way along the banks of the Sang-Wehtu' Spring to a point where the stream joined two creeks to form the wide Ananba River. The two women climbed down from the banks to a strip of sand. They drank there, stripped off their skirts, then bathed.

"That wound has healed nicely," Tani said, eyeing Winyon's shoulder. "And the infection is completely gone."

"Tai, it is only a little sore now," Winyon said.

Tani crept back onto the shore and wrapped her barkcloth skirt around her. "We are not far now."

Winyon washed her ragged shawl then rung it out. "I am nervous," she said. "Under the cover of night there was less of a chance of someone recognizing me. But now…" She shook her shawl out and flung it around her shoulders. "Now I cannot even change into a Hummingbird if I wanted to."

"One is not meant to spin too often, especially when one is weary," Tani said.

Winyon climbed out of the water. She wrapped her skirt around her and pulled a tortoiseshell comb from the folds of her waistband. "It feels so strange to be on the main island again. Five long seasons." She sighed. "I pray we will get inside the Queen's compound before I am recognized," she said as she combed her long silver hair.

Tani gave a toothless frown. "You need training in how to use your Ka properly. Do not be a victim and the Gods will guide you. Like I told you before, remember to keep your sun centered here," she said, placing her hand on her own abdomen. "And do not let anyone bleed you of your light. Never! And never let anyone put you inside a water trough for several days or you will grow moldy and very hungry!" She laughed. "Come! We must go now."

The women stayed close to the river with only a short distance to go before they reached the Queen's compound. They came to a steep bend where the Ananba deepened when a rustling came from the embankment above them. A man's voice rang out. "Stop where you are!"

Winyon stopped, but Tani shuffled along the sandy bank, ignoring the order. The rustling grew louder, hurried and the voice called out again, this time agitated. "I said, 'Stop'!"

Tani continued on, singing softly to herself.

One of Palomei's servants appeared from behind the bushes and came crashing through the grass. The sunlight lit the gold border of his barkcloth wraparound and the blade of his long knife.

"Elder Tani!" Winyon shouted.

Tani scuttled along the sand with no indication that she was going to slow her pace. "If that young man has any sense at all," she said loud enough for the boy to hear, "he will escort us to the Queen personally."

The servant jumped down onto the beach and trotted over to the Elder with his knife held high. He blocked her way.

Tani took a bold step forward and squinted up into the young man's face. "Are you not Shalamin's youngest son, Tu'suling?" she asked, scrutinizing him with her ancient eyes.

The young man was taken back by the question. "Tai, I am Tu'suling, youngest son of Shalamin," he answered.

She eyed the thick blade of his long knife. "You cannot hack a trail with that old relic," she said.

"I know," he said, lowering his sword, "but it was what I was given. The Queen's soldiers and guardsmen have taken up all the best weapons."

"And what is one of Palomei's servants doing out here harassing Elders?" she asked with a twinkle in her eye.

"I beg your forgiveness, Elder," he said and bowed, "but there is trouble between the Believers and Unbelievers. First the Queen makes me a runner. Now I am a Guard. I am under orders to stop anyone heading to the Queen's compound. I am supposed to patrol the western side of the Ananba River as far as Sang-Wehtu' Spring."

"Well, I have just come from the sacred spring," Tani said. "There is no one there, and I saw no one along the way. So, why not be my protector and escort me to the compound? I have important business with the Queen," she said and she shuffled around him.

Tu'suling hesitated for a moment, then looked over at Winyon.

"Be quick!" Tani said. "I do not have all day!"

The young man pulled himself erect and gripped his knife tightly. "Follow me," he said.

Tu'suling took the lead and climbed back onto the high bank, then turned to lend a hand to the Elder. And as they made their way through the river grasses, he took a few self-conscious swipes with his knife to clear a path, continuing on unheeded with a sense of new purpose.

Winyon came up close behind the Elder. "Elder Tani," she started.

"Hush!" Tani whispered. "Stay close!"

Winyon kept a pace away from the old woman when the three came to a large open area of sand with the stone walls of Palomei's compound in the distance gleaming clean and white in the morning sun. There were signs the earth had been dug up around the perimeter of the long wall and bits of debris scattered on the ground.

"What happened to all the vines?" Tani asked.

The boy glanced back at her. "The Queen ordered the vines removed from all the walls. It would be too easy for one of the Rebels to climb a wall covered with vines," he explained.

Something is out of place. The shadows lay differently and so does the sunlight. Tani squinted in the distance and a sudden realization hit her like an ax blow. She stopped in midstride, unable to move, drawing her hand up to her gaping mouth. She looked all around her. Panicked, she broke into a run. Stopping again, this time beside a row of tree stumps, she fell to her knees at the horrible sight.

"In the name of Hianna what has happened to all the royal palms? Who cut them!"

"The Queen ordered them to be cut. If a Rebel climbed one it would be too easy for him to spy over the wall...or even climb over."

"Bi kana lo! What is Palomei doing! Killing the most sacred of trees to the Goddess Hianna! This is a sacrilege!" Tani cried out, which made Tu'suling back a step. Tani's temper turned so hot that it dried any tears she might have shed. She gazed up at Winyon with fire and pain in her eyes.

Neither sadness nor anger overtook Winyon. She began to tremble inwardly from fear. She offered her hand to Tani and helped the centenarian to her feet.

Tani brushed the sand off her skirt with such anger that Tu'suling took another step backward, suddenly frightened of Tani's wrath. "The world has turned upside down!" She spat on the ground and set her hard gaze at their young guide. "The Rebels are still up on Hollow Mountain, are they not?" she asked.

"As…as far as I…I know they are," Tu'suling stuttered, "but I…I am not privileged to know the details of such matters."

The three kept their distance from the western wall and coursed their way around to the southern side. Tu'suling stopped a good distance from the southern gate when he saw an angry crowd of about fifty people gathered there. Five palace guards held them at bay with their shields and spears.

"Back off!" one guard shouted to the crowd.

"We demand to see the Queen!" someone called out.

"Tai," another shouted. "Why have some been allowed into the compound, while the rest of us are left out here? And why can we not sail as far as the Green river?"

"Go back to your boats and go home!" the guard yelled back. "Sail as far as you can and walk the rest of the way!"

A woman holding a child pushed her way to the front of the crowd. "Why can we not sail down to the Green River?" she asked. "I have a sick child who needs to see the Shaman!"

Five more palace guards bolted through the gate to join the other five. They stepped forward and pushed against the crowd with their shields. The people shouted back at them in complaint.

Tu'suling waited until the crowd was pushed back, then motioned to the guardsmen who remained at the gate. Two left their posts and jogged over to the boy and two women.

The palace guards recognized Tani as they approached and drew their swords. "We have been given new orders," one guardsman said to Tu'suling. "You are to see the Head Servant. But first we will take her," he said, gesturing to Tani. "Elder Tani, you are under arrest."

"Again?" she snorted. "What is the charge?"

"Treason!" he answered.

"Oh, and not blasphemy or witchcraft this time? That is fine," Tani said, calmly, "as long as I get to see the Queen in person."

The guard reached down and grabbed the tiny woman by her leathery forearm. He pointed his sword at Winyon. "And who are you?"

"I…?" Winyon started, then stopped and stared mutely at Tani.

Tani gave Winyon a little nod. "It was decent of you to help an old woman through that awful rainstorm. Thank you," she said, and walked off with the armed guards.

Without calling attention to herself, Winyon backed away. She stared in horror and disbelief as the servant and the two guards, who towered over the tiny old woman, disappeared through the southern gate. A chill ran up Winyon's spine as she walked over to the water's edge, keeping a good distance away from the crowd and the other guards. She gazed at the small harbor of empty boats pulled up on the shoreline, the last of the morning mist still clinging to the Ananba River.

I do not know what to do. Where can I go? Where can I hide?

Drifting back toward the river, the crowd began to vent their complaints in the open air.

"Who cut down all the sacred palms?"

"Why are we not allowed past the Ananba River?"

"And why are those, who travel from the opposite direction, not permitted to sail within a quarter of a mile before the Ananba meets the Green River?"

"Tai, and why are only those who live within the compound herded behind the palace walls if the Queen herself did not expect some unwelcomed visitors?" asked another.

"Rebels!" someone hissed.

The voices of the islanders reverberated against the riverbanks and grew louder in Winyon's ears. She kept her back to them as they sauntered toward their boats, shouting in defiance at the guards' use of force. Unaccustomed to people after so many years in exile, Winyon was alarmed by the islanders' presence pressing against her, and dizzied from the storm of their mounting voices.

The people sifted past her, not noticing her, as they pushed their boats out into the water. Winyon began to shake and her breath grew ragged. She staggered over to a log to rest and steady herself. She tried to make herself small, but felt as if her body was rocking like the boats.

She closed her eyes to shut out the sight of the crowd, to still herself against their noisy clamor, to shield herself from their energies shoving against her. She tried to anchor her mind on a single image, but all she could see was her last memory of Mefakani, his face half-hidden in the flickering firelight of his private cavern. It had been two years since Mefakani came ashore to the tiny island where she and Captain Kneller had been exiled. Two years since Mefakani had bound her with his magic and threatened to kill her if the Captain did not reveal why he had gone into Hollow Mountain. Two years since Mefakani cut her husband's head clean off, then made away with it in his boat. Two years of rubbing and grinding the walls of the coral cave with sand to remove the bloodstains. Two long years since the Priest had spread rumors that Winyon, the Exile, the Chokahpeiyape, had murdered her own husband. Two years of having one's tongue cursed so no other could hear the truth. The memories grew bolder, more vivid as the voices from the crowd drew closer, louder.

How life has wedged me into the crevice of nonexistence, she thought. *What the people have not seen in many years I pray is soon forgotten.*

But still she felt the people's anger clawing at the air around her. She shut her eyes tighter, praying they would go away, when a voice broke through the crowd.

"Is that not Winyon sitting over there?" someone asked.

"You mean the Chokahpeiyape?" another answered.

"It cannot be. She has been banished."

"No. It is! Look! See her tattoos!" another replied.

Winyon pulled her torn shawl up over her shoulder and her heart began to beat faster.

A woman's voice rang out close by Winyon's side. "Tai, it is!"

Winyon remained rooted where she sat. She stayed silent.

A sudden hush came over the crowd and then a quiet mumbling. Footsteps drew closer. Winyon flinched and her eyes flew open when her shawl was pulled off her shoulder.

"It is the witch! She is here!" a woman thundered in her ear.

The people retreated and Winyon stared numbly at the mob, feeling naked, exposed.

It is happening all over again! It is as if I have never left the island!

"It is because of her!" someone shouted. "They blocked the river because of her! She has joined the traitors!"

Winyon rose from where she sat… The Exiled, The-One-No-One-Wants, The-One-No-One-Loves…Madwoman! Murderer! Witch!!…

Winyon felt the first stone clip her sore shoulder and she grabbed her shoulder in surprise. She held out her hand to shield her from the sight of her assailant and another blow. But the second stone came from another direction. A sharp pain struck the side of her left knee and she stumbled to the ground. The voices blurred together and she heard the dull sounds of stones hitting sand, hitting flesh. But there was another sound – a voice. A remembrance called out to her. "Give no one your power," Tani had said.

A sharp rock sliced open Winyon's back and her focus raced back onto her pain again. The voices in the mob grew stronger, but so did Tani's singular voice. "Keep your sun centered here." It was as if someone had placed a hand over Winyon's stomach and she felt a heat run through her. She trembled as she drew her legs up beneath her and began to rise.

"Give no one your power! GIVE NO ONE YOUR POWER!" A rain of stones cascaded all around her, but she gave no power to the ones that struck and little attention to the pain. What pain she did acknowledge, she turned into anger, and she used her anger to stand her ground.

"I am not your Chokahpeiyape!" she shouted.

The people fell silent and the stones stopped falling.

"I will not be your shadow anymore!" she screamed back in fury. "I am not a murderer or a witch! I was bewitched by your Shaman! *He* is the one who killed my husband then covered his crime by blaming *me* and spreading rumors!"

Having seen the stoning, the guards started pushing their way through the crowd with their shields.

Winyon saw them coming and stared back at the mob. "Not one of you ever bothered to find out the truth! But Temple Fox did. He is the True Teacher and was the first to hear my story!"

One guard broke through the crowd and drew his sword as Winyon ran to the river. She threw off her shawl and dived into the water, then quickly surfaced.

"Oh, Mother Waters, please protect me!" she prayed. Winyon heard the guards shouting at one another to board their boats and the sound of splashing oars as she swam farther from the shore. The mists enveloped her and she dipped beneath the water, the sounds growing duller, distant.

"Where did she go!" a guard called out.

"I do not know!" another shouted.

The men looked all around them in the mist, but Winyon was nowhere to be seen.

Winyon fought against the current, using her good leg to propel herself. Her ragged skirt was slowing her down so she loosened it from her hips, leaving it to drift in the currents behind her. She swam harder than she ever thought she could, holding her breath longer than she imagined possible, until she sensed she was well hidden from the guards and safe to surface. She emerged cautiously, allowing only her nose and mouth to break the surface, making scarcely a ripple. She gasped in a lung full of air and submerged again to swim further upstream, this time leaving her pain behind her, until again she was forced to surface. This time her entire head emerged so she could see where she might be, only to find herself shrouded by an impenetrable fog. She drank in a few rapid breaths, noting the direction of the guard's voices. She submerged again and continued upstream, this time feeling less panicked and frightened.

Keen to the smoothness of the water flowing over her naked skin, she began to feel as if she had become the water. Suspended out of time, merging with the river, her supple muscles moved through what began to feel like air, and she became like a hummingbird again in effortless flight. Her heart calmed and her slender body sailed beyond the dull murmur of voices to a soundless world. With each confident stroke she gained several yards and when she felt the currents change slightly she knew she was at the junction where the sacred spring merged with the two brooks. She surfaced smiling, sensing peace and safety all around her, her skin goose-bumped from the chill of the spring waters. She took a deep breath and swam into the mouth of Sang-Wehtu' until she could touch bottom and gently pull herself along the sandy bottom. And when she came to the source of the sacred spring she rose shivering slightly from the cold. Winyon felt no pain as she climbed out onto the banks naked, vulnerable, but far freer than she had ever felt before.

CHAPTER TWENTY-THREE

WINYON'S DELIVERANCE

"To the cutting sun that ran me ragged. To every blade of grass that cushioned my fall in the spring of my renewal and the summer of my expansion. To the fire that seared me clear of my old self. To the winds and the rains of the West that washed me clean. To all my Ancestors and all my relatives. To all my friends seen and unseen, and to the Spirit of Sang-Wehtu' Spring, I say thank you. Thank you."

Winyon Kneller
The Makolese Scroll on
The Return of the Ka and the Mending of the Su #23

Winyon crawled up onto the mossy banks of the Sang-Wehtu'. A strong presence immediately engulfed her, roughing her naked flesh and causing her skin to tingle as if she had been swathed in the finest silk impregnated with peppermint. The presence swirled around her, holding her in place where she lay, until Winyon felt she couldn't move and only breathe. She surrendered to its embrace, and a deep sense of holiness permeated her to the core of her being, purifying her very breath and rarifying the air around her.

Winyon rested her cheek on the damp ground and breathed in its goodness. It was like swallowing cool fire. So overcome with this delicate sweetness, Winyon cried aloud in gratitude for her protection and deliverance.

"To the cutting sun that ran me ragged. To every blade of grass that cushioned my fall in the spring of my renewal and the summer of my expansion. To the fire that seared me clear of my old self. To the winds and the rains of the West that washed me clean. To all my

Ancestors and all my relatives. To all my friends seen and unseen, and to the Spirit of Sang-Wehtu' Spring, I say thank you. Thank you."

The prayer was acknowledged and slowly the hold on her seemed to lift, then disappear. There was nothing to mark the powerful presence, only the gentle sound of spring water flowing over stone.

Suddenly, Winyon felt exposed again. Her thoughts darkened for a human moment.

Did the guards think I swam down the river or maybe drowned? Maybe they hold the old belief that witches cannot drown. Perhaps they gave up their search altogether.

Winyon rose and waded back into the water to wash off the sand. She waited for the ripples to play themselves out, then pondered her reflection. Staring back at her was a woman in her late forties, still slender and strong in form, only this woman was covered with cuts and bruises. She leaned down for a closer look, her hair still dripping, causing her image to waver. Her hair had long since silvered prematurely, and the lines on her face were still multiple. But there was life there. New life. And her wounds were healing before her eyes.

Winyon was still beautiful and she smiled at her own reflection.

This time Winyon felt a presence come up behind her before she spied its reflection in the water. She sighed with deep satisfaction when a Hermit Hummingbird, its wings thrumming madly, circumvented her head, then hovered like a specter in front of her face. She watched with fascination as its beady eyes looked into her own to gaze at its own reflection.

"What should I do now?" she asked. "Should I hide?"

The bird circled Winyon three times, then darted into the air. It hovered near a bush crowded with tiny red flowers that had escaped Winyon's notice before. The bird stuck its thin bill deep inside the throat of the blossom, drank in the nectar, then fluttered in front of Winyon's face again. Before Winyon could resist, the Hummingbird slipped its thin beak into her mouth and released the nectar. Winyon couldn't help but laugh with surprise and delight. With an unexpected yawn, she broke the spell and the bird danced around her head again, then darted toward the thick jungle.

Winyon followed where the Hermit had flown and found it doing acrobatic maneuvering in the air around a mammoth hollow cedar lying on its side. She crouched down for closer inspection, and the bird flashed past her inside the hollow log. Placing a bit of moss inside, the Hummingbird flew out again.

"I understand," she said. "I need to hide. And I need to rest."

There was no denying that Winyon was tired and hungry. She had had little rest from the moment she learned how to spin into a hummingbird days before, or even after she had flown to the mainland. Meeting Mefakani again, exploring the maze of underground tunnels that led to the Mother Stone, and now her mad escape from the mob made her dizzy with fatigue. And so she did as her Spirit Ally advised. She ate some fruit from the kamukamu bush, and some fungi, then drank from the sacred spring. After she had her fill, she collected the driest moss for her bedding, and some roots from the uruku to keep the bugs away. She tied the crushed root of some liana vine on her worse wounds for good measure, then climbed inside the massive log. She positioned one eye directly across from a knothole that faced the magic spring. But her eyes quickly closed, and for the first time in days she fell fast asleep.

CHAPTER TWENTY-FOUR

THE HUMMINGBIRD AND THE SWAN

LANGUISHING IN THE AFTERNOON

"The cold pillow
and the longing
led me down
to the weeping willow
at the river bed,
its head bent to hear
the soft voice
of water
spilling over rock,
sweeping the reflections
of cloud and sky.

I languish in the afternoon.

Unless men are dreaming,
sounds not meant for men,
but more gentle beasts,
deepen their minds
to the open sky.

How is it that this body
can hide such brightness?

Close your eyes
and you will see it.
Fill your lungs with it

> *and feel it.*
> *Like a fish in water*
> *with the ocean inside it,*
> *who can say*
> *where the Goddess ends*
> *or where the Goddess begins*
> *as She bends all boundaries,*
> *blending with other oceans of light.*
>
> *The flame of yourself*
> *is the eye of the Goddess.*
> *For She breathed you in*
> *at death*
> *and like a fire eater*
> *spit you out anew*
> *when She blew you*
> *into existence again.*
>
> *What a carnival*
> *Life is."*

Elo Tivluk, popular Makolese poet
The Makolese Scroll on
The Return of the Ka and the Mending of the Su #24

There was a loud splash and the sound of beating wings.

Winyon woke with a start and hit her head on the inside of the log. "Ouch!" she yelled.

Fully aware that her presence had been detected, the startled Swan flapped its wings in a panic and flew up into the evening sky.

Winyon couldn't reckon where she was at first, until the cramped enclosure hindering her movements brought her back to full consciousness. She peered out of the tiny knothole where the jungle was cast in a soft green twilight, not knowing what end of the day it was or what had wakened her. She lay very still and strained her eye in the fading light. Her patience bore fruit when the large white swan splashed down into the spring again and began grazing the bottom of the pool. Winyon admired its beauty and its strength when suddenly it dawned on her. She was halfway out of the log when the startled Swan flew up into the air again and disappeared.

"Bi kana lo!" she cursed, bending stiffly backward and searching the sky.

The Swan circled round, then spiraled down in ever smaller circles until one wing tip grazed the surface of the spring. When the bird landed, the glade burst into resplendent light.

Winyon's eyes adjusted to the evening green again. Before her stood Losha, knee-deep in the middle of the spring, the waters bubbling and pulsating with an iridescence that made the surrounding flowers flash like jewels.

Losha peered at the bruises and half-healed wounds that covered Winyon's body. She frowned with concern. "What has happened to you? What are you doing here?" she asked, the tips of her bushy hair throwing off their last sparks of light.

Winyon had only seen Losha spin and transform twice before. She was lost for words.

"Are you all right?" Losha asked.

Winyon suddenly became aware of her nakedness, but made no attempt to hide herself. She was before one of the Teachers now and felt safe. She simply nodded.

"Where are Tani and O'Juma?"

"O'Juma has gone back to the Shaman's compound. Tani has been arrested," she said more excitedly.

"What? Again?"

"That is what she said. She did not seem to be upset since it was a means to get inside the compound. I think Palomei is preparing for war. She has blocked all traffic along the Green River and is only allowing boats to sail on the Ananba so people can go back to their villages. There was a mob!" She stopped to catch her breath. "They tried to stone me to death!"

Losha climbed out of the spring and up onto the mossy bank. She watched Winyon with an ache that made her want to reach out and enfold the older woman in her arms. "I am so sorry," she said.

"They recognized me. And I spoke to them. I used my Ka, my power. I could not spin to escape, but I told them that Mefakani had falsely accused me of both witchcraft and murder."

"Did they listen?"

"I did not stay to find out. The palace guards came after me and, believe me, they were armed with more than stones."

"You said they blocked the Green River?" Losha asked.

Winyon nodded.

Losha looked away in thought and then back at Winyon. "The Rebel Elders and their warriors will be sailing down the river early tomorrow morning along with some of Palomei's soldiers. Mefakani is planning to meet them back on the mountain in his airship. Temple plans to fly in his Owl form to speak with Palomei's army, but will arrive only after the Rebels have been given safe passage past the troops."

"Then Cranik and Kulo swallowed the bait?" Winyon asked.

"Wholly," Losha replied. "Only now Palomei thinks we betrayed her. She must think we formed an alliance with the Rebels to overthrow her. She may try to stop them on the river."

"I do not know what the Queen thinks," Winyon said, "but she cut down all the royal palms at her compound, fearing the Rebels would climb over the compound walls."

Losha's mouth parted in disbelief. "No one would dare commit such a sacrilege! She must be desperate with fear." Deep in thought again, Losha looked out into her leafy surroundings. "I must go to the Queen's compound quickly…and do so before Palomei has Cranik, the other Rebels, and even her own soldiers killed." She looked back at the naked woman. "We must give both Temple and Mefakani a chance to change the hearts of as many people as they can. If Cranik and his people are killed there will be a civil war for sure."

"The guards will think you are a traitor and arrest you like they did Tani if you do not fly there as a Swan!" Winyon warned.

"I cannot fly," Losha said. "My power has its limits. I cannot change for several hours now."

"That is my fault," Winyon said. "Had you not found me, you never would have changed back into your human form."

"But if I had not seen you, I would have never known about Tani's arrest, and what must be plaguing Palomei's mind."

Losha sat down on the sand, closed her eyes and fell silent for several minutes. She knew that incidents didn't happen by chance. Her mind moved to another place, a still place. And so her mind wasn't racing with plots on how to enter the compound. On the contrary, she was emptying her mind and allowing the Divine Force of her own wisdom to guide her.

Losha opened her eyes and smiled at Winyon. "You are my inspiration," she said warmly. "If you can confront a mob about to stone you to death, I can deal with a few palace guards." She looked up at the darkening greenery. "I am losing the sun. I must go now."

CHAPTER TWENTY-FIVE

LIGHT AT THE SOUTHERN GATE

*"Kill God's messenger who speaks the truth and
the messenger may die, but the truth she has not
spoken still remains the truth!"*

Losha Ninti
The Makolese Scroll on
The Return of the Ka and the Mending of the Su #25

The torchlight flickered against the compound wall causing the Guardsmen's shadows to dance on the ground. Losha stepped deeper into the shadows and edged her way around the wall to the Southern Gate. And as she drew closer, she spied a curious-shaped silhouette where the royal palms had once grown. In the half-light it took a moment to reconcile what she was seeing: a head impaled upon a stake, and with it the stench of decay.

Whose head is this? she wondered and a shiver ran up her spine. Losha's heart rose into her throat and she thought of only Tani. *I have to know.* She stepped forward hesitantly, the buzz of flies growing louder in her ears. She placed her hand on the stake. The blood, still wet and thick, stuck to her palm. Darkness obscured the victim's identity, but the blood she tested with her senses told her the victim was a male, young, probably in his teens.

A voice rang out like a bell. "Identify yourself!"

Losha steadied herself. "Whose life was taken here?" she asked, her voice taking on an authoritative weight.

The voice drew closer. "I said, 'Identify yourself!' or meet the same fate as the boy!"

"I am in service to Queen Palomei," she stated.

Two guards appeared from the shadows, hulking shapes blocking the sight of the Southern Gate.

"Who are you?" a guard asked.

"One who honors all life," she replied.

The guard with the brusque voice answered back. "Not all life deserves to be honored, especially when allies turn into enemies. Who *are* you?" he asked again this time demanding an answer in a tone implying *or* a quick death by sword.

Losha held her head high and gestured with her arms out by her side that she was unarmed. "I am Losha Ninti, Principal Interpreter and Translator to the Queen, and friend of the royal household."

The guards, Maha'oi and Paku', exchanged quick glances. Without saying a word they stepped forward, each clasping Losha by her upper arms.

"You are more than the Principal Interpreter," the brusque voice said, tightening his grip. "You are one of the principal traitors. I will cut off your head now and save the Queen the trouble!" He shoved Losha to the ground and stepped back, drawing his sword with both hands.

"If you cut off my head," Losha said, "please give it to the Queen quickly, for I swear before you now I *will* deliver the important message I have for her – even if I give it with my last breath!" She climbed back onto her feet.

Maha'oi lowered his sword and grabbed her arm again, this time digging his fingers deeper into her flesh. "You will not live long enough to see the Queen!" He pushed her away and took aim again.

"Towa-anash o'besosay pasuntoson, towa-anash anobay oh-a-he,'" she intoned in ancient Makolese.

"What!" he spat back.

"It is an old saying in ancient Makolese," Losha explained. "'The more brutal the man, the more frightened he is.'"

Maha'oi wheeled behind Losha and hit her so hard with the flat edge of his sword she went sailing into the air several feet. But her agility as a swan had taught her how to land without getting hurt, and she rolled on the ground until she was upright again.

"There is no need to be frightened of me," she said coolly.

This made Maha'oi laugh. "Do I look frightened?"

With a short blast of her breath Losha pushed her power up from her solar plexus to the tiny cut between her brows. "'The more frightened the man, the more uncertain he is...'" she said in common Makolese so the guard would understand.

"Shut up!" Maha'oi shouted.

"'…especially when that man behaves like a beast, mirroring the very enemy he wishes to obliterate.' But you see, I am not your enemy."

"I said, 'Shut up!'"

"They are only words," said Paku'. "Hurry up and kill her or we will end up like the boy!'"

Maha'oi swung his sword and Losha ducked out of the way. She looked directly into his eyes and drew his eyes into hers. "Kill God's messenger who speaks the truth and the messenger may die, but the truth she has not spoken still remains the truth!"

"God's messenger, eh? You are nothing but a traitor!" he shouted.

He swung his sword again and the point of the blade missed Losha by inches. Losha pulled him deeper into her eyes. When the tingling in her head intensified, it gathered force at the point between her brows. She exhaled sharply and a flash of light hit her attacker between the eyes. With his head thrown back and his eyes still fixed on hers, he saw the cut on her forehead glowing like a blue ember. The two stood in a silent exchange until the other guardsman interrupted.

"Are you all right?" Paku' asked.

"Tai," Maha'oi whispered. He blinked a few times, looked back at Losha, noticing her calm resolve. A peace fell over him and he lowered his sword and bowed steeply.

"What are you doing?!" Paku' asked, alarmed.

Maha'oi pointed to the Southern Gate. "I will escort you now to the Queen," he said to her. "If I am wrong, then let Queen Palomei take your head. I will not be responsible for your death."

Paku' stared back at Losha, and, seeing her forehead on fire, dropped to his knees and begged her forgiveness.

"As I said before, 'I am God's messenger.' I am not, however, your master. Rise up!" she demanded, "and never bow to me again unless it is with the intent to honor me, not worship me. The same goes for Temple Fox, for he is the True Teacher as well. We two have both fulfilled the prophecy."

And with that brief proclamation the three moved swiftly to the Southern Gate.

CHAPTER TWENTY-SIX

FROM THE SHADOWS

"It is done."

High Shaman Mefakani
The Makolese Scroll on
The Return of the Ka and the Mending of the Su #26

The sound of stone grinding against stone echoed throughout the passageways as the megalithic boulder pivoted on its invisible axis. The smell of smoke and decay escaped into the corridors with a rush of air.

The Rebels, who were half dazed from cold and sleeplessness, jumped to a sudden alertness. The tunnels came alive with the sound of swords being pulled from their scabbards.

"Quick, get me up!" Cranik ordered. Two Rebel soldiers lifted the old man off the cold corridor floor. They placed themselves in front of him as a shield.

The massive stone came to rest, allowing a wide enough entrance for only one person. All eyes strained to see past the dark entranceway, and when the figure of Mefakani finally appeared it was as if the tunnel walls themselves had breathed a sigh of relief.

Mefakani adjusted his headband to make certain his healed scar would not be seen. He stepped into the torchlight and cast his eyes down as if the sight of the light pained him at first. He looked up at the Rebels one by one in silence.

The others shuffled back, startled, not from his weary appearance or in anticipation of the pronouncement the Shaman was about to make, but from the quiet acquiescence that replaced the flinty eyes they were accustomed to. No one knew what pain the Shaman had endured, what spirits had haunted him after death, when he had returned to life again.

His brow furrowed from the pain of the charade he had to play now. His voice fell out into the air like the small cry of a wounded bird, surprising even himself. "Do you wish to see the body now?" he asked.

Elder Cranik ordered his guards aside with a brusque sweep of his hand and stepped forward, yielding to the distance Mefakani's presence demanded. The old man searched Mefakani's face for a thoughtful moment, but couldn't discern with any clarity what he was sensing. There was a different kind of depth hidden behind those eyes, a tender sadness as if the Shaman had yielded to some greater force than himself. Cranik cleared his throat, embarrassed by so long a hesitation on his part. He bowed steeper than he meant to bow, rose, then looked away from the self-proclaimed God, as if looking upon him was too much to bear. He spoke over his shoulder with a kind of nervousness Kulo had never heard before. "Stay here," he ordered the others. "I will go alone with the Teacher."

The Elder took a step toward the entranceway, but Mefakani didn't want to miss an opportunity to play his part fully, and stood steadfast, blocking Cranik's way. "Where is Senior Elder Sahdon?" he asked.

Cranik glanced at Elder Kulo, who stood silently behind a wall of Rebel warriors, then back at Mefakani. "We regret that our Senior Elder had an accident...in the tunnels to the Mother Stone," he said.

Mefakani stared at him hard enough to let the Elder know he could see through a hardened heart.

Cranik turned his head aside to deflect the gaze. "He was asking the Mother Stone to help you kill the Wizard. He fell to his death."

The power of Mefakani's voice cut right through Cranik. "And so you are now the Senior Elder."

"Until there is an election," Cranik answered quickly in defense.

"There are no elections when there is civil war," Mefakani emphasized. "And there will be a civil war unless I can stop it."

"My only concern now is the death of Temple Fox," Cranik interjected.

"Be forewarned, Elder," Mefakani said coolly in a voice more familiar to Cranik's ears. "It would behoove you to think far ahead of the present circumstances."

Before Cranik got a chance to respond, the Priest slipped through the dark entranceway back into the shadows of his private cavern. The others looked apprehensively at their new Senior Elder and waited as he entered the chamber alone.

Cranik felt for the uneven ground under his foot with each hesitant step and made his way inside. Smoke and the stench of rotting flesh clung in the air and played havoc with his lungs, and he noticed the sudden noisiness of his own breathing. For a moment he became confused as the cavern came alive with energies he couldn't comprehend. The Elder struggled to see in what little torchlight Mefakani had provided. When his eyes grew accustomed to the heavy shadows, he spied Tiv sleeping on the floor, and the Priest standing quietly beside the ritual tablet of stone with the body laid upon it on a stretcher made of barkcloth and bamboo. The body was wrapped in barkcloth.

"It is done?" he asked in a whisper.

"It is done," the Priest answered with finality.

The old man started to walk over to examine the body when Mefakani held up a hand to stop him.

"Do not touch him," Mefakani warned, and Cranik drew back. "His body is poisonous and all who touch him may follow the same fate."

"Is that why it took so long? A slow poison?" Cranik asked.

"There were many spirits to call upon," Mefakani said, "and many rituals to follow." He walked up behind the body, out of Cranik's direct line of sight, and lifted a ritual dagger in the air ceremoniously. He cut a tiny slit in the barkcloth behind Elder Sahdon's head and pretended to cut a lock of hair. He pulled out the thick shock of Temple's hair he had planted there before, and held it high in the half-light for Cranik's inspection. "His power," he intoned with awe.

The Elder was wide-eyed. "Is it not poisonous too?" he asked.

"Only I am immune," the Priest answered. He took the longest piece of his shattered staff and bound the hair to the top of it with jute. He lit some herbs in a tortoise shell and used his fan made from the wing of a khala bird to waft the smoke over the remains of his staff. He sang a song of purification while circling Cranik with the smoke.

"I have prepared the body on a stretcher so your men do not have to touch him. They may take him to the swamps now in safety. The Lord Tagheetu will take care of the rest."

Cranik bowed again and ordered his men inside. They lifted the wooden handles of the stretcher onto their shoulders with the stiff bundle cradled upon it. And in the middle of the night, without the benefit of torchlight, they crept stealthily through the Shaman's compound to the swamps beyond, where they left the wrapped body on the banks of the swamp.

The moon was riding high, but barely lent its light to either the dark form lying on the sand or the circle of men surrounding it in silence.

Mefakani prayed aloud, but he couldn't bring himself to invoke the Lord Tagheetu, not after dying and rebirthing in the Light. Just as Tani had always done, he omitted the word "Lord" and evoked Tagheetu, the "Spirit of the Swamps" without worship, but with honor and respect, hoping the Rebels wouldn't notice the difference.

"The Spirit of the Crocodile will take care of Temple Fox's body," he said. "But we must not remain when his spirit is taken. It will be too dangerous for you."

With their new Teacher as their guide, the band of soldiers retreated from the swamps and headed back to the Shaman's compound to receive further instructions.

"Eat well, then rest yourselves," Mefakani advised. "By dawn, use the truce banner and return to Hollow Mountain with fresh supplies. The others will be anxious to hear the news."

"What will you do, Master?" Cranik asked.

"I will fly in the airboat and meet you there. While I am there, I will give the others further spiritual instructions so we all may deal with the armies of both Believers and Unbelievers. It is time to make peace between us all."

Cranik, Kulo, and the Rebels prostrated themselves before Mefakani. They slept that night, lulled with relief, around the warmth of the central fire, knowing the white Wizard was finally dead.

CHAPTER TWENTY-SEVEN

E-LON-E'

"She was no man's wife or lover, nor had ever been."

Temple Fox
The Makolese Scroll on
The Return of the Ka and the Mending of the Su #27

The screen on the Scribe's tablet was dark, and his barkcloth paper had long since dried in front of him, having been abandoned by Maśon during Temple's discourse. And the Scribe's brush laid aside, forgotten too, its fine hairs stiff with yesterday's ink. So enrapt by Temple's story, he leaned forward, straining his painful knee as he waited for the next installment.

"So what happened next?" he asked.

"Well, I wasn't there."

"Where?" Maśon asked. He paused to view the images running through his head, those he had gathered from Temple's mind. "Hold on. I see what you are seeing. You are in the Queen's inner compound."

"But I wasn't there, you understand. I only remember what several people told me so I could piece the story together."

"I see." Maśon nodded. He quieted for a moment. "I see a beautiful woman." He cocked his head in curiosity.

"Ah, yes. That would be E-lon-e'," Temple said. "Naturally, I hadn't met her yet."

"So who was she?"

"Who could forget E-lon-e'? I got to know her well later on. What a beauty she was," Temple said. "A knee-wobbling, wet-your-knickers kind of woman." He smiled and Maśon grinned back in understanding.

"E-lon-e' had a sharp, capable mind, a spiritual calm, and thorough dedication to her job as chief administrator of the Queen's compound.

She seemed unaware of the sensuality she exuded. And, sadly, E-lon-e' was no man's wife or lover, nor had ever been."

"Tragic," Maśon said.

"She ran the compound with a strong arm, with a military-style discipline at the exclusion of anything else in her life. And yet many talked about her devotion to the silk farms, she'd established outside the palace grounds so the worms could work their silent magic in peace. She was obsessed with the cultivation of silkworms, something she had learned from her Javanese grandfather. She taught the people how to feed the worms, harvest the silk, weave and dye it. She always draped herself in the emblematic silk, a not-too-subtle display of her interest in silk trading. She was keen on ending Palomei's war with the Outsiders, and especially the matters of civil war with the Unbelievers. Flaunting her designs was a sly reminder to the Queen to end the war with Outsiders and resume trade.

"She was a spiritual devotee to the Goddess Hianna, but also worshipped Lord Tagheetu. She ate no meat and drank no sha, and some complained that she was completely humorless while others said she had a strong sense of humor."

"A curious creature of contradictions."

"Many alluded to her total devotion to pleasing the Queen to the point of passive servility, while others said that when she disagreed with the Sovereign she spoke out boldly and at great risk to herself. She was obviously the master of diplomacy. To be sure, E-lon-e' commanded deep respect," he concluded.

"All right then. So what happened at the Queen's compound with E-lon-e' at the helm?"

CHAPTER TWENTY-EIGHT

PALOMEI'S WRATH

*"I risked too little when I did not stop Palomei
from cutting down the sacred palms. I pray that the
Goddess Hianna will forgive me, protect me and
give me more courage."*

E-lon-e', the Administrator
The Makolese Scroll on
The Return of the Ka and the Mending of the Su #28

The night was clear. The half moon generously shed its silver light, illuminating the tiled portico and Palomei's yellow-feathered cape as she stormed down the corridor. Her new Head Guardsman, Nijaga, led the way with his shield and spear out in front of him, and his intimidating muscular form as reassurance to the nervous Queen. E-lon-e' jogged by Palomei's side, struggling to keep up.

Sibilant whispers and hurried footsteps filled the night as servants and soldiers flickered in and out of storerooms and pavilions, cutting through the royal gardens and zigzagging across the dark courtyards, charged with a restless energy.

Maome, Palomei's personal attendant, paced herself several feet away in front of Nijaga, while another servant, brought up the rear. Both held oil lamps to light Palomei's safe passage around the palace's innermost courtyard.

A monkey's cry pierced the night and Palomei jerked to a stop.

"It is only a violet howler," E-lon-e' said.

Palomei turned and looked down at her Administrator, somewhat embarrassed. When she spoke she used a scroll she had been holding to punctuate her remarks. "As you know, I have sent a runner to Mefakani to find out what is going on. My runner returned and said he was barred from entering Mefakani's private cavern." The Queen's eyes hardened. "He was not only stopped by the Rebel guards, but our own guards as well!"

E-lon-e' looked up at Palomei's round, flustered face – a face full of blossoming rage.

"They are purposely keeping me in the dark," the Queen said, waving the scroll around in the air, the volume of her voice rising. "I tell you, the Believers and the Unbelievers are all working together against me now!"

Frightened by Palomei's recent order to cut down the royal palms, E-lon-e' spoke cautiously and quietly with sober reasoning. "Have you any definitive evidence to prove your concerns?" she asked. "The last we heard, the Priest was negotiating a peace with the Rebels."

Queen Palomei's nostrils flared. "And what do the Rebels get in return for stopping their fighting? Is a piece of the throne a part of the bargaining? I AM NOT EVEN THERE TO OVERSEE THESE NEGOTIATIONS!!" she yelled. She crushed the scroll in her hand.

E-lon-e' drew back a step. "Naturally, it would not be safe for you to go there, Most Beloved. I have just learned of Tani's sudden appearance at the Southern Gate. Perhaps she has come to report news at the Shaman's compound. Is there a reason for her imprisonment?"

"I will not speak to that old woman." Palomei huffed. "She has caused enough trouble."

"She may know something of what is going on. Perhaps it would be useful if someone spoke to her. I will," she offered.

"NO, you will NOT!" Palomei fumed. "She has a way of bewitching people. I forbid it!"

E-lon-e' bowed her head respectfully and backed another step away. "As you wish, Most Beloved." She paused a heartbeat. "May I ask where your First Advisor and Beloved First Husband is right now?" E-lon-e' continued, unflustered by Palomei's emotional outburst.

Hearing the Administrator's soothing voice speak of Owane helped the Queen regain some composure. "I want all my husbands to be safe. Owane is meeting with them right now to relay my orders that they stay within their private pavilions until I say otherwise." Palomei thrust the damaged scroll at her Administrator. "Here is a list of additional orders to protect the compound. Implement them immediately!"

E-lon-e' took the creased scroll and broke the seal that bound it. She stopped to read it, but couldn't make out the script in the half-light. She held back a moment, mindful of the shadows that swallowed her as the giantess marched down the portico without her.

E-lon-e' called out. "I need a light!"

The servant who had been trailing in the shadows rushed over with his small oil jar close to the Administrator's side.

"Be mindful you do not spill that oil on my dress...or me!" she said, adjusting the silk cascading over one shoulder, the pattern of gold threads that signified her rank catching the light of the oil jar. She squinted down at the scroll again and read quickly. E-lon-e''s arched eyebrows knit into a stern frown. She rolled the scroll up as she scurried off to catch up to the Queen, who was lumbering in huge strides down the portico with her fist-sized pearl on top of her scepter flashing silver and gold in the moon's and lamp's light.

Tall, lean, and long-legged, it was easy for E-lon-e' to catch up to the Queen and match the giantess's hectic stride. She was soon by Palomei's side again discussing the details of the disturbing scroll she had just read.

"May we discuss the details of these new orders?" E-lon-e' asked with an insistent voice.

The small procession turned a sharp corner and came head on into two of the palace guards, Paku' and Maha'oi, and – to Palomei's total shock and consternation – Losha!

The Queen stopped short. "How did she get in here?" she thundered and pointed at Losha with her scepter.

The Head Guard pulled his scimitar from his scabbard and placed himself squarely in front of the Queen as a shield.

The two guardsmen who had escorted Losha through the Southern Gate held their heads down in supplication. Losha bowed, then raised her head to meet the Matriarch's menacing stare.

"Get more guards!" E-lon-e' shouted.

Maome raced down a corridor with the light bouncing against the tiled walls on either side of her.

"You idiots! She is a conspirator! And you bring her into the inner courtyard!" Palomei yelled. "Who is responsible for this?" she demanded, and cast a searing eye at the two guards.

The gruff guardsman, Maha'oi, spoke up. "Most Respected, there has been a terrible mistake."

"GUARDS!" Palomei called out. She pointed the huge pearl on the top of her scepter at Maha'oi. "*You!* Are you responsible for this stupidity?"

Maha'oi stood for a moment, defiant, but still afraid, wishing he had a fraction of the courage Losha had shown him. "Losha Ninti brings a personal message for you from the..."

"She has a message, does she?" Palomei shouted. She pointed to Losha again just as two palace guards came rushing to a stop. "Lock her away like that treasonous old witch! We will get her message out of her in our own way! And when we do, we will get the TRUTH!" she declared with a cruel stare aimed at Losha. "Now take her! And get these two guards out of my sight, before I take their heads MYSELF!"

The two guards grabbed Losha under her arms and whisked her away down another corridor.

Nijaga gestured with his scimitar for the two men to disarm. Paku' and Maha'oi placed their swords and daggers unto the floor cautiously. But Paku' couldn't contain himself. He threw himself onto the floor, not to plead for mercy, but to speak. "If I am to die then I will have my say! Losha bears more than a message! She bears the sacred mark!"

The Matriarch beat her staff on the tiled floor. "LIES!"

"I saw it! We both saw it!"

The Queen stepped forward, her height and mass imposing. "She plays the same game as Temple Fox! You have been bewitched!"

There was the patter of running feet as six additional guards raced to the corner where their towering Sovereign stood bellowing. Owane, her First Husband, sprinted behind the guards with Palomei's other four husbands, Jalok, Kuhil, Tauhans, and Loa'a, crowded behind him.

"I speak the truth!" he argued. "I swear it on the shrines of my ancestors! Both Temple Fox and Losha Ninti have fulfilled the prophecy!"

Palomei's eyes grew large and fiery and she screamed until her cheeks flushed blood red. "Witches! They are all magicians and witches! They have all betrayed me! Everyone has fallen under the spell of ONE FALSE PROPHET!" She took another step forward, towering over Paku', and placed her heavy foot on top of his head.

"But most Beloved…"

"Enough!" she yelled.

"I am telling you the *truth*!" he pleaded.

"I said, ENOUGH!" she screamed.

Palomei picked up Paku''s sword with one smooth sweep of her huge hand and, with a second swing of her massive arms, she struck the blow so swiftly she wasn't certain she had even done so.

E-lon-e' screamed in horror, and one of Palomei's husbands, Tauhans, shrieked in anguish. Her other husbands stumbled backward terrified.

Owane ran toward his wife, then stopped frozen in the moment, frightened for his own life. Palomei's hands were trembling, her yellow cape splattered bright red with blood. Her arm went limp.

Maha'oi held his hands up in defense. "Please!" he cried out. "Please do not kill me!"

Palomei gazed down at the guard who remained. The blood drained from her face, her tattoos a vivid blue against the paleness of her cheeks, her face suddenly ghostly. It was if a fog had wrapped around the Queen and she had vanished inside.

"Palomei! Palomei!" Owane tried in vain to reach her with his words, but the giant stood silent, still trembling. "Not this way! Never in anger!" he heard himself saying.

She turned to Owane slowly and looked down into his frightened face. "I will have no daughter," she said morosely. "There will be no heir." She allowed him to pry the sword from her hand. She lumbered slowly down the portico toward her chamber with Owane walking cautiously behind her. Nijaga and Miyon marched obediently in front of the First Husband and the Queen, while two more trailed after them.

One of the guards yanked Maha'oi to his feet and dragged him out of the courtyard, leaving the Administrator and Queen's other husbands staring in nervous silence at the grisly head and headless body slumped on the tiled floor.

E-lon-e' felt the warmth of splattered blood on her dress, and covered her face with her hands, unable to speak, then ambled mindlessly down the corridor. Hidden in the shadows, she stopped for a moment to slow her racing heart, to recover. She pressed back against the stone wall and slid to the tiled floor, clutching a handful of fabric at her breast. Shaking uncontrollably, she began to weep.

The Royal Husbands huddled together to console one another with the corpse now gathering the interest of the flies. Tauhans, Palomei's fourth husband, was still in shock and quivering heavily. He had been closest to the incident. The others gathered near to soothe him.

The remaining guard stood by the Royal Husbands until they were dismissed. Once Palomei's torches were specks of flickering light in the distance and the royal entourage was well out of earshot, the husbands began to speak.

Loa'a, a handsome man and the youngest of Palomei's Royal Husbands, brushed his thick, black hair off his sweaty brow. He spoke first. "She is crazy!"

Kuhil, who was well acquainted with his wife's tantrums, wiped up a thin stream of blood that ran over his fat belly. He held up his hand to silence Loa'a. "Hush!" he said, looking all around him in the dark. "Do you not know the walls have ears here?" he whispered. "We do not know the circumstances surrounding her actions."

Loa'a leaned closer and whispered. "She lost her mind when her daughter, Shaza, died, and you know it! I will be glad when the last of the race of Giants no longer rules."

"Stop this talk!" Kuhil warned with a harsh reprimand.

Palomei's second husband, Jalok, was a tall, distinguished looking man with sharp intelligent eyes. With the exception of Owane, he was older and wiser than the other husbands. He placed a sympathetic hand on Kuhil's fleshy shoulder. "There is no one here," he said. "Let Loa'a speak his mind."

E-lon-e' pulled her tears back to quiet her sobbing and eavesdropped from the shadows.

"I will not be censored any longer," Loa'a said openly, glaring at Kuhil. "I hear Palomei's twelve-toed, redheaded mother was just as cruel. I pray for an end to the rule by the Si Te Cah. And I pray Palomei has no heirs," he said, spitting the words out with contempt. "Which is why I withhold the most vital essence from my loins when I am forced to make love to her."

Tauhans didn't react. He stood swaying and staring at nothing while Kuhil winced, frightened by Loa'a's frankness.

Jalok looked at Loa'a with surprise, then down at Kuhil's golden skirt splattered with blood.

Loa'a ran his hand through his hair again this time extracting a smattering of blood. "And Owane allows her to get away with all this cruelty. He may be the First Husband, but he is passive – a total limp eel. He does anything Palomei tells him to do."

"Could you do any better?" Kuhil asked accusingly. "Mind you, Loa'a, he is older and more experienced than we are. Have you forgotten he used to be an advisor to Palomei's parents before they were killed? He raised Palomei as his own. They are bound like blood family."

The young man looked at Kuhil on the slant with a hint of guilt, but a trace of distain still lingered.

"You do not understand," Kuhil added. "I believe Owane truly loves her."

Loa'a grunted at the comment. "Like a daughter, not a husband," he said. "I am sure they have never even slept together, which only puts more pressure on us to create an heir."

"Tai, and Temple Fox prophesied she would have an heir," Kuhil said, remembering what Temple had said when he was being interrogated in the Great Round House when he had first arrived.

"When the Su is mended," Loa'a added. "That is if there is anybody left to mend the Su. I tell you she has grown more suspicious and irrational with every passing sun. And did you hear her? Now she does not even believe Temple Fox is the Prophet anymore! She is completely insane!"

After listening, Jalok finally spoke. "I agree. There has been far too much bloodshed. All of this beheading, as you say, Loa'a, is absolute madness. She acted foolishly just now and can no longer be reasoned with," he said sadly as he blotted a spot of blood off his wrist. "And we are soaked in the blood of her actions."

Kuhil looked down at his waistband, trying in vain to wipe the blood away.

"It is no use," Jalok whispered. "We carry her actions as if they were our own. And now we are like a ship floating aimlessly without a rudder in a stormy sea."

E-lon-e' stepped from around the corner and out of the shadows. She paused for a thoughtful second, then took a few cautious steps forward into the moonlight.

Startled, Kuhil jerked his head in her direction, and all conversation came to an abrupt and awkward halt.

E-lon-e' walked up to them with more confidence in her step and bowed to them. "I ask your forgiveness for overhearing your conversation. I, too, bear the burden of your words." Noticing their discomfort, she bowed again, this time steeper, then rose to meet their eyes. "Please, there is no need to hide your comments from me."

The men looked to one another and nodded their consent.

"Then you agree with us?" Loa'a asked E-lon-e'.

"But we are at war now," Kuhil argued. "The throne is threatened by Rebels. Difficult times sometimes call for difficult actions."

Loa'a shook his head in disgust. "She cut down the sacred royal palms! She just imprisoned Elder Tani, and now her own Interpreter! And now we think she does not believe that Temple Fox is the True Prophet! Palomei is killing her own people, even her own guards now, Kuhil! Who will be next?"

"Tai," E-lon-e' said. "The guard, who just sacrificed his life, came to deliver the message that Losha is also the True Teacher. I saw a faint glowing scar between her eyes. It is possible that Losha Ninti and Temple Fox have both fulfilled the prophecy," she announced.

The husbands looked at each other perplexed.

"I know it does not make any sense. I will find out what is really going on," the Administrator said quite calmly.

"You risk too much," Jalok offered.

"I risked too little when I did not stop Palomei from cutting down the sacred palms. I pray that the Goddess Hianna will forgive me, protect me and give me more courage," she said. "In the meantime, to avoid Palomei's wrath, I suggest you all stay together in Jalok's pavilion."

Jalok nodded in agreement.

Tauhans, who had not joined in the conversation, was still staring into the night. "Too much…blood," he murmured as he looked down at his stained tunic and the river of blood that crept toward his sandaled feet.

The sound of hurried footsteps drew closer as they echoed down the portico. Two servants stopped at where the slain body laid, a look of horror distorting their faces. They bowed steeply to the four Royal Husbands and the Administrator then set upon their duties. In seconds the body and head were removed and the blood washed away, the section of tiled floor casting a wet sheen in the moonlight.

Tauhans lifted his foot where blood had pooled beneath his sandal. "Blood," he said again.

"Are you all right?" Jalok asked.

Tauhans heard the question, but the words seemed dull and distant to him. His world had turned into a milky white fog.

"Tauhans?" Jalok said, grabbing Tauhans' arm.

"I must lie down," Tauhans said just as he fainted to the floor.

Two chamber servants kept their gaze glued to the floor as they slid open the tall screens and waited for the giantess to pass into her private chamber, the vast space and cathedral ceiling barely able to contain her dark mood. Palomei paused at the threshold. Owane placed his hand on her huge waist and prompted her forward with a gentle nudge. When the two stepped into the chamber, the servants snapped the screens shut.

Palomei stumbled over to her raised dais and plopped down on her mammoth rattan throne. The bees hurried after her and landed on each white wilted blossom on her crown, spotted now with blood. She placed her feet back up onto the human skulls she used as footstools as she had done thousands of times before.

"I will not have any traitors in my presence," she said, her voice strained.

The private screens were quietly parted again, and a servant entered the Queen's chamber. Silent, he gave a brief bow, and on hands and knees mopped up footprints of blood that led across to the throne where Palomei brooded in silence. When he felt he could go no further without inciting the Queen's wrath, he stood still for a moment and looked to Owane for instruction.

Owane motioned with his eyes and a tilt of his head for the servant to leave. The servant nodded in understanding, bowed and left as silently as he came.

Queen Palomei waited until the screen was closed. She looked down at her First Husband. His face was drawn and gray, his stern eyes pleading, angry, humiliated. She couldn't tell. She glanced from wet wooden floor and the remaining red droplets of blood to her own trembling hands.

"Killing that stupid boy who brought Tani into the compound was one thing," she said, her voice outwardly gaining a modicum of normalcy. "Even killing one of our own disobedient guards seems easy," she said without emotion. "But after seeing Temple Fox survive the ritual sword, there is no telling how we might kill him. How do we even kill our own High Shaman who the Impostor aligns with? And Tani? And now the Interpreter, who has twice betrayed me and has now bewitched her way into this compound?"

"Perhaps one of them is the True Teacher," Owane whispered, forcing his way into the conversation with caution.

Palomei glared down at him, more annoyed than angry.

He coaxed her to look him in the eye. "Who is to say the Believers and Unbelievers have not aligned to find a lasting peace?"

"I say. Only they align against me," she said pointedly, but with a heavy weariness in her voice.

Owane shook his head in bewilderment. "We are ruled by fear," he said. He took a respectful step away and bowed to his wife. "I beg your pardon, Most Beloved."

"You think I acted in haste?" she asked.

"I would sorely love to know why Losha is here. And why Tani came," he said, avoiding the answer.

"It was reported that Elder Tani was spotted with the Chokahpeiyape, a witch!" she said, her blood pressure rising again. "They all plot against me! You cannot deny that my own guards have been disobeying my strictest orders?"

"I do not deny the guards punishment for disobedience, but your actions are harsh and may not fit the crime. Tu'sling was hardly a trained guard. He was a servant boy pressed into service because we are short on soldiers."

"You do not think it is a crime to bring traitors to my doorstep?"

"Are we certain they are traitors? Neither Tani or Losha have resisted. They chose to come. And both are captives now."

"Then we need to interrogate them. But they use magic as a weapon of persuasion," she said, exasperated.

"Well, they have not used any magic to escape," Owane said, hoping his wife would see reason. "We should listen to what they have to say. Then we must use the powers of our discernment to find the truth."

Palomei tossed her aging husband a sour look. "With all this talk about there being two Teachers now it seems like truth changes with the wind."

"Tai. My own beliefs have been like an English weathercock, same as yours."

The Queen suddenly grew quiet. Her puffy eyes took on a distant countenance.

Owane regarded his wife with guarded eyes, frightened that another mood change and tirade was brewing.

"Both of them cannot be the True Teacher!" she announced with a slam of her fist. As if she had forgotten the hope he just offered, she began muttering to herself. "All my hopes have been dashed! All my dreams shattered in a lie. Everything – a LIE! From Temple Fox to this new impostor. All is pretense. Nothing is real. Not prophecies. Not peace. Not even this scepter," she said, sensing the weight of something in her hands. She looked down at him. "Was it all for nothing? NOTHING!"

"I should go now and speak with Tani. Or perhaps I should ask Okon. He is close to her." He turned to leave.

"Please do not leave me now, Owane," she begged. "I am frightened. Please."

Owane turned around and walked up behind Palomei and wrapped his arms around her.

"He promised I would have an heir," she whispered, pulling him closer. "But if he is not the True Teacher then..." She began to sob and Owane rocked her in his arms.

So that no one would notice, E-lon-e' took a circuitous route to the small hut where Losha was being held. She nodded to the guard outside the hut.

"I do not wish to be disturbed," she said.

The guard bowed and stepped aside as E-lon-e' crept in cautiously, all the while praying under her breath to the Goddess Hianna for protection.

CHAPTER TWENTY-NINE

THE DREAM

*"I hold the desires of the river, longing for what is
far and unknown."*

Great Grandfather Okon
The Makolese Scroll on
The Return of the Ka and the Mending of the Su #29

Night sifted down between the uneven roofs of the Queen's compound and drifted along the quiet pathways, causing a gentle breeze to ruffle all the palm fronds. And as the Spirit of the Wind moved stealthily down the tiled porticos, leaving wind chimes singing in its wake, it accompanied Great Grandfather Okon and his servant to the hut where Tani was held captive.

Okon's personal servant, Kaisi, balanced the crooked man on one arm and held an oil lamp out in front of him with the other so the guard would recognize them both.

The guard bowed with respect when he saw the two in the flickering light. Okon handed him the scroll prepared by his Great Granddaughter. The guardsman broke the royal seal and read it, then bowed again and unlatched the door.

Sleep had long ago escaped Tani and she sat quietly in the dark in meditation. When the light of the lamp crept inside the hut and Okon stepped inside, Tani raised her head in surprise. Her delicate honey-colored face came alive with a welcoming smile, warming the room.

Kaisi placed the oil lamp onto the floor as the centenarian staggered forward with his cane.

"Shoo!" he said. "We will be alone now."

"But..." Kaisi complained.

"Be gone!" Okon commanded.

No one could dispute the eldest on the island. The servant left and closed the door behind him quietly.

Okon eased himself onto the floor mat. With his tone taking on a serious note, he said, "My Great Granddaughter has allowed me this visit so I may learn how you, Mefakani, Temple Fox, and Losha Ninti, as well as all the Believers and Unbelievers, plot against her. Such nonsense," he said dismissively. "I will hear you out. But first, I am here for a reason that holds equal importance. I had a dream," he said with no further explanation.

Tani's heart skipped a beat. "A dream? What manner of dream?" she asked.

"The kind that only the eldest on the island has, and one that fulfills a very old prophecy. You know the dream I speak of?" he whispered.

The black slits of Tani's eyes grew large and held a glint of lamplight. "Dear Goddess Hianna! I thought it was I who would bear the burden!"

"Then you have seen this dream too?" he asked, perplexed.

"As clear as stones seen through a clear pool of water."

Okon leaned closer. "Then you know I am as complete as a flower."

Tani spoke softly. "Blossoms wilt and fall so fruit is born. When will the time be ripe?"

"Soon. When the moon is three days from full."

"I was always afraid it might be me," Tani confessed, relieved that the Gods had not chosen her for the task. "In truth, I thought it would be generations from now. So, after nine centuries it is you who will fulfill this prophecy…and at a time like this," she said, shaking her head at the complexity of things.

"I cannot disobey the Gods. You are the second oldest on the island and because you have had this dream as well means I am the Shuntshu Junshi now and you are the Jushinjunshi Shomei. That means I must pass on my ring to you." He touched the ring on his right hand.

A painful look overtook him. "I confess, Tani, I have not the heart to do this thing. I have not even the physical strength."

"I will help you. But it still grieves me. I, too, would shrink from such a task," she admitted.

Tani interrupted her own thoughts. "Are you certain of the timing? This will happen just before the next full moon?"

"Time is of the spirits," he said with sagacity. "They have their reasons. Just as there is a reason you, and now Losha, has shown up at the compound."

"Losha is here?"

He grimaced. "Tai, last night. And my Great Granddaughter has seen to treating her as she has you. She is being held in a guarded hut down the pathway."

The old Healer looked sideways in quiet thought, then turned to face her thin companion. "There is much to tell."

Okon listened intently with only sparse questions and occasional nods as Tani told the whole of what she knew.

"Losha is also the True Teacher!? There are *two*?" he asked, fascinated by the turn of events.

"When the Elders and the Queen questioned Temple Fox in the Great Round House, you mentioned that the ancient prophecy in question was written in archaic Makolese and did not specify whether one or two or more would come."

"I did!" he said, remembering.

"And that single prophecy was written in the archaic script."

"Tai, it was!"

"And now it seems Temple Fox has fulfilled the prophecy as well as one of our own."

"But the Interpreter?" he questioned, disbelieving.

"She bears the sacred mark and can fly. When the Rebels see her flying in the sky as a great white swan, and set their eyes upon her brow, they will know she is the True Teacher."

"A great white swan? And the Rebels will see her first? I see your plan." He leaned closer in the lamplight. "After that dream and now this, I do not know if my heart can withstand many more surprises."

Tani patted his hand in sympathy.

"But what of Mefakani? You just told me he convinced the Unbelievers into thinking he is the True Prophet."

Tani shook her head. "Tai, it is confusing. We trust that the Gods are guiding our actions. Believe me when I say there is no other way to let the people know the truth without them first killing each other and creating a civil war."

"Well, there can certainly still be civil war if and when the Unbelievers think Losha is the True Teacher while the Believers feel Temple to be the same."

Tani leaned forward and lowered her voice even more. "But you see, Okon, they are in love."

Okon screwed up his face. "Who…who is in love?"

"Temple Fox and Losha Ninti. And it is through their love that the Su will be mended."

Okon slapped his thigh with glee, then suddenly grew serious again. "But what of Mefakani? He is a thief of souls and a murderer."

"I have been praying over this. Much depends on how he handles the Rebels in the mountain."

Memory of his dream was swimming in Okon's eyes. "And this all is happening when I have had that dream."

"I think it will make sense in time," Tani said. "We can never second-guess the Gods. And you must do what you must do…no matter what the people think…or how you will be depicted in the History Scrolls."

Tani continued with her story so Okon understood all that had happened and all the implications of what they set out to do. By the time she had finished the weak pre-dawn light had found its way through the air vents between the timber walls and thick thatch roof, suffusing the hut in dark dusty rose-colored hues.

"It is a dangerous business. All of it!" Okon said as a final response.

Tani nodded sadly. "You must know you will not be able to fulfill that dream without this." She stuck her fingers underneath the folds of her sash and pulled out a thin, smoky glass vial. She held it up for Okon's inspection.

"What is it?" he asked.

"The very piece of your Ka that you have lived without for thirty-five seasons. When young Mefakani and his Master came up with that diabolical idea of taking a bit of everyone's life force, they kept them in these tiny jars hidden in a cavern below the Shaman's compound."

Okon squinted harder at the tiny script scratched on the fragile vial.

"Your clan symbol and personal mark are inscribed on it. Every islander has a similar jar, and each will have a chance to have the rest of their life force returned to them. I have several with me." She gestured to her waistband. "I brought yours in case we had a chance to meet since you sometimes can reason with your Great Granddaughter. Now that you have told me about the same dream I have had, you will need all of your Ka without further delay." She eyed the vial in the half-light. "By the will of the Gods, Palomei's guards did not find this when they searched me…or the jar I have for Palomei." Tani let out a little snort. "She needs her Ka more than anyone right now."

A little guilt crept over Okon's wrinkled face. "I should have listened to you when this business about the taking of our Ka came about seasons ago. I am a foolish old man."

"Hopefully, you are not foolish enough to stop me from reattaching your Ka right now," she said.

He raised both eyebrows. "You know how to do this?"

"I do now," she answered. "But I had to wait for Temple to teach me first. It is one of many reasons why he has been sent to us."

Without warning the door to the hut creaked open and Tani swiftly tucked the vial up under her sash. In walked Okon's personal attendant with worry darkening his face.

Kaisi bowed. "I ask your pardon Great Grandfather, but you have been in here for so long I thought you might be in need of something."

"Peace!" the old man snapped impatiently. "I am in need of that! Do not interrupt us again until I ask for you," he said, waving his servant away.

The servant looked down at Tani ruefully.

Tani acknowledged him with a sympathetic smile. "We could use some clean water," she asked kindly. "Boil it first and bring us two cups."

"And some tea leaves?" he asked.

"Pu-reh tea would be good," Tani said. "But do not put the leaves in the water. And make certain the water is boiling."

The attendant seemed pleased with the request, smiled, bowed then left the hut.

Tani grinned at Okon "Nothing happens without a reason. I will need some pure water to reattach that piece of skin of yours that holds a fragment of your precious life force. Hot water will make it heal faster."

The servant returned several minutes later and placed a pot of steaming water on the floor mat along with a bowl of pu-reh leaves. He bowed again, then left without a word.

Tani took out the hidden vial again and opened it, then dropped the shriveled piece of flesh into the pot of hot water to reconstitute it. Then she did exactly as she did for O'Juma, remembering what Temple had taught her. It was time to bring Okon to his natural state of wholeness.

"Lie down," she said. Okon obeyed and she placed a cushion beneath his head.

From the hidden compartments inside her waistband she pulled out two shiny leaves that had been folded into small envelopes. She unwrapped the first, revealing a handful of crumbled herbs that smelled of earth and forest. When she unfolded the other leaf a foul smell filled the hut. Inside was a sticky sliver of congealed blood – menstrual blood – the consistency of liver. She sprinkled the herbs into the bloody mass and worked the concoction into a paste with her fingers. This she plastered onto the tiny scar on Okon's chest.

"When this dries it will drop off," she said. "Then your Ka will be restored. And then, by the Gods' will, you will indeed be as complete as a flower." When she had finished she held her hands over his heart and called forth her healing powers. She sang softly, sweetly, to Okon as he lay before her.

Time passed and the sunlight grew brighter in the hut. When Okon was well rested she helped him to sit up and handed him a cup of water.

"Drink lots of water," she coaxed.

"I am getting too old for this," he said. Although his words were vague he gestured with his hand to encompass the whole of life.

"Oh, remember you are the Shark and will always be the Shark." She gave him a toothless grin.

"Tai, but I have lost my bite."

They sat together quietly, old friends lingering comfortably in full silence.

Okon dozed off soundly for a few minutes and Tani watched the light field around him flicker softly. He woke with a sudden snort and smiled at her, until his expression grew slowly pensive.

"I had the dream again," he whispered. "You know what I have to give you?"

"I know," she answered, aiming her gaze at his ring. "But now is not the time. Not while I am held prisoner."

"Tai. And yet the time grows closer...and dearer."

"You are anxious," she said, her comment sounding more like a question.

The old man nodded. "I hold the desires of the river, longing for what is far and unknown. It is a desire far too great for tears."

A few wisps of smoke from the lamp curled around their heads. Tani's black, liquid eyes smiled back at him. "You hold the blind faith of every groping tendril and root. And for that," she said, pulling his fragile hand into hers, "I love you."

When Okon let out a deep pleasurable sigh the tiny poultice fell off his chest. And while he held her delicate, ancient hand, his free hand explored the smooth, moist skin over his breastbone. "I feel like a young shark again," he mused. "What joy it would bring me if only I could make you shout again as I did when I was young."

Tani chuckled. "Try me," the old woman said teasingly.

The mass of wrinkles that marked Okon's immense age pulled into a smile of pure delight, then a dubious smirk. "Business," he said. "I am here for that now."

"I will make pleasure our business," she said. And before Okon could change his mind Tani pulled the old centenarian into the circle of her leathery arms.

Palomei was so hot with anger that she slammed her fist down and broke the armrest to her chair. "I ask you to find out what that old woman is up to and you are found naked in her arms! I told you, she is a witch!"

Okon's wrinkled face lit up. "Tai, if she can make a hundred-and-sixty-year old-man's limp eel as hard as a cedar branch, you can be sure she is a witch – a good witch!" The old man let out a boisterous laugh that filled the Queen's chamber.

"She has put a hex on you!" Palomei spat back.

"Nonsense, Great Granddaughter. She is innocent of any wrongdoing. Now settle down, child, and I will tell you what has really happened."

CHAPTER THIRTY

IKUS AND KULO

"You cannot fight ghosts naked!"

Elder Kulo Kempok
The Makolese Scroll on
The Return of the Ka and the Mending of the Su #30

The light of a half-swollen moon was lost in the dense jungle when the two Rebel Elders marched their way to the swamp. Elder Ikus, undeterred from his personal mission, cleared the path with his long blade, and the chorus of long raspy snores from the big-bellied frogs came to an abrupt halt.

Elder Kulo sloshed through the mud, lagging behind his smaller companion. Stooping under a low branch, his step faltered, but he caught himself before stumbling to the ground.

"Will you hurry up!" Ikus grumbled in his gravely voice. "You are slower than a pregnant python."

When Elder Kulo caught up with Ikus he was out of breath. "This is not a good idea," he complained. "My back is aching and I am hungry. Let us go back now before something awful happens."

Elder Ikus muttered a deep-throated curse under his breath as he sliced a thick arm of vine with his sword. "May the Lord Tagheetu eat you alive! I have risked my life coming down off that mountain and I will not go back until I see the body with my own eyes! You promised me you would come with me and we are nearly there."

"Lord Tagheetu will probably have my nuts for breakfast for following your stupid ideas," Kulo moaned. "I tell you, Mefakani said it is taboo to go there!"

The thin man pivoted on his heels and stretched his neck from his short wiry frame to match the height of Kulo's chin. He thrust his sharp, rodent-like nose upward. "You worm-minded old fool! Did you ever bother to really examine the ancient prophecy in detail? It stated that the Prophet would become the High Shaman's greatest ally, and conquer his enemies. If it states that, then how can Mefakani, the High Shaman, *be* the True Teacher?"

"Well, you believed him," Kulo said in defense. "Who could dispute such a miracle? You saw that wondrous airboat he was flying in…and the scar upon his brow. He has the most powerful magic anyone has ever witnessed!"

"He hypnotized us!" Ikus spat back. "Mefakani is a fake! He made that scar on his forehead himself!"

Kulo rolled his eyes. "You are mistaken, my friend," he argued. "But if you are right, then we can deal with Mefakani later. What matters now is that the Wizard is dead."

Ikus stood his ground and let his words fly. "Bi kano lo! You are dumber than a coconut husk! I have left our people behind on that mountain because you fools have been absent for three days! Not one word have I heard from you! I will not go back until I see the body myself!" Ikus' veins were popping out of his neck. "Who can trust you! You said you did not even see the body!"

"Of course I saw it," Kulo contested, his face flushed.

"But did you actually see his face? And was he really dead?"

Kulo's voice grew fainter with guilt. "He was wrapped in barkcloth."

Elder Ikus pushed the larger man out of the way as he hacked another vine. "But you said the Shaman did not even deal with the body in the traditional way."

"I did not say that!" Kulo said, the perspiration rolling down his face. "Who knows what the proper protocol is for murdering a Wizard! I said it was unusual that the Priest did not take the Wizard's head!"

Ikus waved the point of his blade at the Elder. "I trusted you, Cranik, and the Senior Elder to take care of this while I was trapped on that mountain practically starving to death. And what do you do? Sahdon gets himself killed, and you and Cranik are mesmerized by a power-hungry priest, who, may I remind you, was our enemy just three days ago!

"Believe me, I have had time to think about this. The prophecy warned against impostors. Mefakani killed a Wizard, but now he plays the part of a man-god so he can have his way with us. I tell you this whole affair is a ruse!" Ikus cut a tangle of thorny saplings from the trail and hurried into the forest with his big-boned friend lumbering after him.

Kulo drew back with a fearful grunt when Ikus took his anger out on a nearby vine. "Ikus, you saw him ride in that airboat. We saw the mark upon his brow. He fulfilled the prophecy! You have been up in the mountain too long with your lively imagination."

Ikus spoke over his shoulder while he hacked away. "Then humor me while I view the body and witness Lord Tagheetu's crocodiles devour that white beast."

The two old men climbed from the edge of dense jungle onto the highest embankment above the swamp where the body had been placed. They stopped to listen to the *c'tunk, c'tunk, c'tunk* of the green-hooded swamp frogs and the rustling of night creatures.

"Come! Make a torch!" Ikus ordered, his eyes straining in the dark.

The swamp frogs ceased their song, and the river filled with the sound of frogs splashing into the water.

Kulo knelt on the ground, wincing with pain from the effort. He collected some grass and twigs, then pulled a piece of flint and iron pyrite from beneath his sash. He struck the flint and iron against one another repeatedly until sparks flew and a dried blade of grass glowed in the dark. Kulo blew on it until the sparks grew into a flame. He lit a coil of dry bark he had secured on a branch of cedar. As he rose with a painful grunt, he noticed streaks of dark purple filtering through the trees, coloring the air above the low-lying mists. He handed the torch to the other Elder. "Ikus, this is crazy," he said nervously. "It is almost dawn. Wait a little longer until we have more light."

"Now!" Ikus whispered back with harshness. "I want to see the Wizard's body now!"

As if his commandment had been heard, a piercing cry struck the air, and a large white owl swooped out from the darkness and flew at Ikus' head. He ducked. Kulo fell face first down into the mud.

"Did…did you see that?" Kulo sputtered, wiping the muck from his face.

"Temple's allies are on guard," Ikus replied. "This place is haunted." He hunkered down into a leathery ball of aging flesh and bones, his hand still holding the torch in one hand, his blade in the other. He searched the jungle above him.

Kulo spoke from the ground in a trembling whisper. "I tell you we should turn back now before something terrible happens!"

"Stay here if you want. I will go without you!"

Ignoring his companion, Ikus stuck his torch into the ground, then cut a bundle of sawgrass with his blade and twisted it around a weathered limb of driftwood he found nearby. He lit this with the torch and threw it far out onto the beach. The firelight bounced and flickered across the muddy ground, illuminating the still, dark form that was wrapped like a mummy.

Seeing no crocodiles, the anxious Elder climbed down the steep embankment, gripping his long knife in one hand while holding his torch in front of him at arm's length with the other. When he was halfway down the slope a fierce screech shook the air. The startled old man turned sharply toward the sound, lost his balance and slid on his buttocks the last few yards. He dropped his torch and lost his barkcloth skirt somewhere behind as he tumbled down.

When the echoed cry had faded, Ikus lay on the beach naked with his heart pounding, his knife still gripped in his trembling hands. He leaped to his feet, cursing and fumbling in the failing light for his torch. But just as he bent to pick it up, the torch suddenly grew brighter with a *whoosh*, and he witnessed his fallen wraparound burst into flames.

Ikus jumped back with a start. Babbling incoherently, he took his blade and sliced the air all around him angrily.

Elder Kulo crawled to the edge of the embankment and peered down at his naked friend. "Are you fighting ghosts?" he asked.

"Shut up!" Ikus snapped back. He looked all around him, shaking.

"What happened to your wrap?" Kulo asked, innocently.

Ikus thrust the tip of his blade into the remains of the charred rag and lifted it into the air. It was still smoking.

Kulo smiled. "You cannot fight ghosts naked! That is not the proper way it is done."

"Shut up!" Ikus yelled. He marched over to the dead body in the fading firelight and raised his blade over his head. His hands shook.

"What are you doing?" Kulo shouted in alarm.

"I want to see his face. Then I will chop up his body so his spirit cannot run after me," he said.

A voice, a familiar voice, cut through the night like a scalpel: "LEAVE MY BODY ALONE!"

Stunned to hear the voice of Temple Fox, Ikus dropped his knife and scrambled up the riverbank so fast he trampled his companion and vanished into the jungle with Kulo screaming behind him in terror.

CHAPTER THIRTY-ONE

SMALL MIRACLES

" 'One without the other is empty.' "

Quote from Prophecy Scroll #12
The Makolese Scroll on
The Return of the Ka and the Mending of the Su #31

Fuming, Palomei paced across the raised dais, her voice battering the rafters of her chamber. She glared under an imperialist brow at E-lon-e', her First Husband, and her Great Grandfather.

"Temple Fox bears the sacred mark? Now you say Shaman Mefakani says he bears the sacred mark and proclaims he is the rightful Teacher? But then you say he has renounced that! Now Losha claims the same! Some of them must be imposters, I tell you! They are all cutting and scarring themselves!" Palomei said. She sat down brusquely and her broken rattan throne let out a heavy groan. She rubbed her head in confusion.

"Great Granddaughter," Okon chimed in. "The prophecy was written in an archaic Makolese glyph. The word 'one' could mean 'many.' The word 'Being' could be plural. So, it was never clear as to whether the Teacher was a single being or more. But it is as clear to me as a calm sea that both Temple and Losha are the rightful Teachers. As the prophecy states," and he quoted:

> "'A human God, who comes from the Heavens, will be Teacher and Prophet to the Makolese. The Holy One will come at a time of peril and help to conquer the enemies of the Makolese. This magical Being will be the High Priest's greatest ally in conquering his enemies.... *(damaged text/short section missing)*... One without the other is empty.'"

The old man interrupted himself and repeated the line once more. "'One without the other is empty.' Here the word 'one' could be singular or plural. If it was plural, was that a reference to Temple and Losha? Temple and the Priest? Or the Priest and Losha? I have just explained to you that Tani says Temple and Losha are the True Teachers, and that Mefakani lured him into his private cavern to try and take his power away by manipulating Temple's Ka."

He cleared his throat and continued.

"'Power multiplies tenfold and then again tenfold, again and again until the time of Purification and Redemption. To be recognized, the Divine One must bear the sign of Wisdom, which is the mark upon the holy brow. Beware of impostors who can fool the elect'.

"I tell you, Great Granddaughter, I have spoken to Elder Tani and she has spoken the truth. Will you not see her and speak to her yourself?"

"Why do I always find it difficult arguing with the eldest on the island," Palomei said, "especially one's own Great Grandfather?"

"And I have spoken to Losha..." E-lon-e' started, but was cut short.

"Without my permission," the Queen pointed out.

"I humbly beg your forgiveness," E-lon-e' said. She lowered her head to the floor.

Owane, E-lon-e', and Great Grandfather Okon looked up at Palomei in anticipation.

"Will you not see them?" E-lon-e' pleaded.

The Queen sat for a quiet minute then nodded in defeat. "I pray I am not surrounded by fools."

★   ★   ★   ★   ★   ★

Leaning over in her throne, the Matriarch winced as Maome, a slight, short woman, pressed her thumbs harder into Palomei's thick layers of fat, deep into her trapezius muscles. The Queen's personal servant paused to shoo the bees away that clustered around Palomei's flowered crown, then ran her fingers down to Palomei's hidden deltoid muscles.

"Perhaps Maome should go for now," Okon suggested.

"Tai, we have delicate matters to discuss," Owane said.

Palomei waved her hand at her First Husband as if he were an annoying fly. "I am in pain. I trust her. She stays."

Maome's eyes remained focused on her task, but the ends of her lips creased into a thin smile.

The Queen straightened her back against her throne and allowed Maome to massage her plump fingers. She squinted at the obvious scar on Losha's brow when the Interpreter and Elder Tani were brought forward. "When this is over," she announced, "I should take everyone's heads! That way the True Teacher would emerge unscathed! And I should take yours, too," she said, pointing her scepter at Tani, whose head was lowered to the floor.

Tani lifted her head and raised an eyebrow at Palomei, then looked to Losha and whispered, "Now would be a good time for even the smallest of miracles."

Losha prostrated herself on the floor before the Matriarch, then stood up and took a bold step forward.

The Queen glared down at Losha with contempt. "Sit down!"

"Most Beloved, please listen to her," E-lon-e' begged.

Palomei's nostrils flared and she made a quick gesture with her head to Nijaga. The Head Guard lumbered over and grabbed Losha's shoulders. He pushed her down on her knees and shoved her head down in supplication.

Losha would not be deterred. She sat in this enforced and humbling position while silently summoning her spirit helpers and allies for help, sensing their energies gathering and filling her with renewed strength and courage. Remembering what the Voice had said to Temple, "Have courage beyond consequence," she deepened her breathing and pushed Palomei's imposing presence out of her conscious mind until she found her center. And when that power had ripened, she rose quickly to her feet again, this time with her right hand firmly on her left shoulder and her left hand on her right shoulder. She was well into her spin, singing her invocation before neither the Head Guard nor the Queen had a chance to react.

Palomei bolted to her feet, knocking Maome to the floor. She pointed her scepter at Losha. "This is witchcraft! Guards!" she ordered.

"No, no, no!" Okon called out. "Let her be!"

Palomei met her Great Grandfather's eyes not in deference to him, but to argue. Before the heat of her temper could penetrate Okon's unruffled evenness, she noticed Losha spinning faster and the space between Losha's brows faintly glowing, creating a thin circle of light around the Interpreter's head.

Maome scooted backward on her buttocks, her eyes wide with terror at first, until a sense of wonder took her over.

The Queen caught a few softly spoken words of Losha's invocation..."sacred" and "holy", "beauty" and "light". The words stopped Palomei long enough to let her witness a bell jar of energy surrounding Losha. The thin wall of glimmering light swirled and shimmered like standing water. Beyond that veil of subtle substance Losha's form disintegrated and her essence spun into a milky-white blur.

Palomei felt a blast of energy slam against her and blow her bees away. And a throbbing energy pulsated in the room that set her heart fluttering.

Okon clapped his hands together in delight. "She spins!" he said in astonishment. "A sight I have not seen in many seasons!"

CHAPTER THIRTY-TWO

SCONES AND SWANS

"We will be able to focus on our formless selves and our other selves contained in all form. We will know once again that wondrous sense of oneness with all creation. And with the return of our complete Ka and our power will come the full memory of who and what we really are in relationship to everything else."

Elder Tani
The Makolese Scroll on
The Return of the Ka and the Mending of the Su #32

Maśon put the scroll aside to dry. He repositioned his painful leg and stopped to refill his ink jar.

"You've barely touched the device I gave you," Temple said.

Maśon flicked a strand of greasy hair out of his eyes and slapped a fresh piece of paper down in front of him. "Believe me. I'm faster." He grinned.

Temple shrugged and stood up and walked over to the small kitchen area. "I'm peckish," he announced. He spied two scones on a plate, pressed a pad of cold butter on one, and ambled back to the woodstove. He held the scone over the heat until the butter ran, then popped it into his mouth. "What had the others remembered of the old spinning magic?" he said, mumbling with his mouthful.

The Scribe flicked a crumb off his paper and dipped his ink brush.

Temple smacked his lips together. "The people back then talked about shape-shifting as if it were a feat only accomplished in secrecy by High Shamans. Others who had performed the magic were only considered legend." Temple licked the butter off his fingers. "Who in that chamber had even remembered seeing such a sight from so many years ago besides Tani and now Okon? Owane was older, but with his Ka having been manipulated, his memories and thoughts had dimmed." He pointed to the remaining scone. "Mind if I have the last one?"

"You've eaten everything else I have. Why not my last bit of food?" Maśon said in a laconic tone.

"Oh, I beg your pardon, my good friend," Temple said. "I do apologize." He walked back into the sparse kitchenette and stood before the nearly empty plate, his back turned toward the Scribe. He mumbled a few inaudible words and walked back to Maśon with the plate in his hand. He lowered the plate in front of Maśon. "Care to have a fresh one?" he asked.

The Scribe looked up at the plate and drew back with a jerk. He stared at a dozen steaming hot buttered scones, then squinted up into Temple's quiet face.

"Forgive me for being so rude," Temple said.

Maśon picked up a hot scone between two fingers as if he were handling a scorpion.

Temple paced the room with the plate as he munched. "Now, where was I? Oh, of course. Okon had just had his Ka reattached, and he was beginning to remember traces of the old magic."

Maśon sniffed the scone, then took a hesitant bite.

"When Palomei rose out of her chair, the old centenarian raised his hand in protest to buffer any further actions to stop the miracle before them."

The Scribe threw the rest of the sweet biscuit in his mouth and grabbed his ink brush to catch up.

"The Queen stood, her mouth agape with wonder as the iridescence surrounding Losha grew brighter, and a field of pointed lights, like tiny stars, formed around her swirling form. The energy field held to a tight spherical formation several feet away from Losha's center, until in a surprising millisecond there was a sudden burst of light that flashed out in all directions, knocking the giantess into her throne chair. And when the Queen had recovered from her momentary blindness, before her stood a magnificent white Swan!" he said proudly. Temple cocked his head. "You want my recipe?"

The large Swan puffed out her powerful chest as she beat her wings. Her trumpeting cry chilled the sweat that trickled down Palomei's spine. The small scar in Losha's forehead began to glow sapphire blue and the sensation of love rarified the air.

"Beautiful!" Okon exclaimed breathlessly. He looked at Tani, who was beaming with pride.

"Now will you believe us?" Tani said to Palomei. "With our precious Ka reattached, all of us will be able to achieve such as this, and far greater things – like we did in the old days, but with no desire to harm another. We will be able to focus on our formless selves and our other selves contained in all form. We will know once again that wondrous sense of oneness with all creation. And with the return of our complete Ka and our power will come the full memory of who and what we really are in relationship to everything else."

Tani peered into Palomei's stricken face. "Now you see, Most Beloved, why we must do as Losha and Temple have asked. Will you not honor the advice of the Teachers?"

Palomei nodded to Tani. "I am listening," she said humbly, and Tani could see the eager reach of her eyes.

"Do not antagonize the Unbelievers," Tani advised. "Let Temple address your troops. Let him teach them. Allow them a chance to withdraw from the foothills of Hollow Mountain. And, although the Shaman is not the True Teacher, let the High Shaman Mefakani preach to his new converts in the mountain so that he may bring them to a wider understanding of who we are as a peaceful people. Give him the opportunity to introduce Losha to them. In their eyes she will fulfill the prophecy.

"Then under the watchful eye of the Swan, let us allow the people the chance to unite again. Give them time to heal while we reattach the Kas that we foolishly gave in trust to Shaman Mefakani."

"Can we trust the Priest?" Palomei asked.

"That is the risk," Tani said. "But I can tell you this. He is a changed man, for not only did he ingest some of Temple's pure essence, but experienced his own death. Then he returned to life. He must have returned to the living for a reason."

Queen Palomei nodded her head again, this time with a shrewd confidence. "It is done," she said.

Tani bowed to the Queen and said, "The Great Swan must go now."

"Where? Where is she going?" Palomei asked, somewhat confused.

"Only after the Elders Cranik, Ikus, and Kulo and their Rebel Soldiers journey back to where the Unbelievers are camped on Hollow Mountain will Mefakani reappear on his airboat. Losha must fly to the mountain and address the Unbelievers herself…after Mefakani has prepared the way for her."

Queen Palomei rocked back in her mammoth chair, her eyes still aglow with the sight of the beautiful white Swan before her and the feeling of love that suffused the chamber. "And when they see her flying…and the scar upon her brow?"

"You understand," Tani said.

"Tai. But will it work?" E-lon-e' asked.

"We must pray, but not to Lord Tagheetu," Tani advised. "We must all pray to the Goddess Hianna."

With that proclamation ending their meeting, the Swan was escorted out the sliding screens onto the tiled portico where she waddled into one of the gardens. She took flight in the direction of the royal ponds to nourish herself and to rest, although her mind was filled with the task ahead on Hollow Mountain.

CHAPTER THIRTY-THREE

IN THE GARDEN

"The body knows what it needs."

High Shaman Mefakani
The Makolese Scroll on
The Return of the Ka and the Mending of the Su #33

In the deepest part of the night, Hollow Mountain seemed nothing more than a huge black mass blotting out the stars. Mefakani rose and walked wearily from his lodge through the quiet compound. Sleep had eluded him, his mind mired in what he would tell the Rebels on the mountain. The darkness was as calm as an approaching storm, yet his mind tossed about with the whirlwind of his thoughts. As he walked past the tall basalt wall that surrounded his private garden, Mefakani ran his fingers along its rough stone. He'd had the wall built six years before, hiding his hybrid plants from Tani. Now, he thought, he would turn the garden over to her and let her glean its secrets.

Mefakani heard a sword pulled from its sheath and saw the glint of metal in the pale moonlight. "Commander Boran," he said. "It is I, High Shaman Mefakani."

"Master," Boran replied, and bowed steeply.

The word "master" made Mefakani shuddered inwardly. He drew closer. "Boran, I have instructions for you. When day breaks, please escort the Elders – Cranik, Kulo, and also Ikus, who has just arrived – back to the Rebel encampment on the mountain. Eight of your soldiers and nine of the Rebel warriors will be with you as well. Remember, we still have a truce with the Rebels. Continue on into the foothills where your army is encamped. Make certain," he emphasized, "that your men allow the Rebels to continue to their own base camp on the cliff. Do you understand? We are not at war."

"Yes, Master, I understand," Boran said, still compliant from having had his Ka altered by the Priest.

"Good." Mefakani motioned Boran away from the garden gate. He unlocked the heavy wooden door. "Please go now and rest awhile, but rise before dawn to prepare for your journey."

"Yes, Master," Boran said, departing.

Mefakani entered the garden quietly and locked the tall door behind him. Jasmine and the delicate raspberry scent of mignonette perfumed the air. And the soothing sound of trickling water filled his ears, calming him further. Beneath this sound, his medicinal plants greeted him with a barely discernible hum. Though the moon lent barely enough light to see by, a distinct glow suffused the air and the garden came alive with Ka.

Mefakani leaned heavily against the door, exhausted beyond what he thought he could endure. He took three deep breaths to drink in the life force and said a prayer of thanks to the Guardian of the Garden and the spirit of each plant, mindful now of the new man he had become. Staggering over to a bed of ferns he laid down into their softness. He swore he had dozed off for several minutes, but on looking up into the night sky, it seemed the stars had not moved. He sat up with a bit more energy and straightened his spine, then prayed to the Source of All Creation to help him renew his strength and courage, to give him the guidance he would require for the impossible task that lay ahead.

He sat in meditation for several minutes until the small voice inside him told him to open his eyes and rise. It was still dark. He gathered himself to his feet and, without thoughts to distract him, found himself feeling the world around him with new senses, deeper emotions, and with a newfound will to surrender to the Divine force within him. He allowed his rational mind – his dangerous mind – and his false pride drop from him, so he could feel the essence of each plant. He moved in a light trance toward the plants glowing bright, and sat beside a hybrids bush teeming with huge five-petaled flowers. Admiring their pink and milky glow, he ran his face over the blossoms. With no conscious thought, he plucked off the soft petals, one by one, with his teeth and ate them each.

The body knows what it needs.

When he had his fill, he turned to another plant with leaves of lavender and gold. He ate some of these as well, then picked off a handful and folded them into a pocket inside his waistband. Licking the pungent oil from his fingers, he cast an eye at the far end of the garden. A vine that ran the length of the southern wall seemed to be on fire, emitting scintillating waves in bands of white and blue. It was a vine that he hadn't planted and had no knowledge of, and a joy ran through him with the thrill of new discovery. He ran like a madman over to the wall and gently fingered the vine, until its flowers yielded up their seed to him. He chewed them well and sat for some time on the earth, sensing the difference in his energy and mood. Lightness of being fell over him and his head began to grow dizzy. Leaning against the wall, he allowed this new earthy energy to flow through him, connecting him deeper to the earth, at once opening his mind. He was certain that he would pass out, but he allowed his body to sink to the ground, and he fell into a deep, deep sleep.

★　　★　　★　　★　　★　　★

Having draped his loins with a soft-leafed vine, Ikus pushed a fan of ferns out of his way as he coursed his way up the trail back to the Shaman's compound.

Kulo paused to pick a pink jungle blossom. He inhaled deeply of its sweet fragrance, then hurried to catch up to Ikus. "Here," he said, thrusting the flower out in front of his friend. "Put this behind your ear. It goes well with the vine skirt."

"Oh, drink rat piss!" Ikus cursed. "I know I will need to find a new cloth when we get back." His gravelly voice was raspy with fatigue. "But first we must warn Cranik." He began to march away.

"He wants nothing to do with you," Kulo blurted.

Ikus stopped cold and turned around. His eyes hardened. "What are you talking about?"

"He knows you came down from the mountain. Why do you think he did not rouse himself from his bed mat to speak with you tonight?"

"He is tired."

"He told me to keep you away from him," Kulo said.

"Bi kana! Why?"

"He does not want to hear a litany of orders from you. He knows how you feel about him being the new Senior Elder. He told me to make sure you were not even in the same boat with him tomorrow."

"Why is *he* Senior Elder? There have been no elections," Ikus complained.

"Because he took the position in Sahdon's absence." The ground leveled off and Kulo stretched his back and yawned. "Forget what I have just said. Come, let us get some rest."

Ikus stared at his friend incredulously. "You idiot! How can you sleep when the ghost of Temple Fox roams around like a demon in the night?"

"Because I am exhausted. And so is everyone else," Kulo said. "I am so tired I cannot think straight." He looked down at his thin companion in the dark. "Your nights on that cliff top were near a warm fire. My body is aching. It is I and not you who had to sleep in the corridor of a dark cavern on that cold, hard, wet…"

"Oh, shut up and quit complaining! That is all you ever do!" Ikus snapped back. "This is far more important than your imaginary aches and pains!"

Kulo was mindful of his large size and Ikus' frail frame. He sucked in his breath. "You are insensitive as usual," he said, controlling his rage. "I told you the Lord Tagheetu will take care of the Wizard. Why else would Mefakani leave the body there? Just go back to camp. I warn you. Do not wake Cranik. And, if you want to continue being the new Senior Elder's ally, stay away from him tomorrow. He has a lot on his mind. I am going now and getting some sleep." He turned his back on Ikus and plodded into the Shaman's compound alone.

Cranik and four of the Rebel warriors were asleep beside the central fire. The other Rebels stood guard around the compound. Even though the two factions had kept the truce during the negotiations, the air was still charged with tension. Palomei's soldiers, who had also been chosen to stand guard within the compound, made certain they didn't converse with the Unbelievers.

Kulo was only a few paces inside the compound when one of Palomei's soldiers stopped him. "Stop!" the soldier called out.

The Elder held up a hand in self-defense. "It is only I, Elder Kulo. I have only gone to relieve myself," he explained.

"Well, next time relieve youself inside the compound." Recognizing the Elder, the soldier allowed the old man to pass and resumed his watchful stance.

Kulo stopped for a thoughtful moment. "But that other old man coming through the forest should not be allowed to pass. He is disguised as a female. You should cut him up into little pieces and use him for fish bait," he said with a snort.

The soldier smiled back, forgetting for a second that the three old men and his former military companions were Unbelievers.

CHAPTER THIRTY-FOUR

A SECRET MEETING

"Remember that part of me is inside you now.
We are apart of one another. You are
made of light."

Temple Fox
The Makolese Scroll on
The Return of the Ka and the Mending of the Su #34

When Mefakani woke, the sky was burning crimson and birds were singing their morning songs. He heard the whisper of men's voices and the crackle of a fire. The smell of cooked food wafted in the air.

Mefakani walked confidently to a little clearing near the western wall where he had landed his airboat days before away from prying eyes. He ran a deft hand down one of the four metal legs that supported the airboat, to see if it balanced and bore the craft's weight adequately. Grunting with approval, he knelt in the dirt to scrutinize each of the crystal spheres that peeked through the brackets from the underbelly of the ship. He rose with another thoughtful grunt and ran his eyes along the ship's frame from bottom to top. The ship had held together well in its maiden voyage.

The metal that formed the bottom of the frame looked no different than it had the day he had found the wreckage on the far side of Hollow Mountain. The metal cast a dull sheen, its sleekness and lightness filling him with a renewed sense of awe for things he had little knowledge of. He murmured beneath his breath at how primitive the rest of the frame he had constructed looked in comparison. Bent lengths of thick bamboo formed skeletal arches from one side of the ship to the other, at the front, back, and in the middle where he had built a seat for himself. Like the basic frame of a woven basket, the bamboo was lashed together with sinew and jute, appearing ridiculous, he thought, next to the smooth metal work of the Mountain Gods. Still, it was far more lightweight than the original iron frame he had forged, and then was forced to scrap due to its cumbersome weight.

Satisfied that the ship would make another journey, he ambled to the gate when a dark form, catching only the faintest of scarlet light in its wings, swooped past his head and landed on a nearby branch.

Mefakani drew back, startled. "Temple," he gasped. The Shaman looked all around nervously. Knowing no one could see or hear them, he walked up to the Owl that perched above him.

The Owl peered down as if he were looking straight through Mefakani's soul.

"If you need to talk, spin and change under cover of the thicker brush," the Shaman said.

The Owl darted back into the air on silent wing, then spiraled downward. The ground beneath an old cedar with heavy branches came alive in a whirlwind of brilliance and the plants below quivered. Lit up from within, darker veins silhouetted each plant's circulatory system as if they had been exposed to X-ray. Their strange inner glow swiftly faded, and Temple's man-form appeared out of the cold fire of transformation.

"I did not expect to see you," Mefakani said, his head turned slightly to avoid looking directly into Temple's piercing eyes.

Temple stepped forward and brushed himself off. "Sorry to scare you, but I had to see you before you left. I had a wee bit of an incident in the swamps," he said. "I ran into that tall ungainly Elder with the white woolly hair, and that thin Elder with the pointy nose."

Mefakani stared down at his feet as he listened. "Ah, Elders Kulo and Ikus."

"Yes, that's what they called each other," Temple said, remembering. "I don't know what they were up to, but it looked like they wanted to see the body. I prevented that from happening, but now they think I'm still alive…as a ghost, I'm afraid."

Mefakani wrinkled his brow. "Our plans are coming unraveled just as Tani said they might." He stole a glance at Temple's face, then lowered his head again to avert Temple's owl-like gaze. "Thank you for telling me. I would not worry. Before anyone brings up the subject, I will tell them that the death of a Wizard comes in stages. First there is capture by trickery, then death by poison and an unspoken magic, and finally, the dismantling of any dark restless spirit comes by the power of the Lord Tagheetu after the Wizard is ingested by crocodiles."

"Well, that's good news," Temple said, "because I stayed in the swamps long enough to witness the crocodiles take Sahdon's body."

"At least there will be no evidence now," Mefakani whispered.

Temple paused and blinked up at the growing light in the eastern sky. "I'm going back into the forest now to eat and rest, and to get accustomed to my newly retrieved soul fragments. If the Divine wills it so, I will see you at Olonopo Crater in a few days."

Mefakani nodded, then gave Temple a steep bow, his eyes still focused on the ground.

"Mefakani," Temple said. "Remember that part of me is inside you now."

Mefakani gave a sluggish nod.

"We are a part of one another."

Mefakani nodded that he understood.

Temple took a step forward and placed his hand on Mefakani's shoulder, and a pleasant energy rushed through the Shaman's body like a stream of sunshine, liquid, silky, but lighter and smoother in viscosity than warm oil.

"You are made of light," the man-god said. "It is up to you to let it shine. I trust you will honor who you really are."

Meeting no resistance, the energy filled Mefakani until it reached his brain, spilling over his crown now, open to the heavens. He lifted his head, drawn by the steadfast gaze of Temple's sky-blue eyes. "I…I will do my best."

Temple smiled and bowed. In spite of the risk taken to spin too often, he spun his magic and transformed back into his Owl form.

Mefakani stood rooted to the ground when the light of Temple's transformation had faded. He watched as the great Owl rose into the air with one flap of its wings and disappeared into the dark forest without a sound.

The Priest, still dizzied from Temple's touch, wasn't sure he possessed a head, a body, a form. His third eye tingled and blazed like a cluster of starlight dancing in place. His heart – an open door now – expanded, reaching toward some unknown horizon.

Mefakani placed his hand over his heart, tears forming in the corner of his eyes.

He didn't know how long he stood there wishing the experience would last forever, but he noticed the monkeys chattering and the sunlight and shadows shift. Slowly, the sensation of lightness waned and he felt his body take solid form and shape again. He said a silent prayer for Temple first and then the others. Finally including himself in prayer, he left the garden and locked the gate behind him.

"Today," he whispered to himself, "will be a day written about in the History Scrolls."

CHAPTER THIRTY-FIVE

JOURNEY BACK TO HOLLOW MOUNTAIN

*"In the shadow of Hollow Mountain morning comes late.
Those who dwell in the East and South broil early.
Those who dwell in North and West do not broil until noon."*

An Old Makolese Saying
The Makolese Scroll on
The Return of the Ka and the Mending of the Su #35

The sun had long since ripened to lemon yellow and the sky was glowing apricot. The heavy canopy of jungle hid the river from the sun and kept it cool and cloaked in low-lying mist.

Temple gazed out across the Green River, drinking in the beauty of every tree and its steamy mirrored reflection. Hidden in the foliage of an old mahogany, he watched as the procession of Believer and Unbeliever approached in seven slim canoes. The men sat in silence, the only sound – dripping paddles, then quiet splashes as their paddles dipped into the river again, rippling a flash of eddies behind them in green, silver, and peach. The paddles lifted again, draped in algae, and the delicate sound echoed once more off the riverbanks as they sailed smoothly through the promenade of trees past the hidden owl.

Moving like a huge sleek serpent, the Green River carried its passengers around a muscular bend into a bright patch of sunlight and, in time, out of Temple's view. His wide, round eyes blinked at the sudden sharpness of the light, and he searched beyond the bend to see where they might reemerge. The prow of the lead canoe reappeared a little further ahead at a break in the trees, until, one by one, the seven canoes emerged, then disappeared round another meandering bend, leading into the foothills of Hollow Mountain.

Temple dived from his perch. With barely a beat of his wings, he was carried by warm moist air high over the upper river, past the canoes, to a point where the Green River met the Ananba River and the waters roughened. Below him stood two of Palomei's soldiers waving their welcome to the procession.

Temple landed in a rosewood above them and cocked his ears in the direction of the approaching canoes. No longer gliding easily in the calmer waters, the oarsmen struggled against the current now and Temple could hear the distant waterfall roar as he surveyed the white water ahead. The oarsmen turned their canoes due east, toward a shallow embankment to the north and set to paddling hard so they would not drift too far sideways. One by one they plowed into the loamy sand, and the two sentries stepped into the rushing surf to help the three Elders out. The others lifted the canoes out of the river and set them upside down on higher ground.

In the shadow of Hollow Mountain morning comes late. The Grandfather Sun, still too low to shine his face on either Believer or Unbeliever, set the sky ablaze in gold.

Temple still couldn't chance being seen in his human from, so he soared from treetop to treetop as an Owl until the group had finally coursed their way up to the Believers' encampment. By then the sun was broiling and directly overhead. Boran stepped forward and, as his Master had ordered him to, he allowed the three Elders and their Warriors safe passage.

CHAPTER THIRTY-SIX

FALLEN ANGELS

*"You cannot impose peace on anyone.
Peace can only come from within your heart."*

High Shaman Mefakani
The Makolese Scroll on
The Return of the Ka and the Mending of the Su #36

The three Elders and their small band of Unbelievers had been given orders to remain silent as they passed Palomei's soldiers high in the foothills. The silence from both factions was welcomed, but uneasy as the Rebels passed through the Believers' camp, all eyes, ears, and nerves at full alert. Their passage proved uneventful.

Weariness came over everyone as they coursed their way far above the encampment. Even Mumbula and Ijebu were exhausted, but they pushed their way up the steep and treacherous trail, mindful of the importance of their mission.

Kulo could barely climb the last hundred yards. Two of the Rebel Warriors offered to carry the heavy man, but he raised an arthritic hand to decline the offer. When they made it to the broad stone ledge that had held their encampment for several days, Pao-ta, a short squat middle-aged woman, was the first to greet them. Kulo broke into a smile and embraced the woman.

Pao-ta pulled Kulo aside, her voice heavy with anxiety. "You were gone for days! Ikus left me in charge. I will tell you straight out that we are dangerously short on supplies," she warned.

"Pao-ta, do not fear. We have brought food and with it the news that the Wizard is dead."

The woman's eyes lit up and she stood on her tiptoes to kiss Kulo on the cheek. But the glint in her eyes quickly faded when Kulo bent closer and whispered that the Senior Elder Sahdon was dead as well.

"We are not to tell the others yet," Kulo said.

The Rebels soon tightened their circle around the small band anxious for the news about the Wizard. The inevitable happened and someone asked where Mefakani and the Senior Elder were.

Elder Cranik climbed onto the stone plinth in front of the gapping mouth of the mountain cave, drawing his attention away from the small dark spot he saw in the sky behind a cloud. He waved his arms in the air to gather everyone's attention.

"Before we talk about the Wizard, we must tell you all that we have lost Elder Senior Shadon. While we were in the underground tunnels he fell to his death seeking guidance from the Mother Stone."

A collective gasp erupted from the mob and many yelled out praises for their dead leader. But they soon grew stormy, pressing Cranik for news about the white Wizard.

Cranik asked for one of the Rebels to hand him a torch. He took the torch and waved it in the air, giving the High Shaman the signal he had been waiting for.

Mefakani watched the Rebels from behind a cloud, waiting for the right moment to land his airboat. He saw the signal fire and prayed that the Divine Light, which had embraced him before in death, and through Temple's magic touch, would give him a safe landing and the proper words to speak.

Mefakani stared at the crowd of Rebels as they gathered to watch him land. Slowly, he pulled a lever back, which engaged a gear that drew a metal sheath over four of the crystal spheres. The craft cascaded gently like a falling leaf until Mefakani engaged another lever. With utmost care he brought the airboat down toward the entrance to the mammoth cave, behind the rise of flat stones the Rebels used as a lookout point.

The Priest blew out a deep sigh of relief, satisfied at the smooth landing, and said a quick prayer of thanks. He leaned his broken staff against the steering pole, and felt a brief moment of anguish recalling the loss of his past magic. He pulled out an obsidian mirror secreted under his sash and palmed it as he stepped from the airboat directly onto the podium of stone. Securing the cloth he had wrapped around his head, he nodded to Elder Cranik.

The old man climbed up onto the platform by his side, waiting for the Priest to speak first.

Mefakani froze for a moment, trying to slow the rapid beating of his heart. He closed his eyes and tried to reconnect with the Divine Light he had met in death.

I call upon the Divine to put words in my mouth.

Cranik grew tense, his eyes flickering between the crowd and the Priest. The Rebels stirred restlessly until, anxious to be the one who delivered the news himself, Cranik shouted so all could hear: "The True Teacher has defeated Temple Fox! The White Wizard is DEAD!"

Cheers stormed from the clifftop and echoed off the mountainside into the chasm below where the Queen's army sat waiting out the truce. The Rebel voices grew louder with song and celebration. Proclaiming the defeat of their enemy, the drums beat louder. And their song wafted in the late afternoon air and made its way down the dark corridors to the little Gods below, into the bowels of their twilight kingdom and into the nether regions of the unseen, resonating with discord. Although it might have sent a chill through the hollow bones of the swallows, and sent a tingling sensation through the fragile ribs of the silent bats deep in the interior of the mountain, another energy was broadcast through the airless air. And this message belied that proclamation, because the animals knew instinctively, as did the little blue Gods who lived inside the mountain, that energy doesn't lie!

The cheers chilled Mefakani's blood and he stood immobilized before the band of Unbelievers. He rubbed his hands together nervously, the absence of his broken staff leaving his hands with nothing to do, with nothing to hold on to, not even his old magic.

The plants he had consumed had renewed his energies to make the journey through the air, but he was still fatigued and frightened. An ache he hadn't been conscious of earlier unexpectantly flared into his awareness. The pain intensified in his legs and shot up into his back, making him want to cry out.

Mefakani bore the pain and set his eyes upon the jubilant crowd below. He was their hero, their Warrior-Priest and now their god in human flesh.

Masquerading as a god and shouting in victory for the death of the True Teacher, even though it was untrue, seemed like a sacrilege to him now. Unlike before, which felt like a lifetime ago, when he pontificated in front of the hoard, killing anyone seemed senseless and abhorrent to him now.

Can I keep up the charade and appear as their Teacher and Prophet, and yet tell the truth as well? Please! I beg the Divine to speak through me!

The conflict in his mind swarmed around his head like a cluster of blue flies in the humid heat. He wanted to tell them the truth and be done with it. But deep within a voice shouted at him to hold on tight to his conviction, to have courage and not allow more destruction to darken his name or the Makolese legacy. It was time for him to make amends. The slightest slipup could end in civil war, pit faction against faction, brother against brother. Although his conscience begged for confession, admitting the whole truth to the hungry people before him now would only mean that he had been defeated by the "White Devil". That would only spur the Rebels on, like coaxing a single, burning coal into an all-consuming conflagration.

Mefakani held on to his resolve and the plan Losha and Temple had prepared to ease both the Believers and Unbelievers out of their bitterness and hatreds, into peaceful coexistence, if not into a state of grace itself.

He reminded himself where they were in their consciousness and whispered a prayer again for guidance and strength. A quiet voice, softer than a she-rain, spoke within him, urging him on gently: *Remember who and what they are. Remember who and what you are. Be your True Self, but speak in their terms.*

He stretched his arms out wide as if to embrace all the people. "The war is over!" he started boldly after the cheers had died down. "And yet when I see into your hearts I see the war goes on. I not only see hatred toward Temple Fox, a most honorable foe, but hatred toward the Believers. Trust me when I say there is no victory in that. I ask you, how can I talk to men and women of war whose hearts are so hardened and confused by fear?"

Mefakani pointed to the crowd. "You must ask yourself this question. Do you truly want a civil war on our small island where neighbor will war against neighbor, brother against brother? When I look deep into your heart of hearts I do not see people of war, but Children of the One Spirit, who have been conceived in Divine Love, who are made of the very substance of Divine Love, and who desire the unity of Spirit with all things – including their brothers and sisters who may not believe as you do.

"I wonder how many of you have asked yourself what the next step is. Temple's followers do not believe as you do and they outnumber you. What are you going to do with them all? Kill them? Divide the island into provinces of Believers and Unbelievers? Exile them?…People! Listen! You may be facing centuries of civil war if you do not desire peace right now!"

A man stepped forward and bowed before Mefakani reverently. "We can impose decrees on them," he called out. "Make laws saying they cannot practice any worship of their White Wizard under strict penalties."

"Do you think the Queen, who is a Believer, would do such a thing? You cannot impose peace on anyone," Mefakani said outright.

"Peace can come only from within your heart. And right now your hearts lay buried beneath all the bitterness you carry. But, good people, I ask that you uncover that desire of peace now to bring about the changes that await us. Do not be fooled and think this is an unattainable goal, for it is the natural state from which we came and which we are destined to return."

He drew in a deep breath, then let out a surrendering sigh as the words flowed forth.

"We all have been born out of Divine Love and Peace," he said with absolute conviction. "No…peace is not something that can be imposed on a people. Only order can be imposed on people. That is not at all the same as peace and will inevitably fail.

"Within the deepest chamber of your hearts I see wise men and women who ultimately desire harmony. You choose peace. You have made choices in the past and have acted on them bravely. Now I ask you to be even braver. Let your fears fade as your shadow fades when you stand in the light of the Father Sun."

Mefakani remembered the Light he had been reborn into and his voice took on a tone of awe. "What others believe or do not believe cannot possibly harm you when you stand inside such a powerful Light. Let your fears, and your worries, and all your sad projections of what may or may not happen here fade from you now like a vanishing shadow. If you are Warriors, then let you be Warriors of Peace! Surrender to the Divine and trust that the Divine will guide and protect you, for you are the Children of the Light. You are the Children of the Greater God of Love and Forgiveness. Be bold and lay down your arms!"

There was a stirring in the crowd and the murmur of voices grew louder and agitated.

"What is all this talk about the Divine and the Greater God? He makes no mention of Lord Tagheetu or the other Gods," Ikus pointed out to the other Elders.

Mefakani pitched his voice above the rising outcry. "Yes, lay down your arms! When the others see this, and see the light pour from your opened eyes, they will recognize the greater truth as you do. And the truth is – you and the Believers are kin. You all are one! You all are ultimately apart of a greater mind. One mind. It does not matter if you think that your brothers and sisters have flawed vision. They are made of the same Divine Love as you are. Soften their hearts with your patience, compassion, and understanding. Show them your true selves first and they will follow in time. Love knows no other face, but itself. There lies the greatest 'weapon,' the greatest power, the 'weapon' that will unify the island."

"You say we should lay down our arms? Even the lightning spears and power shields you invented?" a Rebel soldier asked from the crowd.

"Yes!" Mefakani answered.

"You say we can walk down this mountain safely, that the Queen's army will not attack and killing us all?" someone else called out.

Mefakani found the face in the crowd and called out to him. "We presently have a truce. The Believers have allowed myself, and others, to come and go without incident. Leave here and no one will harm you. Show your courage. Yet show it in such a way without the need to raise a hand or weapon against them. But first," he emphasized, "you must learn to rid yourselves of fear."

"But how?" one woman asked.

CHAPTER THIRTY-SEVEN

THE TEACHER TEACHES

*"I won't force you to change your mind, nor do I
propose to force a change in the hearts of the
Unbelievers. It's not in my power to do so. I only
mean to change my thoughts about you and, in
doing so, correct a flaw in my thinking. By seeing
you as wholly Divine, I hope you'll come around
and see yourself as I do. When you see yourself
and the Rebels in such a glorious, harmonious
light, there'll be little chance for the fear on this
island to escalate into war. You see – I'm
your mirror."*

Temple Fox
The Makolese Scroll on
The Return of the Ka and the Mending of the Su #37

"You must first know beyond all doubt that we're collectively of one
heart and one mind," Temple said, answering the same question for the
Queen's army that gathered in the foothills of Hollow Mountain. He
stood above them on a boulder, speaking smoothly and clearly in their
native tongue, a nacreous glow emanating from him. And from this
pulpit of stone he embraced these strangers with his compassion and
understanding, his message riding on a current of truth.

"You're inseparable from the Rebels because you all come from
the same loving Source. It's truly that simple. Holding this knowledge
close to your hearts will help you move beyond any fears you hold.
But don't mistake me," he called out. "I don't ask that you withhold
your feelings of fear or mask those fears simply because I ask. Don't
hold any emotion at arm's length. If you do, those emotions will well

up inside later and fester like a sore. Holding such emotions back will only keep you from healing.

"Listen to me. All of you are Warriors – incredible Warriors, whose minds are as intelligent and as disciplined as the best the world has ever known. But now I ask you to learn something new, to embrace with as much conviction, discipline, and courage as never before. You have trained your mind. Now it is time to train your heart and bring both into balance. You have been soldiers of war. Now I ask you to forgive your enemies and be soldiers of peace!"

Not a word was uttered as the Queen's army listened to Temple, their attention testifying to the charisma he carried and their willingness to learn.

"I ask you to center and ground yourselves as you have been taught before, and focus on your out breath. When you enter this meditative state, I ask you to be truthful with yourself – truthful as to how you feel toward the Unbelievers. Take one feeling at a time and feel it fully. But don't judge it. Don't see any emotion as either good or bad. See it as neutral. See it as the Gods see it. See it simply as energy.

"If you feel hatred toward the Unbelievers, recognize that you perceive them as your 'enemy' and know that that's all right. Focus on that feeling no matter what it is and let it intensify inside you. Is it fear? Is it resentment? Frustration? Find the feeling first, then find where you feel it."

Temple gestured with his hands. "Is it in the pit of your stomach? In your throat? If it is forgiveness you feel for your Rebel brothers, do you feel it in your heart? Your head? Whatever it is you're experiencing, move it toward your heart. Your heart is where energy becomes balanced and purified. Once you have it centered there, move it toward the opening in your heart. There's a doorway there. Take that emotion, that energy, no matter what it is and push it through the door as a beam of pure Light and send it out into the universe. By doing this you transform any emotion into Divine Light.

"This is a holy act," he emphasized, "and a powerful action that will bring you back to wholeness again and ripple outward to transform others. This is what the Makolese were born to do. This is your destiny. Learn this. Then teach others."

"But, Master Temple, what of the Rebels?" a soldier asked. "You ask that we withdraw our troops. But reason tells me this is too dangerous. When the Rebels see us withdraw they will come down from the mountain and engage us in battle!"

"Tai! Your plan is fraught with danger! We should wait here and starve them out!" another shouted.

The soldier looked all around him and saw others nodding in agreement.

"You must trust that Spirit is working to bring peace to the Rebels' hearts as well," Temple said. "While your reason may tell you my plan is foolish – reason is what got everyone into trouble to begin with. Reason can conjure up the darkest, most nightmarish fears and delusions. The intellect is where limited notions of reality are first formed. You know this from your training with the power shield. It's reason that has convinced you that you're separate from the Divine, and when you perceive yourself that way, it's easy for you to see your brothers as enemies, when, in fact, you are all apart of one whole energy – the Divine Force known as Love. Think about it. If you saw yourself and others in that light, there would be no war. There would be disagreement, naturally, but never the violence of war."

Someone else called out: "But even if we learned to see ourselves this way, there is no guarantee that the Rebels could do the same."

Temple found the face in the crowd. "As I said before, there's a greater plan working as we speak. That's where trust comes in. Still, I will not stand here and give you hope that your lives will not be threatened. Instead, I will tell you the truth. There might be a civil war. It's possible, but not entirely inevitable. Only you can choose if this is what you really want. Only you can choose the degree of destruction it brings and the duration of it. My aim is to give you a detour, to offer you a path to peace and hasten your spiritual development.

"If you do as I ask, you can change time itself. I pray that you choose wisely and set the wheels of peace in motion."

"This is madness!" yelled a soldier in the distance. He shoved his way through the crowd and stood before the Teacher, clutching his sword in his fist. "My brother was a trained Warrior the same as I. He was butchered by the Rebels! They will destroy our entire culture if we do not stop them now! I, for one, will stay here and fight them until none are left alive!"

There was a smattering of cheers from the farthest reaches of the army.

A single voice erupted above the others. There was anger in the voice. "Are you doubting the Teacher? He has risked his life for us and is standing before us now calling for peace. Maybe you are becoming an Unbeliever!"

A different tone overtook the army. There was shouting between soldiers.

Temple held up his hands and the soldiers quieted down. "Thank you! I am grateful for your candor. But see what has just happened.

Fighting among yourselves! We already have two factions warring with one another. What will we have now – three?" He waved his fist in the air and yelled out, "The war is over! Now is the time to unify!"

The soldiers shouted back in agreement, and the Teacher stood in silence, waiting until the noise subsided. The soldier who had stepped forward with his sword stood his ground, silent, before Temple.

The Teacher spoke evenly, his penetrating gaze aimed at the very soul of the soldier. "I won't force you to change your mind, nor do I propose to force a change in the hearts of the Unbelievers. It's not in my power to do so. I only mean to change my thoughts about you, and, in doing so, correct a flaw in my thinking. By seeing you as wholly Divine, I hope you'll come around and see yourself as I do. When you see yourself and the Rebels in such a glorious, harmonious light, there'll be little chance for the fear on this island to escalate into war. You see – I'm your mirror."

The soldier's brow furrowed and his jaw tightened.

"It's your choice to live in fear. But fear blocks your self-awareness, your understanding that, in fact, your essence is Love Divine. It's the very foundation of who you are.

"You can only be awakened to Love's presence by passing through the fear, by rising through from your dark, unconscious, self-imposed illusions, to emerge beyond the limited mind and fuse with the feelings in your heart. Recognize that love, like sunshine, doesn't shine on some and not on others. It's for everyone because, simply put, love is everything. It's what we're all made of – you, me, the Rebels in the mountain and the mountain itself."

The soldier could no longer stand the forceful gaze of Temple's intense blue eyes and turned his head away. "All this talk of love and forgiveness!" he said, his face twisted in anger and exasperation. "Look at the ground you stand on! It is soaked with our people's blood!"

"The war is over," Temple repeated in a calm tone. "If you want it to continue…then the choice is yours. I only ask that you're clear as to what you really want."

The soldier blinked nervously and swiped the sweat from his forehead. "What do you mean?" the soldier asked.

"What is it that you really want?" Temple asked and captured the man's eyes again. "Is it your choice to spend the next few months, even years, in continuous battle with the Rebels? Do you want to stand out here in the heat and rain without shelter, with little food and sleep, so you can maybe kill one or two of them? This can't bring your brother back to life. So what possible fulfillment could this bring you?"

"Knowledge that I have done an honorable thing to save my people," the man answered forthright.

"An honorable answer in your mind, but one that lacks the power of forgiveness," Temple said. "With the war dragging on, what happens to your culture that you vow so bravely to protect? If all the other men feel and act as you do, what happens when they are gone for so long? Who will fish and hunt for food to keep the people alive? Who will perform all the sacred rites and dances? Who will be there to teach the old songs and to keep the tradition of prophecy pure? Who will teach the children? And what will they learn when they see their older brothers and fathers at constant war? Will they learn fear and anger? Only fear and vengeance and nothing else?"

Temple could read the man's mind and addressed him before the man could respond.

"The children have already witnessed your amazing courage, which you have taught them by example. Now, when will they learn compassion and tolerance? When will they learn forgiveness? Will they be brave enough to learn that? And who will teach them by example? Truly, how will they ever learn what peace is? Isn't that what you are ultimately fighting for? But peace comes with the courage to forgive. Think, man! Think how your neighbors will feel about you once you return to your village and they find out you have killed their brothers or their children? You know you can destroy a culture in just one generation. It has happened countless times before. The bitterness will escalate and can go on for several generations. Think, man, and *feel*! Feel the bitterness now, then push it out through your open heart!

"By chosing to engage in war, no matter how noble you think the cause is, you may lose all you set out to protect. And you may even lose your life in the process. How would your parents feel about that? They've already lost one son. The cycle of darkness begets more darkness, and put into motion it's a hard thing to break. The only thing that obliterates the darkness is not more darkness, but light. And that is the light of forgiveness. So, tell me what you truly want? The island divided in civil war? More hatred? More death? More chaos? Do you want revenge simply for revenge's sake?"

Temple drew the man deeper into his energy field and his piercing eyes. "Or do you want time to honor your dead brother and the others who have fallen? Do you desire peace of mind? Peace in your heart?"

Temple held up his right hand, palm outward, and aimed at the soldier's hardened heart.

"Do you want to melt that dark spur that's churning inside your guts right now? Do you want to dissolve that hard lump in your throat?" the Teacher asked.

The soldier stood motionless, speechless, his breathing becoming labored. He gripped his sword tightly until his knuckles turned white. His teeth clenched in resistance.

"Do you want that burden you carry to be lifted from your shoulders?" Temple asked gently. "Hatred and revenge are heavy burdens to carry by yourself."

A stillness overcame everyone as the man stood there in silence.

"You loved your brother," Temple said with deep emotion. "You *loved* him," he said in an intense whisper. "This is a time to grieve, and by grieving you honor his memory. But after grieving, do you really want to carry the dead around all your life?"

Beads of sweat formed on the man's brow and he began to tremble.

"Hand your troubled heart over to the Divine," he said softly. "Trust you'll find peace in time, my friend, in time. There's none other to turn to but the Divine." Temple held his arms out. "Why delay the inevitable? Why not simply *let it go?*"

Waves of invisible energy washed over the soldier and his breath came in shallow gasps. His chest tightened and he tried desperately to pull back the dam of tears that wanted release.

"Breathe," Temple said. "Beloved brother of the Light, don't hold back what troubles you. Breathe…and let it go."

The soldier took a deep breath. When he exhaled a stream of tears fell from his eyes. He let his sword fall from his hand and he dropped to his knees sobbing, holding his hands over his face to hide the act.

Temple knelt down in the dirt with the man and held him while he cried. "There's no disgrace in crying, brother," Temple whispered. "It's a sign of the greatest warriors. It's an act of bravery. Let it out and be purified. There's strength in surrendering."

The other soldiers stood around in an uneasy silence at first. But after seeing the most hardened of them fall into Temple's healing embrace, there were few dry eyes, and many threw their weapons in a great pile beside their weeping comrade.

CHAPTER THIRTY-EIGHT

CONFESSIONS

*"This is not a time to talk about death. It is time
for reconciliation and renewal.
It is the time for forgiveness. But first, there is
confession."*

High Shaman Mefakani
The Makolese Scroll on
The Return of the Ka and the Mending of the Su #38

The Shaman wrapped his cloak around him, not to protect him from the sun or wind, but so no one could see him trembling.

"That is what I wish for you to do," Mefakani said.

"You want us to surrender?" someone in the crowd asked.

"I speak of surrender in a larger sense," Mefakani explained. "I ask that you surrender your personal will to the greater will…to Divine Will. I ask you to forgive your enemies."

A Rebel Warrior interrupted. "I, for one, will not lay down my arms! I do not care if I am seen as a coward. I will keep my sword to defend myself and any other man or woman who will join me!"

Mefakani looked out across the crowd of a hundred Rebels. "But it will not be necessary," he said. "The Queen's army will not move against you."

A woman stepped forward and looked up at the imposing figure. She bowed, and rose to meet Mefakani's eyes. "I know you are the True Teacher, and I wish to honor your wishes," she said, "but I cannot do as you ask either. I admit I am not brave enough to walk down from this mountain unarmed. But I am brave enough to stay here and fight the Believers to my death – armed!" she cried out. There was a thunder of cheers behind her.

When the cheers died down a young man drew closer to the podium of stone and prostrated himself before Mefakani. "I beg your forgiveness, Master. Perhaps we could learn to be as brave as our Teacher if you shared with us how you killed the Wizard."

"Tai!" the Rebels yelled out. "Where is the Wizard now? Let us see his head!"

Mefakani froze for a minute and did not speak.

Cranik gazed at the silent Teacher. He spoke instead. "The White Devil is being devoured by the Lord Tagheetu."

A voice called in excitement. "So, how did you kill the Wizard? Tell us!"

It is time, he thought. *Time for the truth.* But he shuddered inwardly, feeling the truth of what he knew jostling against the lies he had to tell them. He placed his hand behind his back. Without anyone noticing, he took the obsidian mirror he had palmed. He aimed it at the sun and sent the first of three signals to Losha, who, he prayed, was waiting somewhere above him hidden on a rock ledge.

He spoke again. "This is not a time to talk about death. It is time for reconciliation and renewal. It is the time for forgiveness. But first," he said, "there is confession."

Cranik met Mefakani's eye. "Confession?" he asked.

Losha followed the Green River just as Temple had done as an Owl. Landing in the river for a respite, she shook her long serpentine neck, drank some water, and nourished herself on the algae by the shoreline. Yet, something within her sensed the energies were out of balance. She raised her head to test the energy in the trees, the river, the air, and felt a sudden chill course through her hollow bones. Something felt wrong…or was about to go wrong. The Great Swan cast an eye toward the mountain and shook her powerful neck to shake the feeling, but it pervaded her senses, and a dread overtook her.

Losha shook the water from her wings to take flight in haste. Just as she flapped her wings, her webbed feet skimming the surface of the river as she lifted into the air, a river snake lunged through the water at her. And she tumbled back into the water with a splash.

Mefakani nodded to Cranik and spoke to the crowd. "There are things I must tell you first." He drew in a deep breath and braced himself. He flashed the mirror again. "It concerns your Ka." He touched the spot in the center of his chest as if the act could ease the ache in his heart. "As everyone knows, I took a piece of everyone's Ka. But I want you to know that I did not just take them. I stole them! And I stored a sliver of everyone's Ka in my private cavern. Now, I wish to return them to you."

"What do you mean?" Kulo called out.

"It means I will return a piece of your soul to you, a piece of your life force, your power and free will. It was not my right to take it in the first place, nor was it my right to control you in any way. You will be free of me."

"But then witchcraft could break out on the island again. You collected our Ka to prevent that!" someone shouted.

"Tai. You helped restore the order. Now the order will be broken!" someone else said in agreement.

The crowd began to stir and a voice rang out. "What do you mean, 'free of you'? Are you not here to teach us and prophesize?"

Mefakani shook his head. "Believe me, I am not worthy of teaching you."

Ikus pulled Kulo aside and drew his mouth close to the other's ear. "That is because he is not the True Teacher! I knew it! And now he is going to trick us somehow. Just wait!"

"You cannot just abandon us now!" a woman shouted.

Mefakani found the woman's face in the crowd. "From now on you will have to take full responsibility for your every thought and every action. Jabal and others will be taught to reattach the bit of Ka I have stolen from you."

"Jabal? Your First Apprentice?"

"Tai."

Ikus yanked Kulo's shoulder down toward him and whispered harshly. "You said Jabal acted as a spy for us and claims to be an Unbeliever. You told me he was the secret Informer that Sahdon was working with. But what if he and Mefakani have planned something else? What if Jabal and the Priest plan to do something else to us under the ruse of reattaching our Kas? What if Jabal actually murdered the Senior Elder!"

Kulo stared at Ikus, finding himself unable to speak.

"And you?" someone shouted from the crowd. "If you will not teach us, what will you do?"

"I must leave you," he said. He moved the black mirror back and forth again to catch the light, signaling for Losha to get ready to make her dramatic appearance.

The crowd grew anxious. "Why?" they asked in unison.

Mefakani's heart started racing, and he began to sweat, the weight of his secret yearning to burst free. "As I said before, I am not worthy." He flashed the mirror again. Then he held his hand up to quiet the crowd while scanning the sky for a sight of the great white swan. "Because..." He held his breath for a heartbeat. "I am not the True Prophet!" At last the words were spoken and Mefakani breathed a sigh of relief.

Ikus glared at Kulo, then at Mefakani angrily. "What are you saying?"

Knowing Losha would appear soon, Mefakani unwrapped the cloth from around his head to reveal the wound had healed.

Kulo, who was standing to the right of the Priest, scrutinized the wound and spoke loud enough for all to hear. "That does not mean you are not the True Prophet. The prophecy said the sacred mark upon the brow was a sign of the True Prophet. It did not say the scar would never heal."

Mefakani shook his head. "You do not understand. I know I am not the True Prophet."

A hush came over the crowd and a great wave of fear fell over them like dark settling smoke.

"You must be wrong!" Cranik said. "You killed the Wizard! And you said you were the Rightful Teacher!"

Mefakani fixed his eye on Cranik. "I know," he started, "because I fooled you into thinking I was. I had to in order to gain your trust...so I could deal with Temple in my own way."

Cranik's jaw tightened. He and Elder Ikus moved toward the Priest, but Kulo held them both back.

"Say this is not true!" Cranik shouted.

The crowd grew noisy. Elder Kulo held up his arms to quiet them. When he looked at the Priest and spoke, his voice called for reason and clarity. "You lied to us so you could kill the White Wizard, is that not so?"

Tiny rivulets of sweat began to streak down Mefakani's tattooed face, and the silence grew thick with anticipation. He looked to the skies, but Losha had not yet appeared.

Kulo was close enough to see Mefakani sweat, and watched as the Priest took a deep power breath. He drew Mefakani's eye. "If you knew Temple Fox was an impostor, why did you not join us in the Council?"

Mefakani searched the empty sky. He wiped his brow, pausing a moment to think of how to talk around the question and stall Kulo.

"Each of you," the Priest shouted to the Rebels, "is of Divine origin! And each of you has the potential to be a man-god…to prophesize…to teach…to heal, and to love without reward. It is your true destiny. That is why I must return your Ka to you and ask forgiveness for having taken it."

Kulo shot a worried glance at Cranik and Ikus.

Ikus squinted at the Priest and called out. "You did not answer his question."

The Shaman continued to preach more forcefully, ignoring the Elders.

Ikus realized he had lost control over the discussion. He pulled Cranik aside and out of Kulo's earshot while keeping a watchful eye on the Priest. "Listen to him!" he whispered. "He sounds like Temple Fox when Temple preached to the Councils. He is possessed, I tell you!"

Cranik's jaw fell open. "Possessed?" he whispered, his eyes bold with terror.

"Kulo and I heard Temple's spirit in the swamps."

"You went to the swamps?" Cranik asked.

"Tai, I needed to see the body myself. And now I see by this fine performance that Temple Fox has possessed the Priest! Listen to all this talk about trusting the power of love, and surrendering your personal will to Divine Will. I tell you, Temple Fox is talking through him! Mefakani is possessed by the dead Wizard!"

"Bi kana lo!" Cranik said, shaken.

Ikus leaned closer. "Do not trust anything he says. This moving confession about stealing our Ka is a ruse! He has something else planned. I am sure of it! If he returns our Ka to us, what do you suppose will happen?" Cranik hesitated for a moment, waiting for Ikus to give him the answer. "Witchcraft, Cranik! Witchcraft will break out on the island as it once did years ago. He will drive us into chaos! We will be warring with one another, only we will not be doing it with swords and spears. It will be a war of curses and spells."

Cranik stole a quick, nervous glance at the Priest. "So what do we do now?"

"Do not bend to his demands," Ikus whispered. "Do not consent to having your Ka returned. There is some trickery behind it."

Ikus looked over at Kulo, who was still listening to the Shaman intently. "We need to warn Kulo," Ikus said. "But listen to Mefakani? There is no way to stop him."

"Master, I will follow you to the ends of the earth," one soldier said. "You have taught me discipline, and have helped me to train my mind. You are too humble. Please let there be no more talk about how you are not the True Teacher."

"I am not," Mefakani said. He scanned the vast sky again to see if he could spot the Swan. Seeing nothing, a deep dread fell over him, and he sensed that all connection to the Divine had been broken.

Thrown off balance, he stopped his discourse for a moment to try and raise his vibration, but the thought that harm might have come to Losha began to gnaw at the edges of his mind.

He wondered what to say next, when his guilt and shame pulled at him, causing him to lose even greater focus. "There is more I wish to confess," he suddenly blurted out, and Elders Cranik and Ikus turned their heads to listen.

Mefakani forced himself to speak with as little passion as he could muster so he could get through his confession. "I am not only able to take a portion of your Ka. I am able to take more of your Ka if I choose to. I can extract the most vital component of your life force and your will power." He stopped and looked into the eyes of the Unbelievers to glean what he could from them. "It is the most advanced form of Makolese magic ever performed, and I alone possess the knowledge of how to do this." The Shaman took a deep breath, glad to have gotten this far in his confession. "I want you to know what I have done, and how I have wronged you."

"He is crazy!" Cranik hissed between clenched teeth.

"See!" Ikus said. "This is a trick! He is practically admitting to us what he plans to do to us when he pretends to give our Ka back!"

"Shhh!" Kulo warned.

Ikus moved behind Kulo and whispered in his ear. "Fool! He will pretend to give us back our Ka so he can take it all!"

Mefakani called for his servant boy, and the crowd waited restlessly until Tiv climbed to the podium of flat rock. The Shaman positioned the boy in front of him and took him gently by the shoulders. The Rebels stared hard at the boy, giving Tiv all of their focused attention.

Mefakani began slowly, but the sad confession tumbled out all the same. "Tiv was my First Apprentice…and a very gifted one. He would have made a great Shaman, even a High Shaman someday. But I felt he was getting too... too ambitious. I… I." Mefakani glanced up into the empty sky, and his words jumped out of his mouth without any forethought. "I was scared," he confessed. "I thought Tiv might try to use his powers to overthrow me as your High Shaman. So I lured him into my private cave for a special rite of passage. I…I used him in an experiment to perfect my means to create a more obedient servant…a…a slave."

The word "slave" hung in the mountain air like a spectre from the past, causing a chill to run up Mefakani's spine, but he was not alone. He scanned the sea of frozen faces.

"He is mute now." Mefakani's voice suddenly lost its power. "That is because the experiment went horribly wrong. I damaged his brain. He does not have the ability to remember because I drugged him."

He scoured the empty skies with his eyes, knowing something had gone horribly wrong. There was no Swan.

The Rebels listened without comment or criticism, immobilized by shock and a need to hear more.

"After I drugged him, I took his will power. I took his free will and then – " Mefakani's voice cracked and he stopped, his mind reeling from the memory of what he had done.

The people waited in anticipation. No one spoke a word. Kulo didn't interrupt either, but studied the Priest's every nuance as he listened to Mefakani spill out his confession.

Mefakani began to sweat more profusely and to visibly shake. "I am a High Shaman! A Warrior Priest! I have battled Lord Tagheetu and the Outsiders! I have fought Demon Spirits and defeated them all! But this war within me has made me feel so helpless! So out of control!"

He wrapped the cloak around himself more tightly to control his shaking, but he trembled so violently that Tiv turned to him, placing a consoling hand on the Master's shoulder. Yet this simple act of compassion caused Mefakani to come undone. He wept.

The crowd became one body, one mind in shock, as they watched the man who they believed to be their Prophet fold up into himself. Panicked whispers filled the air.

The Priest's confession had consequences so dire it strained the Rebels' imagination and all credulity. They hushed one another as they strained to hear Mefakani's confession. Only those close to him could hear his story as it came out in uncontrollable sobs. He described what he had done to Tiv, giving no reasons or excuses. Those who could hear the story whispered to those who couldn't, and the story was passed on in fragments. The Scribe's brush moved in quick strokes. As soon as a scroll was finished it was whisked away, still wet, for the people in the back to read.

Mefakani gained some composure, but his voice had weakened further. He sat on the edge of the platform, his head hanging low.

"I participated in the same ceremony with my own Master. I was only twelve. Master Tagon gave me a potion to drink." The telling made his tongue come alive with the memory of its taste – sticky sweet. "I had little memory of what happened afterward…but…but my body held a memory…a horrible memory…no boy should have," he stuttered. "I thought the rite had been sanctioned by Lord Tagheetu as the principle act that would allow me to become a Shaman and Priest, servant to both Master Tagon and Lord Tagheetu. It was so utterly perverse. I know this now because I have been reborn in the Light."

The three Elders looked to one another for help, but remained speechless except for Ikus, who grabbed Kulo's shoulders from behind.

"Kulo, listen! He is possessed!" he whispered. "He speaks too much like Temple Fox!"

Kulo spoke over his shoulder. "Then why is he confessing these horrible acts?"

Ikus didn't have an answer. He couldn't find a reason for this sudden confession.

One woman spoke up and broke the silence. She addressed the Priest in the familiar.

"Mefakani," she shouted, "you are not alone."

The Priest raised his head, and looked out into the crowd to find the voice.

"Like you," she began, "my Father was killed and my Mother taken by the Slavers. Master Tagon made certain many orphans would not feel abandoned…especially the girls. He used to take us into his lodge – *alone*," she emphasized. "I know because I was one of them." She paused briefly to allow her thoughts to catch up with her feelings. "I was no initiate for the Priesthood. I was only a little girl…without parents, without my aunts and uncles. Those who did take care of me were still traumatized by the massacre. Everyone," she said, glancing around her, "lost someone in the massacre."

Mefakani managed to speak. "You, too, then?" he asked.

"Tai," she answered, "only it was done without ritual or ceremony." She looked the Shaman in the eye. It was time to end her shame and let the hidden truths be boldly exposed. "At the time, I dared not question the authority of the High Priest," she added sharply.

Mefakani's heart was moved, and though the comment stung, he understood her pain. He told Tiv to leave the podium, to go to the woman who had spoken, and as the boy made his way through the crowd another voice rang out. The voice was that of an older woman.

"Tai," she said, "I experienced the same. Tagon had his way with me as well, and I carried his baby."

There was a gasp heard on the clifftop, and a muttering within the crowd.

"I told Elder Tani," she said.

The Elders looked to one another, and then to Mefakani.

"She never reported this to the Elder Council," Cranik replied.

"I do not know if she did or not," the woman said. "But I do know that High Shaman Tagon died soon afterward."

Mefakani raised an eyebrow, remembering that his master had died in his sleep. *Poison?*

A man called out so all could hear. "It sounds like Elder Tani took care of the problem herself."

Cranik bristled at hearing Tani's name. "She still should have told the other Elders," he said.

"And who would have challenged the authority of a High Priest with such accusations?" the woman shouted back. "*You?*"

★　　★　　★　　★　　★　　★

Temple's sharp sense of hearing caught a familiar cry above his head before the others detected the sound. He shaded his eyes and scanned the sky. A smear of white with a thin darker spot below it appeared and started to circle high above him.

The form sailed lower, and it became apparent to everyone that a magnificent white Swan flew overhead. And as she flew closer, her wings making a raspy noise, the soldiers could see that the feathers of the beautiful Swan were bloodied and that she carried a dead snake in her beak.

Temple pointed. "Behold!" he shouted.

As Losha swooped down, she dropped the snake at Temple's feet and let out a trumpeting cry, then rose high into the air again toward the clifftop.

Temple waved to her, then set his gaze upon the dead snake at his feet.

"This must certainly be a sign – an omen of some kind. But what does it mean?"

A sense of foreboding crept over Temple as Losha disappeared from his view, and tremulous pain clutched at his intestines.

★　　★　　★　　★　　★　　★

Mefakani felt the conversation float around him, and he withdrew into his private mind, detaching from his former self, yet not fully present with the new identity he was forging. In truth, it felt as if the Rebels were talking about someone else, someone he hardly knew.

"The only person who had the power to punish or execute someone was the Queen," the woman shouted. "But she was only a child. Elder Tani must have done what she did very quietly, and at risk of being accused of witchcraft!" She aimed this last comment at Mefakani, which brought the argument fully back to him, for only days before he had accused Tani of both witchcraft and blasphemy, both punishable by death.

All eyes turned back onto the Priest.

Someone deep within the crowd spoke out. "Too bad Tani did not kill Mefakani! That is if she knew about his hideous crimes!"

The Priest stood up and addressed the crowd with his voice gaining power as he spoke. "Few," he started, "are brave enough to question authority, be it the Queen's authority, our Elders', or a High Shaman's. But you all did just that when I represented Temple Fox in the Council. You had a right to confront me then, as you do now. I have committed crimes against you all, and willingly accept the punishment of exile." He opened his arms wide. "I will do to myself what I have wrongly done to Winyon, the Chokahpeiyape, and her English husband, Captain Kneller. I confess I murdered the Captain with my own hands. Both are innocent of the crimes I accused them of. Winyon Kneller is not a witch, and never was!"

His heart was bounding out of his chest.

"Murderer! Why should we allow *you* to decide your own fate?' a Rebel shouted. "Exile? I say, death!"

"Tai, we should kill you now!"

"But he has confessed his crimes and shows great remorse," a young woman said.

"Tai, and he saved us from the impostor," said another.

"It does not negate what he has done," said a Rebel, and an argument broke out among the people.

"But he killed the Wizard and saved us from…"

"I DID NOT!" Mefakani screamed above the fracas.

The people stopped and stared at him in shock.

"I DID NOT KILL TEMPLE FOX!!" he yelled, shaking his fist in the air. "I tricked you! I wanted Temple Fox for myself! Do you not see that!? I wanted the power of the True Teacher for my own! And that is what I did! I took his Ka, and took his power to magnify my own!"

Ikus stepped back from the podium to distance himself from Mefakani. "I knew it!" he shouted, pointing to the Priest. "You are more than possessed! You and the Wizard are one!"

Mefakani fastened his eye on the Elder, but Ikus was deaf to the Priest's self-pity and miserable plea for retribution, begging almost to be put down like a wounded animal. Ikus only saw the fire in Mefakani's eyes, and the fire was threatening.

"I cannot explain who I am anymore," Mefakani confessed. "I do not know. I only know that I died while trying to take Temple's Ka! When I died, I saw the Light! I saw my life over again! And the Creator gave me another chance to complete myself! To make amends!"

"You took Temple's power, but you did not kill him?" Cranik howled in anguish. "You did not kill the Wizard?"

Mefakani took a step toward Cranik, and the Elder moved back in defense. "That was Sahdon's body that you saw."

"I knew it! I knew it!" Ikus said.

"Sahdon got himself killed!" Mefakani explained.

"Then where is the White Wizard?" Cranik shouted.

"*He is not a Wizard!*" Mefakani shrieked, losing total control. "I told you that from the start! I took his power and it changed me! Can you not *see* that?" he pleaded.

A wave of terror fell over the Rebels like a tsunami. The Elders fell into one another as they backed away from the podium, and the crowd shoved against one another to retreat.

"I have been embraced by Divine Love!" Mefakani cried out, his voice growing hoarse. "I was reborn in the Light! I was not judged! I was accepted for who I am, and was given reprieve to correct what I have done!"

The Rebel soldiers in the rear pushed forward through the crowd, but Ijebu and Mumbula remained steadfast on either side of the podium beside the Priest.

"It is a supreme privilege to be given life in physical form! And I have been returned in this same lifetime to make amends – only my crimes are many!"

Cranik grabbed a shield. "Ijebu! Mumbula! Quick!" he yelled, and gestured for the two to back away. The two Warriors turned their head to acknowledge the Elder, then gazed up at their Master to wait for his command. The Shaman said nothing, and the two did not move.

Ikus crouched behind Cranik's shield. "They have turned against us!" he said to Cranik. "They have been enslaved like the boy. Quick! We must get to Kulo!"

"If Temple Fox is alive, as you say, where is he now?" Cranik shouted over the maelstrom.

"He is with Palomei's troops below," Mefakani answered. "He is convincing them to lay down their arms. Losha Ninti has already persuaded the Queen to withdraw her troops to spare your lives, and grant you safe passage. And there is more. It involves Losha. People, listen!" He raisied his arms and shouted full force. "You must understand that Losha, the Queen's Interpreter, is also the…"

Ikus interrupted with hysterical shouting. "Troops withdrawn! Are you crazy!" He turned to address the people. "Their troops have not withdrawn! It is just another trap!"

Ikus and Cranik pulled Kulo behind the shield. They shouted to the others to gather their weapons and create a wall for defense. The mob pulled some of the rocks down from the wall they had built on the cliffside to arm themselves against the crazy Priest.

Mefakani ordered Ijebu and Mumbula to kill no one, but to make ready with their shields to protect themselves. He held his arms out wide in surrender. "Kill me if you want to, but do not kill your own people! Please wait for Losha. Losha is…"

Cranik gave the first command. *"Now!"* The first volley of gaffs, rocks, and lightning spears were thrown.

Mefakani saw the lightning spears flying and could have repelled a couple, even though he vowed to never use his magic again. But there were too many thrown from different angles. Death was welcomed, but death by electrocution was not. Out of instinct, he jumped behind the plinth of stones. Sparks flew all around him, and his cloak caught on fire. He leaped onto the airboat, but the flames engulfed him, and he fell against the steering rod. The anti-gravity mechanism engaged, and the airboat lifted off the ground at an awkward tilt.

Mefakani screamed as the flames rose around his face, at first singeing his eyebrows and hair, then searing one side of his face. His hand was burnt raw when he finally ripped his cloak off, but his barkcloth skirt had caught fire. He rolled back and forth to smother the flames, and the airboat wobbled in response. Pushing past his agony, he grabbed the steering pole. The airship rose higher with a sudden lurch and veered sharply to the right. Mefakani cried out in torment as he pulled himself up onto his knees to gain control of the stabilizer.

There was a second volley and the sound of stone hitting metal.

Mefakani's head snapped back, and he fell against the seat. Seized by a new, sharper pain, he lost his grip, and the airboat listed to the port side. He toppled sideways, and clawed the air blindly. His left leg fell through a crossed length of bamboo, wedged tight, and snapped in two, trapping him there. The pain was past his bearing. To ease the pressure from his broken leg, he grabbed another section of the bamboo framework with his burnt hand, until he could throw his right leg over another beam. He slid into a better position, and the airboat ascended higher, but too fast, and wobbled out of control.

More stones pelted the metal and bamboo frame. Shattered fragments filled the air. Mefakani's vision cleared for a moment, and he spotted an eyeball, strangely familiar in the changing light, swirl like an egg yolk in a bowl, then slip off the edge of the platform into the smoky air. And as his good eye watched it disappear into the mob below, he spied a lone lightning spear arc into the air, its crystal point rushing closer into view. He held out his good arm as if to greet death, relieved that his pain would end soon, when the ship swayed too close to the mountain, and scraped its side, leaving a shock of sparks in its wake. The ship rolled, and the spear that was meant for him struck one of the crystal spheres instead. A flash of brilliant light filled his head. The electrical charge that raced through the ship leaped inside Mefakani's right hand, and marked a ragged path through his body. Burnt from the inside out, unable to let go of the metal frame, he howled in anguish, convulsing uncontrollably, until the charge shot out of his right foot.

The remains of the ship flipped upright, and pitched sharply forward. It began to descend back and forth slowly like a falling leaf. As its final death dance, it rolled over in the air like a dog surrendering. And as it plummeted to the clifftop, Mefakani's flesh, melted now to the metal frame, pulled loose from its bone, allowing what was left of him to drop like a stone.

The Rebels watched the smoking figure fall from the sky. The body came crashing down off the cliff's edge onto a screw pine, snapping twigs, and smashing limbs of both tree and man, until the raw husk of the man hung from the branches upside-down like a bundle of burnt rags.

The Rebels had only seconds to run for cover as the airboat tumbled to the ground, splinter into fragments, and exploded with a thundering roar. Amid an avalanche of rock, the air filled with a scintillating display of rainbow light.

★   ★   ★   ★   ★   ★

High above the deafening explosion, a trumpeting sound resounded above the frightened mob. But no one heard the beautiful white Swan's plaintive cry, or saw her circle high above them. The shock wave threw her back into the sky. Her left wing scraped across the face of the mountain before she slammed into it, and fell to a shelf of rock – unconscious.

CHAPTER THIRTY-NINE

BURNT OFFERINGS

*"It was oblivion that he wanted now. Not peace,
but nothingness."*

Rebel Scribe
The Makolese Scroll on
The Return of the Ka and the Mending of the Su #39

Like butchered carrion hanging in a tree, Mefakani's lifeless body rocked to and fro when the shock wave hit him.

And something deep within him stirred.

Ash drifted to the ground, and shattered slivers of quartz crystal danced in the sunlight and showered down on the land, until the clifftop looked as if it were silvered in hoarfrost. So consumed by the sudden silence, and paradoxical beauty of the moment, the Rebels didn't notice Mefakani far below them when his body jerked alive. The vision in his good eye was blurred, but he could feel and see well enough to know that he was hanging upside down. Shifting his weight slightly, he turned his shattered hip, allowing his body to slide down the trunk, until he fell limp to the ground like a rag doll.

He was numb to the pain at impact, cold from the shock and the fire that had seared his nerves. Dizzy and nauseous, he struggled to breathe, wishing he would die. His breathing grew even shallower, and he was about to lose consciousness when the life forces of Ijebu, Mumbula, and Boran reinvigorated him, and his breathing eased. But he couldn't feel his legs anymore. He didn't quite know where he was either, but he could smell the smoke.

Smoke!...

Distant memories came to him in brief flashes. The sea appeared before him, waves pounding the shore rhythmically, musically. Then all at once the sea disappeared. The percussive pounding grew fainter, the only sound, the desperate beating of his heart. He felt the moist ground again against his cheek, and his senses leaned toward his heart pumping...pumping. And out of the corner of his good eye he watched his blood flow into thin rivulets on the ground, the miniature red stream turning blades of stock weed into trees, a rock into an island mountain. The blood reached its limits, and soaked into the ground before him, and the pounding grew louder in his ears. Pounding... pounding. The sound of pounding feet matched the pumping of his heart. The image of the sea returned, and with it Arab dhows rocked on the horizon. He heard people running, and babies screaming. Smoke filled the air. The images were disjointed at first, but he saw swords flashing.

Mefakani's mother pulled the young Mefakani by the arm through a thick curtain of smoke, past the burning Common House to a grove of banyans. She found the largest niche at the base of a tree, and quickly dug a hole in the sand. She tucked him into the niche, and ordered him to stay as she covered him up with debris. She left him there and ran. She ran! A sound came to him and caught his breath up short. Metal against metal. Swords clanging. Chains rattled madly to the rhythm of running feet. A spray of sand pelted the leaves that hid him as a shadow streaked past. He heard a dull thud, and a deep groan, and something being dragged over dry sand. The rattling of chains grew louder, and his heart leaped as he watched his mother being shackled at her feet and dragged down the beach. She fought furiously with her arms flailing until a second Slaver appeared, and the two chained her wrists together and dragged her off.

Mefakani tried to push through the hole as he once did forty years before when he had darted from his hiding place and ran after the men. He had to get to her, had to save her, but one arm was useless, and his legs wouldn't move. So he started crawling. He used his one good arm to pull the rest of him. Slithering through a cluster of dianella, as he once did as a snake, he made his way past small burning heaps of wreckage that lay scattered on the slope all around him. He dragged himself over embers and ash, choking on the air, oblivious to the burning debris, that was once his airship. He inched along beneath patches of stinkweed, powdered now with the sparkling dust, and found he had made his way up and over the lip of the cliff to the mouth of the mountain cave.

"Mama! Where are you!"

The screaming in his head stopped, and the images faded, and he didn't know where he was again. Moving out of pure instinct, he paused only once to look above him and noticed the sky had turned a milky white, which glistened. There was some kind of serenity there and hope, even eternity, he thought. But death came too hard. It was oblivion that he wanted now. Not peace, but nothingness. He looked down at the charred ground he had just traversed, a trail of blood littered with scraps of black scorched flesh, shimmering with the same starry substance as the sky. He listened to a voice within him that seemed to whisper about the brutal beauty of things, and he understood. And so he turned back toward his destination, not knowing what it might be, but knowing he must go. He crawled on his belly around the rough edge of the mammoth cave. And with his vision growing darker, and his strength waning, he slipped into one of the seven tunnels to the world below to find his nothingness.

CHAPTER FORTY

THE BLIND

*"Believe what is false, and that is blindness.
Refuse to accept what is true, and that is also
blindness."*

Elder Kulo Kempok
The Makolese Scroll on
The Return of the Ka and the Mending of the Su #40

Palomei's startled army witnessed a flash of brilliant light fill the sky. Seconds later they heard a sharp clap like thunder, and a low rumble roll off the clifftop that shook the ground beneath them.

"Losha!" Temple shouted, but his voice was lost in the muffled roar.

The army scattered, and Temple dived for cover behind a stone overhang. The boulders marked their descent with the sound of crashing branches. He flattened himself against the stone wall as the deep grumble grew louder, and two boulders the size of small dugouts came thundering past him to the foothills below. An avalanche of debris followed, raining down on the encampment like hail.

Several minutes passed. The pelting of stone against leaves diminished, until there was a span of quiet. The only sounds that filled the encampment were the soft patter of heavy dust and the distant shout from a scout, who was posted on the mountain slope above. His voice echoed through the foothills. No one could understand what he was saying, until the scout scurried down the mountain slope, shouting to see the Teacher. The scout slipped, and fell the last few yards, jumped swiftly to his feet, and ran behind the shelf of rock where Temple had taken refuge. Caked in sparkling dust, he doubled over to catch his breath with his magnifier still clenched in his grasp.

"The airboat!" He coughed, and gasped. "I saw it rise back into the air, and then explode!"

"Was Mefakani in the airboat?" Temple asked.

"Yes! He was attacked!" the scout said.

"And the Swan! Did you see the Swan that flew overhead? Did you see what happened to her?"

The scout shook his head, and a cascade of fine powder clouded the air. "I did not see any swan. I was focused on the airboat, and momentarily blinded by the flash."

Temple left his small refuge as Palomei's soldiers gathered. "Is anyone hurt?" he asked. There was a quick assessment of casualties, but nothing serious was reported.

It took several minutes before the dust cleared. By then Temple's mind had also cleared. He looked above him and saw a column of white smoke rise from the clifftop, enshrouding the Rebel encampment. He ordered a courier to run to tell the Queen what had happened.

★　★　★　★　★　★

When the wind had thinned the smoke and ash, two Rebel soldiers gathered at the tree where they had seen the imposter fall. But Mefakani's body was gone! They moved to the edge of the cliff by the tree, and strained their eyes below. One body was caught on a thin ledge of stone. Two more were snagged on the scattering of trees that twisted up through the steep cliffside rock. They were too far away to identify, so the men gathered some ropes to lower a soldier down.

The rubble tumbled from Elder Cranik's back as he rolled over and looked around him. The mountain cave had a huge chunk missing from it, like teeth broken in a gaping mouth and now snarling. And the earth all around the Elder was dotted with boulders that had not been there minutes before. The sight caused Cranik's blood to run cold. He craned his neck over one of the boulders, afraid of what he might find, and spied a figure sprawled on the ground. Rising slowly to his feet, he inched forward, still shaking, the shock of everything that had just happened causing his head to spin. He grabbed hold of a broken boulder, and leaned on it to steady himself. Before him lay the twisted bodies of Ijebu and Mumbula, hardly recognizable in the wreckage and sharp debris. A sudden movement caught his eye, and his heart jumped. What appeared to be a pile of earth moved, and old Ikus drew himself up on all fours, coughing, and spitting out blood, a huge slab of sharp rock that had impaled the earth just a foot from his side.

Cranik came to his senses. He dusted himself off, and called out, "Are you all right?"

"No! I am not!" Ikus sputtered and spit out a broken tooth. "There is something in my eyes." The crooked man stood up in a pall of glittering grime.

"We need to find Kulo," Cranik said, noticing he couldn't even hear himself because of the deafening ringing in his ears.

Ikus kept blinking, but managed to open his eyes. "Bi kana lo! I cannot see!" he managed to cough out.

"What?" Cranik asked. He shook his head, and wagged a finger in each of his ears. "My ears are still ringing from the blast."

"I am blind!" Ikus said, blinking furiously.

"I cannot hear a thing until that confounded noise stops!" Cranik said.

"I said, I AM BLIND!" Ikus shouted.

Cranik watched Ikus' mouth move, but heard no sound, only a thunderous ringing in his ears. "Let us move away from the noise and see if we can find Kulo," he said, and started to walk away.

"There is no noise! I said, I am blind, you whale anus!"

Cranik spotted Kulo in the distance and strode over to him. "There he is," he said.

Ikus could hear Cranik's voice, and the gritty sound of his footfall fading away.

"Where are you going you idiot? I cannot see! Help me," Ikus cried.

Kulo's flesh was powdered pale as the moon. He had a few scrapes on his body, but they were minor.

"Kulo, are you all right?" Cranik asked.

"Tai, I am all right," he said, "but there are many people wounded. Where is Ikus?" he asked in a sudden panic.

Cranik watched Kulo's mouth move, and he began to understand.

"I said, where is Ikus?" Kulo asked again, his alarm mounting.

"Can you hear me?" Cranik asked. He saw the Elder nod. "Bi kana lo!" he said, cupping both his ears. "I think I am deaf!"

A short distance away a deep gravely mumble turned into a panicked cry. "Will someone please answer me? Where has everybody gone?" Ikus wailed.

When Kulo heard Ikus' voice he beckoned one of the women to attend Cranik. He stepped over newly broken boulders and debris, and lumbered toward Ikus. He gathered the frail man up into his huge arms. "I thought I had lost you!"

Ikus' face was hidden under his quivering hands. "I am blind, Kulo! Blind!" he sobbed.

Seeing that Ikus was not suffering from any broken bones, Kulo placed his arm around the old man's thin shoulders, and walked him back to where the others were gathering. "It is not your fault," Kulo said. "If we had listened to you to begin with we might have seen that Mefakani was an impostor from the start. If anyone is blind it is us."

"No! No!" Ikus cried again. "I am blind! *Really* blind!"

Kulo patted him reassuringly, and a little white cloud of quartz dust rose from his shoulders into the chalky air. "Now, now, there is no need to place the blame solely on yourself. We are all equally responsible."

"No, you pile of crocodile dung! My eyes! My eyes!" Ikus screamed. "I CANNOT SEE!" The wiry figure shook as he swung at Kulo blindly.

Kulo backed away, and caught the Elder's wrists with his large hands.

"What is going on?" Cranik complained.

Kulo held the squirming figure, until the fight in Ikus was all played out. "He is blind," Kulo answered.

"What?" Cranik asked.

★   ★   ★   ★   ★   ★

Kulo sat in the glistening dirt watching the women tend to the wounded. Cranik sat opposite him on a boulder, dazed, expressionless. Elder Ikus leaned against the same boulder in the dust. Both of his eyes were bandaged. He moaned softly when Kulo explained that Mefakani had been blasted over the cliffside.

Cranik looked over at Kulo. "We will have to reorganize as swiftly as possible, and go down and fight Temple and his army," he said. "There is no other way."

Kulo looked back at Cranik and shook his head. "This is no time to simply react to what has happened. We have the wounded to think about. We need time to think this thing through."

Cranik's voice was edged with the acid of his physical pain, anger, and bitterness. "You know I cannot hear you, but it does not matter what you are saying. I am telling you to reorganize everyone and get them ready to battle Temple's men. We will never surrender!"

Kulo's nostrils flared. He stood up to his full height, towering over Cranik. "I will not listen to you anymore," he began. "It was you and Sahdon who drew us deeper into this mess! If you had listened to Ikus from the start we would not have made such a hasty decision to declare a truce, and allow Mefakani to take Temple!" Kulo's voice grew louder, and his spit flew in all directions.

"And if Sahdon had any brains he would have had Ikus come to the tunnels and have left me up here! Then Ikus" – he pointed – "could have taken over as leader instead of *you*! But, no! You took over! And you had me come and sit with you for days on the hard, cold ground, until I was so pained I could not think straight when Mefakani came out, and *you insisted* to go in *alone* to inspect the body!"

Cranik looked over at Ikus, worried that Kulo had lost his mind. "What is he shouting about?" he asked Ikus.

Ikus turned his bandaged head in Cranik's direction. He pointed to Cranik's head, and left a small space between his index finger and thumb. He knew Cranik couldn't hear him, but spoke anyway. "He is saying you have brains the size of a plum pit."

Cranik glared back.

"You are right, my friend," Ikus said to Kulo. "We need time to think this one out. But Cranik is also right, too. We must not surrender."

Kulo stood his ground. "No one is talking about surrendering. Surrendering only means a quick death. But not surrendering means a slow death by starvation, unless the gods show us some favor, and give us a miracle."

Cranik looked at the other two, his eyes full of loathing. "What we need to do is find Mefakani, and take his head! Do it like our ancestors have always done. We could use some of Mefakani's power now." He looked all around him. "Get the body!" he ordered.

Kulo shook his head, too remiss to explain that all the bodies hadn't been retrieved yet. He sat back down in the dirt, and turned his back on Cranik.

Tiv, who had been sitting a few yards away listening to the conversation, stepped forward, and bowed to the Elders.

"Go away, boy!" Cranik growled.

"Who is there?" Ikus asked.

"It is Tiv," Kulo answered. "This is talk for Elders, boy. Go and help the women."

Tiv shook his head and wouldn't leave. Though he couldn't speak, he could hear. Kulo watched with fascination at how easily the boy conveyed what he had overheard from the Elder's conversation by gesticulating to Cranik.

Cranik was excited that he could communicate with someone. "So you know where Mefakani's body fell over the cliff?" he asked the boy.

Tiv nodded, and motioned for the Elders to follow him.

Curious now, Kulo took Ikus by the arm, and the four walked around cracked boulders down the trail to the broken screw pine. Tiv squatted at the base of the tree, and pointed to a pool of blood. He hopped a few paces away from the tree to where another few drops of blood were smeared on a flat stone.

Cranik leaned down for closer inspection, his eyesight his only means to gather information now. The plants had since been flattened, but Tiv turned back some leaves, revealing scraps of burnt flesh, some which had faint traces of tattoos. Tiv got down on all fours. As he crawled through the blue clusters of dianella flowers he discovered a clearly marked trail of burnt flesh and blood.

Cranik looked up at Kulo, and raised an eyebrow.

"Does anyone care to tell me what is going on?" Ikus asked, annoyed.

Kulo called for the trained Warriors to gather. While Ikus listened to the sound of footsteps, someone grabbed his arm, and led him through some foliage. Leaves slapped against his ankles, until he was led to a cluster of stinkweed, over rockier terrain littered with metal debris. Ikus stumbled a few times trying to keep up with his companions as they followed the trail like a pack of wild dogs tracking a wounded deer. Then the guiding hand pulled him back sharply, and Ikus heard their voices rebound off the cave walls. When he understood that the trail led to the fourth tunnel inside Hollow Mountain, he agreed with the others, and Kulo ordered the tunnel to be sealed.

CHAPTER FORTY-ONE

THE BAT SHAMAN

"Where is Death?
When will its sharp blade draw the last of my life
out of me?"

High Shaman Mefakani
The Makolese Scroll on
The Return of the Ka and the Mending of the Su #41

With the order of the encampment quickly delegated to others it didn't take Temple long for him to spin into an Owl to find his beloved. The soldiers watched with awe as the god-man spun his magic, transformed in a brilliant burst of golden light into the magnificent bird. And as he flew toward the Rebels' clifftop refuge, his only thoughts were on Losha.

His heightened sense of sight and hearing proved his greatest assets as he scanned every rock ledge and tree, every cliff face and form below him far beyond the Rebels' range of sight. It took only a minute or two before he spotted Losha, her limp white form draped precariously on a thin shelf of rock, her bloodied feathers ruffling in the wind. His heart skipped a beat and he let out a panicked cry. Swooping down for a closer look, he passed over her once, twice, three times to inspect her body, anticipating the worst, postponing anymore horror he was certain he would be unable to endure. His heartbeat eased when he noticed that she was breathing.

With one strong beat of his wings, he banked to the south, sailed low, and landed lightly by her side. He used just the right amount of pressure with his talons to feel her spine, her neck, and then her wings.

Nothing is broken. But her spine is out of alignment.

Temple used the flat of his feet to press each vertebra back into place. And there he sat in vigilance with only brief excursions to forage for healing mosses and minerals to bind her wounds and lessen her pain. Using his Owl instinct and his human knowledge, he returned with the right elements, mixed them with his saliva to make a poultice and pressed the kumbab to her wounds.

A day passed. Night fell. Temple's Owl eyes scrutinized every twitch Losha made, every beat of her pulse, every quiver she made as her bloody wound congealed and her breathing strengthened.

Temple regurgitated a masticated mouse he had found by happenstance as Losha roused out of her reverie. He was about to feed her when her eyes opened and locked onto his.

Do you think you could find something less atrocious than a chewed-up mouse, like fresh algae or a bug or two? she conveyed with her mind.

Temple answered with a shriek of happiness and nudged her neck affectionately.

My little pigeon, I thought I had lost you, he said telepathically.

Losha's serpentine neck grazed against the sides of Temple's feathery head and she gave him a weak peck. She raised a wing to feel for any damage, managing the pain with a breathy grunt then rearranged her wing feathers with her beak. When she started to groom herself, Temple knew that she was on the mend.

Mefakani pulled himself along with his good arm and let the rest of him drop like a wet rag to each tread on the stone stair, the rough-hewn rock cutting him, driving him deeper into misery. The lower he descended into the caverns, the deeper the pain penetrated his damaged nerves, tissue and bone. For Mefakani, oblivion was hope. Numbness, salvation. And any notion of a greater peace had become nothing more than the absence of pain.

Where has the Great Light gone that had once embraced me, spoken to me, given me life again?

Mefakani could barely think past the harrowing pain, but in his delirium he could curse and plead and pray, and, escaping death with another breath, curse again and start the cycle of misery over once more.

Where is Death? When will its sharp blade draw the last of my life out of me?

He fell the last few steps and rolled to the bottom of the stairs to the cold stone ground.

The Bats, long since stirred up by his presence, danced in the musky air above him, wondering what creature he might be.

Face melted into black-and-red buckled flesh, with only the bone of his nose remaining, gave Mefakani a batlike appearance. The news that a shamanic initiate wished to become a bat-shaman was spread swiftly with a series of high frequency squeaks, and the other bats quickly gathered in great numbers. Mefakani was now a brother and was to be treated as such. So the bats took turns feeding him blood to replace the blood he had lost by regurgitating food and placing it inside his mouth. By doing this with great diligence and patience, they all kept him alive...and in anguish.

CHAPTER FORTY-TWO

PRAYING FOR A REVELATION

*"Just as there are vague fissures in a peaceful soul
that allow the black, sticky tar of hate to seep
through, there are cracks in a warring soul so the
light of love passes through."*

Elder Kulo Kempok
The Makolese Scroll on
The Return of the Ka and the Mending of the Su #42

Powdered with chalky rock and crystal dust, the Rebels moved like pale ghosts on the cliff of Hollow Mountain. They removed the rock that had crushed Ijebu and Mumbula, wrapped their bodies in barkcloth and placed them out of the hot sun inside the cave. Others meandered to and fro bandaging the wounded, sifting water through clean baskets, reconstructing the defensive wall and counting their stores of food.

Ikus was attended by two women and bore his pain with the traditional Makolese stoicism, while Cranik walked around, numbly mystified by his surroundings, barking orders at people who largely ignored him.

Kulo sat alone on the bough of a broken tree far apart from the others, watching the Rebels work like ants. His back was bent in pain, his mind overburdened with worry. He was about to lift a water gourd to his lips when he spotted a praying mantis on the end of it. The insect reared back with its forelegs, wings spread and jaws opened, ready to boldly strike out at his mammoth adversary in defense.

The Elder placed the gourd down. The creature inched its way onto the log beside him and began its mesmerizing sway, rocking side-to-side, keeping all its eyes on the old man. Kulo watched with fascination in total stillness for several minutes until the mantis began washing its head and bulbous eyes from the white powder it, too, was covered in.

"Here, let me help you," Kulo said. He tipped a few drops of clean water from his gourd to make a puddle from which the creature could draw water.

The praying mantis dipped its spiky forelegs into the droplet and ran its legs along the length of its long antennae.

"Seems like you are the only one I can talk to now," Kulo whispered. "Cranik cannot hear what I hear now. And Ikus cannot see what I see now. Why do I listen to them?" he said in a distant tone. He spat a piece of grit from his teeth.

His most private thoughts pressed out into the open air, uncensored. "I have been such a coward I had to wait until Cranik was deaf before I told him what I really thought. And now it is up to me to lead. Are you listening?"

The praying mantis stopped grooming, cocked its triangular-shaped head and froze in place.

The old man bent over and patted his white wooly hair and watched a rain of crystal dust drift lightly to the ground. Rubbing his gnarled, arthritic hands together, he noticed his tattoos were no longer indigo, but powdered to a pale blue. No matter how many times he dusted himself off he couldn't rid himself of the ash that had turned his dusky brown skin to a sickly beige, leaving him more Caucasian in appearance than he could endure. He thought about Mefakani, the ghastly trail of charred flesh they had tracked, bits of identifiable tattoos scattered on the ground as if the man, Mefakani, was some kind of coherent text that had fallen apart glyph by glyph.

Remembering how Mefakani stood before the Rebels in bold resignation and surrender, professing in the last minutes of his life how he had stolen Temple's essential Ka, made Kulo stir uneasily.

And yet, stealing Temple's Ka transformed the Shaman, he thought.

Kulo knew. He had been close enough to witness the change that had overtaken Mefakani. Whatever happened in Mefakani's private cavern, it had completely undone the Priest. Of that Kulo had no doubt.

The words, "Temple Fox is, and has always been, the True Teacher," echoed in Kulo's ears like a temple bell. It was one of the last things Mefakani had proclaimed, knowing the proclamation could end his life.

The praying mantis resumed its grooming while Kulo sorted through the clutter of his mind, seeking clarity.

Mefakani said the same things Temple did when Temple taught in the Great Round House. Both have taught that we all hold the magnificent ability to love and be loved, to heal, to forgive, to prophesize, and, knowing our present, correct our past. We are to become co-creators in partnership with the greater part of ourselves, which is the Great Creator.

He spoke in a hoarse whisper. "Are we the Gods of our own destiny?"

As if to respond, the praying mantis ceased grooming and turned its head toward the muted sun to dry.

Kulo rubbed his head in thought. *Those are not the words of a usurper. Those are words that come from the white Wizard who stopped our own corrupt High Priest – a priest who had become our abuser and enslaver without us even realizing it. Temple did not even kill the Priest. Instead he transformed him out of what Mefakani described as mercy and compassion.*

Kulo looked behind him for a guilty moment, as if someone might overhear his thoughts as in the old days.

In the end, Mefakani confessed to stealing our power and left us all with a message for our self-empowerment.

The Elder breathed out a sigh of frustration. "I have been fooled before," he whispered with new doubt, remembering Mefakani's clever speech that convinced the renegades tthat he, the Shaman, was the True Teacher.

He looked out into the chalky sky with the sun trying to force its way through the clouds and dust. "How am I to know what is true and what is not?" he prayed.

All at once, a breeze stirred the air, and thin fragments of crystal were drawn into an updraft. A single finger of sunlight pried the clouds apart and a shaft of light filled with rainbows struck the tiny crystals, and they swirled and glistened in the air. They shimmered for one exquisite, nacreous moment, then landed lightly on a spiral symbol on the back of his hand. That ancient symbol defined who Kulo really was, a boundless, moving, dynamic spirit, one infinite spirit, inseparable from his native land, all people…even Temple Fox.

His secret thoughts had found their limits, when all at once the praying mantis snapped its mandibles shut. Kulo stared down at the mantis. In its jaws struggled a Makolese war-beetle.

"Bi kana lo! I did not see that coming!"

Suddenly, the trauma Kulo had lived through hours before on the remote mountain ledge, on an island surrounded by vast oceans, on a spinning planet surrounded by endless space, seemed small. He decided at that moment what he would do and he called for one of the Scribes to lend him her brush, ink, and a scrap of mulberry paper.

If I am willing to die on the roof of this world, I am willing to do this.

Elder Kulo watched the fragile flakes of quartz fall into the drying ink as he scribbled a short note. And when it had dried, he rolled it up into a tiny scroll. He bound the scroll and called for the Scribe again, demanding that she keep the scroll a secret until it was time to be delivered.

It didn't take long for the flies to find Mefakani. A great churning cloud formed around his body, and the echo of his cries rang out again and again against the rock walls, lost to human ears. The buzzing of flies and screeching of bats drove the Shaman deeper into madness as the bats feasted on the flies, and the flies feasted on Mefakani's dead flesh.

CHAPTER FORTY-THREE

FALLING INTO GRACE

*"If I am willing to die on the roof of this world, I
am willing to do this."*

Elder Kulo Kempok
The Makolese Scroll on
The Return of the Ka and the Mending of the Su #43

With every footfall, Elder Kulo's thighs tightened up and his knees began to ache. He had hiked in the twilight of early morning and had persevered without mishap, though the meandering trail was the widest and easiest at the onset. But he was hungry and thirsty now, and exhaustion chipped away at his resolve. Still, he was better than halfway to the Believers' encampment and didn't want to stop to rest.

The foliage thinned on the cliffside as the path narrowed. He slowed a few paces to look all around him. If any of Palomei's soldiers waited in ambush up ahead, he wouldn't be able to detect them, his attention so focused on his sandaled feet and the sheer drop to his left. He could only pray that when the Believers' army spotted him, they'd honor the white sash he wore, signifying a truce.

The path dropped steeply. Kulo took shorter steps to keep his balance and study the length of trail ahead that disappeared into sky, marking a lookout point and a sharp bend to the northwest where there would be little to hold onto but the mountainside itself. No great feat for a young man, but Kulo was eighty-eight and tired already. He groaned at what lay ahead, when his foot came down on a loose, uneven stone and his ankle turned awkwardly. He caught himself by balancing with his other foot, but his sandal slipped over some pebbles and he slid several feet. Reaching out to the mountainside, he caught a thick woody vine and hung there for a moment, listening to the small avalanche of stones that cascaded off the mountainside. His heart beat a ragged rhythm as he struggled to regain his balance.

With his foothold secured, Kulo steadied himself by pulling a vine into the crook of his arm. One by one he pulled splinters from his hand with his teeth and a dirty fingernail, all the while deciding about returning to the Rebel camp or not.

"I am risking my life to meet with the True Prophet," he whispered, "if he is, indeed, the True Prophet. If I am wrong about him, I will be killed anyway."

Kulo looked behind him at the trail littered with rough rock. He glanced over the ledge, sensing the distance below.

"Better to die on level ground among my friends than to fall off the mountain and have my bones scattered by birds," he muttered. "But I have come this far."

Every decision seemed to spell danger for Kulo, and seeing no better alternatives, he licked his salty wounds, dried them on his truce banner and, with no further thoughts to thwart his mission, continued his descent.

The worst of events can happen in a moment of distraction. Kulo's eyes strayed from his feet for a fraction of a second to roam the distant hills, when the lip of his sandal caught on the edge of a root and he fell helplessly forward. He threw his arms out to break his fall, but his chest hit first, and he slid down the pebbled slope toward the cliff's edge. Twisting his body slightly, he clutched onto an outcrop of rock, but his hold wasn't firm enough and, having slid sideways, he rolled down the path and over the cliff.

It happened so fast. Kulo felt the air rush all around him and saw the clean slab of vertical rock run past his vision. Pawing the air wildly, he grabbed at a mass of thin vines that ripped through his hands and managed to slow his descent, breaking his freefall. The large man hung there swaying for a frantic moment in the tangled web of greenery, his heart pounding dangerously harder, when suddenly the vines pulled loose and he fell again! To his shock, his feet struck a shelf of rock with a painful jolt. His legs buckled under him and he collapsed safely onto his backside with a dull thud.

Kulo sat panting, mystified that he was still alive, his hands stained green, still clutching the loosened vine, his body tangled in it like a fish caught in a net. His buttocks were sore and bruised, and the full length of his body was scraped and bleeding. And to add more trouble to his dilemma, the white truce banner he still wore was now scarlet and shredded, which would send no other message to the soldiers below but a call to war.

Kulo caught his breath and untangled himself from the vines. When he dared to look behind him, he began to shake. Six short steps away, on the rock ledge he had fallen onto, was open sky. The blood from Kulo's face drained, and he crept as close to the edge as his nerves would allow. He peered over. Below, lay the tops of trees, and a little distance beyond, he watched thin streams of smoke from the army's campfires rise into the late morning air.

Beyond the camp, below the soft distant foothills, a small lake loomed larger now and looked up at him like a huge eye. White fluffy clouds passed in its reflection, then slowly rippled in the wind as if the great eye was blinking up at him.

He backed away until his spine pressed against the warm cliffside and looked skyward where he had fallen. Plumb rock towered over him with not one cleft to use as a hand or foothold for climbing. And the edge of the cliff he had fallen from, which stood fifteen feet above him, seemed like a mile away.

CHAPTER FORTY-FOUR

THE WOUNDED

"Our plans had collapsed. While Losha needed time to repair her body, I needed time to empty my mind. I had to allow enough space to let the Divine step in. So, I rested and reentered my heart to replenish my spirit."

Temple Fox
The Makolese Scroll on
The Return of the Ka and the Mending of the Su #44

Come on, my little pigeon, Temple said encouragingly.

Temple nudged Losha to coax her to her feet and lifted her damaged wing with his head. The kumbab he had made her had worked its magic, and she was feeling little pain. But she was uncertain if she could fly and let her wing drop by her side. Annoyed by his persistent prodding, she struck out at Temple and gave him a quick bite. The Owl shrieked and, with no heed to her warning, lifted her wing again. This time Losha flapped her wings and thrust out her chest to push Temple away.

Temple cried out again, and Losha realized that she was well enough to escape the ledge. She nuzzled Temple, and with a literal and confident leap of faith, she jumped off the scarp.

Losha fell for several yards, until Temple came swooping beneath her to bear her weight and balance her. And together in tandem they flew together back to where Palomei's soldiers stood guard.

★　　★　　★　　★　　★　　★

It was mid-morning when Cranik pulled the strip of bark off the tiny scroll and unrolled it. "What is this?" he grumbled to the Scribe who had handed him the scroll.

The Scribe waited with a stick ready to write in the dirt as a way to communicate.

"What!" he said. "Where did he go?" Cranik asked.

The Scribe drew the sign for "no word spoken" in the dirt.

Ikus came to full alert while he listened. "Where did *who* go?" he asked.

Cranik handed Ikus the scroll absentmindedly. "Will you look at that?" he said.

"Look at *what*?" Ikus asked.

"Well, when did he leave?" Cranik asked the Scribe. The Elder looked at what the Scribe had written and turned to Ikus. "That stupid Kulo left here well before dawn. The Scribe does not know where, but Kulo said if he does not return in four days then we should consider him dead!"

"Bi kana, he has gone to negotiate with the Believers by himself! The fool! They will kill him!" Ikus said.

"What?" Cranik asked.

★　　★　　★　　★　　★　　★

Temple sat facing the mid-morning sun with his back to the soldiers and his beloved resting comfortably by his side. In the distance below, the hills blazed in hues of gold and green, and a veil of pale blue shadows pooled softly in the valleys. Southeast of the rapids, he gazed absentmindedly at the round lake, its sapphire blue surface ruffling in a quiet breeze, shimmering in the sun. He felt an energy approach behind him and drew his attention back from the far-off place he had been beckoned to in meditation.

"I beg your forgiveness for the interruption," the voice behind him said.

Temple turned his head to meet the soldier's eyes.

"One of our scouts just spotted a Rebel on the trail."

Temple spoke in a faraway tone. "Thank you, Asin. Yes, I know. It's one of the Elders – the tall, big-boned fellow, I believe."

"Tai," Asin answered. "His name is Kulo Kempok."

"I've been feeling his energy draw closer since this morning. I sense he is alone."

Asin nodded. "Tai. We do not know how he got there, but he sits on a narrow cliff just below the lookout point that leads to the most constricted part of the northwest trail. He wears a red war sash. I can show you in my magnifier if you like."

"Thank you, that won't be necessary," Temple replied. "I'll go to him myself – alone." He placed his hand on the Swan's back. "See to it that no one harms this bird or they'll have me to reckon with. She's a sacred bird. Whatever happens to her, happens to us."

CHAPTER FORTY-FIVE

THE VINE

"Not only are we called upon to see beyond those judgments, and transcend the kind of consciousness that sees all experience as only good or bad, but to do this while still living in polarity consciousness. That means moving beyond fear while still living in a fearful world. It's something to master. It's living in a dangerous world and a beautiful world simultaneously."

Temple Fox
The Makolese Scroll on
The Return of the Ka and the Mending of the Su #45

Kulo ripped off his tattered sash and mopped up the blood from his chest. His nerves calmed a bit as he examined his dilemma with quiet trepidation. Gathering all the vines he could reach, he wove them together to make one strong vine. But the vine wasn't long enough to braid into a knotted ladder. He felt hopelessly trapped, and he uttered every phrase meant to injure another, blasphemy the gods, and insult one's mother. The words, useless, sailed out into the open sky, falling on no one's ears. The late afternoon sun crept over the edge of the cliffside as he grumbled to himself, and he managed to curse the sun as well, for no other reason than it was there.

Temple sat in a tree, a gentle breeze ruffling his feathers. He watched with keen owl eyes, waiting for the old man's energy to reshape itself and change hue. He groomed a few feathers and sharpened his beak when he noticed a subtle shift in Kulo's energy field.

"Does no one hear my plea?" Kulo cried out. The Elder tossed a pebble over the cliff and waited until he heard it land far below. "Where are all the Gods and Spirits when you need them?" He held his arms out in surrender and his energy turned inward in prayer. "Bi kana lo, if I am to believe the teachings of this Temple Fox, then I ask the divine forces of compassion to send me a way to get off this cliff!"

Temple saw Kulo's energy field expand and deepen to a lavender hue. He took this as his signal and leaped down from his perch to the jungle floor where he had gathered a mass of fox grapevines. He grabbed one in his talons, and with several beats from his enormous wings, he lifted high into the air. He soared over the unsuspecting captive, banked around until he was facing the cliff. Diving lower, he dropped his load on top of the old man and caught a thermal updraft.

At first one imagines happenstance. A lone vine loosens in the rough wind and falls from the jungle high above. A second vine and Kulo was craning his neck, scanning the ledge above him to catch a glimpse of his rescuer. By the third vine there was mirth and excitement, but no glimpse of his liberator.

"Thank you! Thank you, whoever you are," Kulo cried. He pried a handful of the tiny grapes into his hand, rolled them around his parched mouth, then spit out the pits. Then he tied the vines together and made knots at evenly spaced intervals.

After the old man tugged on the vine to test its strength, he made a huge lasso. He threw the lasso high above him to the cliff top, but it wouldn't catch onto anything. The Elder tried three dozen times, but could not throw the end of the vine far enough above him.

The Owl saw him struggling. When Kulo threw the vine again, Temple, risking disclosure, caught it in his talons, flew to a sturdy branch of the closest tree and looped the vine around it.

The Elder caught a glimpse of the bird. "Temple's animal ally!" he called out in a hoarse whisper.

The old man tugged hard on the vine, then tested it with his full weight. And when he began his arduous ascent out of his cliffside prison, Temple flew down to a wider point on the trail, out of Kulo's sight, where he spiraled around to make his transformation.

By the time Kulo pulled himself up, halfway over the ledge to level ground, he was drenched with sweat and racked with pain. He swung one arthritic leg over at a time, still clinging to the vine for life. Filled with a mixture of fatigue and exhilaration, he crawled along the vine to where it was anchored. Knowing he was safe now, he lay on the path he had fallen from, struggling to calm the wild pounding of his heart. He rolled over, shaded his eyes with his stained and swollen hands to search the sky for the Owl. But Temple was nowhere to be seen.

Should I return to the safety of the Rebel camp or press onward? he wondered. *The worst of the trail is yet to be passed... And yet, I cannot ignore the miracle that just happened.*

In spite of his injuries, Kulo was confident of what he needed to do. He grabbed hold of the tree stump and pulled himself up onto his feet. He faced the sky from where he had fallen and thanked Henakaga, the Spirit of the Owl and the animal ally to Temple Fox. With great passion, he prayed out loud to the Earth Mother, the Spirit of the Wind, and the Spirit of Hollow Mountain to grant him safe passage. He squeezed a drop of blood from his bleeding hand and let it fall into the wind to let the Spirits know he meant business. Then he found himself a good, strong stick and limped down the narrow mountain trail. As he edged his way over the hardest part of the path, with the wind howling at him, he wound down through the treacherous passage, then around another twisted bend to where the mountain sheltered him from the sun and wind. As the path widened, Kulo spotted Temple sitting placidly on a log, waiting for him.

Temple's bright blue eyes met Kulo's old weary ones. His smile broadened as the old man approached. Temple stood up and gave the Elder a respectful bow, then held out a long owl feather as a gift.

The old man stopped and stared at the man, upon whom only two days before he had wished death.

Temple coaxed him further with his dismantling smile and Kulo limped a little closer. A warm wave of energy enveloped the old man and his breathing became even: the pain in his joints began to ease. He hobbled up to Temple and accepted the gift with a nod, his eyes locked with the Teacher's blazing eyes. And for the first time, he saw Temple for who he really was. Without knowing he would do so, he lost control and burst into tears.

Temple stepped up to the Elder and the two embraced. While Temple held him for a long moment, he felt all the old man's tensions and suspicions drift away like dark clouds parting to make way for the light.

The Teacher pried the old man from him gently and looked up at him with an impish grin. "I've been expecting you all morning. What took you so long?" Temple asked.

Kulo's weeping turned to laughter and he wiped his face with a dirty hand. "I had to fall off a mountain and face death first. Sorry, I am late," he chortled.

"Come and sit," Temple insisted, and pointed to the moss-covered log situated in a shady spot beside the path. "I brought some water and a little food for you."

The old man sat down. Temple handed him a length of thick bamboo, which Kulo accepted and drank from gratefully.

"Thank you," he said and returned the empty container. "And thank you for all those grapevines you brought me. You saved my life." He turned from Temple and looked out over the green foothills for a quiet moment, watching the tops of trees below sway in the wind. When he turned back around he lowered his head, averting the intensity of Temple's steadfast gaze. "I owe you an apology," he said, his voice weighted with guilt.

"No apology is needed," Temple replied. "Please understand how courageous you are. You've come farther in your consciousness than most who believed I was the Prophet from the start."

Kulo engaged Temple's eyes again. "That last bit of the trail is the windiest and the most treacherous for an old man like me to travel alone. How did you know I would even make it this far?"

"Because I know your heart. I saw you coming, and what I foresaw I base on probability," Temple replied.

The Elder nodded with understanding. "You are the Prophet after all." Kulo grew pensive. "I have a question for you," he finally said. "If you know the magic of spinning, why did you not spin back into your man form so you could haul me up?"

"What's the point of learning life's lessons if someone else is going to do it for you?" Temple answered. "I am a Prophet and a Teacher, not your savior, as many mistakenly believe me to be, which," he added, "is a great misinterpretation of the Prophecy. I gave you those vines as a tool to help you, but you needed to climb out on your own. You needed to do it by yourself."

"I do not mean to sound ungrateful, but it is a cruel thing not to help an eighty-eight- year-old man in distress," Kulo said.

Temple stared back with a focused calm. "And yet it is old men such as yourself who keep the fires of hatred burning and instigate others to commit violence," he said.

Kulo dropped his head and fell silent, feeling the frank reproach was deserved.

"Besides," Temple began again, "I needed to know just how serious you were about meeting with me. I had been feeling your energy and your desires since yesterday, but wanted to see if you would have the courage to follow through in spite of all the obstacles."

"Tai," Kulo nodded. "I considered going back."

"But you came anyway, and at great peril to yourself."

Kulo nodded again. "If the others knew that I thought you were the True Teacher, they would have my head."

"Now that we are meeting face to face, how may I serve you?" Temple asked.

"I would not be here were it not for Mefakani," Kulo began. "He told us how he betrayed us. He confessed his crimes and risked his life doing it. You know what we did to him?"

"You attacked him."

"Any traces of a truce have been obliterated. The Unbelievers are calling for revenge against you and the Queen. Temple, you are the True Teacher. You must stop this madness! We must bring an end to this war and create peace!"

Temple nodded. "I understand what you ask," he said. "You may find peace, but may not be able to end the feud between the Believers and your friends."

"I do not understand," Kulo said. "How can I find peace if this war does not end?"

"You find the peace within yourself first," Temple answered. "Peace isn't something you can impose on someone else.

"You must understand that all is happening according to a Divine Plan," Temple continued. "It's true that the island has never been this divided before. Each faction feels they are morally right and that the Gods are on their side and demand justice. But what if the intensity of recent events was designed to press everyone into a corner, so that they *all* learn something *magnificent* about themselves? What if the true reason for all these extreme, polarized feelings – anger, fear, hatred – appearing at once is intended for people to *transmute* those feelings?

"Civil war lurks on the horizon. What if this civil war isn't solely designed as an external war played out with spears and swords, but primarily as an internal experience? What if the grand plan is to allow this conflict to occur, to bring you all to a pivotal point in consciousness? Each faction draws the other faction to itself. What if all are mirrors for one another? What if the Divine Intelligence gave you freewill to create whatever you wanted? And what if you all provided yourselves with as many scenarios as you needed, but no more than you could handle, to bring your worst fears to your doorstep…so that you might look those fears in the face and conquer them? And what if that Divine Intelligence gave you all the tools to accomplish this?"

"But that is what we do by battling the Lord Tagheetu when we are first initiated," Kulo said.

"And yet that one time initiation is not enough to solve the problems your people are facing now, is it? That initiation was designed as a rite of passage so your young people could become adults. I speak in larger terms now, which deals with how your entire culture views itself through fear. Look," Temple said, "you live in dangerous times right now. And you live in miraculous times."

Kulo shook his head sadly. "I do not feel these times are so wonderful. I am frightened."

Temple nodded his head in understanding. "What if this harsh experience is to lead you to your true nature, which is a wholly compassionate nature? Could you also see that harsh experience as being wonderful – even miraculous?"

The old man shook his head again. "I have already expressed my compassion by supporting our Senior Elder and our people. You may call us traitors and renegades, but we did what we did to protect our culture because of what we thought you really were. That is why we tried to kill you."

Temple smiled with his eyes. "And yet you are sitting with me now. You no longer believe as you did before. Now you accept me as the True Teacher and feel you're acting out of compassion by trying to stop this civil war."

Temple leaned forward. "Elder Kulo, no matter what the outcome of this war, it isn't designed by the gods as being right or wrong. The gods have no attachment to what the Rebels believe, or what Queen Palomei and her Council believe. The war is neither moral nor immoral. Try to reason from a more expansive perspective and without all the emotional chaos. If you do, you might give yourself breathing room to allow events to unfold and simply be what they are – a blessing divinely disguised. It's seemed to work for you so far," he added.

"That is a cold way of looking at war," Kulo said. "I cannot. I have survived the Great Massacre."

"I'm not suggesting you dismiss the horrors of war. Although the gods do not judge you, they may feel disappointment when humanity continually wars against itself. For violence lowers your vibration, which, in the end, keeps you at a base level, preventing you from aspirating to a higher purpose and finer vibration. Where there is violence, there is fear. And where there is fear there is no love," Temple said. "But you see, the Gods are forever patient with us as we learn to move toward love. This war, however, is unpreventable."

Kulo leaned back and grimaced at the thought.

The Teacher spoke again. "It would serve the highest expression of yourself to understand that all the events in your life are consequences of your choices and not rewards or punishments. Human beings have a tendency to see the choices in their lives through the screen of judgment they've placed on their previous experiences. And they also see their lives through the opinions of others. Not only are we called upon to see beyond those judgments, and transcend the kind of consciousness that sees all experience as only good or bad, but to do this while still living in polarity consciousness. That means moving beyond fear while still living in a fearful world. It's something to master. It's living in a dangerous world and a beautiful world simultaneously."

"You expect us to be like the gods," Kulo said with a huff. "Impossible!"

"I've done it, and I expect no less of you," Temple said sharply, "for it's what the Makolese were born to do. It's why I'm here, to teach you how. The gods don't make such requests without giving you the tools to accomplish this.

"Tani once told me that the plant that cures the Makolese truklum rash grows near the ivy that causes the rash. When problems arise, the answer to that problem is always close by.

"Elder Kulo, you are in a unique position to see both sides of this conflict. If the war continues anyway, please realize it will be both horrible and wonderful. It's not a bad thing…and not a good thing either. The war will simply provide a means for learning about your true compassion nature. That is all."

Kulo spoke again. "But does that not mean I am condoning the war?"

"No," Temple answered. "If you choose to, you can see the war as a gift and accept the gift as an opportunity to express your true essence in a fashion you've never expressed before. It's time to temper logic with the perceptions of an ever-expanding and purifying heart. It's time to bring the wildly swinging pendulum of emotions to center, to rest. To become pumped with anger harms the physical body and darkens and weakens the spirit. To fear and hate others only serves to slow our understanding of who we really are in the larger scheme of things. We are spiritual beings living very human experiences in brutal and wonderful times."

Kulo let out a deep sigh. There was a long silence before he spoke again. "If only I could make the Rebels see what I see now. But you saw what they did to Mefakani? Maybe I am just a coward."

"You aren't a coward, I assure you," Temple said. "Humanity often kills those who frighten them the most. And those who frighten humanity the most are usually the ones who are helping humanity empower itself. I imagine possessing your innate power seems frightening to a Makolese, especially since the Makolese, I have heard, have a history of abusing their power when they did possess it."

"Tai," Kulo said. "Mefakani is a perfect example of that."

"No doubt, Mefakani spoke the truth to you all," Temple said, "but the Rebels attacked him anyway. Right now he suffers greatly and is learning an ocean of knowledge."

"He is not dead yet?" Kulo asked with one white eyebrow raised in surprise.

"Not yet, but he will leave his body very soon and go into the Spirit World."

"And not into the jaws of the Lord Tagheetu?"

"One's passage from this world into the next is designed by one's belief system, to make the soul comfortable as it makes its transition from one place of consciousness into another. But all end up in the Spirit World eventually, where they will receive healing and rest. Once there, their Spirit Guide, who is their personal Teacher, receives them. This loving Guide takes the soul, you'll be pleased to know, before a Council of Elders."

The old man made a face to convey he approved of what he heard thus far.

"These Great Elders," Temple explained, "have already experienced what the returning soul has experienced. They've known every sorrow, every joy, every pain and human guilt. They've experienced, firsthand, every human frustration and every imaginable shame and have mastered it all. That's why they're Masters and are called Elders. Energetically, they've embodied every human emotion and understand those emotions with the greatest compassion. That's why, when you're brought before them, you're not judged by them. You're simply understood by them with great love and caring. They ask what you believe you've learned from the last lifetime. You're given praise for your accomplishments, and encouragement for the progress your soul has made. And you're reminded of your responsibilities, and asked to take a cold, hard look of what's yet to be mastered."

Kulo took this all in with silence.

"After meeting with the Council of Elders, all souls are returned to their original soul clan for a kind of reunion and celebration for having even dared to journey to this harsh plane of suffering and intense learning. You can be sure," Temple said, "there'll be jokesters in this soul group to remind you of every banana peel you ever slipped on and every petty action and indiscretion you took in your own self-interest. But they care about you and do this with great humor and love.

"After this, you're given an opportunity to examine in great detail all you had learned from the life you just left and how it relates to the lessons from your other past incarnations. There is much studying and contemplation that goes on in the Spirit World.

"When you're ready, you're shown anywhere from two to five new lifetimes the Elders, or what some call the Masters of Karma, have chosen for you. These proposed lifetimes hold the lessons you need to learn the most, and are designed to give you the greatest opportunity for learning. Since the greatest gift we are given is freewill, we have a choice of incarnations we'd like to test out and live through, or even if we want to incarnate again or not. When we're certain which incarnation we want, we come here again to learn more about how to become compassionate."

Kulo looked askance for a second. "But no jaws?" he asked. "No Lord Tagheetu?"

"Well" – Temple grinned – "maybe when you first get there, to give you a bit of a fright because that is what you may expect to see. But even if seeing your Lord Tagheetu was a part of your belief system, you may very well never see her."

"Her?" Kulo asked, wide-eyed.

"Yes," he answered. "That bit of gender switching was one of the many misrepresentations passed down to your culture by some very jealous male Priests. When you have your Ka returned, many things will become clearer to you."

"Ah, the Ka," Kulo said. "Then Mefakani spoke the truth. It is very important that we all have it returned to us."

"Absolutely," Temple replied. "Which is why I sent a runner for yours." Temple stuck his thumb and forefinger into the inside pocket of his waistband and pulled out a small obsidian vial with Kulo's clan symbol and name etched on it. "The procedure is quick and easy. Would you like me to return your Ka to you in its entirety after we go down to the camp and get you cleaned up?"

Kulo took the tiny vial and held it up in the sunlight for inspection. "Tai, very much so," he said.

CHAPTER FORTY-SIX

NIGHT OF THE TWO SUNS

"I'm here to tell you I am a man same as you. I'm not some untouchable, unfathomable, unknowable God. Like you, I am of Divine origins. In truth, the only difference between most of your people and myself is that I know what I am and they may not."

Temple Fox
The Makolese Scroll on
The Return of the Ka and the Mending of the Su #46

It was dusk. Two suns blazed at the horizon where Temple and Elder Kulo sat together, the foothills giving them a vantage point over the island and out to sea to the west. One sun hung like a great orange ball in the sky, the other rippled in the waves beneath it.

"We call that the Dying Sun or *Maut Mati,*" Kulo said of the former, "and the Water Sun or *Mizu Mati,*" he said of the latter.

Temple and the old man watched the sun as its reflection shimmered to a dark red and drew together until they touched.

"That is the Twin Sun or *Judavaan Mati,* or what lovers refer to as the Kissing Sun or *Chumban Mati,*" Kulo explained. "Cynics say the Sun is kissing its own reflection and call it the Vain Sun or *Sia-Sia Mati.*"

The two merged into a fiery ellipse and became the Eye Sun, or *Mata Mati,* and slipped silently into the sea.

"The great Sun God blinks and we are shut into darkness," Kulo said. "Were it not for the sparkle in His eye, we would not see our shadows. But there is time for sleep, and even so great a God as the Sun must rest. It is then that His Wife, the Moon, a great Goddess, takes over to guide us through the night and through our dreams, for in our dreams we see our sleep shadows."

Temple turned to Kulo and smiled, and the two watched the sunbeams fan out and set the sky blazing in hues of magenta and lavender. "Of course, there is a time when She gives us no light and we all enter the Shadow Time. But a Husband and Wife must have their time alone together."

Temple's eyes smiled back.

The two men passed the time together in the easy silence of prayer and meditation while Kulo's newly attached Ka healed. The soldiers, who were not on watch, were asked to pray for the Rebels, and the encampment grew quiet and peaceful. The great Moon Goddess rode through the night sky with the stars as her companions. When she reached her zenith, Temple turned to look at Elder Kulo.

The firelight flickered against Kulo's broad tattooed chest and he let out a deep sigh of satisfaction. "I am amazed," he said, "and deeply grateful." The old man watched the last of his scab and the foul-smelling poultice drop from his chest. He touched the tiny pink scar at his breastbone and took a deep breath. "Even the air tastes cleaner, more full of life. And you!" he said with a look of delight. "You are glowing like the Moon!"

"That's nothing," Temple said, grinning. "You should see Losha Ninti."

"Losha Ninti? She...?" Kulo leaned on the broken end of a question.

"She has fulfilled the same prophecy, as I have," Temple said. "Remember, 'Two multiplies the power tenfold. And then, multiplies tenfold again and again,'" he said, reciting the ancient prophecy.

"I know it well," Kulo said. "I never realized what it meant. But Losha, the Queen's Interpreter? It seems impossible."

"Any more impossible than me becoming the True Teacher?" Temple grinned.

"Well, I suppose not."

"And believe me when I say there will be more like Losha and I. That's why she must fly to see the Rebels."

"Fly?"

"Tai," Temple said. "She flies in the form of a large white Swan. And this is the form she will use when she flies to the Rebels' encampment. The Unbelievers may not believe I am the True Teacher, but they will accept her when they see her fly with the sacred mark upon her brow. She, by the way, is resting right now. You will see her in the morning."

Kulo shook his head as if his brain was rattling inside of his skull. "Truly, we live in a world filled with surprises."

The curtain of night drew over the encampment and Temple sat in silence until Elder Kulo could catch up with his private thoughts.

A soldier approached and bowed, then placed two steaming pots over a bed of coals, one filled with stew and the other with sha. He handed both men a bowl and a cup made of coconut and each a wooden spoon, then ladled a spoonful of stew into each bowl.

Kulo raised the bowl to his nose and breathed in the aroma. "Ah, turtle soup."

"Is there anything else I can get you?" the soldier asked.

"Thank you, Asin. Nothing for me," Temple answered.

"No. Thank you," Elder Kulo said. He looked up at the soldier and noticed that the man showed no bitterness and carried no weapons.

The soldier bowed and left.

A quizzical cast in the old man's eyes drew Temple's full attention, and he waited for the question that had bothered the Elder the most.

Kulo's head tilted slightly and he squinted at Temple through the firelight. "When we were on the mountain pass, you said you were not our savior. Yet you admitted to being the True Teacher and Prophet."

Temple chewed a bit of turtle meat and nodded. "As I tried to demonstrate to you before, I'm not here to solve your problems for you," he said with a mouthful, then swallowed. "And I'm not here to save your soul or, like the Christians believe, wash your sins away. I'm here to tell you I am a man same as you. I'm not some untouchable, unfathomable, unknowable God. Like you, I am of Divine origins. In truth, the only difference between most of your people and myself is that I know what I am and they may not. I know who I am, where I come from, and why I came here. I know the lessons I came here to learn, as well as the lessons I came here to share with your people. It wouldn't serve you to see me as greater than yourself. I don't want to be worshipped, nor do I need to be. I don't need your love or adulation. I love myself already and am greatly loved by the Source of all Creation, which is, in essence, the greater part of myself. So please don't waste your time kowtowing to me, calling me Master and giving me your power. You all did that with Mefakani, and look where that got you. You need to draw from your own innate Divine Wisdom now."

Kulo pursed his lips together.

"Is my Makolese good enough to make myself understood?" Temple asked, taking another spoonful.

Kulo snapped alert. "Oh, tai, tai," he said. "Your grasp of our language is excellent. It is my grasp of understanding that might be in question." He laughed.

"Good," Temple said. "Any other questions or concerns?"

Kulo drew his hand up to his mouth and coughed, a bit too nervously, Temple thought. "Are you a newly created god-man?" He cleared his throat and began again. "What I mean to say is, have you come here as a young soul, a new soul?"

Temple shook his head and ladled some sha into the Elder's cup and handed it to him.

"Actually," Temple began. "I'm a very old soul. Now, don't mistake me when I say this. Being an old soul doesn't necessarily mean being wise. In fact, some old souls are simply old because they are slow in mastering life's lessons. They keep incarnating over and over again until they get it right. Most old souls, however, are, indeed, wise and more experienced than the younger souls." Temple paused for a moment, knowing how the old man would respond to what he had to say next.

"Elder Kulo, I am tied to your people more intimately than you might have imagined, for in a former incarnation your ancestors knew me as Gadji."

Kulo dropped his cup and exhaled as if the wind had been knocked out of him.

Temple picked up the cup and refilled it. "Maybe you could use another drink." He laughed.

Kulo chortled in response and took the cup and drank the liquid in one huge gulp. He placed the cup in front of him, signifying he needed no more. "Now, I am confused," he said. "You were a god back then, and now you claim you are not?"

"That's another misconception," Temple explained. "I wasn't a god back then either."

Kulo scratched his head and Temple pointed to the caldron of sha simmering in front of them. "Mind if I have a cup?"

"Please, take your fill. But I warn you, by the end of this evening I may have to drink it all," Kulo quipped back.

Temple swallowed the brew deeply, then set his cup before him. "What I did in my incarnation as Gadji was to unify people. I fought for the awareness of Oneness to make people realize we are all equally of Divine origin. I tried to end a corrupt Priesthood that believed the animals were less sacred than human beings. Humanity started to become a bit too arrogant about themselves back then and were slaughtering some of the animals needlessly, without any respect, without honoring them. My ancestors weren't killing them to protect themselves or even using them for food or clothing. The killing had become a blood sport.

"We had taken one large step in separating ourselves from creation, which is god in its many forms. I could see where this was leading us and was simply trying to restore the true spiritual order of things. Treat the animals, the plants, the water, land and sky as you wish to be treated. Respect all forms of life. I did succeed in ending that belief, but one Priest remained, who, after killing me, created a whole new religion that was as dangerous as the first."

"Naweze Ka-Seipa," Kulo surmised.

"Tai." Temple nodded. "After he murdered me, he fed my body to a great crocodile that embodied the soul of Tagheetu. When storm clouds gathered and the sky grew dark at the moment of my death, Naweze Ka-Seipa became frightened of those who shared my belief that all life is born from one Source and is sacred. So he formed a way to placate them. He deified the Spirit of the Crocodile and deified me, too, and concocted the creation myth about Tagheetu and myself and the Goddess Hianna, though there is some truth to the tale. Better to deify a dead man who can't speak for himself, I suppose.

"Naweze Ka-Seipa became what the white people call a power broker. He became the intermediary between the people and the governing power of Lord Tagheetu, who was also considered part god because he had ingested me – as Gadji. Does any of this make sense to you?"

Kulo's eyes grew larger. "It is beginning to," he said.

"I wouldn't have told you this much had I not returned and healed your Ka for you. You must understand, as Gadji I wouldn't think to place myself above another. What Naweze Ka-Seipa did was contrary to everything I held sacred. Like I said, I wasn't a god back then and Tagheetu wasn't either, and yet, though it sounds contradictory and blasphemous according to your people's beliefs, we all are in a sense god, a fragment of the Source itself as It seeks to replicate itself in other forms. We are all part of the Divine, which is why I've no objections to being called a man-god. When everyone's Ka is fully restored I hope your people don't mind if I refer to them in the same terms. More sha?"

Kulo declined with a wave of his hand. "While you are rewriting our history I think I need to be sober."

"I must tell you one more thing about myself and then we will be done talking about *me*," Temple said in his straightforward manner. "You see, the quality of one's soul, the depth of one's wisdom, is revealed when people speak less about themselves. It's the message that is important, not the messenger.

"You can tell the spiritual depth and the intelligence of not just one person but an entire culture by how they treat women, children, the land, the water, and animals. Creation is the body of God. Creation is the Divine in physical form. It doesn't matter if a person professes an allegiance to what they feel is the superior of all the Gods or Spirits, to Jesus or the Budaloto or Krishnaram or even Hianna. It is how they treat all of Creation. Truly, you have to ask yourself: Does this culture speak of only the messenger and not the message the messenger brings? Or do they act upon the message? I bet a million cowry shells the culture that focuses on only the personage of a man, since it is usually a male, is a culture ruled by young souls inhabiting male bodies.

"So you see, I'm not behaving at my best today because I have talked about myself too much. But then, there is a whole culture fighting over a single personage, namely me, and so I feel compelled to set the record straight.

"You may also be surprised to learn that in this incarnation I was born to a Caucasian English mother and a Caucasian American father. I was raised in both America and England, and spent a good part of my life in East Africa. In my adulthood I became a pilot, you see."

"A pi-o-let? What is a *pi-o-let*?" Kulo asked.

"A pilot is a person who operates a flying machine, like the airboat Mefakani invented, only it's far less sophisticated. It's what I fell out of when your people found me floating in the sky. I drowned and was born anew in the Great Light I have spoken of, when Tiv, not Mefakani," he emphasized, "resuscitated me and brought me back to life."

Kulo retrieved his cup. Forgetting all polite custom he dipped his cup into the caldron, knowing this would be a long, long night.

Kulo fingered the small scar on his chest, which was healing very nicely. "Do you feel Losha will be able to do the same for the Elders Ikus and Cranik as you have done for me?" he asked.

"Why her?" Temple asked. "Why not you?"

Kulo stared back at his Teacher as intensely as Temple was staring at him. The old man hung his head down for a second until he was able to look Temple in the eye again. "You have caught me up again."

He laughed. "Naturally, I feel she would do a better job of it, and would be far more convincing than I."

"There's no time like the present to begin becoming who you were born to be."

Kulo let out a self-conscious laugh again and bowed from where he sat. "Thank you."

Temple bowed back. "Besides, there will be many people who need their Kas reattached. The more who learn to do this, the better.

"Right now, you need to rest and get reacquainted with your Ka again. Let it align you to your Greater Self and to the Divine Will. Let it rejuvenate you and empower you. It's a long journey back for you tomorrow."

"I will do as you want, my friend," Kulo said.

"I do not *want* anything," Temple said, correcting him gently. He backed away slowly, signifying their meeting was ending.

Kulo watched as Temple slipped into the darkness. He sat by the fire deep in thought, watching the smoke curl around his head as if his thoughts had escaped and lingered in the night air for examination. He allowed the sha to make him drowsy, and even though he knew any of the soldiers could kill him sometime during the long night, he felt safe, perhaps safer than he had felt in weeks. He curled up on a bed of fern that Asin provided for him and fell into an untroubled sleep.

CHAPTER FORTY-SEVEN

LOSHA'S GIFT

*"There's no time like the present
to begin becoming who you were born to be."*

Temple Fox
The Makolese Scroll on
The Return of the Ka and the Mending of the Su #47

A gentle hand rubbed Kulo's shoulder and he jolted awake. He found himself staring up at Asin. It was still dark, but emerging red streaks in the eastern sky hinted of dawn. The fire yet blazed, but the woodpile stored nearby had been used up.

"Asin is your name, is it not?" Kulo asked.

"It is," he answered and bowed. "I have brought you breakfast." He handed the Elder a large leaf filled with fat slices of bilimbi sprinkled with rock salt, a generous handful of acai and a couple of sapodilla to counteract the sour taste of the bilimbi. "Temple Fox would like to meet with you again after you have eaten." He handed the Elder a bamboo length of coconut water.

"Very well," Kulo said. While Asin waited by his side, he bolted down the breakfast and drank from the length of bamboo until it was empty. With his fears assuaged and his hunger appeased, he allowed the soldier to help him to his feet. As he rose, he sighed a curious grunt, not from pain, but from the absence of it. He touched the tiny scar in his chest and breathed deeply of the clean mountain air.

As the two walked together into the heart of the encampment, every soldier they passed greeted Kulo with a respectful bow. When Kulo reached Temple, the two embraced like old friends. The man-god gestured behind him in the distance to where a large swan stood, her white chest puffed out, her powerful wings flapping, releasing a cloud of loose white down.

Temple turned back to Kulo. "I would like you to meet Losha, although I am sure you have met before."

Kulo stared past Temple at the beautiful bird with the strange red gash in her forehead where several feathers were missing. "Tai, but not in this form," he gasped.

"We woke you to witness her transformation."

"Thank you. I am honored," he said.

Temple ran his hand over Losha's long neck and back, then stepped away and nodded. Losha wasted no time and took a short running start before she lifted into the air. She flew high above the encampment until she dipped down and soared into a spiral.

The soldiers moved out of the way as the bird descended rapidly, signaling them to know where she would land. She marked the spot with a wing tip, constricted her spiraled flight with the last lap, then spun in the center in a whirlwind of light. Sparks flew off her wingtips until there was a sudden burst of blinding light.

When the witnesses had recovered their eyesight, the dark beauty stood before them in her human form, beaming a warm smile of welcome, the wound in her forehead glowing like a blue flame. She bowed to them and they all bowed in return.

Kulo watched the play of what he thought was the morning light as it gathered around Losha's body, encapsulating her in a glowing soft white bubble.

His mouth parted in wonderment. *She is radiant!*

Kulo peered through the crystal-clear light, his eyes set upon the deep scar on her forehead. He bowed to her again and she nodded in acknowledgment as she sauntered up to him.

"I will escort you back to your camp the way you came, to make certain you do not fall again," she announced in greeting. An engaging smile lit her face and the Elder noticed that the glowing sphere around her suddenly engulfed him.

A wave of calm and the fullness of her compassion fell over him like a soft blanket. He let out a sigh of satisfaction and blinked back at her. "I am safe in your presence," he said. "Thank you."

After a brief meeting and more prayers offered for the Rebels, Elder Kulo and Losha set out together arm in arm up the steep incline. They talked about their families, the rebellion, Mefakani's demise, and how Losha received the mark upon her brow when she had first learned to spin while being held as Mefakani's captive.

Losha explained in depth the prophecy, of which she had no foreknowledge, which dealt with the blossoming of the starflower during a rare star formation. She confirmed much of what the Shaman had told the Rebels, too, but added events from her own perspective.

Kulo spoke about the loss of his wife, and Losha listened intently, commiserating with him as she related her own feelings about her recent widowhood.

"Believing as you do now," she warned, "you may lose others... family…friendships."

Kulo nodded his head in understanding. When they reached a point where Kulo could continue on safely alone, she turned to him.

"I will leave you now. The next time you see me I will be flying overhead in a tight spiral and make my change when I have landed. Please make sure no weapons are aimed at me. It would ruin the moment," she said, laughing.

"I wish my wife were here to see this," he said, smiling sadly.

"I am certain she is with you here in spirit," she said, and patted his large hands. "Before I take leave of you, until we meet up ahead, I wish to give you something."

Losha lifted the old man's huge hands into hers and held them for a quiet moment.

A spike of sublime energy surged into his palms and he cried out sharply, falling to his knees and weeping. The old man looked up at the dark woman with tears streaking his face. "I know what you have given me and I thank you. Thank you," he cried.

Losha gave Kulo a reassuring hug and watched as the old man, his energies renewed by the new hope and the gift he had just received, climb the trail that would lead back to the Rebel camp.

CHAPTER FORTY-EIGHT

THE FEMALE PROPHET

"You will also remember the old ways. No Makolese should forget that our heritage is rich and must never be forgotten. To have your Ka returned to you means you will begin to perceive the world through the heart and not solely through the mind. And to see through the heart is pure magic!"

Losha Ninti
The Makolese Scroll on
The Return of the Ka and the Mending of the Su #48

Kulo ambled into the camp as if he had never left. Several Rebel scouts, who had seen him first, escorted the Elder over to the makeshift headquarters where Cranik sat by a campfire with his ears bandaged.

Cranik wasted no time flailing him with accusations and curses. "You penis head! Where have you been?" he yelled. "And do not lie to me. You had this silly cryptic message sent to me saying you were going off to meditate and pray just like Sahdon was supposed to have done at the Motherstone. Have you lost your mind! You abandoned us! I have never known such an idiot be so totally irresponsible!"

Kulo waved him away. "You cannot hear me even if I tell you," he said. "In truth, you have never been able to hear me." Kulo walked away from Cranik, which sent Cranik into a frenzy.

But his friend Ikus heard Kulo and called out. "Kulo! Is that you? Are you all right?" Ikus asked. His eyes were still bandaged and he reached out with his thin arms, desperate for his old friend.

Kulo lumbered over to Ikus and embraced him. "I am more than well, my friend. And you will be soon as well. I have seen things as I have never seen them before."

"See them for me then, my dear friend," Ikus said, patting Kulo's thick hands.

"I wish for you to see something very soon, but sadly you cannot. And yet it will be something written about in the History Scrolls."

"What is it?"

"Something wonderful!" he said. He smiled although Ikus could not see him smile.

"Tell me. Tell me where you have been and what you have seen."

Kulo remembered well what Temple had told him. The man-god had said: "There's no time like the present to begin becoming who you were born to be." Remembering the gift Losha had given him, the Elder's hands suddenly burned hot. He looked down at them, knowing what he must do, but suddenly feeling self-conscious.

Kulo stood over Ikus and invoked a prayer for healing. "I call upon the Divine Healers, the Ancient Ones, and the Masters of Karma to do whatever is needed for the benefit of the soul of my friend Ikus Galo-ao'. Thank you for helping him see again through Divine eyes."

Kulo placed his hands over Ikus' eyes and held the image of Ikus whole and healed as if his old friend had never become blind. He felt a great heat fill his body and course through his limbs and out of the center of his palms.

"What are you doing? I feel hot," Ikus complained.

Kulo's closed his eyes and a river of fire poured forth without his control and his hands began to shake violently.

Ikus cried out. "I am on fire!"

By then others had gathered around the two, including Cranik, who pushed the others aside. He stared with alarm and reached out to grab Kulo's arm to stop him.

"What are you doing, you idiot!" he yelled. But the others, who seemed to understand what Kulo was doing, pulled Cranik's hands back.

Kulo felt the power surge through his hands until he sensed a void had been created inside Ikus. All at once Ikus was filled with a cool blue light, which slowly turned to a soft vibrant violet. When Kulo felt the healing was complete, he let his hands drop by his side and sat down next to Ikus. "Ikus, how do you feel?" he whispered.

"I feel as though I have been removed from myself, licked clean by some strange blue fire that turned purple, and then returned to my body. At least, that is what I saw and felt in my mind. I feel so clean –

so full. And...and..." He hesitated as he searched his feelings. "The pain is gone."

"Let us remove those bandages," Kulo suggested. He very gently unwound the bandages over Ikus' eyes.

Ikus saw a smear of fuzzy light, too strong for him to bear. He blinked rapidly until he grew accustomed to the brightness. He squinted up at the blurry form, which was unmistakably that of his large friend, until Kulo came sharply into view. The first thing Ikus saw was Kulo's wide grin and a mirthful twinkle in his eyes.

"I can see again! I can see! Thank you. Thank you, my dear friend." He grabbed his friend's hands and held them in his own. "But how did you do this miraculous thing?"

That was Kulo's cue. He glanced above him and let out a sharp signal whistle. Losha, who had been watching from a great distance above on a rocky ledge, began her long descent. And when Kulo drew his attention to the white bird circling above him, the others looked up as well.

"Draw no weapons," he warned. "She is a friend."

No weapons were drawn, for all the Rebels stared up in awe at the magnificent creature above them, knowing a swan flying so high in the mountains was an omen...a good omen.

"Behold!" he said just as Losha's wing tip traced a circle in the stony ground and her bird form burst into a cyclone of resplendent light.

The light was so intensely radiant that some could not see through it. Within seconds a dark form took shape, and out of the dazzling shimmer stepped a woman. And as she approached the astonishing crowd they could see the glowing scar that marked her brow. They dropped to their knees.

"The True One!" they shouted. "The True Prophet has arrived!"

"I see her! I see her!" Ikus cried. "But it looks like...like the Queen's Interpreter."

Losha walked up to Kulo and kissed his hands. And together they walked arm in arm across to where Cranik sat in stunned silence, his head to the ground in reverence.

Cranik lifted his head when the two approached. He swallowed hard before he could find his tongue. "Tell me this is truly happening. Am I dreaming?"

Kulo shook his head so the Elder would understand. Losha placed her hand on top of Cranik's balding head and allowed the flow of Divine energy to pour forth.

Cranik closed his eyes. A strong beam of white light entered the crown of his head, gently at first, then grew with more intensity, until a pronounced tingle filled his skull, causing him to lose all sense of proportion for where the limits of his skin ended. The sensation rushed through him until it entirely filled every cell of his body, obliterating his fears and filling him with a peace he had never known before. Like a warm waterfall cascading over him and expanding past the boundaries of his flesh, he became part of the energy.

I feel like I have become a particle of light...or have turned into the air itself, although this exquisite force is far more subtle than that, he thought, then sank back into the sensation without trying to analysis it.

After several minutes the Elder let out a deep sigh of surrender. Losha sensed the brightness within him and lifted her hands off his head and repositioned them onto his ears. The effect was immediate. Cranik suddenly heard murmurs from the crowd, the sound of his own breathing, and the wind in the trees. His entire soul opened to the world that had been shut off to him.

With his head still held gently between her loving hands, Losha bent down and kissed the Elder on his forehead and then on both cheeks.

Cranik looked up at Losha. Although he remained silent, his tears spoke for him in profound gratitude.

There were no dry eyes as Losha backed away and bowed to Cranik. And they watched her silently and in awe as she and Kulo walked around the camp, healing the wounded and listening to their stories about their losses and fears.

It was midday after many healings had been performed when a woman came up to Losha and bowed her head with respect. "I never thought I would live to see this day," the woman said, her eyes full of wonder and hope. "The Gods are with us."

"The Gods are always with all of us," Losha said as she touched the top of the woman's head in blessing.

The woman lifted her head, her face streaked with tears. "Please, we beg of you. Please kill the Wizard. Just like our own Shaman, Temple Fox is poisoning our people with his lies and clever deceits."

The voices of the Rebels slowly grew increasingly agitated and joined with the woman in a cry to "Kill the Wizard."

Losha felt a cold chill rush through her blood. She forcibly calmed herself one heartbeat at a time until she was able to address the woman, and she faced the crowd down with an implacable presence.

"There will be no more fighting," she said when quiet had returned.

"But what about the Wizard? The Shaman claims he did not kill him," a voice rang out.

"Tai, we cannot just leave this mountain," said another. "If we do, Palomei's army will cut us to bits."

"They have been ordered to withdraw their troops," Losha said.

"How is that possible?" yet another yelled.

"I have met with them already," she said without further explanation.

The crowd stared at one another, rattled by her answer.

"They have seen you?" the first woman asked.

"Now they know who the True Teacher is!" said a Rebel far back. Still at odds with each other, the voices of the crowd fought for dominance, some crying "Kill" while others cheered with hope.

Losha raised her hand to silence them again. "Eventually, each of you will have to return to your villages. If any of Palomei's soldiers remain when we leave this place, then I suggest you pass them in silence and provoke no one. I will protect you. But before we leave Hollow Mountain, we must first tend to an important matter."

"What?" The crowd pressed forward.

"I will reattach the small portion of your Ka that Mefakani stole from all of you. You will need your entire life force to be able to bring the Makolese back to wholeness. You see, one cannot bring an entire culture back to wholeness unless they are whole themselves."

The crowd looked to each other, stirred with amazement and disbelief at the same time, as Losha gestured to Kulo. "Elder Kulo will assist me."

For all his massive size, Kulo seemed to shrink into himself. "Me?" he asked.

"I will teach you," Losha said reassuringly. "And once a few others have their Ka back, you and I will teach them how to do this wonderful healing. Within three days everyone will have their life force returned. The restored energy will reinvigorate all, clearing and purifying hearts and minds. Then we will leave this mountain and take our place among the people again."

"So what the High Shaman said was true. We all will have our Ka returned?" Kulo said.

"It is of paramount importance," she answered. She turned to address the gathering again.

"With your Ka returned, you will feel complete again – whole. You will begin to remember things long forgotten, and true healing will begin to take place.

"You will also remember the old ways. No Makolese should forget that our heritage is rich and must never be forgotten. To have your Ka returned to you means you will begin to perceive the world through the heart and not solely through the mind. And to see through the heart is pure magic! In truth, if you have your Ka returned and healed, the great shadow that has been cast over each of us and our land will be lifted. Then, together we will mend the Su!"

CHAPTER FORTY-NINE

STAR FLOWERS

"Leave it to the women of old to keep their secrets."

Temple Fox
The Makolese Prophecy Scroll #118
The Makolese Scroll on
The Return of the Ka and the Mending of the Su #49

Mason lifted his head from the scroll he had just written. "It sounds like Losha was well received by Palomei's soldiers, and Elder Kulo, even the Rebels," he said.

"Most definitely."

"But where did the little obsidian jars come from that held pieces of everyone's Ka?"

"I flew ahead of the soldiers when they left the mountain and collected as many vials as I could carry from Mefakani's private cavern. Well, not exactly," he said, pausing to collect his thoughts. "It took me several trips. Losha had Kulo take an account of all the Rebels' names so I knew which vials to gather. She and I met in our bird forms on the same ledge I had carried her to when she had been wounded by the blast. She had the list ready for me by the time I brought the first load.

"Meanwhile, Tani was busy like a mad bee reattaching Palomei's Ka first. She was hoping that the healing would help restore Palomei back to sanity. Tani made a point of doing her second and third healings on Owane and E-lon-e', who had not gotten their knickers in a twist like the Queen had.

"O'Juma and Jabal were nowhere to be found in the Shaman's compound so, with a little bit of mentoring from me, I taught the Lesser Apprentices how to reattach and heal the Ka. They began the work of healing as many people as they could find.

"I gave some of the Apprentices the list of Rebels and had them sort through the vials from Mefakani's private chamber. Placing as many as I could carry into a sack, I flew them back to the mountain. I flew seven loads in all before I was able to get the vials for over one hundred Rebels. It was exhausting!"

"But didn't the Rebels see you come and go to drop off your rather special deliveries?" Maśon asked.

"I delivered them at night." He paused and ran his hand over his bald head. "I had a wee bit of a mishap with the last load."

Maśon raised an eyebrow.

"I was completely knackered," he confessed. "The heavy sack began to slip out of my talons. I grabbed it in time, but not before a few vials slipped out and came crashing down to the rocks below." He let out a sigh as if the memory made him weary.

"How many did you lose?"

"There was no telling at the time. But I found out later I had lost twelve of them."

Maśon nodded and began to dip his brush back into the ink when he stopped cold. "You mentioned O'Juma and Jabal before. What in God's name happened to them?"

Temple suddenly became alert again. "People in the Shaman's compound said that Jabal was gravely ill and had been taken into the jungle by O'Juma for a ceremonial healing. No one knew exactly where they went."

"Did he die?"

"Who's telling this story?" Temple said. "I'll tell you when I'm good and ready."

Maśon rocked back a bit. "No need to fuss about it. And Winyon…what happened to her?"

"I see you want to fill in the gaps of my story. Fine," Temple said. "You will have to rearrange the order later on.

"She spun into a Hummingbird and flew into the Queen's compound unnoticed. By the time she got to Palomei, the Queen had already been convinced that Losha had, indeed, fulfilled an old, obscure prophecy no one could even remember. Winyon was given the task to collect healing herbs at Sang-Wehtu' Springs so Tani could begin reattaching everyone's Ka."

"Wait! Wait a minute! What ancient prophecy are you talking about?" Maśon asked, his brushstrokes unable to catch up to the narrative.

"Maybe it was providential that Mefakani in his arrogance ignored the female prophets. It had to do with astronomy."

"Astronomy?"

"When there was a rare celestial alignment between the triangle of the constellations Cygnus, Vega, and Lyra with the Pleiades constellation, it would mark the return of the Divine Feminine through the embodiment of the Divine in a visage of Cygnus…meaning the Swan.

"Actually, Losha never even knew about this seventeen-thousand-year-old prophecy. She decided privately on her own to align with the Swan as her power animal ally.

"Mefakani should have watched for this heavenly sign since he had learned astronomy from his older friend, Fazail, the Arab sailor. But he didn't. Tani did," Temple explained. "There was one salient detail that Mefakani overlooked, or maybe didn't even know about, which Tani was alert to. It had to do with the blossoming of a particular flower that looked like a tiny white star. It only grew in one, very small, very specific spot in the forest near Dolphin Bay. Tani, in her incalculable wisdom, had built her hut right next to the spot so she could keep her eye on it.

"This minuscule star flower only blossoms once every fifty-five years. Mefakani wouldn't have remembered this because he hadn't been born yet to see it blossom. This celestial alignment came and went hundreds of times over the centuries, but the star flower never blossomed at the same time."

Temple paused. "The day that Losha was born, Tani said there was a profusion of star flowers around her hut. She had only seen the phenomena once before, but the flowers had never grown in such abundance! Naturally, she checked the skies that night and found the unusual alignment."

Mason's jaw gaped open.

"Leave it to the women of old to keep their secrets."

Mason grunted with a grin, then poised his wet brush above a blank barkcloth scroll. He cocked his head in Temple's direction.

Temple nodded and continued his tale. "It took three days for Losha, Elder Kulo, and others they had taught to reattach everyone's Ka, to bring the Rebels back into a cohesive energetic wholeness. Apparently, supplies were running low and the Rebels were growing anxious. Losha was running out of ideas on how to evade questions about how she was going to kill me. Although they were two days ahead of schedule, Losha knew it was time for the Rebels to leave their mountain fortress.

"On the morning of the fourth day Losha gathered the people before her."

CHAPTER FIFTY

NAFFA

"Let there be no mistake what twelve patriots can do!"

Naffa, the Young Rebel
The Makolese Scroll on
The Return of the Ka and the Mending of the Su #50

Losha stood on the same flat boulder where Mefakani had addressed the Rebels days before. Encrusted with quartz dust that had vitrified to the stone, leaving it glazed and gleaming in the early morning sun, the spot remained filled with a palatable power.

She called them to gather and spoke loud enough for all to hear. "It is time for us to leave this place. We have been invited to the Great Round House so that the Queen may thank you all in person. Gather your things! We will leave right away!"

"Do we take our weapons with us?" someone asked.

"I will leave that up to you," Losha answered. "Either way, you will be safe."

Knowing events could change like the breath of the wind, Losha led the people in a prayer of protection.

After the prayer, without speaking another word, Losha started her rapid descent down the mountain path with Tiv by her side, and Elders Kulo and Ikus right behind her, paying no heed as to whether anyone was able to keep up with her pace.

Several men carried the bodies of the dead and wounded on stretchers made of barkcloth and broken tree limbs. The majority scrambled frantically to collect their assortment of fishing gaffs, nets, swords, long knives and water supplies to march behind her. The departure was so swift that many lingered behind not knowing how to react.

"Where are we going?" one Rebel asked perplexed.

"Could you not hear the Teacher above the chatter? Losha Ninti is taking us to see the Queen at the Great Round House. She said the Queen wants to address us personally," answered another. "We are heroes now!'

The Rebel pulled out his dagger and tested its sharpness against his fingernail. "If anyone ambushes us along the way…I will be ready for them."

★　　★　　★　　★　　★　　★

It took better than two hours marching in silence before the Rebels saw any evidence of the soldiers' outpost below. One by one the Rebels stopped and waited for Losha to stop. But Losha didn't falter. She continued in the lead with Tiv by her side and a few of the braver Elders and Rebels, who followed in full trust that Losha, the True Teacher and Prophet, knew what she was doing.

Losha put her arm around the boy's shoulder, wrapping him in a cocoon of soothing energy, her heart open to the raw grief and confusion she sensed the boy was suffering. While keeping the healing energy flowing, her mind scanned the area and the wariness of the Rebels behind her.

Losha motioned to one of the trained Warriors who walked a few paces behind her. He hurried to her side and bowed his head in respect.

Without stopping her pace she whispered to him, "Please tell those two young men who are hiding behind the huge red boulder that they are not safe here. Tell them to join us down the mountain where I can protect them."

"Are they Palomei's soldiers? Are we to be ambushed?" he said. He cast a concerned look out of the corner of his eye at the large boulder they had just passed.

"They mean no harm. They are simply curious, but foolish young men."

"But we scouted the area in advance. We saw no one."

"That is because they are tucked in a deep niche behind the boulder under a cover of leaves."

Realizing that the Teacher was using more than her sense of sight, he motioned for two men to follow him.

The three marched cautiously behind the boulder with their spears aimed at a pile of leaves. One Rebel poked the leaves and heard, "Ouch!"

"Come out, you two!"

Tauk, a thin young man with straight black hair that hung loosely over his shoulders, climbed out of the crevice, his hair covered in leaf litter.

Bek-no, a chunkier young man, rolled out of the niche and dusted the debris out of his thick, curly brown hair. They both held their arms above their heads.

"Please place your weapons on the ground!" the Warrior ordered.

Bek-no shrugged. "We have no weapons."

The Warrior gestured to the others and the two Rebels ran a hand around the inside of the young men's waistbands.

"They have nothing," one Rebel said.

"Check their hiding place," the Warrior commanded.

One Rebel got down on his hands and knees and stuck his head inside the hole. He rummaged around in the leaves and found only two lengths of bamboo filled with water and two sacks. He lifted each sack with the tip of his sword to test their weight, then tossed them onto the ground.

Empty.

"Nothing in here, just water," the Rebel reported.

"Well, we will not deny them water. We will not harm you," the Warrior said.

The two young men lowered their arms and retrieved their bamboo containers.

"I told you we should not have come back," Tauk admonished his friend.

"But they came two days early!" Bek-no complained to Tauk.

The Rebel pressed the tip of his spear against Bek-no's flabby stomach. "How do you know that?"

"I heard the soldiers say so," Bek-no answered. "They said you would not come down for another two or three days."

"Is that so? Well, we are here now. Why are *you* here?" the Rebel asked pointedly.

Bek-no looked at Tauk and decided his friend should speak for the two of them again. "We have been runners for Palomei's troops. We have brought them food and water. We saw them leave and decided to return here."

"Why? What business do you have here?" he pressed. "Were you expecting to see a great battle between the Believers and the Unbelievers?"

Bek-no's voice faltered. "No, no, not at all. We thought we might find some neat stuff…that the soldiers left behind."

"Scavengers!" the soldier spat to one side. "Are there any others of you in these foothills?"

The two shook their heads frantically side to side.

"Go back to the Queen's compound now," the Warrior said. "We will protect you if you join us down the mountain."

The two runners stood rigid and the Warrior waited for them to move. Suddenly, the two young men jumped forward nervously and walked slowly through the camp.

The Warrior motioned for them to join the line of Rebels.

"I need to relieve myself first," Bek-no said, somewhat embarrassed.

The Warrior rolled his eyes and ordered the other two Rebels to watch the young men as he jogged to the front of the procession to catch up with the Great Teacher.

"Hurry up!" said one of the Rebels.

The runners walked back toward the boulder. While Bek-no emptied his bladder Tauk retrieved the sacks that had been left on the ground.

"I knew we should not have come!" Tauk whispered anxiously to his companion. "I should never have listened to you!"

Bek-no waved to the two Rebels signaling that now Tauk had to urinate.

The two Rebels nodded their heads, but one grew too impatient and left to fall in line with the other Rebels.

Bek-no gestured to the remaining Rebel that he needed to do more than urinate and would be awhile.

The last Rebel nodded his head. After three minutes passed he shouted, "Hurry up!" When another minute passed the Rebel sucked in his breath and glowered.

"Bi kano lo!" Bek-no said.

"What?" Tauk questioned.

"I really do have to go."

"Well, hurry up!"

"Tell him I am sick," Bek-no said.

"Tell him yourself," said Tauk.

Bek-no grunted with the effort. "I cannot hurry this. Tell him!"

Tauk gestured that they would be longer and called out. "He is sick!"

Disgusted, the Rebel turned away and joined the line with the others.

"Tell me when he is gone," Bek-no said.

"He is already down the hill. What is taking you so long?"

"I *am* sick and am running like a muddy river," Bek-no offered.

★　　★　　★　　★　　★　　★

One Rebel, a robust man in his forties named Chabon, stopped to lower his heavy sack of bamboo water containers and rub his sore neck. He turned to his walking companion, a tall, slender, and muscular woman in her early thirties who had a lean, angular face. "I need a rest," he said, wiping his brow. "Besides, we must ready ourselves if any of Palomei's soldiers are still left in their camp."

Arma kept her pace as she passed Chabon on the trail and turned her head to meet Chabon's eyes, her own copper-colored eyes burning with new light. "You must learn to trust, Chabon. Losha Ninti is the one we have been waiting for. Do not give up hope now," she said.

"Tai," he said. He picked up his load again and followed, but not before he pulled a dagger from his sheath.

Arma pulled out a slim club from her sash and grinned.

One of the younger renegades in his late teens caught up with Chabon and Arma. He wiped a thick crop of black hair off of his sweaty face and pulled out his long blade. "We are almost at the enemy camp now. I am ready," he said.

"Did you not hear, Naffa?" Arma asked. "The Teacher said the soldiers have retreated. She will protect us. We must put our trust in her now."

Naffa stood on the trail alone with everyone passing him by until he quickened his pace to catch up to Chabon and Arma. He waved his long knife in the air. "If any soldiers are waiting for us, I will deny them another breath!"

Arma looked over at the impulsive boy and frowned. "Save yourself for the real battle, Naffa. We have the Queen's full cooperation now. Together with Losha, Palomei's troops, and our army, the Wizard is as good as dead."

"But what if we have two enemies now?" Naffa asked, frowning.

Arma paused on the trail, which caused Chabon to stop and listen. "Mefakani is dead now," she said. She aimed her gaze up the trail at Mik-lon, a traditional warrior who had turned renegade and had joined the other Rebels from the beginning of the rebellion. Mik-lon still wore his crocodile chest band and buskins, and carried a spear with its sharp obsidian blade. "If you are worried about some of Palomei's soldiers, do not forget, we have some of Palomei's trained warriors in our own group as well," she said with proud defiance.

"Unless…" Naffa paused mid-sentence.

"Unless what?" Arma gave the boy a hard stare.

The other Rebels hiked around Arma, Chabon and Naffa on the trail as the three huddled together. Chabon pulled a length of bamboo from his bundle so the other two could have a sip of water. He handed the first length to Arma who accepted it with a nod of thanks.

"Unless the very person who Temple Fox has spent most of his time with is now conspiring with him," Naffa whispered.

Arma lowered the water container before it reached her lips and glared harshly at the boy. "You think Losha Ninti works with the Wizard!" she hissed at him between her teeth, then glanced all around her to make certain no one had overheard them.

"Temple Fox is the most clever of all Wizards. It is possible," Naffa said, almost off-handedly.

Mik-lon, who was bringing up the rear on the long trail, stopped before the three. Towering over them, his presence provoked obedience. "You three should keep moving and keep pace with the others," he advised.

Much to Arma's annoyance, Mik-lon's muscularity proved to be an unwanted distraction for her. She scowled as much at her private weakness as the imposing figure leering down at her with half a smile. She willed the obvious flirtation from her mind with a shake of her head, her eyes taking on a deadly serious cast when she told him what Naffa had speculated.

Mik-lon leaned on the shaft of his spear and listened intently. "No, I do not believe this. She came from the sky as predicted and fulfilled the prophecy. She even bears the sacred mark. We witnessed her heal so many. Surely, she is the Great Teacher."

"Tai, but the Wizard has also healed others," Naffa reasoned. "And so has Mefakani. That would make three now who have claimed to be the True Teacher. There can only be one."

"What if Losha Ninti is the real Teacher, but is unknowingly walking us into an ambush?" Chabon suddenly offered.

"What if you are wrong?" Naffa questioned. "What if Losha is *purposely* walking us into a trap? Does anyone know that Palomei's soldiers have withdrawn?"

Arma looked askance. "Because our own scouts have confirmed this."

"It still could be a trap," Mik-lon warned. "There are many ways to make a camp look empty. They still could be hiding and waiting for us."

The four looked at each other, a gap of silence filled with a groundswell of dread. When they began to discuss what to do, others were drawn into the conversation as they ambled by – energy attracting like energy. Minutes passed as they compared their thoughts with one another, which drew the attention of Elder Cranik, who was being carried on the back of a young male servant.

Cranik saw the Rebels clustered together. "What is going on here?" he asked, his tone clipped.

The group opened its circle and allowed the Elder entrance.

"Put me down! Put me down!" he ordered, and his carrier gently lowered the Elder to the ground. "Go ahead!" he ordered. "I will walk on my own from here."

The servant left with a bow, then joined the line of Rebels and resumed his descent.

The few others who had gathered waited until the servant could not overhear them and filled Elder Cranik in on their concerns.

Cranik's peanut-colored skin turned three shades of red. "It is not possible," he blustered. "Ikus' blindness was healed by Elder Kulo, who said the power to heal was given to him by Losha. Losha, in fact, healed my deafness. Or did you forget that!"

"Did you get your Ka reattached?" Chabon asked.

Cranik's bushy brows knit together. "No. Kulo explained there had been some mix-up with either the list that had our names on it or the obsidian vials that held each of our Kas. I do not know. He did not explain. Why is this important?" he pressed, growing more annoyed.

Naffa gestured to the circle gathered together. "We have discovered that all of us have not had our Kas reattached."

"So?" Cranik questioned.

Naffa pointed to the line of their fellow Rebels who were slowly passing them by one by one. "But they all have had their Kas reattached and healed."

"Tai, and I plan on having mine reattached later," Cranik offered.

A short, stocky, middle-aged woman named Pao-ta shouldered her way into the center so that she could be seen and heard. "Elder Kulo told me in confidence that there were twelve vials he could not account for," the older woman said.

"Meaning?" Cranik shrugged.

For Cranik's benefit, Pao-ta began to count out loud all who were present until she counted twelve – five women and seven men, which included Cranik. "There are twelve of us."

"Pao-ta, I have not got all day! Make your point!" the Elder grumbled.

Pao-ta lowered her voice and jabbed her finger in the direction of the Rebels as they passed by. "Naffa believes Losha may have altered *their* Kas just like Mefakani did to Tiv, and to Mumbula and Ijebu. And just maybe, Senior Elder, that is why they are so obediently following her. Losha could really be..."

"...another false prophet," Naffa interjected.

A sudden doubt clouded Cranik's thoughts as he was beginning to form a grim picture in his mind. His face turned from red to gray. He let out a heavy groan. "It does not add up," he said, trying to gain a modicum of optimism, testing what he knew through his feelings.

Illa, a sight girl of only fifteen, chimed in. "It does add up if Losha is another imposter and is walking us into an ambush," she concluded. "Furthermore, where did she get those vials from?"

The others looked to one another and shrugged their shoulders.

Cranik sucked on his long yellow teeth as he walked a few paces away to search his feelings again. A chill came over him, and he felt he would come unraveled, but he gnashed his teeth together in a strange kind of grimace. He ran a self-conscious hand over his sweaty head as the others politely waited for him to speak.

"I felt her power and that power was pure love. How many of you were healed by her and felt her power?" he asked.

Everyone shook their heads.

"Out of the eleven of us only two of us had injuries and they were minor," Arma offered. "And they did not feel they needed such a healing when others were suffering far more."

The others nodded in agreement.

"Then you could not possibly know. You are all mistaken," Cranik said. "I know Losha is the True Teacher."

The others stood motionless, but Naffa and Illa shook their heads in disbelief and disgust.

Cranik shielded his eye from the sun to gauge the others' responses with more scrutiny while the others looked at each other warily, waiting for the Elder's instructions.

"Respected Elder, I believe as you do," Arma said. "We will do what you tell us to do. But should we not simply yield to caution?"

"I say we stay behind and see what happens to the others as they pass through the camp," one man suggested.

Arma questioned the man with a sharp look of reproach. "Are we such cowards that we must wait to see if Palomei's soldiers will pounce on our friends first?"

"But we have only twelve of us," Mik-lon pointed out to Arma.

The sweat began to trickle down Cranik's face in thin streaks. "You must trust me. Losha is the True Teacher. Still, let the crowd pass us by," he whispered with his head lowered to hide his embarrassment. Without turning his head, he glimpsed the last of the Rebels out of the corner of his eyes as they coursed their way down the trail.

After the last stragglers passed he spoke again. "Let us take what precautions we can for now. Let us find a vantage point above our people as they pass through the enemy camp. That way we can search for any of Palomei's soldiers if they are hidden. We must try and protect our people if they are attacked. If nothing happens, then we can keep ourselves paced well enough behind them and out of sight to make certain there are no ambushes ahead…or behind," he added nervously and looked over his shoulder up the path behind them all.

The twelve nodded in agreement and continued down the mountain path at a slower pace until the enemy's outpost was spied below them in the distance. Cranik hid behind a lengthy wall of rock and a crop of stinkweed. The rest splintered off and hid behind thicker bushes and boulders where they had a good vantage point for a reprisal. They watched in silence as their own people wound their way through the camp, the air around them cramped with nervous expectation.

While Arma crouched in silence she fingered the two tiny orchid bulbs she had secreted beneath her waist sash days before. To her it was a symbol of life – her life and the life of some unknown man she hoped to marry someday. She mindlessly ran her thumb over one bulb when she spotted something below. "Psst!" Arma caught the eye of Mik-lon who was poised behind a boulder with his spear in hand. She tilted her head in the direction directly below her and to the left, where two young men were crouched behind a huge red boulder, alert to the last of the Rebels as they ambled by, but oblivious to the twelve Rebels who lurked above them.

Arma and Mik-lon whistled to the others, and the remaining ten came out of hiding. They kept their heads low and drew together. Arma pointed to the two young men below and they all nodded. They waited longer until the Rebels were well past the camp and the two young men came out of hiding, resuming their search with their sacks in their hands and their heads bent low in concentration.

"Looks to be only two young men. They are not from our group," Arma whispered to Mik-lon. "It does not appear they are there to ambush anyone."

"Not unless they have an ardent desire for a swift death," Naffa stated flatly.

"Then why are they there?" the young girl whispered.

"Let us find out," Mik-lon replied.

Arma gave the signal to advance, but stopped short to address Cranik first.

"I beg your forgiveness, Respected Elder," Arma said and bowed. "I think you should stay up here with two of us to protect you. We can handle this."

Cranik nodded and hid behind a boulder with two others and the bundle of bamboo water containers as the others proceeded down the stony slope to where the two young men had resumed their curious hunt.

Arma strode down into the empty camp with her nine companions marching behind her. They quickened their pace as they drew near.

"Who is the True Teacher?" she called out boldly to the two young men.

Tauk and Bek-no looked up at the approaching renegades and stood erect, stiff with fear.

"Say nothing," Bek-no mumbled beneath his breath to his companion.

"I told you we should have caught up with the others!" Tauk complained. "But no, you wanted to stay behind to search for more!"

"Do you want the Rebels to find them?" Bek-no whispered back in exasperation.

"Well, they will find them now!" his friend conceded.

Arma motioned to her friends to spread out at a safe distance and surround the two men.

"Look at their wraps," Pao-ta whispered to Mik-lon. "They are from the Queen's compound and have the markings of runners."

Mik-lon stepped forward and spoke first. He pointed his spear at them. "Answer the question! Who is the True Teacher?"

The two men looked to one another, tossed their sacks aside and got down on their knees. They bowed until their heads touched the earth, a plea for mercy.

"Well?" Arma asked, tapping her club in the palm of her hand.

"Losha Ninti is the True Teacher," Bek-no answered. *At least I am not lying,* he admitted to himself.

"You saw her spin...into a great white Swan?" Arma asked. "And you saw her fly with the sacred mark upon her brow?"

"Tai." Bek-no nodded.

"And so you renounce your belief in the white Wizard known as Temple Fox?" she pushed.

Bek-no didn't answer.

"Answer me!" she insisted.

Arma advanced, close enough to deliver a hefty blow.

Naffa glanced over at Illa to make sure the girl was watching him. "Perhaps a soft blow will hurry his answer," he offered, his eyes full of mischief.

Arma glared at the young man who was egging her on.

"Why do you not answer?" Arma asked Bek-no. "Can you not see that Losha is the True Teacher and Temple Fox is an imposter?" Arma could feel heat rising up through her belly and into her arms.

Bek-no bowed his head lower.

"Has the Lord Tagheetu bitten off your tongue?" she asked, taunting him.

Naffa took a step forward and pointed at the young man, who was barely older than himself. "Look at him. He still believes the Wizard is a man-god! Pathetic!" he concluded with a huff.

"ANSWER ME!" she shouted.

A surge of anger built up inside her. She took a sudden step to the side and aimed her contempt onto Tauk instead. She shouted her question to Bek-no again. "Do you still believe Temple Fox is the True Teacher? Answer me now or I will give your friend a headache he will not soon forget!" she said to Bek-no.

Naffa couldn't contain his anger. He bolted forward and pushed Arma roughly out of the way. "I will handle this!" He lifted Bek-no's head by a handful of his curly hair and placed his blade against the man's neck. "Renounce your belief in Temple Fox now or I will kill you!"

Bek-no shook uncontrollably. He bit his lip and remained silent for several tense seconds.

"Well!?"

The adrenalin pumped madly through Naffa's veins. Driven by raw impulsiveness and anger, he drew the blade across Bek-no's throat and a fountain of blood gushed forth onto the earth.

Tauk let out a sorrowful yelp like a wounded animal. The others let out loud gasps and drew back in horror. Naffa released his grip on Bek-no, and the man slumped to the ground clasping his throat and gurgling for life-giving air.

Naffa aimed his bloody long knife at Tauk. "Do Temple Fox and Losha Ninti work together?"

Tauk cried out, shaking with fear, his hands held out in defense.

Naffa grabbed Tauk by the hair as he had done to Bek-no. "Answer me!"

Tauk wailed.

Naffa leaned down into Tauk's tormented face. "Do they?"

Tauk nodded his head, immediately regretting his actions.

Naffa released Tauk. Tauk bolted to where Bek-no lay squirming on the ground. Bek-no's voice came out in liquid gasps and grunts, a puddle of blood growing beneath his head. Tauk pressed his hands against his friend's neck wound, but he could see that Bek-no's life was spilling out too quickly.

Knowing it might be the last thing Tauk would be able to say as he watched his friend die, he looked up into Naffa's savage eyes. "They *both* fulfilled the prophecy. If you cannot see that…then I pity you."

Naffa's nostrils flared and his face reddened. He lunged forward, grabbed Tauk by the head in a tight grip and drew his blade across Tauk's neck so swiftly the others had no time to react. Tauk slumped over his friend, and the scarlet blood of both runners mingled together and spread across the thirsty earth.

The others looked over at Naffa who appeared to have spent himself.

"Was that necessary?" Pao-ta asked in reprimand.

"It drew the truth out of him," Naffa panted. "Now we know what we are up against!" He wiped his long knife clean against his barkcloth skirt and shoved it back into its sheath.

A frightened and worried look darkened everyone's faces.

Arma plopped herself down on a boulder next to Mik-lon and hung her head down. "Losha and Temple are together! How can that be? Losha Ninti must have somehow gotten drawn into Temple's influence. Maybe he gave her the power to transform into that magnificent swan and convinced her that she, too, was the Great Teacher. Or have they made some sort of deal together?" She raised her head and looked at Mik-lon. "Maybe he offered her Queenship!" She shuddered.

"Tai," Mik-lon said. "And she is walking our friends right into a trap like a school of clownfish led into a circle of sharks."

Arma cast an eye at the Senior Elder as the old man frantically scurried down the path with his two bodyguards.

"Now we cannot even trust Cranik," Arma whispered. "Not with his continual misjudgment or his inept leadership. We can only trust ourselves, and there are only eleven of us."

"Tai," Mik-lon said. "We are hopelessly outnumbered by an entire culture of blind and misguided…"

"Idiots! Fools! And Wizard worshippers!" Naffa yelled with his teeth clenched. "Now we have two Wizards to kill! Temple Fox *and* Losha Ninti!"

Cranik overheard the comment and blushed. He was panting as he reached the spot where the two bodies lay. "Is that true?" he asked.

"One of the boys just told us." Arma buried her head in her hands in exasperation. "What do we do now?"

Naffa's heart was still pounding with the thrill and power of having taken life. "With the power of Lord Tagheetu we take our fight to them!" he announced. "Let there be no mistake what twelve patriots can do!"

Cranik stared at the two bodies dumbfounded. He looked from face to face as the conversation swirled around him.

Arma continued, paying no heed to the Senior Elder as she spoke. "When our people are ushered into Olonopo Crater we must…"

Naffa cut in. "Our own people are probably being ambushed somewhere below right now!"

"But if there was to be an ambush, why did not Palomei's soldiers do it here?" Mik-lon reasoned.

Naffa wiped the sweat out of his eyes and shook his head. "I do not know, unless the Believers wish to make a public display of our execution at the crater."

"Then one of us needs to warn the others," Mik-lon said.

"Wait!" Cranik called out. "I do not believe what you are saying. You all must be wrong!"

Pao-ta bowed to the Senior Elder. "We have proof," she said, pointing to the two slumped bodies on the ground. "We have a witness who said that he saw them both together…here."

Arma spoke. "Senior Elder, our people need to be told about Losha Ninti and Temple Fox working together. And we must warn the Queen, for I believe Temple and Losha's ultimate goal is to take Palomei's throne!"

Cranik was paralyzed into silence.

Illa, the slender girl with long gangly arms and legs, stepped forward. "I will go! I am the fastest!"

"Then go now!" Mik-lon ordered, ignoring Cranik. "Be quick and tell the others what we have just learned!"

Illa took off down the trail at top speed.

"What do you suggest we do now?" Chabon asked the Elder.

The Elder sat down on the boulder opposite Arma. "This is so hard to believe. How could we have been fooled again?"

"Elder Cranik, we all believed that High Shaman Mefakani was the True Teacher, did we not?" Pao-ta pointed out.

Cranik gave a sluggish nod.

"We always saw Temple Fox and Losha together. They must have made some sort of deal to share the power because, as rumors run,

Temple desires Losha Ninti. And frankly, he needs her just as he has needed her since he first fell from the sky."

"Bi kana lo!" Cranik groaned. "My concern now lies in the fact that Losha had Kulo take all of our names down on a scroll," he said, his frustration building up inside him.

Kulo! The sound of Kulo's name cut into Cranik like a blade. *Kulo – a traitor! He was always the weak-minded one,* he thought. *He is the one who led us into this dangerous farce.*

"Even if Illa tells our people to run away, Temple and Losha know who we are now," he said. "None of us will ever be able to get close enough to the Queen to warn her. And we need to warn the Queen quickly," he emphasized, "before Losha Ninti takes the throne for herself!"

Mik-lon scratched his chin in thought. "We still have our weapons. I think we should head to Olonopo Crater while one of us sneaks into the Queen's compound before Palomei leaves. And there is only one way to get inside such a guarded compound unnoticed."

Mik-lon took his spear and scratched a map into the dirt. And as he worked out the details of his plan, Arma noticed how the tiny grooves on the edges of his scrawl turned to red rivulets from the pool of blood nearby.

CHAPTER FIFTY-ONE

THE OLD ONES

THE LIQUID EYE BEHOLDS
"The liquid eye beholds
the curved sky
dancing with spinning stars,
a goblet of pure water,
a drop of blood,
the turning over of the soil
by worms in the moist field.
Every sealed secret
is revealed
by the keen eye
and the curious hand
pulling away the moss
to find the mirror."

Elo Tivluk, Popular Makolese poet
The Makolese Scroll on
The Return of the Ka and the Mending of the Su #51

The palms and ferns towered over the diminutive forms of Great Grandfather Okon and Elder Tani as they ambled through the royal gardens of the Queen's compound. Okon ran a gnarly hand over the few strands of hair on his scalp, and adjusted his new barkcloth skirt. He walked up to Tani slowly with his cane, smelling of spearmint and orange.

Tani shuffled by his side, her skirt in near tatters, her white hair unkempt like a palm tree that has been hit by a hurricane. Together they strolled arm in arm stopping to admire the pond apple and the lime, the bilimbi, and gardenias, delaying the inevitable.

Okon paused by a fork in the path. The pathway to the left circled back into the royal gardens. The pathway to the right led to the main causeway that would lead them through the inner gate of the compound to the outer courtyard and beyond.

A gray-and-white shark parrot, known for the tuft on its back that looked like a shark fin, called to them from a pandanus with its melodious tune. Without warning it dropped from its branch with a screech, and swooped passed their faces so close that both could feel its wings stir the air.

"Another omen. It is time," Okon announced.

"Have you ordered supplies?" Tani asked, shoving her emotions aside and forcing herself to be practical.

"I have," he said. "There is a servant who I can trust to keep his mouth shut. I told him to put what I will need in the boat. The supplies should be waiting for me when I get there."

"I will make sure you get there safely."

"Thank you," he said and patted her thin arm. "I was going to ask if you would."

"Of course, you old shark. Do you think I would have you leave alone?"

Okon smiled as the two veered onto the right pathway that would take them to the outer courtyard. Just as they were making their way through the arched gate they heard the fast clip of footsteps draw close behind them. Both turned in unison.

Okon's personal servant, Kaisi, bowed then raised his head. "I beg your forgiveness for the interruption, Elder Okon, but where are you going?"

Okon flicked an eye of concern at Tani then back at his servant. "We are going for a walk…by the shore…alone."

"But there are still Unbelievers in every village. I should follow in case…"

"Alone, I said! Can an old man not enjoy some privacy with a pretty woman?"

"Oh! Tai. Tai." The servant backed away and gave a quick bow. "And when will you return?" he asked.

"When I am ready," Okon said.

Kaisi looked up with knitted brows.

Tani stepped forward. "He will be in my care," she said.

"Tai," Okon said. "And, frankly, I do not wish the Queen or anyone else to know about this. She has enough weighing on her mind."

"But…"

"No buts," Okon said. "This is an order that I expect you to honor."

Gossip traveled fast in the compound and all the servants had heard the rumors about Okon and Elder Tani having been found naked together when Tani had been held captive. Kaisi was beside himself and apologized profusely. "Of course. You have my complete discretion."

"Good," Okon said, and resumed his stroll down the path.

Tani turned her head and gave Kaisi a wink. "Bye. Bye."

Kaisi arched an eyebrow and bowed. He stood staring in disbelief.

When they were out of earshot of the servant, Tani let out a loud cackle to mask the sadness she knew would soon follow. "Perhaps he is embarrassed that such an old man as you should be enjoying the better pleasures with someone so much younger."

"Tai." With the help of his cane Okon pivoted on his heels to face Tani. "How old are you now?" he asked, squinting at her.

She gave a toothless smile. "Oh, I am one-hundred-and-ten…or maybe one-hundred- and-twenty. I forget."

"You are much younger than I by forty or fifty years. What will people think?" he chuckled.

"Tai. People will gossip."

The garden was suddenly flushed with the agitated chatter of monkeys.

"Hear that? The purple howlers are gossiping already," Okon quipped.

The leaves from a nearby tamarind rustled, and a purple howler swung from a branch and jumped onto a milipalm. Its lustrous fur shimmered in prismatic hues, changing from green, blue and violet to a golden sheen and back to blue-green and violet again. A long strand of pearls clenched between its teeth swayed to and fro with a clatter. When the agile creature spotted the two Elders it froze, then leaped to a higher branch, dashing out of view with such vivacity and speed that the Elders didn't know if they had seen the monkey or not.

"Am I getting old or did I not just see a purple howler with a strand of pearls in its teeth?" Okon asked.

"Tai, you did. Little thieves! They have overrun the compound! But that is what you get when you cut down all the sacred palms near the compound walls! Now they are trapped inside and eat all the fruit!"

"That was not my fault!" Okon snapped.

"Well, you should have tried to stop Palomei!" The heat of Tani's anger started rising and her face flushed.

"I did try to stop her!"

"You should have tried harder!"

"I did, but I failed!"

"There is no excuse for committing such a crime! I feel like we are walking in a graveyard! Now there will be no food left over for the pigs. And the howlers leave such a mess!" She turned away from Okon and spit on the ground.

Okon was aghast by Tani's sudden contemptuous rage. He stepped back and scrutinized Tani's disheveled hair, the grime beneath her fingernails, the stench of her sweat – things he purposely avoided noticing before out of respect...out of love.

"Everything is a mess right now," he said, "but there is no need to get so mad at me. Nothing can be done for the sacred palms now. They are gone." He placed a tender hand on Tani's arm and turned her around to face him. "And the servants will find a way to get rid of the howlers and feed the pigs."

Knowing she was madder for the things that had gone unspoken, the old Healer forced herself to calm her sudden fury one heartbeat at a time, aware that life was too precious for arguments now.

"Ah, the pigs." She grabbed Okon's forearm again and drew him close, settling into a quiet truce, sorry she had made such a fuss. They continued down the walkway together arm in arm. "Having pigs was a brilliant idea on your part years ago. They are closer to human flesh and kept the giants from eating us."

"Tai, you have no idea what it was like being married to Palomei's Great Grandmother. I am happy I did not end up roasted on a spit."

No one stopped the two eldest on the island as they amicably ambled past the outer gates, over the river on a small boat and onto a trail that provided a shortcut through the jungle.

Okon pushed back a tree branch with his cane so Tani could pass. "Remember the time you fell from a tree?" he asked.

"Tai. I thought I was falling to my death. But you caught me!"

"And yet you were only four feet off the ground and another twenty feet from the coconuts you were climbing after," he chortled.

Tani's gummy grin stretched from ear to ear. "Well, when you are five years old it feels like you are a mountaintop away from the ground. Of course, being caught by a handsome man did not hurt."

"Tai, I was in my prime then. Now I am very, very old." He turned and looked her in the eye. "Why do you think we never married, you and I?" he suddenly asked. "I mean, before Palomei's Great Grandmother made me her fourth husband?"

Tani stopped in her tracks. "Marry?" she squawked. "I am married to the jungle...to my work...to monitoring the prophecies, and to mentoring Losha and Temple Fox."

"But you did marry."

"Tai, but most of my many husbands drifted like thirsty bees to other luscious blossoms...except for the last one who died in the..." Her voice trailed away, hopelessly tangled like the vines before them.

"But you became an even more magnificent healer because of it," Okon whispered.

"Tai. The massacre sealed my fate," she said, her voice morose and lost for a moment, still remembering the horror.

"It was your destiny," he said. "Just as what I do now is mine."

Tani could feel the air cramp. There was a sullen silence between them.

"I wish I could accompany you," she said, breaking the silence. "If only I could still spin into a Dolphin again I could go with you to see you through to the end."

"No," Okon said. "There are sure to be sharks around. It is better this way."

Tani gave a sad nod and bent to sniff a sweet-scented jungle blossom. She raised it to Okon's nose and he inhaled deeply and smiled. She pinched the blossom off and put it behind Okon's ear, then gave him a peck on the cheek.

"This will calm you," she said.

"But now my heart is all aflutter," he teased.

"Not the kiss, you old fool. The flower!"

Again a stiff silence followed, but neither felt a need to close the gap in the conversation, realizing that what was not being said lay beneath the surface and would never be voiced.

CHAPTER FIFTY-TWO

AT THE RIVER'S EDGE

"We are one people now!"

Losha Ninti
The Makolese Scroll on
The Return of the Ka and the Mending of the Su #52

Losha stopped at the base of the mountain when she came to the river. She turned to face her bedraggled band of followers and spoke for the first time since she had set them on their fast pace down the mountain, and safely through the abandoned enemy camp.

"I ask that you follow me to the Great Round House in Olonopo Crater where Queen Palomei awaits you now. Take heed!" she said, loud enough for all to hear. "The High Shaman took a piece of everyone's vital life force to control us. Your Ka has been freely returned to you now, which allows you to become whole again, to think clearly with your heart once more, and to fulfill your potential as the great Makolese people. But remember, not every islander has had their Ka returned to them yet and many will still view you as their enemy. I have made arrangements with the Queen for everyone to return to wholeness, but it will take some time. Have patience. Treat our people with respect regardless of how they believe. We are one people now!"

The people cheered, until the clamor of their voices subsided, and the sound of water rolling over rock could be heard echoing against the foothills.

Losha bowed to them, which greatly pleased them, then turned on her heels and marched forward in the direction of the grand escarpment that led to the Great Round House.

★   ★   ★   ★   ★   ★

By the time Illa made it to the riverbank all but four of the Rebels had already waded across the river and were on the foot trail that would lead them to the crater.

Illa climbed onto a boulder high by the riverside and waved her thin arms in the air to draw their attention. "Stop! Stop! I have news!" she shouted, her breath reduced to short, shallow puffs.

The last four who were still slogging through the water turned to listen.

"It is just as the Shaman said! Temple Fox is still alive! But he and Losha Ninti work together!"

"What are you saying?" someone shouted back.

"We have been fooled *again*!" Illa announced, still struggling to catch her breath. "We were told…by two of Palomei's runners…back at the Believer's outpost! We have been LIED to!" she screamed.

A man who was waist deep in the water turned to argue. "Then why did Palomei's soldiers not kill us on the way down here? Answer that?"

"We have seen Losha Ninti fulfill the old prophecy with our own eyes, child," one woman shouted. "We have witnessed her power and her healing."

"Tai. You are seeing shadows where there are none," another called out. "It is all over with. We are going to the Great Round House. Come and join us."

"No! You are all wrong!" Illa shouted. "Stop! Do not go there! You will be slaughtered!"

The remaining Rebels turned their backs on her.

"Please, we must warn the Queen!" Illa pleaded. "Losha plans to take the throne! It is what they were planning all along!"

The few who had heard the girl climbed up onto the banks on the other side of the river and continued their journey to Olonopo Crater.

Illa stood alone dumbfounded. Then she began to cry.

CHAPTER FIFTY-THREE

THE HOLLOWED LIGHT

*"What you sense – what you feel deeply – rides on
a river of truth, for truth never lies."*

Elder Tani
The Makolese Scroll on
The Return of the Ka and the Mending of the Su #53

"Is there any food around here?" Naffa complained as Mik-lon scratched the details of his plan in the dirt. "I am starving."

Arma glanced up from the complex diagram Mik-lon had drawn in the dirt. "Go and look yourself...and bring us back some if you find any extra."

Naffa wandered through the camp. He searched the campfires that had been doused two days before and combed through the charcoal. Ignoring the two dead bodies, he came upon the sacks that had belonged to the two runners he had killed. He lifted both in the air, sensing their lightness in weight when he felt a slight tingle in his hand.

"Feels empty," he mumbled to himself.

Curious, he rummaged through the bag anyway, but there wasn't any food inside. His fingers brushed against something clinging to the bottom – something soft – something familiar. Suddenly a stream of electrical energy jumped into his fingers and coursed up his arm. Naffa snatched his hand back as if he had just been electrocuted and flung the sack to the ground!

"Argh!" he howled. He stared down at his hand.

Arma looked over at Naffa with an annoying scowl, then lowered her head again to examine Mik-lon's sketch in the dirt.

"What in Tagheetu's great name is in that sack?" Naffa muttered to himself. He lifted the bag into the air with the tip of his long blade.

At risk to himself he pinched the bottom seam of one sack with the tips of his thumb and index finger and turned the sack upside down to empty its contents.

A dozen feathers drifted lightly to the ground. "Feathers?" he whispered to himself. He stared down at the ground, then stooped for closer scrutiny, which caused his head to throb. *Bi kana! Owl feathers!!*

Using the tip of his knife he raised the second sack and tipped it over as he had done with the first sack. A dozen or more white feathers spiraled to the ground at his feet. One landed on his foot and he let out a yowl.

Pao-ta lifted her head and gawked at the boy. "What in Lord Tagheetu's name is that boy doing?" she asked, irritated.

Arma raised her head again and spied Naffa doing a tortured kind of dance in place as if he were walking on hot coals.

She walked over to him slowly. "Snake?" she offered.

"No!" he gasped. "Feathers!"

"Ah, feathers," she said coolly and grinned. "They are so dangerous."

"No! No! Be careful," he warned and blocked her with his arm. "I found a whole cache' of them, about three dozen in all. " He pointed to the ground at the mixture of horizontally striped brown and yellowish-beige Owl feathers and a smattering of long white Swan feathers and white fluffy down.

"A-ha! Swan feathers! And Owl feathers!" She leaned down to pick up one of the long Swan feathers for her examination. As her fingers drew close, an electromagnetic pulse emanated from the plume. Arma drew her hand back hesitantly.

It is only a feather, she told herself, *even if it did belong to Losha Ninti.*

She started to complete the action, but before she had reached the white feather, it rose delicately into the air, then drifted downward, alighting gently into her open palm.

Arma stared down in wonder. *There is no wind. No breeze.*

A strong thrumming and prickly sensation slowly crept into her fingers. All at once a sudden jolt of electrical energy hit her. Arma bolted backward and, losing her balance, stumbled to the ground. The sensation coursed into her arms and raced through her body, creating the sensation that she was on fire.

"Bi kana lo!" she shouted.

The others immediately dropped what they were doing and sprinted over to Arma, who was still lying on the ground gyrating on top of the pile of feathers as if she had just been wrapped up inside some terrible invisible force.

"Were you bitten?" Mik-lon asked, concerned, but Arma couldn't speak.

"Whatever you do, do not touch those. They are poison!" Naffa said, pointing to the feathers.

Mik-lon stared down at Arma, who was now sprawled face down on the ground, her hair disheveled, her fists balled tight. "Are you all right?" he asked.

Arma managed to roll off the pile of feathers to face the others, her eyes and teeth clenched tight, white down stuck to her cheeks and snagged in her hair. Without realizing she had done so, she succumbed to the strange and powerful sensation and relaxed into the experience. Her eyes remained closed, and she allowed herself to be hugged by the energy until her head lightened and her heartbeat calmed. She peeled a feather off her cheek and squashed it inside of her palm.

"What in Lord Tagheetu's name are you doing?" Naffa complained. "Drop it! It is dangerous!"

Cranik pointed to the litter of plumage on the ground. "What is all this?"

Naffa pointed to the rumpled sacks. "I found Owl feathers inside one sack, and Swan feathers inside the other! And from the distinct vibration on them, I would say they belonged to one very infamous and very pale Wizard, and, our liar of all liars, Losha Ninti – further proof that they were here together."

"Did you read the pattern of feathers before she picked one up?" Cranik asked the boy.

"What do you mean?" Naffa asked, thrown by the question.

Ignoring Arma's apparent state of mind, Cranik grabbed the boy's forearm. "Before she started rearranging them like a chicken scratching in the dirt, did you read them?"

The boy's mouth parted, stupefied. "Why…no," he answered. "I did not think to. I do not know how to read signs."

Cranik pushed the boy aside and leaned down to read the pattern the feathers had made in the dirt. Feeling the intense vibration that rose in the space above the pile he backed away a step. He squinted at the order of feathers from a distance of three feet, but the radiation was too strong for him and he backed further away. A flush overtook him and he began to sweat until the sweat ran into his eyes. Suddenly, he felt light-headed and began to sway. "Who knows how to read these?" he asked.

Pao-ta stepped forward cautiously. She bowed respectfully to the Elder then leaned down to read the pattern of feathers on the ground.

"Shew!" she said as she tried to shield herself from the energy with her hand. She tried to focus on the delicate pile Arma had rolled into, but her vision blurred. "Bi kana, I think I am losing my sight. Everything is turning to a milky white brightness." She stepped away.

"Here, let me try," Chabon offered. "Mind you, I am no great reader of the signs." He kept his toes well away from the soft mound and leaned his head over. But the emanations proved too intense. He grabbed his head between his hands and stepped away. "I cannot," he confessed.

A smile spread across Arma's face. "It is all right. I think I am growing used to the energy." She sat up and opened her hand to examine the white feather. "I think I will keep this and make a charm out of it." She gazed up at the others.

"Tai! Tai! A charm, of course," Naffa added. "Anyone care to have a trophy of the enemy and wear one as a talisman?"

"You think it is safe?" Chabon asked Arma.

"No, it is not safe!" Naffa answered for Arma, his tone full of acid. "At least this way we will get used to their awful energy."

"Actually, it is a pleasant sensation after you get accustomed to the initial shock," Arma said.

Chabon gestured to Mik-lon to go first. "It is your turn," he said. The Warrior nodded in consent and boldly pulled a long Owl feather from the pile and tied it into his hair braid. The others stood waiting for a reaction. Mik-lon bore up well with a forced grin, then reached down for a Swan feather. He tied it onto the shaft of his spear.

Arma laughed out loud. She took the shaft of the long white plume she had been holding and tied it to the center of her necklace made of shells and bone where it hung down between her breasts.

"Well, it is now or never," Pao-ta said. She plucked a Swan feather off the ground with her chubby fingers. All at once a powerful electromagnetic current spiraled up her arm and collided inside her chest, which caused her to double over. The discharge snaked up inside her skull, and a quick flash of brilliant light filled her head. Rocking back on her heels, she let out a deep moan. "Oh my Lord Tagheetu!" she exclaimed, clasping her large bosom.

"Just stay with it a minute or two," Arma instructed.

"Maybe we should not make talismans," Naffa said. "Maybe they are too poisonous!"

"Shut up!" Pao-ta snapped at Naffa. She waited until the intensity of the experience subsided. Her eyes glazed over as she settled into a state of bliss. "This is better than a pot of sha!" She giggled.

Not wanting to be shown up as a coward, Chabon lurched forward. "Give me one of those," he said brusquely. He grabbed an Owl feather first, then snatched up a Swan feather. He clasped both to his chest, then walked away to avoid embarrassment.

Standing several paces away, Cranik studied everyone's reaction while the rest of the group, with the exception of Naffa, took their turn choosing feathers. A couple made feeble groans to mask the obvious pain they felt. One cried out in anguish. Others wept softly to themselves.

The Elder cast a mercurial eye over at Naffa, who stood silently gaping in horror at everyone. Arma still lay on the ground, smiling. Pao-ta hummed quietly to herself with her hands pressed to her breasts. Mik-lon was down on his knees, wrenching up something black and vile. Chabon was nowhere to be seen.

Naffa stood in the center of the Rebels and glanced all around him, bewildered and shocked.

"Look at them! Look at them all! This is dark magic," he worried out loud, suddenly feeling alone and isolated. "Do something!" he finally said to Cranik. But Cranik just shook his head signifying he had no control over the situation.

The Senior Elder witnessed the sheer joy on Arma's and Pao-ta's face and sank into his private thoughts.

Was I wrong? Were we all wrong?

He walked back over to the pile of plumes and reached down and plucked up one long Swan feather. He held it up, delighting in how the sunlight trimmed its edges in gold, relishing its beauty and the warm feeling that spread through his chest. Cranik slowly rolled the feather between his fingers. Tears formed in his eyes and he bent down to retrieve an Owl feather. He held both feathers close to his chest as he walked over to a flat boulder, the powerful loving resonance rushing through his body. He plopped himself down – spent – defeated, his face streaked with new tears.

I was wrong? he cried. *I know it now. Kulo knew. Something happened to him on the mountain that made him change his heart. Even Mefakani admitted that Temple Fox was the True Teacher and then confessed that he himself was an impostor. He did so knowing we would try to kill him.*

And I was right about Losha. She has fulfilled the prophecy. Palomei must believe it too. And now all but ten of the Rebels believe that Losha is the True One. But in all truth, there are two – one male and one female – the True Prophets! Bi kana, I have been so miserably wrong about everything!

Naffa saw the disturbed look on the Elder's face and spoke, hoping someone would listen. "This is a powerful omen. It is as if we have defeated Temple Fox and Losha Ninti already!" he proclaimed in a voice full of strained optimism. The boy tried to smile to convince himself as much as the others, but dropped his smile when he saw that no one was listening to him. "So keep your feathers like you would the head of our enemy," he said, trying to rouse some hope for his cause. "By doing so, you gain some of their strength and some of their power!"

Cranik glanced around him. *All but Naffa understand now what I felt when Losha first touched me. Temple and Losha are the True Teachers. I thank the Gods. I thank all the Spirits for this moment.*

Cranik cast a leery eye over at Naffa, who still stood alone watching the others in silence.

He does not believe. He does not understand. If I explain it to him, will he strike me down?

He glanced at the bodies of the two boys on the ground attracting flies.

We must leave this place. Still, I do not understand what Losha plans to do with the rest of our renegades at the Great Round House...

"She must be merciful," he muttered to himself. "She must! For in time, they all will understand as we have."

"Elder Cranik," Naffa called out weakly, shattering Cranik's private thoughts. Seeing that no one was paying him any attention he drew up beside the Elder. "How do we kill the White Wizard and his woman?"

Cranik looked up at the boy with a sorrowful gaze. "Kill them?" he asked, not quite taking in what Naffa had just asked.

"Tai," Naffa pressed in a quiet tone.

Cranik shook his head. "It is no use, Naffa. Our purpose has been for nothing. Look no further for we have found our answer."

"And what is that?" Naffa asked, his eyebrows furrowed in sudden fright.

"What do you feel?" he whispered.

Naffa took a step back, wide-eyed. "No!" he insisted. "It is not true."

Cranik spoke again, his face flushed with new energy, the weight of his world slowly lifting. "It is true. We have been wrong from the beginning. And now we must stop our own people from doing something stupid."

"Your mind has been poisoned!" he spat. "Look at Mik-lon! Look at *you*!"

"Tai, look at Mik-lon," Cranik whispered hoarsely. "He is releasing all that negativity – all that hatred and anger – all the doubt. He is being purified."

"No!" Naffa shouted defiantly.

"Tai. And look at me," he said, his face taking on a soft and a beatific glow. He locked his eyes onto to Naffa's frightened eyes.

"NOOO!!" Naffa said. He broke into a run.

The boy bolted over to where Mik-lon was resting against a boulder, his retching having subsided, his spear resting in the dirt beside him. Naffa stared into the Warrior's face.

"Mik-lon, tell me what you feel. Tell me!"

The Warrior shook his head in surrender. "It is over. We were wrong."

"You have been charmed! You have been poisoned!" Naffa's face reddened and he backed away and shouted at Mik-lon. "Coward!"

The boy turned and sprinted down the trail to find Chabon, who had disappeared several minutes before. He lumbered around a bend when he spied Chabon crouched on the edge of a steep cliff peering into the distance. He was rocking and weeping softly to himself.

"What are you doing, Chabon! Get up!" Naffa commanded.

Chabon shook his head, signaling he wanted to be left alone.

"You are a traitor!" Naffa shouted in his ear. "You hear me! TRAITOR!"

"I do not know if I can live with myself," Chabon whispered, his voice watery and full of grief. "I killed one of the Believers."

"And now you are one of them," Naffa spat.

"I do not know if I can live with that. I have been so wrong," Chabon cried, and a new wave of tears overtook him. His shoulders heaved with heavy sobs.

"Well, let me help you then," Naffa offered in a muted venomous tone. With the flat of his foot he pushed Chabon off the cliff.

★　　★　　★　　★　　★　　★

Naffa continued his journey down the mountain in a silent rage. Paying no heed to Chabon's twisted broken body on the path, he coursed on. He thought solely of reaching Illa and the Rebels she had hopefully persuaded. When he finally reached the riverbank, Illa was sitting on a mossy log, alone, the sound of water over stone resounding off the riverbank and foothills.

"Illa!" he called out.

The girl turned her head and rose quickly to her feet to greet him.

"What happened?" he asked anxiously.

"Where are the others?" she asked in a sullen tone.

"Never mind about them. What happened?" he asked again.

"They did not listen to me. No one believed me," she cried.

Naffa grabbed her arm and dragged her behind some bushes. "Are they all gone?" he whispered.

She nodded, staring down at her feet, melancholy and fear immobilizing her.

"We are alone, Illa. It is just you and me now."

She looked up puzzled, terrified.

"It is true," he started. "They have all become traitors to our cause – all but you and me. And we are the only ones who know the truth."

"Even Elder Cranik?" she asked.

"They have all given up," he said. "They have surrendered to this mad idea that both Temple Fox and Losha Ninti are the True Teachers. They have been overtaken with a kind of sickness, maybe even possession by evil spirits."

Naffa told Illa about the discovery of the strange Owl and Swan feathers.

"You can still reach the Queen so she knows the truth."

"Me?" she questioned in alarm.

"Here is how you will get into the compound to warn her without being seen." He started to draw a map in the sand when he heard the distant sounds of voices far above them on the cliffs. He grabbed her arm again. "Come quickly! The others are coming! Let us hurry and make some distance from them and hide ourselves so I can explain my plan."

The two scurried down the bank of the river and, when they were out of breath, they ducked behind the thicker bushes in the sand where he explained Mik-lon's original plan to get inside Palomei's compound. He redrew the map in the sand. Illa nodded that she understood until all conversation stopped between them. The distant sound of sandal grating against stone could be heard above them on the windy trail.

"They are getting closer! You have the map memorized?"

"Tai."

"Good. You should go now!" he said.

"You are not coming with me?" Illa asked in panic.

"I have other things to do."

Naffa looked through the heavy foliage above him to where the sounds grew nearer, but Illa didn't follow his gaze, her eyes never leaving Naffa's face.

"Go now so they do not see you," he warned. He brushed away the diagram he had scrawled in the sand. "I will tell them you were gone before I got here. I will play their little game and make them think I am a Believer as they are now."

When he turned to face Illa again her eyes were full of want and fear.

"What are you waiting for? Go!" he insisted.

Illa leaned forward and planted a quick wet kiss on his cheek. She bolted from the bushes and, with nimble feet to avoid leaving footprints, she dashed onto the tops of one boulder after another up the river, until she rounded a steep bend and disappeared from view.

Naffa watched the slight girl slip away beyond his sight. He touched the wet spot on his cheek for no other reason than to remember the moment.

Why do I find a pretty girl just when I know I may never see her again?

Naffa wiped the wetness from Illa's kiss onto his blood-splattered wrap-around and the tender moment was rubbed out. Blotting the sweat from his eyes, he noticed his hands trembling. He stilled one hand with the other.

His heart jumped in his chest, and he willed his racing blood to slow, when he heard their voices more distinctly. He drew his knees up to his chin and pulled his energy inward demanding of himself calm and calculating control. He sat quite still and feigned a brooding pose as the footfalls drew closer and louder.

Mik-lon was in the lead and spotted Naffa first. He called to him from the water's edge.

"Naffa!"

Will there be a spear waiting for me? the boy worried.

Naffa raised his head and rested it on his knees. "Mik-lon," he whispered weakly in greeting.

Mik-lon moved a branch out of the way with the tip of his spear, uncovering the figure partially hidden by leafy branches.

Naffa's nerves came suddenly undone by the sight of Mik-lon's spear and the Warrior's large and imposing presence. His heart began to race again, but he didn't let his panic show.

"Where is Illa?" Mik-lon asked.

"I do not know. There was no one here when I got here."

"Did you see Chabon on the way down the trail?" he asked with suspicion.

"We spoke briefly. He seemed depressed," Naffa offered, his voice growing quiet.

The others came down the trail one by one and stood at the edge of the foliage.

"Did he say anything to you?" Mik-lon prodded.

"He said he regretted killing one of the Believers in the skirmish on the mountain."

"And then what happened?" Mik-lon asked, and the others pressed forward.

Naffa looked from one to the other, but adverted Cranik's gaze. "Why do you ask? Where is he?"

"He is dead!" Arma stated flatly, almost accusingly.

"From an ambush!" Naffa asked in sudden mock alarm.

"We do not think so," Arma answered.

"Then how did he die?" Naffa asked. He unfolded himself from his closed posture, pretending he was interested.

"It appears that he fell to his death," Arma said. "We found his body along the trail. You did not see him fall?" she asked, her eyes gleaning what they could from the boy's demeanor and tone.

Naffa shook his head. "I am sorry. He was a fine man, and a very brave and dedicated patriot."

"Then you did not witness his fall or hear anything?" Mik-lon asked.

Naffa shook his head again. "Was it suicide?"

"It could have been," Cranik said as he stepped forward pushing branches aside.

Feeling Cranik closing in on him, Naffa willed himself to respond calmly. It was an effort, but he spoke quietly – cautiously. "What a waste," is all he said.

"We took rocks and covered his body, and that of the two young men," Pao-ta added. "That will have to do until we can return to retrieve them later and give them a proper funeral rite. At least the birds will not find them."

Naffa nodded and rose. "There has been too much death this day," he said sadly, his head hung low. "And I too feel regret."

"For what?" Pao-ta asked.

"For killing those two men up there," he gestured with a twist of his head in the direction of the mountain. "Maybe I was wrong," he lied.

"Maybe you were," Cranik stated without sympathy.

Arma's voice was suffused with more compassion. "We were all wrong."

"Tai. I am just a stupid boy. I admit it," Naffa confessed, his voice purposely falling flat and weak, his bold undetectable lie taking root.

This is what they want to hear – a confession – some declaration of regret.

There was a span of tense silence until the moment drew out too long, leaving a heavy awkwardness between Naffa and the others. He looked directly at Cranik and broke the silence. "What are we to do now, Senior Elder?"

"We go to the Olonopo Crater just as Losha Ninti instructed us to," he answered. "But we must hurry. It is going to rain."

"But what about the others?" Naffa embraced his role more easily now, improvising as he went along. "Illa must have gotten the chance to speak to some of the Rebels and tell them what we had initially discovered. Should we try and stop them?"

"We do not know where Illa is or any of the others that she may have convinced," Cranik explained. "We will still proceed as planned and go to meet with the Queen."

Who will probably kill us, Naffa worried.

Feeling he had been returned into their confidence, Naffa fell in line with them. And together the band of ten silently waded in the shallowest part of the river and headed to the trail leading past the Queen's compound to Olonopo Crater.

★　★　★　★　★　★

Arma found herself slowing her pace so she could walk side by side with Mik-lon. She made a quick study of his muscular chest, the bulge in his crotch, then met his waiting eyes.

He smiled at her. She grinned back somewhat embarrassed until her brows furrowed and she resumed an overly serious demeanor. Her voice was barely audible above the rising voice of the rapids.

"I offered him one of the Owl feathers," she said to Mik-lon.

Mik-lon leaned down closer. "What? Who?"

Arma craned her neck, her lips close to his ear. She felt one of his hair braids brush against her bare shoulder and she shuddered with delight. "Naffa," she began again, shaking off the momentary distraction. "I offered him one of the Owl feathers."

Mik-lon raised an eyebrow, but didn't comment.

"He visibly flinched at the offer and said he did not deserve it. Then he walked away from me. I think he was scared."

"And what did you draw from this?" he asked.

"He is frightened of the power the two Teachers hold. Maybe he is even lying about his sudden conversion as a Believer so…"

"…we do not kill him."

"Which we would not have done anyway," Arma added.

"Speak for yourself," Mik-lon said. "I will defend the True Prophets."

Arma snorted at this. "Somehow I do not think they need our protection. As I recall Temple Fox pulled a sword out of his own gut during the exorcism for Losha's dead husband. They have the power to take care of themselves."

"So you think Naffa has suddenly become agreeable so he can get inside Olonopo Crater."

Arma nodded.

"Perhaps he hopes to join in some spontaneous rebellion with the others Illa has convinced."

Arma nodded again in reply.

"It will not do him any good. Two True Prophets who work together against a handful of Unbelievers, who still believe Losha is or is not the one and only True Prophet, is unlikely to make any significant impact. Still, I will keep my eye on him," he whispered back.

"As will I," Arma said.

She fastened her gaze onto Mik-lon's light brown eyes a bit too long, then turned away self-consciously.

"Do you like orchids?" Arma suddenly asked.

"Of course," Mik-lon said. "They are beautiful."

Arma grinned up at him. As was her way, she quickened her pace to distance herself from Mik-lon and rejoined the others ahead. She glanced behind her to see Mik-lon quickening his pace to follow her and she smiled to herself.

CHAPTER FIFTY-FOUR

LAMENTATIONS

INVITATION
I stand alone,
an invitation
for the Light
to take
my flesh and bones.

I am still,
Light filling
hollow places
with the splendor
of a million suns.

I am one
and many faces,
my will fused
with the will of God,
spilling over into Love.

I am the Lion
and the Lamb.
I am Light.
I am Love.
I am Joy.

I am.

Elo Tivluc, popular Makolese poet
The Makolese Scroll on
The Return of the Ka and the Mending of the Su #54

The two centenarians shuffled down the well-worn path with the beach in sight. Tani tightened on Okon's arm to hold him back. He followed her gaze as a root snake slithered slowly across the trail. The color and pattern of its scales changed rapidly from the ocher-spotted roots it had been hiding under to the khaki-and-saffron colored leaves it was creeping into in the dappled light, camouflaging itself as it passed.

Okon watched every detail of the transformation with fascination, noticing the air about him grow crisper, cleaner, the colors of the snake growing more vibrant.

"Beautiful," he said in a breathy voice. He squeezed Tani's hand.

"Another omen," she whispered back.

They waited until their poisonous guest slipped out of striking distance.

When they reached the beach, the stern of Okon's boat was already breathing with the sea as it rose and fell in the swelling tide. His boat was filled with the needed supplies – a fishing pole, a box of bait, bamboo pipes filled with clean water and sealed with beeswax, string bags packed with fruit and nuts, and dried fowl covered in honey and berries wrapped carefully with waxy leaves and tied with jute.

"I need for you to tell Palomei what I have done," he said, staring out to sea.

Tani looked at him with apprehension…for him…for herself. "I will find the right moment."

The eldest of Elders turned toward the old Healer and placed his gnarled hand on top of her disheveled mass of white hair. He blessed her, and Tani felt a pronounced prickling on her scalp that cascaded through her body. He removed his hands and leaned over so their foreheads touched. When he pulled away, he set his gaze on his ring. "You still have the ring?"

She fingered the heavy gold ring that was too big to wear and had been tied around her neck with jute. Like a stepped pyramid, each tier was set with a series of faceted gemstones, starting with meteoritic iron at its base, then ruby, aquamarine, and iolite. The square flat top had been fashioned from several pieces of green tourmaline that fit like a jigsaw puzzle. At the center of the ring sat a slightly raised dome of faceted amethyst surrounded by another thin band of gold. The whole design was reminiscent of a miniature ancient temple.

Great Grandfather nodded his head in approval. He looked at it as if to weigh its importance one last time. "And you have the Mimi-ishi?"

Tani pulled the black ear-shaped stone from her sash and held it up to him for his examination.

"And do you have the ceremonial gris?" she asked Okon.

Okon pulled the dagger from a hard leather sheath by his side and placed it into her hand. The blade was a tapered, clear, double terminated quartz with twelve long facets, each end a sharp point. The hilt had been fashioned from fossilized whalebone for firm handling, while the peculiar handle had been forged from an unknown metal. Six metal spines that spiraled down to its fat pointed base were set with rough rubies, garnets, meteorites, and rare metals of titanium, thulium, iridium, and ilmenite.

Tani inspected the dagger with a discerning eye. "Curious. The metal looks much like what the Sea Bells are made from."

"Iridium perhaps."

"Ah, you know metals like I know plants," she admitted. "It holds an odd and very powerful energy."

"Tai," the old man said. "We could not have fashioned such a thing. It is from the gods."

Tani nodded and handed the dagger back to Okon with care. He placed it safely back into its sheath, then clasped both of her bony hands in his.

"You are not just the Jushin-junshi Shomei anymore. You will be the eldest of Elders and the Shuntshu Junshi now. Wear the responsibility well."

There was no saying good-bye for Tani. "I honor you. I will remember you," she said and bowed her head.

They kissed tenderly and embraced for a lingering moment. Then both stepped into the surf, the rising tide pulling on their ankles. She helped him climb into boat, making certain he was safe.

"I will not be needing this any longer," he said. He handed Tani his cane.

She took it and pressed it to her long flat breasts. "I will keep it forever."

Okon looked at her amused. "Do not be so soppy."

He hoisted the heavy anchor up and struggled to pull the donut-shaped rock over the gunwale. Tani sucked in a sharp breath as it came crashing to the bottom of the boat with a loud thud, setting the boat rocking. Okon looked up, embarrassment reddening his face until he broke out in nervous laughter. He grabbed a long oar to push off from the shallows, and the bow of the boat slipped free from the shore with the sand grinding against its underbelly. The boat bobbed in the surf as it coasted out to sea, until he raised the small sail and secured the sheet to the cleat. The boat picked up momentum. He hurried to the bow to see Tani one last time.

Okon lifted a string bag filled with bananas. "Look!" he shouted. "My favorite!"

"They are easy to eat when you have no teeth!" she called back, and they both laughed.

"May the gods bless and honor you. May Tahneyah fill your sail," she shouted. "I will be watching and listening for you."

"Bless you." Okon held up his hand in praise and blessing. And as the wind caught his sail he waved good-bye.

Tani watched from the shore until she could no longer see his boat on the horizon. She remained long after he had gone, too stunned and numb to cry.

"What have I done?" she whispered.

CHAPTER FIFTY-FIVE

TRUST

*"You must know beyond belief, trust without
doubt, and be courageous beyond thought of
consequence. And above all else, forgive and love;
love the one who threatens you most and throws
you into disbelief, doubt, and fear."*

The Unknown Voice
Reference to the Makolese Scroll on The Education of Temple Fox #5
The Makolese Scroll on
The Return of the Ka and the Mending of the Su #55

Temple sat crossed-legged on the floor in the long room behind the Queen's empty chamber. High windows constructed from a latticework of intricate mahogany carvings filtered the early morning light, showering beams of light on his quiet form. Behind the windows grew a tall, spiky gris palm. As each breeze stirred it cast sharp shadows across Temple's eyes, and his eyelids fluttered in the flickering light.

Temple's attention was split in several directions, so he breathed more deeply to enter into a light trance. The sudden awareness of something unexpected stirred at the corners of his mind, grappling for his attention. In his mind's eye he saw a small band of Rebels who had fallen far behind Losha and the other Rebels. An Elder was leading the small group and there was a light around him. But there was also a gray cloud of darkness in the group, and the cloud grew blacker, thicker. Temple took careful note of this and tucked the vision away just as his thoughts were interrupted by the the bamboo screen sliding open.

E-lon-e' entered the chamber quietly and closed the sliding screen behind her. She lifted her silk dress slightly up off the floor and bowed before him.

"Master," she intoned.

"Please, simply address me as 'Temple,'" he said, his eyes still closed as he drew his senses back onto the room.

"I beg your forgiveness for the intrusion. I am E-lon-e', the Queen's Head Administrator. I am responsible for the running of the Queen's compound."

Temple caught the scent of coriander and mint. He opened his eyes and beheld the comely Administrator. His eyes roamed over her tall and slender form, noting that unlike the other women in Makol, her dress was covering her breasts and was buttoned up to her long, graceful neck. The stark contrast of her long black hair and bourbon-colored skin against the subtle sheen of her peach silk dress pleased his senses. He forced himself to refocus on what she was saying.

"We have had a runner come with a message for the Queen," E-lon-e' announced. "She wishes to share it with you."

Temple nodded to the Administrator from where he sat.

"Losha Ninti is midway to the crater now. And she is being followed by the Rebels without incidence."

Temple nodded in acknowledgment. "We will give them a few more hours, or until the sun is three-quarters in the sky to the west, as planned. By then they will be well fed and rested and ready for quite a show." His brow suddenly furrowed and his eyes took on a faraway cast.

"Are you all right?" she asked.

"There are many things that are troubling me. I was just thinking about the prophecy."

"May I sit?" she asked. She gestured to a cushion nearby.

Temple nodded. He ran his eyes over E-lon-e' as she gathered her dress to the side and sat with her legs askew. She waited until he spoke again, her palms resting gracefully in her lap.

Temple forgot where he was for a distracted second and cleared his throat. When he came to his senses he repeated the old prophecy – a prophecy he knew now by heart.

> *"A human God, who comes from the Heavens, will be Teacher and Prophet to the Makolese. The Holy One will come at a time of peril and help to conquer the enemies of the Makolese. This magical Being will be the*

High Priest's greatest ally in conquering his enemies.... One without the other is empty."

The words of the ancient prophecy haunted him.

"Power multiplies tenfold and then again tenfold, again and again until the time of Purification and Redemption. To be recognized, the Divine One must bear the sign of Wisdom, which is the mark upon the holy brow. Beware of impostors, who can fool the elect."

He looked at the Administrator. "Frankly, I don't understand the prophecy. Losha and I have been Mefakani's greatest ally and did help him to conquer himself. But he fell into darkness again through his own guilt and grief. How on this good green Earth can Losha and I help to conquer the enemies of the Makolese when they war among themselves?"

Temple idly ran a hand over the pronounced scar on his brow. "I don't give a damn if someone believes that Losha or I am the True Prophet or not. But this whole thing has turned into a bloody mess! To what purpose have Losha and I truly served but to divide the people and bring the Makolese to war?"

"Perhaps you should breathe deeper and center yourself. I will invoke the Goddess Hianna and support you with prayer," she said. She bowed her head.

"That's exactly what Losha would've told me. You're right. I must remember what the Light said to me in the Great Round House a month ago. It said, 'You must know beyond belief, trust without doubt, and be courageous beyond thought of consequence. And above all else, forgive and love; love the one who threatens you most and throws you into disbelief, doubt, and fear.'"

He closed his eyes and took three deep power breaths, reminding himself of what he was told.

A few minutes passed and his eyes flew open. "The only one who threatens me the most right now is *me*," he breathed between his lips. "It seems I must continually relearn to trust the Divine within me. But I'm so bloody human."

He looked into E-lon-e''s sympathetic eyes for an embarrassing second. "Thank you for letting me share my thoughts and feelings."

She lowered her eyes and bowed her head slightly.

"And so the plan this evening must work or..." He stopped short.

E-lon-e' gave in to the slightest hint of a frown.

"You're troubled by this as well?" Temple asked.

"May I ask the Teacher a question?" she asked.

"Of course."

"What are the chances that this will work without any incidence of violence?"

Temple closed his eyes for a quiet second, then opened them. "There's a ten percent chance there'll be no violence."

"Then there is a great probability this will not work at all?"

"Tai," he said.

"Then I fervently pray to what you refer as to the Divine within you that this plan of yours will work."

"I pray as well." Temple returned a weak smile and beheld the Administrator's beauty for a long second, savoring what he could of what was left of any beauty on the mysterious isle.

CHAPTER FIFTY-SIX

THE GREAT GATEWAY

*"Some said it was a hollowed stone wheel. Some
said it was a smooth tunnel, while others knew it to
be a slim ribbon of rainbow light made from
crystal quartz suspended in midair. Whatever it
was made of it had been put in place by the Gods
to keep the Makolese inside the Barik Limits like
crabs trapped inside a crab trap. Traffic was
regulated by the Gods and the Makolese were
barred from leaving."*

Makolese History Scroll #119
The Makolese Scroll on
The Return of the Ka and the Mending of the Su #56

Most Makolese fishermen, having tested the boundaries of the Barik
Limits, knew where it was. The doorway that led beyond the Limits,
however, was another matter.

One old fisherman, named Sabayon Kuf, who had a habit of
fishing alone right up to the edge of the Limits, describe this portal as
the lens of a great eye that one could sail in and out of when the iris
opened briefly at dusk and dawn. He claimed he had sailed through it
many times. Sabayon Kuf, however, also drank a great deal of sha and
once claimed to have killed a whale single-handedly. When he had
returned with no evidence of such a fantastic catch, he claimed he had
left it behind as an offering to the Mother Sea.

Other fishermen described the gateway as a mammoth arch that
rose high in the air and spanned a quarter of a mile in width at sea. Its
uppermost part was reported to be hair-thin, its base widened at the
waterline to a hand's-width, while its lower parts were submerged in

the sea where it formed a thick ring made from some strange metal that never rusted like the Sea Bells.

Having examined it with spears and oars, others claimed it had been formed from some clear unbreakable volcanic glass, which is how theories arose about its origins being volcanic.

Some said the Great Gateway was the slim mouth left from a mighty volcano that had tipped on its side from drinking too much sha. Still others believed it was the womb of the Mother Sea herself, and the very portal where fish, birds, and other life-forms were first born. When the Wind is blowing hard, they say, the Wind is making love to the Great Mother, and often you can hear her moaning in ecstasy. Those who believed this said that even the most horrid enslavers, who sailed from the Mother, were her creation. What lies beyond the Barik Limits, they claimed, is the amoral, impersonal, un-manifest world of great nothingness where all lies in unrealized potential, and that this tunnel somehow connects to another gateway that leads to the Outside World.

Great Grandfather Okon, of course, thought this all was complete nonsense. He had been to the edge of the gateway more than anyone alive and knew full well that the ancient portal was nothing more than the upended remains of the jawbone from Mao-Atua, the great Shark God.

All of this was very much on Okon's mind when a great gust of wind tipped his boat precariously close to the water's edge nearly swamping it and toppling most his of food supply into the ocean. He reached for the food bouncing on the surface of the water, but the more he leaned over the more water the boat took in. Abandoning his efforts, he quickly drew back to balance the boat and set it right again. And then he bailed…and bailed. By the time he had finished bailing, his string bags stuffed with food were long gone…an offering to the Mother Sea.

"Why feed a dying man?" he said out loud.

The night had fallen and the stars ripened and marked the pathway for Okon. Tongues of water lapping against the boat became many voices in a lullaby he had heard from childhood. The boat became a cradle…or a coffin…he knew not which, but he slept and had the dream again.

CHAPTER FIFTY-SEVEN

CURSES AND CURES

CRY A HEALING FOR ME

*"Cry a healing for me
with your best intent.
Blow it onto a feather,
then tie it to
a bush in windy weather,
praying it is sent.
Cry a healing for me.*

*Cry a healing for me,
whether it's done with fists,
or by calling a fawn
to prance lightly
over my heart at dawn
in the morning mist.
Cry a healing for me.*

*Cry a healing for me.
Sing it loud in song.
Dance it in the air
in twists, knowing
your breath and wind's a pair
that sweeps the Earth along.
Cry a healing for me.*

*Cry a healing for me, please.
Suffer it if you must.*

> *But weep it 'til*
> *your chest is soaked*
> *and heart is fire filled.*
> *My pain will turn to dust,*
> *when you -*
> *Cry a healing for me."*

Elo Tivluk, popular Makolese poet
The Makolese Scroll on
The Return of the Ka and the Mending of the Su #57

Losha placed her arm around Tiv's shoulders. "Tiv, I think you should go back to the Shaman's compound. Where we are going could be dangerous for you."

Tiv shook his head and placed his hand back into hers, reluctant to leave the warmth and caring he found from this great lady.

"No, Tiv. You really must go now," she said. "I need for you to go back and let Jabal and O'Juma know what has happened. Will you do that for me?"

Anxious to please, he nodded his head.

"Good," she said, smiling, and rested her hand on his shoulder to reassure him. "I need for you to do something else…something different."

He looked up at her with wanting eyes.

"I would like for to take the long route to the Shaman's compound by way of Sang-Wehtu' Spring. When you reach the sacred spring, bathe there and rest awhile before you venture further to the compound. You know the route?"

Tiv nodded. He knew it well.

"All right, then. I bless you. And I thank you, dear boy, for you have been a courageous and most valuable servant." She placed her hand atop his shaved head. A river of soothing energy poured from her hand like liquid light into his crown until it cascaded down and through his energy body.

She lifted her hand off his head, then knelt a little to touch her forehead to his forehead as was the Makolese custom when one older person blessed a younger one.

Tiv bowed. When he walked a few paces he turned and waved good-bye to everyone.

"Bye, Tiv!" a scattering of voices called out.

"Poor boy," Kulo whispered to Losha. "He has been so traumatized. Will he ever be healed?"

★　★　★　★　★　★

The ten reformed Rebels marched down the banks of Anaba River with the view of the sheer walls of the Queen's compound in the distance. Naffa paced himself several yards away from the others so he could think and plan his next move.

How in the name of Lord Tagheetu can I kill a Wizard?

He ran a dirty hand through his rumpled hair nervously.

Temple Fox has survived several attacks on his life. But he cannot be invincible. All creatures have a weakness – some hidden vulnerability.

Mighty Lord Tagheetu, he began to pray in his mind, *if I have been chosen to slay the White Wizard, then please send me help, a sign, or a message of some kind as to how to do this great thing. I will do it in your name, Lord Tagheetu. I will do it for my people so we do not become the slaves of Temple Fox and the traitor Losha Ninti. Please help me!* he begged.

No sooner did Naffa say this prayer when Cranik held up his hand to stop everyone.

"We must stop and rest," the Elder insisted.

"But we are so far behind the others," Arma complained.

Cranik pointed to several empty fire pits by the riverside. He held his hands over the coals. They were still hot.

"We have paced ourselves well and have almost caught up with the others," he said. "Judging from the heat of the coals we are only several minutes behind them now. The rest of the walk will be easy, but the climb up the escarpment to the crater will be arduous. So please, let us find something to eat like the others did and rest awhile so we can gain some strength."

"Tai, we are all starving," Pao-ta said. "We can easily stir these embers to life again if we only had something to cook."

Naffa squinted into the distance upriver at the figure of an old man with a fishing pole. He broke into a sprint and called out. "Great Uncle, is that you?"

Mik-lon grinned at Arma. "I think Naffa just found us something to eat."

The leathery old man heard the pounding of familiar feet draw nearer. He dropped his string of fish and threw his arms out as the boy fell into them. "Naffa! My dear grandnephew! Your parents and I have been worried sick."

Naffa hugged the old man. "I am sorry, Great Uncle. Are they all right?"

"Tai, Tai! They know, as I know, where you have been, boy." He patted Naffa's bare shoulder and stared blindly at the boy's face. He ran his long bony fingers over the boy's eyebrows and then his cheeks, touching him lightly with deftness and sensitivity. When he ran a finger beneath Naffa's eyes and caught a tear he patted the boy's cheek. "Now. Now. You have seen some horrible things and are frightened. But I know how brave you are. We are all proud of you."

Not wanting the others to see him, Naffa sniffed back a tear and wiped his face with the back of his dirty hand.

"I have come to the river every day to catch a whisper of some news. No boats are allowed to sail to the Green River or the rapids. Still, I have heard the rumors. When you did not come home we realized you must have gone to Hollow Mountain with the Rebels. We heard there was a skirmish with some of Queen Palomei's soldiers. And then days later there was a great explosion that we could hear from the village! We thought you were dead!"

"I am sorry," Naffa apologized again. "I could not tell anyone where I was going. There was a great explosion and Shaman Mefakani is dead."

"Then he did not succeed in killing the White Wizard?"

"No, he did not! And now the Queen's Interpreter has joined Temple Fox and pretends to also be the Great Teacher. They work together now as *two* Wizards!"

The old man grimaced, revealing a row of missing teeth. "Losha Ninti?" he asked. "I know her voice. She was just here...with many others."

"She appeared to us as a great white Swan and bears the sacred mark upon the brow."

The old man shook his head. "There is much confusion, and now more than one imposter. And you say she and Temple Fox work together?"

"Tai."

The old man patted Naffa's cheek again and drew the boy's forehead to his own brow in blessing. "I bless you, boy, for your strength and courage," he said, then pulled away. "Your parents and I believe as you do. The white man is a false prophet. And now it seems the Interpreter as well has joined this dangerous ruse. Bi kano lo, if I were younger and had not been born blind, I would have joined you."

"I believe you," Naffa said, feeling more at ease.

"Although the river has been closed to all traffic to the north, Losha Ninti and a troop of people came through here just a few minutes ago. I could smell the fish they stopped to cook. Sounded like there may have been a hundred of them. I know it was her. I heard her voice. She insisted that all who had taken life be bathed and blessed by her in the river...to wash the stain of death off of them."

"Tai, you are right. Losha Ninti and the other Rebels did come here, I am sure. Only now, Great Uncle, they believe she is the Great Teacher."

"Temple Fox must be stopped," the Elder said emphatically. "Both of them must."

"But how, Great Uncle? How?"

Just then Mik-lon strode up to the two.

Naffa whispered in the old man's ear. "Say nothing. A Believer approaches."

"And who is this?" Mik-lon asked Naffa and bowed to the Elder.

"This is my Great Uncle, Kal," Naffa answered.

"Who has many fine fish," Mik-lon joked.

"Tai, he does," Naffa said. The boy stooped and retrieved the string of fish and handed them to the warrior. "He has graciously offered his fish to us for our midday meal."

"I have?" the old man asked.

"Thank you." Mik-lon bowed again to the blind man, then trotted back to the others, who had already stirred the coals into a nice fire.

When the footsteps had faded, the old man leaned over. "That was a Believer?"

"Tai, they are everywhere. No one is to be trusted anymore. The people I am with are one small faction of former Rebels who now believe that Temple Fox and Losha Ninti are both the Great Teachers. I have aligned with them so I can get into Olonopo Crater where the Queen will be waiting for us."

Kal furrowed his brow. "Oh, there will be danger. Come back with me, Naffa. Come home to your parents."

"I cannot, Great Uncle. There is a list of all the Rebels and my name is on it. If I do not go now, they will only find me later."

"You have a blade of some kind?"

Naffa placed the Elder's weathered hand onto the hilt of his long blade.

"Ah," the old man said. "This is the fine blade your father gave you."

"But this will not be enough to kill the two Wizards."

The old man's lifeless eyes grew solemn. "So," he said, "tell me what you know of this White Devil and this traitor to our people, so I can figure out how to kill them."

While the others cooked the fish and ate, Naffa and his Great Uncle sat on the ground huddled close together in conversation.

"They know how to spin…into an Owl and a Swan, you say?" Kal said.

"Tai," Naffa whispered.

"Well, that is your key," the old man whispered. "Find the shared enemy of all Swans and all Owls, and you have your answer."

Naffa scratched his head in thought with his dirty nails. "The Owl has no enemy on this island, but the snake."

Kal nodded.

"And a snake may also kill a Swan."

Kal smiled.

"Snake venom?" Naffa asked.

"Tai. And I have some."

"You do?"

"Of course. Elder Tani always keeps a fresh supply for me. I use the venom from the horned saw-scale viper as medicine for my heart in the most minute doses. But in larger doses it could kill a whale!"

"The mighty Lord Tagheetu has answered my prayers!" the boy said excitedly.

"But if I gave it to you, how would you use it?" the old man pushed.

"I…I do not know," Naffa said.

"Think, boy!"

"In a cup of sha?" Naffa asked, his eyebrows drawn together.

"Do you plan on offering the Wizard a cup of sha anytime soon?" the old man asked.

"Well, no," he said embarrassed.

Kal pulled out his short blowpipe. "Use this." He placed a length of bamboo pipe into Naffa's hands, and the boy secreted it under his clothing close to his thigh and the knife he carried. Then Kal handed Naffa a tiny bottle carved from black obsidian and a leather pouch holding three darts. Naffa slipped the objects into the folds of his sash.

"Do not dilute the venom as I do. Use it full strength."

"This is undiluted? Why in the name of Lord Tagheetu would Elder Tani give you a bottle of this full strength? Is she crazy?"

"Now, quiet down. She did not give it to me full strength. I took this bottle from her hut after she was arrested. I needed my medicine and knew where the catalyst was. I dilute it myself. Thank the Lord Tagheetu not all of her potions were taken by Palomei's Guards."

"So, you drink this stuff?'

"Tai, but only one drop per jug of clean spring water. You will have to dip my darts in the full-strength potion. And you will have to get close to your targets. It is a short pipe," his great-uncle warned.

Naffa grabbed his great-uncle's hand, then squeezed it tightly. "I hope to be as good a shot as you are."

"Ah, when you have no eyes, you use your ears and other senses. That is why I am such a good hunter. I can tell you what animal is close just by the rustling sound it makes."

"Thank you, dear Uncle."

"Are you forgetting something?" the old man asked.

"What?"

Kal pulled another small bottle from beneath his sash. "The antidote. You do not think Elder Tani would give me such a powerful medicine without an antidote, do you? Feel the bottle," he said, placing the fat glass bottle in the boy's hand. "Feel the difference?"

"Tai."

"Good. Do not mix them up. Now you better join the others," the old man said. "They are ready to go."

Naffa turned around with a start and leaped to his feet just as Elder Cranik, Mik-lon, and Arma came up behind him.

"We are leaving, Naffa," Arma said. "And we have saved you a fillet." She handed the boy the steaming fish cradled on a banana leaf. She turned to the old man. "We thank you for your kindness."

The old man nodded and smiled up at the voice. With no further delay the group veered from the riverbank to the trail leading to Olonopo Crater.

CHAPTER FIFTY-EIGHT

BEAUTY AMIDST BROKENNESS

SILENCE BEFORE THE WORD

Think I am mute?
Don't interpret my silence
with such severity.
There are no words
for the radiant self.
I am soaked in a light
that cannot be described –
a language that precedes
and exceeds the first preverbal grunt,
is far beyond all the star maps
of the written word
that flashes like the moon
on the first dark waters.

Breaking the silence,
I am here now
ready to burst upon the scene
with new words
poised like the crane -
one leg tucked up against its belly -
the other a pillar of perfect balance
set firmly in the amniotic mud -
its keen eye dancing
with star language,
until urged to strike!
The gasping prey

pierced like the swift
finished stroke
of a bamboo brush,
wet and dripping
in the open air.

It all starts there in a quiet rush,
and even on dry land
where the geometry of stones
speak of themselves in hushed tones
of pulsating rhythms.
And the tree limbs sway
to form new meanings and new words
with a clatter
and smatter of birdsong.

All matter laid out on the world altar
in symbol form.
All sound played out
in the grand architecture of light.
All giving the same radiant message.
I am divine design
and I am made of love.

Elo Tivluk, popular Makolese poet
The Makolese Scroll on
The Return of the Ka and the Mending of the Su #58

Tiv passed by the palace guards who stood on the riverbanks that wrapped around the compound's southern gate. A tightness began to build inside his chest and his breathing grew shallow. Feeling like he was being mauled from the inside out, he plucked at his skin to pull the annoying sensation out, but his agitation increased. In spite of his physical fatigue and the persistent clawing, he ran swiftly down the river, his need to serve Losha pressing on him. He wound his way above and around the marsh reeds, down the river where it narrowed, until he came upon the quiet spring.

Winyon sat on a log staring into the waters with a bundle of herbs in her hand. She looked up in surprise.

"Tiv?"

He bowed and walked up to her.

She embraced him, but he pulled away, his head hanging down.

"What is the matter?" she asked. "What has happened? Can you write it out for me in the sand?"

The boy shook his head.

"You can no longer read or write?" she asked in disbelief.

He stared at her blankly.

"Damn that Mefakani!" she cursed. "I understand, Tiv. Mefakani once cursed my tongue so I could speak to no one."

Tiv pointed to the mountain. He grabbed a stick and drew an oval in the sand, then three loops perpendicular to the top of it.

"Ah, but you can draw." Winyon squinted at the scrawl. It looked like a basket with three handles. "What is that?" she asked.

He made a motion in the air as if his hand were a bird flying with no flapping wings.

"The airboat?"

He nodded and drew back his arm as if he were throwing a spear, then took his stick and jabbed the drawing over and over again in the sand. With a final strike from his stick he obliterated the image.

"The airboat was attacked by the Rebels? It was destroyed?"

He nodded his head vigorously and drew the glyph for Mefakani, which was the same symbol that was tattooed on the Shaman's cheek – a zigzag. Tiv drew a line through it and obliterated it as well with his foot.

"Dead? The Shaman is dead? Oh, Great Tagheetu's Ghost!" she breathed. "Mefakani is truly dead."

Tiv nodded his head, emotions he had been holding back beginning to well up inside of him, searching for a way out.

He scribbled in the sand again, this time drawing a well-delineated swan. He flapped his arms in the air to denote her flying.

"Losha came. And then what happened?" she asked.

He touched his heart and his countenance brightened at the remembrance of Losha. He took a sharp breath and placed his hands on top of Winyon's head.

"She healed people? She blessed them?"

His head bobbed up and down.

"She is with the Rebels now? And they know now that she is the Great Teacher…or, at least, one of them?"

He gave an enthusiastic nod, then pointed past the river onto the direction Losha and the Rebels were heading. He pointed to the figure of the Swan again and drew the glyph for Rebels, which was a crooked X, then drew the symbol for the Queen, which was a bee. He pointed in the direction of the crater and scrawled a bird's-eye view of the crater with the Great Round House at its center.

"The Rebels, Losha, and the Queen are meeting at the Great Round House as planned?"

Tiv nodded. He threw the stick aside and, facing the spring, he squatted in the sand and redrew the zigzag glyph again. He wiped it away with a sweep of his hand, redrew it, then obliterated it again.

"Tai, tai, he is dead," Winyon said. "Mefakani, your Master, is dead."

The boy struggled to breath. "Mmmm…" he mumbled. "Mim…mim…my fault," he said.

Winyon looked up with surprise. "You spoke! Tiv, you just spoke!"

"My…my fault," he repeated.

"Oh, no, no no!" she said. "It was not your fault. You had nothing to do with it. Tiv, you can speak!" she said with new joy.

"My…fault," he stuttered again and dared to look into Winyon's excited eyes.

"Oh, Great Tagheetu! You have done no harm, dear boy. *He* harmed *you*. Do you understand? If they killed Mefakani in the end, then he brought it upon himself."

"Ba…ba…But…wha…what will I do?"

"Well, for one thing, Tiv, you have found your voice. You will speak your own mind from now on. Do you understand what I am saying? You are no longer a slave to anyone. You are free of him!"

"But…my…my parents?"

Winyon drew closer. "What about them?"

Tiv's face screwed up and his eyes filled with tears. "Mmm...my…fault."

"That they died? Oh, Tiv. No. It was not your fault."

"Could not…heal them," he cried.

"But neither could Mefakani or Elder Tani," she explained.

Tiv held his face in his hands and began to sway. A deep-pitched groan rose from deep within him, up from his gut and into his throat, rising in pitch as it moved. And then the boy vomited on the sand a blackness that caused Winyon to draw back in horror, until he had emptied the contents of his stomach and was spent of all his energies.

When she felt he had finished vomiting, Winyon placed the flat of her hand squarely on his sweaty back. She buried the soiled sand with her other hand.

"Come, Tiv," she coaxed. "Come closer to the water to rinse your mouth and to drink from the sacred spring."

Tiv nodded his understanding. On hands and knees he crept over to the water's edge and leaned down, first to rid himself of the vile taste from his mouth, and then to drink. He drank several handfuls from the sacred spring, then rocked back on his haunches, his shoulders slumped forward. His breathing became labored.

Winyon put her arm around his shoulder circumspectly, and without realizing she was doing so, she repeated the same prayer Tani had done for her. She dipped her fingers into the spring and gently tapped his chest.

Winyon saw tears well up in the boy's eyes again.

"It is all right," she cooed. Tears began to brim in her eyes.

She put her other arm around him and rocked him gently as he cried. And together they wept in each other's arms for what was once beauty cherished, beauty spoiled, and beauty found again; for lives shattered and healed, and, in their imperfect state, now valued even more with graceful acceptance. They cried together for their shared suffering, for the loneliness, despair, and the isolation so painfully endured. They cried as one for the quiet sadness and wistfulness of all things past.

Kintsuki waabe-saabe

CHAPTER FIFTY-NINE

THE SEA BELLS TOLL

WAKE UP!
"Has the sun been blocked
from waking the world
with the light of God,
the jealous clouds
having thrown
the coverlet of themselves
over his glory?
Good news.
Bad news.
It does not matter!
What are they afraid of?
Wake up and face the day!"

Elo Tivloc, popular Makolese poet
The Makolese Scroll on
The Return of the Ka and the Mending of the Su #59

The sun rose above a somber horizon, a sliver of light narrowly visible through a cape of ruddy crimson clouds.

Tani knelt in the bottom of her boat, half draped over the gunwale. Although her knees and back ached, her resolve to communicate with Okon rekindled in the dawn light. She stared harder down into the ocean in the weak light, but the columns of Sea Bells and the Guardians proved barely visible. She was just able to hear the six dolphins squeak and squeal as they swam in and out of the Sea Bells with their coded song and underwater dance. Weaving strands of invisible energy, they helped initiate Tani's first visual contact of the morning with Okon.

Tani lifted her head skyward and measured the sun's rise by two fingers. It was still early. She noted with worry a steady wind pushing down from the north where Okon would be, and the hulking mass of black thunderheads pressing down on her from overhead. She felt the air stir, and a sudden jagged bolt of lightning illuminated the muddy pall and scuttled across the dark morning sky. The air shook with thunder, and then the rains fell.

Tani pulled a thin tangle of wet hair from across her face and searched the sky again.

She held the whale ear bone in one hand and clutched the gunwale with the other. The boat began to rock harder.

"The sun has just risen and now it is growing dark again! I am losing him in the storm!" she called out to any spirits who were listening.

She pressed her lips together and called out to the Guardians with a series of squeaking sounds, whistles, and buzzing clicks.

What is happening? Is he still alive? She asked the Dolphins.

One Guardian broke the surface of the nappy sea, clicked in response, then dived back beneath the waves. Tani knew the Dolphins would have to leave soon because of the thunderstorm. If they couldn't help to form a visual for her, she prayed they would recalibrate her message in coded frequencies that would traverse immense distances to another pod of Dolphins, who would relay the message and return an answer about Okon.

She bent, nearly touching the water. The old Healer watched the six sleek shadows weave in and out of the twelve thick metal rods that were anchored to the seabed in varying heights and thicknesses, knowing it might be the last thing she'd see until the rains subsided.

Successive flashes of lightning ripped across the darkening sky followed by a grumbling roll of thunder and then a boom that caused Tani to jerk back with a start. She leaned forward again, hoping for the first glimpse of Okon since dusk. The sky lit up with more silver streaks, and thunder pounded the air with sound waves that shook the boat. Tani felt as if a fist had been driven into her gut.

In the watery depths the magic gathered force. A light in the center of the ancient Sea Bells converged and she caught a vision of Okon's boat. Its sail was tattered, and the wind lashed and tossed the vessel violently. The image faded quickly.

"OKON!" she cried. Tani dropped the ear bone to the bottom of her boat and grabbed the gold ring swinging from her neck.

Swords of lightning sliced through dense cloud, momentarily blinding her, and causing the hairs on the back of her neck to stand on end. A deafening crash sounded above, and she saw the flash of a metal blade pass through her vision as if she were witnessing the massacre again. In her mind she heard people screaming, saw children running, and smelled smoke and fire roaring all around her. She doubled over, trembling uncontrollably, but the wind and rain scourged her so hard it drew her back to the present.

When she came to her senses she raised herself up and set her gaze back to the Sea Bells beneath her, the vision long gone and the circle of metal rods obscured now. Remembering the last vision of Okon, she watched in mournful silence as the Dolphins were driven away by the storm.

Daring to lose her handhold on the gunwale, she searched the bottom of the boat with the flat of her hand in the blur of rain, found the ancient whale ear bone, and pressed it to her heart. Consumed with the horror of not knowing what lay ahead in the future, if, indeed, Okon did not complete his mission, she prayed fervently. And when she could pray no longer, she slumped to the bottom of the boat and curled up, the beating of the rain deafening, leaving her isolated and alone in the dismal noise. And the old woman rode out the storm throughout the day, seeing no images, and hearing no sounds but the beating of the rain and the thumping of her grieving heart.

CHAPTER SIXTY

ILLA

"I will do as you ask. I will behead no one."

Queen Palomei
The Makolese Scroll on
The Return of the Ka and the Mending of the Su #60

"What happened next?" Mason asked, rapt with attention.

"Illa is what happened next."

Mason cocked his head, waiting for more of the story to unfold before he put brush to paper.

"Luckily for Illa, the heavy rains obscured her actions and aroused no interest from the Palace Guards," Temple said. "She found her way to a deep trench flowing with water from a small waterfall that runs from the foothills of Hollow Mountain to the Queen's compound. The waterfall's rushing waters are channeled into a narrower canal that is lined with rock and runs through a small hole in the outer wall of the compound.

"Mind you, the Queen's compound is a vast village onto itself. It is built around several springs that provide fresh water. But because the Su had been broken, and the life force of the island had been severely disturbed, two springs had dried up. But the village has this alternative water source that feeds into the complex from the outside. Before Mik-lon's sudden conversion as a Believer, his original plan was to swim down the northwest canal and up into the Queen's compound. But what Mik-lon hadn't anticipated was that a hand-forged mesh had been placed over the hole in the wall to catch debris that might plug up the hole. It was a recent addition that E-lon-e' had thought up to improve the water and sewer system for the compound, and to keep water snakes out.

"In spite of the obstacle, young Illa took her knife and pried the metal brackets that attached the mesh to the stone wall. She propped her knife between the cage and the stone wall and managed to squeeze through.

"She knew the top of the canal was covered in heavy tiles. She was told to lift a tile and climb out once she was deeper inside the complex where the channel narrowed. But she was a slender girl and decided to venture further along the waterway as long as she still fit in the niche.

"I've been told she often had to swim holding her breath for lengthy periods until she could poke her face up and catch her breath."

"Then she almost drowned," Maśon said.

Temple nodded. "Illa swam several meters following the map in her head to what she thought was Palomei's private bathhouse. Mind you, she was doing this in total darkness, feeling her way around and not knowing when she'd be able to take her next breath. She bore to the right as instructed, until she encountered a second fork in the canal that wasn't on the map.

"According to the story, Illa swam, then crawled to the right as the passage narrowed, thinking she'd emerge inside the Queen's bath, which wasn't far from her private quarters.

"You remember Tauhans?" Temple asked, interrupting his own narrative. "He was the husband, you'll recall, who had fainted after Palomei cut off the head of the disobedient guard."

Maśon nodded that he remembered.

"To sooth his jangled nerves Tauhans decided to quietly enjoy a bath at the bathhouse where the Royal Husbands often bathed together."

"The husbands's bathhouse?" Maśon asked.

"Yes. It was somewhat Roman in design, only they never needed for the water to be heated underneath like the Romans did. It has a circular pavilion with a high-pitched roof covered in thatch to allow for airflow and protect bathers from the rains. The walls are made of stone that are only thirty feet high."

"Only?" Maśon was puzzled.

"Designed by giants," Temple said, a bit too nonchalantly. "Fish, aquatic plants, dolphins, whales, and stylized wave designs were carved into the stone in bas-relief with various holes chiseled through the stonework in geometric patterns to allow air to flow and to allow a modicum of privacy. Although the Makolese never truly had a concept of privacy, the royal household did.

"Out of the center of this pavilion rises another smaller round structure, namely the bathtub. The bath is large enough to accommodate maybe twenty husbands...or maybe five giants."

Maśon raised an eyebrow.

"This great round pool depicts the same images carved on the outside walls, but the materials are tiny colorful gemstones and volcanic glass that make a smooth mosaic, covering the bottom and sides of the bath. In fact, the entire floor is covered in gemstones. I remember seeing a lot of green opal, green and blue tourmaline, peridot and eyeball jasper," he added, remembering the beauty of the place.

Temple snapped his head up, breaking from his reverie. "According to the story, while Tauhans was bathing, there was a sudden rush of water behind Illa. The girl was pushed out of the water niche and surfaced between Tauhans' legs. Thinking a python had made its way through the canal, Tauhan let out a scream that echoed throughout the palace. And then he fell into a dead faint again!"

Maśon broke into a raucous laugh.

"Meanwhile, the poor girl shrieked in terror, thinking, she, too, had rubbed up against a water snake. She let out another horrible scream when she realized she was in a pool with a naked man – a naked man who was one of the Queen's Husbands!"

The Scribe's reaction was so contagious that Temple convulsed with laughter.

Temple wiped tears from his eyes. "By the time the other husbands ran to the bath, a breathless Illa was seen cradling Tauhans in her arms so he wouldn't drown."

"Oh, it gets better," Temple chortled. "Initially, the others thought the timid Tauhans had risked the Queen's wrath by taking up a young lover, and had fainted during his marital transgression."

Maśon got caught in another wave of laughter and slapped his thigh.

"But Illa quickly set the record straight and confessed to slithering her way into the compound to deliver an important message to the Queen."

Maśon's laughter subsided. "I must say, in spite of the fact that the message she bore was wrong, she was a brave young girl."

"That's not how Queen Palomei saw it."

★   ★   ★   ★   ★   ★

The soothing drumming of rain against the thatched roof of Palomei's bathhouse fell over the pavilion like a bell-jar, quieting the nerves of Palomei's personal attendant. Maome treasured the cocoon of privacy the sound made for no other reason than the intimacy it offered between herself and the Queen. The tiny woman scurried over to Palomei's dressing table to tidy up the Queen's combs and jars of oils and perfumes, when a roll of thunder shook the structure.

Violet howlers punctuated the air with a cacophony of shrill screeches.

Maome jumped with a start and clutched her bosom.

"You are jumpy today," Palomei said. Having finished her morning bath, the giantess sat on a tall fat cushion before her writing table with only a blue silk skirt wrapped around her bulbous waist.

Maome blew out her breath and let out an embarrassed laugh. "Tai, I am," she admitted.

Palomei finished writing four small scrolls, which she blew on so the ink would dry. She rolled them up, sealed them with beeswax and her personal stamp embossed with a queen bee, then handed the scrolls to her servant.

Maome took the scrolls and looked at the Sovereign questioningly.

"Give the first scroll to Owane after he returns from the meeting with the Rebels at Great Round House."

"But you are going together," Maome complained.

"Did I ask for a commentary? You are to give this to him if I do not return from the meeting with the Rebels," she said pointedly.

"Oh," Maome said.

"Give the second scroll to my other husbands. The third scroll goes to Great Grandfather Okon."

Maome's lips puckered in thought. "I have not seen Elder Okon for days."

"I have not seen him either. I have been too busy. Is he ill?"

"I have heard nothing except that he spends all of his time with Elder Tani."

Palomei let out a soft grunt. "No telling what they would be doing together."

"I will check on him myself," Maome offered with a shallow bow.

"Good," Palomei said. "Give the last scroll to Losha Ninti and Temple Fox. Understand?"

Maome nodded and tucked the four tiny scrolls away beneath her sash.

"Keep all four scrolls on you for safekeeping. I trust you," she said, looking into Maome's round brown eyes.

The Titan pushed her writing paper aside and pulled her obsidian mirror closer. She leaned forward with her head dropped and squinted up at a slant, parting her black hair at the top of her scalp with one hand. "I have neglected myself this past month. My red hair is showing at the roots…and I distinctly see more gray."

"Would the Most Beloved like for me to dye her hair this morning?" Maome asked.

Palomei held up her hand. "There is no time today. Maybe I will let it go red and gray like my Grandmother did. I am after all from the Si Te Cah Clan. It was such a ludicrous idea to dye it black in the first place. But Owane thought the people would accept me better if I looked more like them when I first became Queen." She swung around on her cushion to look at Maome. "Imagine a child dyeing her hair."

"One never knows what one has to do in harsh circumstances. The war…it causes people to do strange things." Maome took a tortoise shell comb and stood on her tiptoes to run it through the Queen's long black, red, and gray hair.

"Do you ever think about the Great Massacre?" Maome asked.

"Never," Palomei replied sharply. "There is no point in remembering. It only brings heartache."

"Such loss," Maome murmured as she combed her Sovereign's hair. "I am older. I remember well. There is not a day the memories do not haunt me."

"I have no time for such things," she said. "You can stop now."

Disappointed, Maome lowered the comb and placed it neatly back onto the dressing table.

Palomei rose to her full height, her back still turned, her attention on the drumming rain outside, and the sheet of water that splattered onto the tiled portico. "Besides, I was only seven years old. I remember nothing."

"I am afraid for you, Most Beloved," Maome admitted, then hid her face by bowing low.

Palomei turned to face her servant. "Why?" she asked, suddenly more attentive.

Maome rose and looked up into the giant's face. "The Rebels. It is so dangerous for you to meet with them. I do not understand why you could not have kept them trapped up on Hollow Mountain. Now they are being treated like special guests at a great feast at the Great Round House of all places."

"It is a fitting place to meet so many," Palomei offered. She paused for a thoughtful second. "Maome, we have a standing truce. And I do not completely view them as Rebels any longer. They think, and rightly so, that Losha Ninti has fulfilled the old prophecy. They are halfway in their understanding of the truth. Now all they have to do is accept Temple Fox."

"I realize that," Maome began again. "But if they do not accept both of the True Teachers a schism could develop among the people and continue to divide us. They have weapons," she emphasized.

"Tai," Palomei said. "They do. Disarmament is something we could not agree on in the negotiations. They do still, indeed, have their weapons."

"While our own soldiers do not," Maome added, then threw herself into a steep bow, embarrassed for speaking out so boldly. "I beg your forgiveness."

Palomei nodded and signaled for her servant to rise. "My precious Maome, you do not need to worry about me." A sly grin crept across her face. "Do you really think I would meet with the Rebels with only my own personal guards? Did you forget that Losha and Temple Fox will be there too? I will have their protection as well."

Maome blotted the moisture from the corner of her eyes.

"Truly, Maome, do you think we would enter into such a precarious situation without a good defense?"

"But I thought…"

"Do not worry. The Rebels have been told one thing, but you can rest in absolute certainty that we will be well armed. Our weapons – which I might add, are far superior to anything the Rebels possess – will be out of the Rebels' sight, however." Palomei squinted down at her servant. "You will keep this information confidential, of course."

"Of course. But the scrolls you just wrote…" Maome pressed her hand against her bulging sash.

"A precautionary measure. I did so during the last battle that took my precious daughter, Shaza, from me. It would not be the first time I have written such scrolls."

Maome bowed, satisfied that her worries had been quelled. "I apologize for probing."

"I take no offense. I am the Mother of my people. You are concerned for my welfare. I value that in you. Now," she said with a sweep of her hand. "I have bathed, prayed at the altar of my Ancestors to solicit their help, and have written the scrolls. Now dress me."

Maome rose on her tiptoes to help the giantess slip out of her blue silk skirt. The small woman climbed up onto a stool to hang the fine silk onto a frame made of polished mahogany. She smoothed out the wrinkles from the back of the long silk skirt, admiring the rich design that had been hand-brushed with images of white gardenia blossoms and a swarm of small bees, rising to meet their larger queen. With utmost care she retrieved the Queen's traditional sash and barkcloth skirt trimmed in gold thread, stepped down from the stool, dashed up onto another stool to wrap the skirt around Palomei's thick waist, and tie the sash.

"You are quite quick and nimble today," Palomei said. The Queen opened her mahogany chest inlaid with mother-of-pearl and abalone, and rummaged around in it.

Maome smiled. "I had my Ka attached."

"I see. Naturally, I had mine attached first, but I confess that I feel no different." She let the lid to the chest slam shut. "Do you have any idea where my long strand of pearls are? They seem to be missing."

Maome shrugged. "I am sure they are around here somewhere."

Queen Palomei glared at Maome.

"I will search for them. Perhaps the Most Beloved could try these instead." The servant slipped several bone and shell necklaces over her Sovereign's head, rearranged them so they hung nicely, then bolted down off the stool and up onto the other stool again with limber alacrity. Maome lifted the Queen's long yellow feathered cape off another rack and waited for Palomei to back herself into it. Next, Maome placed the crown of red blossoms onto Palomei's head, which immediately attracted a throng of bees. The servant slowly backed down from the stool one foot at a time and stepped back to admire the powerful Queen.

"You still have the scrolls?" Palomei asked.

Maome blinked back, her worry rekindled by the question. "Well, of course I do."

Maome knelt on the floor to slip each of the Sovereign's six-toed feet into a pair of sandals, when they both heard the first scream.

Palomei turned her head in the direction of her Husbands' bathhouse. "Tauhans!" she called out, recognizing the shriek.

A second, higher-pitched screech from an unrecognizable voice was muffled by the rain, but echoed over the first. Palomei bolted into the corridor that separated her private bathhouse from that of her Husbands' bathhouse.

"No! Do not go! Wait for the guard!" Maome warned, but Palomei pushed the small woman aside and rushed into the hall in a blind panic where she heard the scurry of feet.

Owane, Jalok, Kuhil, and Loa'a scurried into the bathhouse with Palomei, Maome, and a guard pressing behind them. All stared in disbelief at the young girl, who was standing in the pool, cradling

Tauhans in her arms, her breathing labored, her long hair dripping. Her face was flushed with confusion and terror.

"What is going on!" Palomei yelled. "Who are you!" She pointed at the girl accusingly.

"I...I am Illa. Illa Lanba," she stuttered.

Seeing that this might be a personal matter, Palomei waved Maome and the guard away. She spoke again when the bath screens were closed.

The Queen raked her eyes over Illa's young and slender form. "What happened to Tauhans, and what are YOU doing in the bath with him?" Palomei bellowed with her cheeks puffing.

"I did not know I would end up here. I swear it," the girl began to cry.

"What were you two doing in here?" Palomei asked again, her panic building.

"I...I think he fainted," the girl said.

"Get him out of there!" Palomei yelled.

Kuhil and Loa'a climbed into the pool and pulled the limp man from Illa's thin arms, and placed him gently on the tile floor. Jalok knelt down to check his pulse.

"Tauhans. Tauhans! Wake up!" Jalok said. He patted Tauhans' cheek.

Tauhans let out a weak groan, then suddenly came to and looked all around him. "Palomei," he said to the familiar pair of huge sandaled feet beside him, and the face looming down from her towering heights.

"What were doing with that girl?" she shouted as if he were deaf.

"What girl?" He looked up with incredulity.

"THAT GIRL!" She said, pointing at Illa, who was wet and shivering with fright.

"I do not know! I never saw her before."

"Get her out of there!" she barked.

Jalok stayed with Tauhans while Kuhil and Loa'a yanked the girl from the pool. They searched her, and finding no weapons, they stood her up between them with their hands firmly gripped around her wrists.

Palomei pointed at the girl. "How did you get in here?"

"I crawled through the northwest canal...that runs from the waterfall...and channels underground into the compound," she said, trembling.

Palomei broke into a sweat. "You what!"

"You broke into the compound?" Owane asked, taking over the questioning.

Illa nodded to Owane, then peered up at the giantess. "I had to. I have an important message for you. This is the only way I knew how to reach you without being stopped at the gates and arrested before..."

"What message? From who!" the Queen asked, frowning with anger.

"I… We have…"

"Who is WE?" the Queen snapped.

"I am one of the Rebels," Illa said, plainly, almost defiantly, regaining some of her courage.

Palomei sucked in her breath and the room seemed to lose all air. Her face reddened, and sweat ran down her puffy cheeks. She started to reach down to grab the girl by the neck.

The girl struggled against Palomei's two husbands, who held her in a tight grip, but she managed to take a step backward.

The Queen withdrew her hand and balled her fist instead. "What is this message that is so important that you have gotten past ALL OF MY SECURITY MEASURES?" she ended up shouting.

The girl spat out the words. "The two work together against you!"

"WHO?" Palomei asked, her face darkening.

"Temple Fox and Losha Ninti!" the girl said, relieved to have finally given her message of warning delivered to the Queen in person.

Jalok eyed Palomei on the slant. The Queen fell silent, her feet anchored far apart, her hands firmly planted on the rolls of her huge hips.

"And why would you think such a stupid thing?" Jalok asked on behalf of the Queen.

The girl blurted out the details of her message. "Suddenly, the Queen's Interpreter possesses great powers to spin and change into a Swan. She can fly and heal people. And now we know she has been seen consorting with the White Wizard. Two of your runners told us," Illa explained. "Temple Fox and Losha Ninti are BOTH Wizards! And they plan on taking the throne!"

"No one will ever take my throne!" Palomei said in bold declaration.

Loa'a, the more handsome and younger of the Royal Husbands, stepped in. "Illa. Is that your name?" he asked gently.

Illa gave a sheepish nod.

"How old are you?"

"Fourteen," she said meekly, and looked to Palomei's youngest husband for empathy, then glanced back to the furious Matriarch.

Palomei's nostrils flared. She let out a deep breath to calm herself and lowered her voice. "Child, I know you and those murderous friends of yours believe Temple Fox is an impostor. But we know" – she gestured with her hand circling to encompass all her five husbands – "that, in fact, Temple Fox and Losha Ninti are BOTH the True Teachers, who, indeed, work together. But they work together to bring us back to wholeness. In truth, the prophecy has been fulfilled in a most usual way."

"That is a lie!" Illa said. "They charm people!" She struggled against the strong arms that held her in place. "They have bewitched you, as well as Elder Cranik and a small band of nine other Rebels."

"So, one of your own Rebel leaders has become a Believer?" the Queen asked.

Illa nodded with regret.

Palomei looked at each of her husbands, a slight smile stretching her fat cheeks. "That is good news!"

"No it is NOT!" Illa shouted. "They were bewitched!"

"How?" Loa'a asked.

"By feathers," she said, looking again to Loa'a for understanding.

Palomei gave out a hardy laugh.

Illa craned her neck out to emphasize her point. "Owl feathers and Swan feathers! It has been rumored that Temple Fox has an Owl as an ally. We believe he can actually spin into an Owl! If you touch one of the feathers they poison you! It is how the two Wizards charmed my friends!"

"I see," the Queen said smugly. "And two of my runners told you this?"

"The runners who told me are dead now!" Illa let her words fly out vehemently with defiance. "And everyone else will die too if you touch one of their feathers, or as much as look at them! But it is too late because YOU have been BEWITCHED!"

Palomei's eyes hardened. "How did my runners die? Were they killed by your Rebel friends?"

Illa fell silent. She remembered the last time she gazed upon Naffa's face, savoring the memory of his youthful beauty, his bravery, and his leadership.

I have been captured already, she said to herself. *But he is still free and still has a chance to save us all.*

"I did!" she announced boldly. "I slit their throats!"

Palomei glared down at the girl, her jaw tightening. Sweat rolled down her cheeks in thin rivulets.

The girl spoke coolly, spitting her words out. "I would have thought our Most Beloved would be grateful that a Rebel risked her life to bring you this warning. But I see you have been charmed by the Wizards!"

Angered by the obstinate young Rebel, Palomei stared down at the girl harder, more menacingly. "I will make an example of you," she said with equal coolness. "You will be executed for murder. And ALL others will be executed as well," she declared loudly in the open air, "who do not accept, as we do, that Temple Fox and Losha Ninti are the True Prophets. And I will do it in the caldera where the sacred bones of Lord Tagheetu rest!"

Owane looked up at his giant wife aghast. "Palomei, no! There has been enough bloodshed. Why not simply trust the Teachers? You told them you would. Let them handle this."

She folded her arms over her bare bosom and stared down at him. "I will do as I must to keep the peace."

"But do you not see that will not bring peace?" he argued. "Just as Losha has told us, violence breeds more violence. You cannot strong-arm the entire island."

"I can do as I like," she announced brashly.

"Even if you are known in the History Scrolls as a butcher?" Loa'a butted in.

Owane glanced at the Queen's other Husbands out of the corner of his eye. They returned the look askance, frightened for young Loa'a.

Palomei turned her head slowly, a stabbing stare aimed at her fifth husband. "I do what I must for the good of the people."

"Please," Owane pleaded now, his frustration rising. "DO NOT DO THIS!"

Owane's voice was loud enough to be heard by the guard outside, and Palomei shot her first husband a venomous look. "Speak no more!" she commanded. "We cannot afford to have religious divisions among our people. I will be seen as a heroine who united her people, and protected them all from fanatics," she offered.

Owane took a cautious step back from the Sovereign, out of the reach of Palomei's long arm.

Tauhans drew himself up into a sitting position while trying to cover his nakedness and vulnerability. "Please, Palomei. Owane is right," he said. "I, too, cannot take anymore of this killing."

Palomei stood erect in a resistant pose. "This girl has killed two of my runners and deserves to be punished!"

"But the rest of the Rebels, too?" Tauhans questioned. "They realize that Losha is the True Teacher now, but have yet to understand that Temple is as well. Why not let Temple and Losha do as they have planned to bring the Rebels to a greater understanding? Please," he said quietly, calmly. "Think it over."

The room became a blur of fury when Palomei backhanded a water jug and sent it smashing to the tile floor. The gritty sound of shards crushed beneath her immense feet could be heard under the patter of the subsiding rain as she paced the bathhouse for several tense minutes with all her Husbands watching her in stiff silence. She stopped before Illa for a second, mumbled something inaudible under her breath, then stood before her five husbands. When she spoke again it was in a forced, but civil tone. "I will allow the Teachers to do as they planned, but if it does not work…" She let the sentence linger.

"You will kill them *all*!" Tauhans asked, his panic resurfacing.

"It is not the way," Owane said cautiously. "You cannot turn this thing around in a single day!"

"I can and I will," Palomei declared. "It is more expedient to cut a tangled knot than to unravel it slowly and painstakingly bit by bit. Let it be done! And let us get rid of all these renegades once and for all! Bind and gag that girl!" she ordered.

Kuhil and Loa'a found some silk sashes that had been discarded in the bathhouse. The two Royal Husbands moved swiftly to gag Illa, then tied the girl's hands behind her back.

Palomei pointed a finger at each of her husbands in warning. "I want only Owane to go with me today. The rest of you stay in your lodges. It is not safe for you to be in a crater with half-witted militants. And I do not want anyone to talk about what I have planned. Not to E-lon-e', My Great Grandfather, Elder Tani, or even the Teachers. Understood!"

Everyone nodded except Tauhans.

Tauhans saw the swift blade from the sword Palomei had picked up from the disobedient guard again in his mind, remembering the golden arc it made in the torchlight as it came down against flesh and bone, the sound of blade against bone echoing in his ears. Tauhans felt the warm blood splattered against his skin again, and he grabbed his wet cheek as if he were reliving the experience again. He lay back down on the cool tiles and curled into a ball, covering his face with his hands. He began to sob.

Palomei looked down at him, annoyed.

"No more beheadings," he wept, his pleas barely audible.

"What did you say?" Palomei leaned down, concerned now that her meek husband had finally lost a grip on his sanity.

"No…more…beheadings," Tauhans said plainly between sobs.

Palomei let out a loud groan of resignation. She gathered the front of her yellow cape in one hand and leaned down to offer her hand to Tauhans. He took her huge hand, and the powerful giantess pulled him up onto his feet effortlessly.

She cupped his wet face in her enormous hand. "For you my sweet, Tauhans, I will make a promise."

Tauhans looked up at her with terror...with hope...he couldn't say which.

"I will do as you ask. I will behead no one," she whispered. She released her hold on her third husband's face.

Tauhans let out a deep sigh of relief. He looked over at the others with surprise, then up at his wife again.

"Truly?" he asked her.

Palomei's face became expressionless, her tone flat. "You have my promise."

CHAPTER SIXTY-ONE

FRAGILE HOPE

"You may question my convictions, my faithfulness, and my loyalties to all the Gods, the Spirits, even our Ancestors. You may even question the ancient prophecies that foretold about me. But what I have to say must be said because you are no longer to be treated like children and deserve the truth."

Losha Ninti
The Makolese Scroll on
The Return of the Ka and the Mending of the Su #61

The rains subsided and the sun came out of hiding. Palomei stood on the crater rim, her pearly scepter gripped tightly, her yellow feathered cape ruffling in the damp wind. Silent, alert and unusually tense, her guards stood at a distance from their Queen to form a shield of privacy around her as she and her First Advisor and Principle Consort, Owane, gazed out to sea.

Palomei absentmindedly fingered the sore spot where her Ka had been reattached. She spoke over her shoulder to Owane with her eyes to the far horizon. "With my Ka restored, who knows what power I have now, good husband. So long we have lived in a shadow world of Mefakani's half lies, convinced that we would only use our powers to bewitch another. And so," she said, turning toward Owane, "these are the great powers Temple Fox spoke of a moon ago, and what Losha Ninti spoke about days ago? Our power is our own now."

Owane shook his head. "I think they define power differently than you, Most Respected." He came up beside her, his face drawn and grim. "I pray that the Rebels do not force you into brutal actions," he whispered.

Palomei tossed an irritating look down at her older husband. She gazed out over the harbor again, far into the distance, where she watched men pull in their fishing nets, and flocks of hungry gulls rise into the sky. The greedy gulls dived at the boats in droves to steal the catch, squabbling with one another. She heard the voices of children playing far below in the surf.

Palomei glanced to her left side where her troops lined up across the curved backbone of the crater. She grinned with satisfaction, knowing that small weapons were concealed beneath their clothing, and long knives were hidden in every recess of brush and rock. Their lightning spears and power shields remained inside cavities in the earth they had dug out earlier and covered with green foliage for quick retrieval.

She spoke to Owane without looking at him, her tone curt and demanding. "I pray that Losha Ninti and Temple Fox do not disappoint me. Please leave me now so that I may think in peace. I will join you inside the Great Round House before the Rebels arrive."

After Owane left, the Matriarch paced, her scattered thoughts begging for focus. She stopped on a precipice of rock to gaze into the distance again, thinking about how so much had changed in the past month because of the Stranger. Her thoughts turned to Losha, her Interpreter, who possessed miraculous powers. Losha had absorbed all the lessons of the Stranger, and worked in equal partnership with him. She was the first of the Makolese who truly understood what Temple Fox had tried in vain to explain to everyone. And she, like Temple, was the first to live that truth.

I desperately want to learn from the two Teachers. I want to trust the Divine as they do. I want to be as powerful as they are.

Palomei leaned against a barrow rock and closed her eyes. Practicing what she had been taught, she took a deep breath and centered herself, and asked the Spirit within her for guidance. Slowly, an almost imperceptible tingling glanced her brow. Her eyes flew open and the sensation blew away like dust. She tried again, this time keeping herself calm. The sensation returned with intensity. Palomei felt a distinct tightness draw together in the center of her forehead. Only this time a flood of memories, held hostage for years, spilled out onto the screen of her mind. She heard shouting and the sound of running feet surround the small pavilion where she, a young child of seven, and her tutor sat huddled on the floor. Asan pushed the trembling child from the safety of her arms and rushed over to the windows, pulling the bamboo blinds closed as if the very act could muffle the noise and shut out the horror.

"Hide!" she'd said to her pupil.

The young Palomei ran to the lap of pillows in the corner of the room and hid her bulk beneath them just when the door was bullied open. A slab of dusty light hit the room and a silhouetted figure, barely seen through the tumble of pillows, stood panting in the room like an asthmatic.

"There is nothing for you here!" her tutor shouted.

The figure lumbered forward, and the sound of heavy blows came again and again, until Asan's cries were bludgeoned out of her, and her voice became a whimper, then no more. The only sound remaining was the assailant's heavy breathing as if he had spent himself.

Palomei's soft cries would never have been heard were it not for the sudden stillness in the room. She heard shuffling feet, a table kicked over, and the crackling of scrolls being crumpled beneath heavy feet. A footstep fell beside her ear. She froze and stopped breathing, her heart pounding wildly. The pillow lifted from her face, and the man, dark eyes set beneath a pugilist brow, loomed over her with a bloodied club in his hand. He snorted aloud and threw the pillow roughly to the side.

The smell of the sea, and the stench of sweat rose into the Queen's nostrils again as if all the years she had lived were balled into a single knot. He was vivid in her mind, the leer of rotting teeth, the dark creases in his ruddy face where the grime had settled. And the club – most of all she remembered that – and how he had held it over her. Palomei watched in her mind's eye as if in slow motion a drop of blood formed at the tip, puckered like a tiny bud, and released onto her quivering brow. She didn't move, feeling the drop sting like a nettle. Then the assailant's hand came down like a claw and ripped the cloth from her tender loins, exposing her to the muddy light.

The greater part of the child's being hid somewhere deep within her, secreted away behind her eyes, behind her head.

He fell on top of her with a grunt, the club pushed against her neck, his weight on her chest, and the force against her throat suffocating. He splayed her legs apart, until she thought her joints would splinter, and he pushed and pushed himself trying to gain access into her. But the child was not wide enough. And the two of them gasped, she for air and he for entry. He found a wet spot and bore down with his full weight, determined to have his way. And the child twisted like a bug impaled on a pin, her eyes wide open, watching, but her mind in some distant place.

She remembered him grunt again, and his weight lift, and a sharp pain and a sticky wetness between her legs. She gained her breath, and her eyes readjusted to the room as he strode away, her mind hovering somewhere outside of herself: she didn't know where. The spattered light was too dim to absorb the darkness, and a heavy stillness hung in the room. The only sound, the buzz of flies clustered now over the body of her tutor.

Queen Palomei watched as the child covered herself up to hide the deed that had undone her. From that moment on she kept the secret tucked up between her legs, behind the wounded heart, beyond the dark chambers of her memory, until now. Only now, after the tiny portion of her Ka had been returned, had her memory been restored completely. She saw herself again, rising slowly past the slumped body of her tutor, past the swarm of flies, past the stench of the foreigner clinging to the walls. Outside the room everything was fire and smoke. She remembered hands, warm trusting hands reach down and picking her up. Then running, running...

The Queen's memory had faded in spots, but what she saw now was as vivid as the royal palms lining the edge of the crater. Bodies, too numerous to send to the swamps, had been lined up in rows on the beaches. The memory choked her senses and confused her mind all over again. And she could still feel the large warm hand that had rescued her, Owane's guiding hand, press the heavy scepter into her small palm.

"Stand," he had said, coaxing the child with a sad smile. "Show the people their new Queen. You are their only hope," he had whispered in her ear. "You understand. You suffered with them. Shed not one tear, child. Be brave."

The memory scattered in a sudden breeze, and she felt a slight touch on her shoulder. Expecting to see one of the guards behind her, instead she heard one distinct word: "Mother."

Palomei turned sharply. No one but her personal guards stood near. A sudden gust rocked her backward, and the wind wailed.

"Shaza?" she whispered, but there was no answer. Other memories resurfaced: Three Warriors carrying her daughter's limp body to the shore. A searing heat overtook her. Tears welled up in her eyes. She tried to will them away, but the swell of emotions proved too great, and she let out a bellowing cry like a wounded animal.

Nijaga rushed over to her, but she waved him away. "Stay away!" she commanded. He bowed and backed away with a frightened and worried look on his face, and took his place again on the edge of the caldera.

Palomei slumped to the ground, the anguish pressing down on her. "Why?" she cried. "Why did it have to be you?" But Palomei felt no presence, no invisible hand, only the deep well of grief.

A swarm of mad bees hummed around her red flower crown, and one dared to sting her royal arm. She squashed it between her thick fingers and flung it into the air as if to shake off the memory of buzzing flies. Using her scepter, she pushed up onto her feet and wiped tears away.

Nijaga called her attention to the thicket below that led to the base of Olonopo Crater. She acknowledged the signal and spotted Losha leading the approaching Rebels.

Palomei rubbed away the last traces of tears and stuffed the most horrible of all memories away.

While the Rebels made their arduous climb up the switchback stairs, the giant Matriarch stayed inside the coolness of the Great Round House away from the scorching heat of the day.

Owane watched his wife pacing to and fro, her reflection casting distorted facsimilies of herself on the nacreous abalone wall and the black obsidian floor. Owane was grateful for any interruption from watching his brooding wife when Nijaga came into the great hall.

He prostrated himself on the black floor. "Losha and the Rebels have just arrived," he announced.

"Any incidents?" she asked. She searched his face for the answer.

Nijaga lifted his head. "No, Most Beloved. Our men did as you asked and greeted all of the Rebels with respectful bows. Nothing out of the ordinary happened."

Palomei tilted her head toward a sack that lay several yards away. Still tied and gagged, Illa had been placed inside the sack with a guard watching over her. "Carry her out if and when I order you to." She glanced at Owane with a wry glint in her eye, but he turned his head away in disgust.

"Let me know when the Rebels have assembled. I am sure they will be grateful for some food after so long a journey. Have some of the guards bring them water and a little sha as well, but not too much sha," she insisted. "A little sha will help loosen them up before I address them. When I have finished with my speech, please escort Losha to the podium. Let them see Losha and me together."

Nijaga nodded, rose to his feet, then sprinted through the low arch of the chamber door into the garish light and heat of the day.

"I do not know what you are planning, Palomei, but I do not like it," Owane whispered.

"I will keep my promise," she said.

Queen Palomei crawled out from the small archway of the great Round House on her hands and knees into the glare of daylight. With the help of Owane, she rose to her feet and crossed the raised platform of stone surrounding the entrance to the Round House, her stride swift and deliberate.

The sky was streaked in gold, lavender, and pink with the last of an armada of thick bluish-gray storm clouds drifting over the caldera. She unconsciously scanned the sky, searching for Temple in his Owl-form. Confident that he would make his appearance as planned, she nodded to Owane.

Owane stepped forward and called for the blowing of the conches to bring the people to order. The haunting sound reverberated in the belly of the crater, and the people fell silent.

Palomei took her place by her First Husband's side. She raised her pearled scepter in the air, her bright cape and scepter catching the late afternoon light.

Losha, who had been standing before the Matriarch with her back to the crowd, bowed to the Queen. Elder Kulo and the Rebels followed her lead.

Holding an ancestral skull up high, Owane recited his greeting: "Good people. The Queen's Council wishes you a long... and... and prosperous life." Owane's words stumbled when he realized what he was saying. *How long would life be?* he thought.

"It has been our Sovereign's wish to have you all assembled here. If the Queen permits?" He looked to his wife beside him.

Palomei deliberately stepped in front of him, towering over him on the platform of stone. "I make no personal apologies, nor confessions," she began frankly, to the surprise of the crowd. "I ask for your patience, understanding, and complete obedience.

"I wish to give thanks to the Lord Tagheetu and His legion of Spirits, to give profound gratitude to our Ancestors, and to the Spirit of this sacred place. And I wish to thank all who are before me now," she prayed. The giantess gave a long-suffering bow to the Rebels.

"As your Queen, I thank each one of you in person for your tremendous courage, your openness, and for your fierce tenacity. Hear me now! Let the past be the past. And let the future unfold like a star blossom with the rarity of beauty so becoming of our great people. Our future is now in your hands. May forgiveness fill your hearts. May peace prevail. May our honor among the Gods be restored. And…may the Su be mended soon, very soon."

The Queen bowed again in all four directions, then to the Earth, and to the blazing late afternoon Sun, her huge hands held upward in prayer. She bowed again to the people, then gestured with an outstretched hand toward Losha, who was obviously pleased by what the Queen had said. She was smiling.

"I place you now in the good hands of the True Teacher and Prophet, Losha Ninti, who has been twice spoken about in the old prophecies. She is our future. She is the great White Swan!"

Losha took the cue and climbed up the stone staircase onto the platform, kneeling before the Queen to show her respect, and, as Palomei would have it, displaying the pecking order of authority.

The Queen bowed deeply to the Teacher, then stood up rigid and erect to her full height.

Losha rose gracefully to her feet.

The Rebels pressed forward to hear the Teacher, and placed their heads to the ground to honor her.

Losha gave a long, steep bow in return, then raised her outstretched arms as if to embrace the crowd. "I honor you as you have honored me," she began. And upon that declaration, the tiny space above and between her eyes began to glow a fiery green, then blue, until a violet hue grew brighter and colored the space around her.

The people gasped in awe.

"Thank you for following me down the mountain to this sacred place. I greatly value your trust in me. As you know, the energies in and around Hollow Mountain have been greatly compromised by Shaman Mefakani and the presence of death, grief, and conflict. My intent was to leave that dangerous place until the energies from the mountain might be cleansed and revitalized once more. The ritual I performed with you in the Ananba River was essential for our peace as a people. Taking life distorts a soul, and all needed to be washed clean of all the violence and death. My intent was to deliver you to safety in a sacred place where the energies are more balanced and amplified for either unity…or disharmony. That will be a choice you all will make collectively today.

"In order for you to decide which course you will take in your own personal futures, and for the future of the Makolese people, I speak to you with utmost honesty – an honesty that will make some question all credulity. You may question my convictions, my faithfulness, and my loyalties to all the Gods, the Spirits, even our Ancestors. You may even question the ancient prophecies that foretold about me. But what I have to say must be said because you are no longer to be treated like children and deserve the truth."

The Rebels gazed at her in silence and listened intently with an edge of anxiousness stirring within them.

"Do you know how important your Ka is?" she asked the crowd. "To have it returned to you is a great gift. But please know that it was and has always been a gift from the Gods, which is your birthright. To have it taken from you was a travesty. To have it returned is a blessing. Treasure it because in the decades ahead the Makolese will have to fight to keep it. Without it we lose heart. Without our Ka we lose hope, and it is hope that anchors us.

"I want you all to know that with the return of your Ka comes a responsibility. Will we use it to harm another as we did in our dark past? Or will we use it now to heal old wounds…to show compassion to one another…to treat others as we wish to be treated…and to spiritually grow into the magnificent Makolese we are destined to become?

"Yes, you are in the process of becoming. And when we work together in trust and love, we become beacons for others. This is our true destiny! To return to the Light of the Creator. To join with the Mind of God. To be the very Heart of God, and be an example to others."

A murmur of assent rang through the crowd, signaling approval of what had been heard…thus far.

"You have had your whole Ka returned to you. Feel the power of your love right now. Feel your minds clear up, and your hearts heal from the horrors and lies of the past. That is not to say you will forget the heartache. But find it in your heart to forgive those who have harmed you, those who took a life, those who deceived you. Love them anyway," she shouted. "Show your true selves. For the greatest warriors are the ones who can forgive."

"You have fulfilled the prophecy!" someone shouted. "We thank you for coming in our time of need."

"Yes, thank you!" they called out en masse.

"We trust you because we have witnessed you heal our physical wounds," someone added. "Now, with your help the healing will go deeper."

"It is not *I* who heals you," Losha explained, "but the power of the Divine which runs clearly through me and through you. You can do this for others just as Elder Kulo did. You all aspire to the same abilities. Now I ask for you to heal your own hearts."

"But no heart can be healed unless you kill the Wizard who plagues us all!" a young man yelled out.

Kulo stepped forward to prevent the man from speaking, but Losha held up her hand to stop the Elder.

"Let him speak," Losha insisted, and Kulo took a step backward with a nod of understanding.

"Can you kill him?" the man continued.

"I have come so peace returns," she shouted above the growing roar of voices. "We must end our differences. We have challenges ahead of us that demand we all work together as one people. Whether our people think Temple Fox is a Wizard or not, his prophecy of an armada of Arab dhows arriving on our shores in two moons still stands in the realm of probability."

There was a growl of voices among the Rebels, until Losha held up her hand to quiet the crowd again.

"Do not fall into fear again! The Slavers' approach may not be imminent if we first silence the mind and work to see a more positive and hopeful outcome. Warring with one another, chastising each other, even creating laws against your neighbors who may not believe as you do, will not only drive us deeper into separation, but will draw the Slavers to our shore. We must work together to have one heart, one purpose."

"Then what do we do?" someone asked.

"Silence the mind. Go to the place in your mind, body, and spirit that troubles you, and move it forth into the space in front of your heart. See through your heart, and all frustration, pain, grief, guilt, anger, fear, and hatred will be purified."

"Tai, that is what Mefakani told us to do. It is the same teaching, but with different words."

"Then he spoke the truth," Losha said.

There was a span of silence as she waited for her words to take hold. She watched as their frenetic energetic fields settled down before she spoke again. "I suggest you begin now – right now. Close your eyes and go deeply into your fears. Bring them forth so they can be purified. There is no moment like the present to begin. As you begin, I will pray and send you all a grand healing to assist you."

The crowd did as Losha asked and sat on the ground to quiet their minds. They remained so still and quiet that the rustle of the royal palms around them was heard in the soft breeze. And in the distance, the sea breathed rhythmically and in harmony with the rest of the world.

Losha watched their energy fields flicker and change hue, until she sensed a growing peacefulness. And when the color of their auric fields vibrated into blue and purple bands, she sent the first of two hand signals to Temple, who had been waiting at the remote perimeter of the crater.

"And now I want you to stay in that state of peacefulness, but open your eyes."

Losha waited for the crowd to return to normal consciousness before she spoke again. "And now for the harder truths," she said. "I would not have gained my godhood in this human body I occupy without a great deal of help from the Gods, the guiding Spirits, the Spirit of the Swan, and those who are incarnate. If it were not for Elder Tani I would not be standing before you now."

"We have heard rumors that she was arrested for witchcraft and blasphemy," someone called out.

"That is true," Losha stated. "She was arrested, but the charges brought against her by Mefakani were false and have been dropped. She has been released and resides as a guest in the Queen's compound as we speak. She works day and night to restore the missing piece of Ka to as many islanders as she possibly can. She is also teaching others how to do this, for it is of paramount importance to return everyone's Ka to them and to restore the Su together.

"The truth is, Elder Tani is neither a blasphemer nor a witch. She is the highest of Shamans and holy women, and a grand teacher who has awaited this day for over a century."

The Queen nodded in agreement as Losha spoke.

"So, I am beholden to Elder Tani, and, it might surprise you, to High Shaman Mefakani as well. If I had not been captured and imprisoned by him I might not have been challenged to learn to spin and fly, and in the end, to fulfill the ancient prophecy."

Losha allowed the information to sink in before she confessed the rest. "And most of all…I am beholden to the God of old…known to all of us as Gadji."

"Gadji? Gadji?" the Rebels mumbled, looking to one another, some shrugging their shoulders.

"Yes," Losha said. She let her words draw out. "Gadji has returned…in a new embodiment…for Temple Fox is the reincarnation of the great God Gadji."

Losha waited for a reaction.

Elder Ikus looked up at Losha. "Gadji was no Wizard!"

Losha spied where Elder Ikus stood glaring up at her. "Nor is Temple Fox," she replied. She gave the second hand signal, so subtle that it was only perceptible to an Owl. "It is time you learned the truth. Temple Fox is the True Teacher...as I am."

"But that is impossible!"

"Remember the prophecy, 'One without the other is empty.' He and I needed each other to learn and grow to become what we have become. Remember the rest of the prophecy. 'Power multiplies tenfold and then again tenfold, again and again until the time of Purification and Redemption.' The rest of you are destined to spiritually grow as Temple and I have."

Residing in his Owl form, Temple dropped silently off the branch of a royal palm and flew high above the crowd.

"And the warning against imposters?"

"That was High Shaman Mefakani," she answered.

Temple circled round and round in a slowly descending spiral, until he was certain he had been noticed by the Royal Swans who swam in the pond below the Great Round House.

A great commotion ensued as the birds beat their wings against the waters and rose into the sky to meet Temple.

Kulo, who was the first to notice the Owl, pointed upward. Soldiers, guards, and Rebels alike tilted their heads skyward.

"Look!" one Rebel called out, alerting the others. "An Owl...in daylight...with the Royal Swans!"

One by one the Rebels shielded their eyes from the western sun to spot the silhouette of the large Owl, its wings spread out in grandeur. And the Swans circled around Temple.

"It is Temple Fox...in his Owl form!" someone shouted.

"Tai! The Wizard is coming! And the Swans have him surrounded!"

The Rebels looked to Losha, and she began to spin and sing her invocation to the great White Swan. Losha's body revolved round and round into a bell jar of such brilliance that the crowd had to shield their eyes. And then all at once the shimmering prismatic bubble burst into one blast of blinding light. A wave of exquisite energy pulsated outward in concentric circles, enveloping the crowd. And out of the Light the Swan pivoted to a halt.

The white Swan spread her great wings, her feathers aquiver. In a heartbeat she closed her wings and thrust upward, rising into the sky.

Below, everyone watched, dumbstruck, as the Swan soared above them, ascending to meet the herd of Swans and the Owl.

CHAPTER SIXTY-TWO

THE SWAN AND THE OWL

"It's true. I realize it appears I'm contradicting myself somewhat. But then I am human, living in a frighteningly polarized, schizophrenic world."

Temple Fox
The Makolese Scroll on
The Return of the Ka and the Mending of the Su #62

Temple rubbed his hands together over the woodstove when he spoke again. "There is something Losha and I had talked about in depth days before she left with Elder Kulo to address the Rebels on the mountain. She said it was human nature to take a story and bend it to one's own perception. We decided to do what we needed to do by what we knew to be the truth, knowing there would be various versions of our remarkable story in the end."

"Well, I hope I'm getting the real version," Mason huffed.

Temple cleared his throat. "But, Mason, aren't you getting only *my* version of the story?"

"Well, yes, but…"

"There are many versions of this story," Temple said. "You see, Losha recognized that it wasn't in our power to convince anyone that we had fulfilled the ancient prophecy. We just decided to be our true selves. There was no holding back our light.

"We didn't care about who they thought the True Prophet was, and who they thought wasn't, though initially we had been concerned that conflicted beliefs would create a civil war. And in the beginning we manipulated events so that wouldn't happen. Naturally, the original plan fell flat on its face. But by the time we got to the Great Round House we didn't hold that fear any longer. We were now willing for events to unfold as they might, for no other reason than to allow the people to learn what they must from the conflict...even if it meant blood was spilled."

Maśon blinked in surprise.

"What we did care about was the message," Temple clarified. "And the message spoke of equality...of everyone being born of the same Divine origin. It spoke of self-empowerment and having freewill to do great things by exhibiting true compassion in all circumstances no matter what one believed. It spoke about embracing unlimited possibilities with a bold heart and strong focused will – a will aligned with Divine Will and True Compassion."

Temple opened the door to the woodstove with a creak and tossed a log onto the fire. "Everyone in the end was going to believe whatever they wanted to believe. What we decided to do was allow that to happen naturally. But," Temple emphasized with a mischievous grin, "we kind of helped things along...at risk to any ego need we might have had for fragile fame or any hidden fears that still lingered about us creating a civil war, of course."

Maśon blew out his breath in exasperation. "You are diabolical."

"It's true. I realize it appears I'm contradicting myself somewhat. But then," he said, holding his arms out, "I *am* human, living in a frighteningly polarized, schizophrenic world."

Temple turned to warm his rump by the fire. "I may be viewed as a man-god and con man rolled into one, a paradox if you want to call it that, but I am one who also speaks the truth."

Maśon stared up at Temple, his mouth agape. "You admit that?"

"Well..." Temple paused. "It's only *my* version of what I think I am." He shut the woodstove door and laughed.

Maśon shook his head as if to untangle some debris from his black greasy hair. "I have to remind myself I am only a Scribe and must only record and not interpret what I am told."

"Impossible," Temple said. "You're a master storyteller. Your unique energy and perceptions are woven throughout this story whether you're aware of it or not."

"Well, I will do my best to be impartial and remove all traces of subjectivity when this is over, " Maśon offered.

"Good luck." Temple smiled, then gestured with an outstretched hand. "Shall we continue?"

The Scribe nodded in defeat.

Temple sat down on the floor across from Maśon. "It was quite the aerial show in the crater at the Great Round House, and that's saying something for a pilot." Temple grinned. "I was given the agreed-upon signal by Losha when she felt she had the Rebels' complete confidence, and they were sitting together peacefully in harmony. And then I flew into the picture."

He recalled the event with a glint in his eyes. "With our inner wisdom glowing from our brows, we danced in the growing twilight like feathered ballet dancers. We drifted in graceful arc after graceful arc as the other Swans, along with Losha and me, soared around each other, exuding only beauty and pure light. It was the most beautiful experience of my life," he said, breathlessly.

Maśon scribbled swiftly with his ink brush, looking up now and then to catch Temple's expression.

Temple stopped and smiled at the Scribe. He pulled a well-worn scroll from his cloak and handed it to Maśon. "Here's a gift for you, my friend."

Maśon placed his brush down and received the scroll with both hands and a gracious nod. "What is it?"

"This is something I've been carrying around for almost one hundred years now. It's an account by one of the Rebel Scribes of what happened that day. Apparently, it was discarded and left behind in the crater. As a scribe and a historian I thought you might appreciate it."

"Oh, I am! Thank you so much," Maśon said. "I will treasure this forever."

Maśon careful unwound the bindings and unrolled the fragile scroll and read, his eyes racing over the faded script. His eyes grew larger. He looked up from the text at Temple. "Really?" he asked.

Temple chuckled and lay down on the blanketed ground, his arms raised under his head as a pillow. "Go ahead. Read it out loud. I know it by heart, but would love to hear you read it to me."

Maśon cleared his throat self-consciously and began to read the scroll aloud. "'The Royal Swans rose bravely into the sky above the Great Round House. They surrounded the Wizard in his Owl-form to protect the great White Swan from attack...'" He stopped and frowned. "It says you attacked her!"

"I know. Go on," Temple said, prompting him.

"'The powerful Owl lunged at the great White Swan...and the two fought in midair, tumbling, gliding, striking out against one another. The Owl screeched in pain when, in one deft maneuver, Losha banked around to Temple's left flank and landed him a blow, nearly knocked him out of the sky. He fell several meters like a leaf spiraling downward, until Losha soared in a figure-eight configuration and came around his other side to deliver a second serious blow. Feathers flew and scattered onto the crowd. Temple scrambled furiously with his sharp talons, clawed the air, and, by wild luck, clipped one of Losha's wings. Then he swooped under her. She too fell several meters and collided on top of Temple's back, which seemed to knock the air out the Wizard. Losha swiftly compensated for her damaged wing and lifted off Temple's back, but not before she bent her serpentine neck and hammered the Wizard a brutal blow…"

"Why, this is incredible!" Mason said. "It's not what happened at all!"

"But it's what they chose to see at the time," Temple explained. "Some of it is true, though. At one point she soared too close and bloody well nearly poked out my eye." He laughed. "All gracefully done, of course.

"You see, the Rebels who believed Losha was the one and only True Divine Teacher thought she had defeated me in battle. And then they thought she had tamed me in the end – me, the great and powerful White Wizard." Temple let out a hardy snort. "In the broader reality, of course," he said, with seriousness that added weight, "we are all Divine. We are surrounded by the Divine – soaked in it. We have never been apart from it because it's present in everything. The God force we know as the Divine is the Spirit Which Moves In All Things. But I digress.

"Losha spun back into her human form first. When she made her way back to the podium, she raised her arm in a signal we had agreed upon earlier. I swooped down and landed on her arm. She stroked my chest feathers gently. I hopped onto her shoulder, confident that we'd done the best we could to show our alliance with one another."

"And?"

Temple smirked and rolled his eyes. "Every weapon the Rebels possessed was waved at me. Before the crowd could mob me, I regained enough power to spin and transform back into my human form."

"And then you bowed to her. That's what I heard," Mason said.

"Yes, but it wasn't in defeat. It was out of genuine respect for the Goddess I knew her to be in human form, and, of course, out of my love for her. And she bowed back to me. Naturally, the crowd claimed victory over the wicked white man-beast."

"And then what happened?

"I told them I was there to serve them. Then Losha and I took each other by the hand and bowed to the Rebels. It probably wasn't the smartest move we made, but we were being true to ourselves. Well…and maybe we were being a mite naïve."

Maśon raised an eyebrow. "And? And?"

"The Rebels rushed me," Temple replied with nonchalance. "They clearly wanted my head. Palomei's soldiers held them back as the Queen proclaimed that the pair of us had fulfilled the prophecy and would now be considered human gods. But her attempt to create order misfired.

"Within seconds all the weapons concealed by Palomei's soldiers – in their clothing, hidden in the brush, buried in shallow trenches – came out of hiding. Palomei's forces made a show of raw power.

"And then, without Losha's and my foreknowledge, Palomei called for Illa to be brought forward."

CHAPTER SIXTY-THREE

KEEPING PROMISES

"There's no judgment on how you have learned."

Temple Fox
The Makolese Scroll on
The Return of the Ka and the Mending of the Su #63

Nijaga came out of the Great Round House with a sack slung over his shoulder. He followed the Queen down from the platform while other guards and soldiers formed a tight shield of protection around her. Nijaga lowered the sack to the ground and pulled the barkcloth sack off the girl.

Terrified, Illa stood before the frightened crowd, still gagged and bound, screaming without being heard. The Queen grabbed the girl by the hair and dragged her over to the pond beneath the Great Round House. The powerful giantess lifted her into the air and placed Illa feet first into the water.

The Rebels stopped in horror.

"It is the girl, Illa!" Arma said to those around her.

"Illa!" Naffa cried out.

"Great Tagheetu's Ghost!" Cranik mumbled. "What is she doing?!"

"Accept the two rightful Teachers! Bow to them now!" Palomei commanded. "If you do not believe this great miracle and do not obey me," she shouted, "then each of you will suffer the same fate as this traitor!"

"Oh great Goddess Hianna!" Losha exclaimed. "Absolutely everything has fallen apart! Temple…" She turned to Temple, but he remained silent, unmoved, deep in an altered state.

"Stop. Palomei! STOP!" Owane shouted over the angry roar of the crowd.

Palomei stopped short and turned around to face her husband. "You still do not understand," she said to him.

The crowd watched as Illa sank beneath the water with only her head exposed and her eyes rolling white with terror. Then Palomei parted her yellow robe, her pendulous breasts draped over the great round of her belly. She lifted her heavy foot in the air, steadying herself with her scepter, then placed her foot squarely on top of Illa's head. She pushed the girl's head under the water.

"You are all possessed by demons!" someone shouted from the crowd.

The swords, spears, and long knives, fishing gaffs, daggers, and clubs suddenly flashed with new life. The Rebels aimed their weapons at the giant Queen.

"Let her live!" Arma shouted.

"She has admitted to killing two of my runners!" Palomei shouted. "But I will grant her pardon if you all declare your obedience to the two rightful Teachers…and to *me*!"

Losha shouted above the crowd. "Queen Palomei, stop! Please stop!"

The Queen lifted her foot, and Illa came bolting to the surface struggling for breath.

"This was a trap from the beginning. What do we do now?" Mik-lon asked Arma.

"Bow," she said. "Bow!"

"But –"

"This is Palomei's doing. The Teachers have nothing to do with this. Do it to save Illa!" Arma insisted. "Bow!" She called out to the others to do the same, then placed her head to the ground.

Following Arma's lead, Mik-lon lowered himself to the ground, as did Pao-ta and many others. Cranik wound his way through the crowd to where Elders Kulo and Ikus stood immobilized with horror while Losha worked energetically to comb the knots of turbulent energy from the surrounding space.

Mik-lon gripped the spear at his side until his knuckles turned white. "Why do the Teachers do nothing?" he asked Arma, his voice muffled and harsh. "They are a part of this! Arma, listen to me!" he pleaded.

"Trust me," she whispered. "Trust the Teachers."

Palomei pointed her scepter at the crowd and shouted with vehemence. "All of you! DOWN!"

Pao-ta lifted her head off the ground and looked over at Arma and Mik-lon. "We are surrounded!" she said. "She will kill us all! And the Teachers do nothing!"

Palomei shouted again. "Profess your allegiance to the two rightful Teachers now or the girl will feel the weight of my foot for the last time!"

Having already surrounded the mob in the caldera, Palomei's palace soldiers tightened their circle around the Rebels one ragged heartbeat and one step at a time.

"We surrender!" several called out.

"I believe! I pledge allegiance to the True Prophets!"

"Let her go!" a few yelled. "She is only a child!"

Elder Ikus waved his arms in the air and started shouting: "DO NOT SURRENDER! Losha has betrayed us! All of this has been a sham!"

A wave of cacophonous cries bellowed out from the congregation and a few shouted back in agreement. Ikus turned to face the Queen. "I will never follow you or any of your Wizards! We will finish this and finish this here before the ancient bones of Lord Tagheetu!"

"ALL OF YOU!" the Queen screamed, pointing her scepter at Ikus. "NOW! It is all of you...or none of you!"

The majority of Rebels bowed with their heads to the ground, but the remaining few gathered in a circle facing outward with Ikus at their center, their weapons still drawn in defiance.

Palomei gnashed her teeth together, and the crater reverberated with her angry roar of frustration. She pushed her foot down on Illa's head hard, and the girl, once more, was forced beneath the water.

The glow between Losha's eyes faded and she let out a panicked cry. "This is not the way!"

Palomei looked over at the Teacher, startled. She removed her foot from Illa's head and the girl leaped to the surface in a rush, gasping for air through her nostrils.

Naffa crawled his way through the mob closer and closer, his eyes flickering back and forth between Illa, the Queen, and Temple.

He is making her do this! Losha and the Queen have been bewitched!

Naffa set his gaze firmly on Temple.

"Everyone, surrender! Please!" Elder Kulo yelled. He motioned for several of his friends close by to move behind the soldiers for protection, then held his hands up and shouted. But no one was listening, until Cranik pushed his way through the crowd and got their attention.

"People, stop!" Cranik shouted. "I have witnessed the power of both Losha and Temple Fox! I have been healed and transformed by both of them!" he confessed.

Kulo stared at him with surprise.

"It is true, my friend," Cranik said to Kulo to the side. "I am not just saying this to save the girl."

Kulo raised his hand to silence the crowd. "Listen to him!" he shouted. "And listen to me, as well! For I too have experienced a complete transformation thanks to Temple Fox and Losha Ninti! It was, in fact, Temple Fox, who returned my Ka to me!"

"Noooo!" several shouted.

"You are either lying or have been deceived!"

"They are bribing you with power!" one of the Rebels shouted.

"I am not lying," Kulo explained. "Losha and Temple are the True Teachers who have both fulfilled the prophecy!"

"We have been fooled before and will not be again!" Ikus shouted from a distance with his new followers poised with their weapons.

"There can only be one True Prophet!" a man shouted. "YOU ARE TRAITORS!"

Kulo and Cranik grabbed each other by the arm and stepped backward behind the wall of soldiers, who allowed them entrance. The old men motioned for others to join them.

Naffa snaked his way on his belly to position himself closer. He stopped and pulled the blowpipe from beneath his waistband, then the bottle of venom. He fumbled with the stopper, his hands shaking. He dipped one dart into the bottle and loaded it inside the length of bamboo.

"All must profess your belief now!" Palomei bellowed. She waited for a long second, then placed her foot back onto Illa's head and held it in place.

"You test my patience!" she roared.

Losha began to lurch forward toward the Queen when Temple held her back with a look of perfect peace. She hesitated.

A Rebel pleaded. "If either of you are the True Teacher, then do something!"

Losha tugged at Temple's arm and shot him a look that could sheer off mountain tops. He gazed deeply into her eyes with such softness and assurance that she yielded again. It was then that he silently conveyed what he knew. When Losha finally understood, she stopped resisting.

Enraged at the Rebel's obstinacy, Palomei thrust the girl down under the waters with her heavy foot and held her there, until she felt no struggle beneath her foot.

The crowd cried out in horror, and a flurry of spear and rock throwing filled the crater. But the well-prepared soldiers bounced them off their power shields.

Pao-ta, Arma, and Mik-lon flattened themselves to the ground as the rocks and spears flew overhead.

Bitterness and rage filled Naffa's soul and he crept closer, determined, driven.

The crowd struggled against the Queen's soldiers with two power shields of their own. One Rebel finally threw his lightning spear.

"There is something I've been meaning to teach you," Temple said to Losha.

"And what is that?" she asked.

The lightning spear hurdled in the air with a whistling sound toward Temple. Having spotted the spear with his keen vision, Temple drew power up through his spine and into his arm, until it welled up inside him with great potency. He aimed his arm at the projectile. With a quick flick of his wrist the power he had conjured deflected the spear, which veered wildly at an obtuse angle.

"That," he said with satisfaction and a sense of relief.

The lightning spear bounced off the air in front of him, somersaulted end to end in midair, its trajectory heading for the polished stone dome of the Great Round House behind them.

Temple stopped for a moment as he noticed the spear repelled from some unknown force field surrounding the dome.

A thunderous boom and a crackling shook the newly charged air, and the energy field three feet from the dome lit up in a shower of electrical sparks until it played itself out, leaving the air suffused with ozone.

Distracted, Temple was momentarily blinded by the display of lightning and sparks bouncing all around him. Then another of the Rebels' conventional spears was thrown, this time slipping past the soldiers' power shields just when one soldier pivoted to repel a hail of rocks.

Temple was just turning back around, after witnessing how the lightning spear had been repelled off the dome, when he heard Losha draw breath. She was well into a spin and beginning to dissolve into a blur of white light, when with split-second timing, she altered her gyrations and moved her arm back as if she were swimming the backstroke. The spear missed Temple's chest, but clipped his earlobe, and went flying over the heads of the soldiers beyond the great dome.

Losha slowed her spinning before she transmuted her form to that of a Swan and came to a halt. She grinned at Temple. "Teach me what?"

Temple placed his forefinger to his ear. He drew it away to examine the spot of blood on the tip of his finger, his eyebrows raised in surprise. His eyes smiled back. "Smart ass. And you did it your own way as well."

Seeing what had just happened, the mob, having pressed forward, stopped short and retreated a few steps. The last of the small contingent behind them threw their remaining conventional spears, but the soldiers repelled them again, leaving a litter of weapons piled yards in front of the platform of stone.

Still flattened to the ground, Mik-lon's hand tightened on his spear and he broke out in a sweat. "Arma!" he pleaded gritting his teeth. "The Queen! We must stop the Queen!"

Breaking into a run, Ikus' followers pushed their way up to the line of soldiers, this time forcing Palomei's guards into hand-to-hand combat with swords and fishing gaffs slicing the air all around them.

Losha leaned forward and grabbed Kulo's arm. Temple took the cue and pulled Cranik behind him, to shield the old man from harm.

The sounds of metal clashing against metal, shouts and groans, piercing war cries and howls of anguish rippled through the caldron of battle. The Rebels who had reacted violently were so outnumbered that the battle was over quickly, and a dozen or more bodies lay bloodied on the ground wounded, but still very much alive. None of the wounded were Palomei's men.

Ikus retreated further from the Great Round House, several of his men protecting him with their shields. He pushed his way out of the defensive circle and began to shout, his eye aimed at Kulo. "It is because of you that we are here…SURROUNDED!" His face blustered, and he waved his sword high over his head. "If we cannot kill the Wizards, then you and all your idiot Believers friends will die this day! TRAITORS!" He lunged forward at the crowd and swung his blade wildly.

And another battle ensued this time between the new Believers and Ikus' Rebel faction.

Palomei's soldiers threatened the fighting mob with their own lightning spears. They marched forward, then stopped and drew back their arms to take careful aim with their deadly weapons.

One by one the new Believers tossed their weapons onto the ground. Only the closest to the Unbelievers continued to defend themselves until Elder Ikus saw the soldiers advance, tightening their circle around him. In a vehement storm of anger, Ikus hurled his sword into the crowd, hoping it would strike someone. Seeing the hopelessness of their situation his followers tossed their weapons to the ground and held up their hands in surrender.

All but Naffa, who was far from the fray.

A disquieting hush took hold inside of the caldera. Losha heard the mournful cry of one of the wounded, and she instinctively pressed past Palomei's guards and trotted over to the man. She ripped the bottom of her barkcloth skirt off and quickly bound his wounded arm to staunch the bleeding, then laid her hand over his head to accelerate the healing. And while she called forth her powers of healing, she looked over at Temple.

Naffa followed Temple with his eyes as Temple wove his way confidently through the crowd to where a guard stood at alert in front of his Sovereign with a spear and shield in hand.

Naffa took aim.

Nijaga gave Temple a steep bow, then stepped out of the way so Temple could reach the Queen, who was standing in defiance with her arms laid across her large bosom, and her scepter resting in the crook of her arm.

The boy lost his aim when Temple moved. He paused for a second and repositioned himself as he struggled to control his breathing.

Ignoring the Queen, Temple slipped behind her to where Illa floated in the water. He stepped into the pool and scooped up the lifeless girl into his arms, climbed back out and placed her gently to the ground. He rolled Illa's head to one side.

Naffa stopped short and stared in shocked silence, his palms sweating, his heart beating out of control.

Temple breathed into the girl's mouth.

"Leave the girl alone," Palomei insisted. "This is my business and my business alone!"

He is poisoning her! He is trying to take her soul! "Leave her alone!" Naffa found himself shouting.

Temple continued to breathe life back into the girl.

"Stop *touching* her!" Naffa whispered.

Realizing his efforts weren't working, Temple rose and stood before the limp figure on the ground. Clasping his hands together in prayer, the burning coal of Divine fire in his brow began to glow again, until the space around him grew brighter.

"LEAVE HER ALONE!" Naffa said, between his clenched teeth.

Seeing he was being ignored, Naffa wiped the sweat from his eyes and took aim, commanding his hands and his breath to obey his will.

Temple closed his eyes and placed both palms out in front of him toward the girl and called forth the Divine power that ran through him now like lightning. He drew in one long, deep breath. One tense second passed and his exhalation became a shout! And just as he shouted, "In the name of God…BREATHE!!" Naffa blew the dart with one short blast from his breath.

Illa instantly gasped for air and began to choke up water. She sputtered, and a fountain of pond water poured from her mouth onto the wet ground.

Palomei took a short step back in shock. And the people, who still sat with their heads bowed to the ground, lifted their eyes to witness the miracle unfold.

Naffa stared hard, but saw that his dart had missed Temple. He swiftly retrieved the second dart, dipped it in the venom and took aim again, his heart pounding faster this time but his hands steady.

Illa coughed up the last of the water and began panting.

Palomei's face twisted in horror. "No!" she said and clutched her heart.

Losha saw how the power of Divine energy poured through Temple and brought Illa back from the dead. She stopped what she was doing and walked over to Temple, his eyes still closed, his arms still outstretched in Illa's direction. He dropped his arms by his sides when Losha came up behind him and wrapped her arms around him in a warm embrace.

Having gained her breath, Illa eased herself up onto her knees, and stared up at Temple. She bowed her head to the ground with profound gratitude.

A million words on a hundred scrolls could not have spoken more clearly to the crowd. Losha's and then Illa's reaction to Temple was so clear, so sincere, and spoke with such purity of love, that the Rebels stared up in wonder.

"Behold, the two True Prophets!" a woman declared with jubilation.

Naffa stilled his breathing for a mere second and steadied his aim. Using his rage to fuel his actions, he drew one deep breath, then let out one terse, sharp blow, and watched the dart streak through the air several meters. It struck Temple in the thigh.

Temple grabbed his thigh, and seeing the dart, plucked it out and threw it to the ground. He turned to warn Losha. "Be careful, love. Don't touch that," he said, then stumbled to the ground.

When the people realized what had happened, a deathly stillness filled the green.

"Nooo!" Illa cried.

Losha quickly dropped down and crouched by Temple's side. She cradled his head in her lap and placed his face between her hands like a prayer. "Stay with me, Temple!" she whispered.

Temple looked up at Losha, his eyes full of love. He smiled. As his head rolled to one side, he saw the Queen clasping her breast, her breathing labored and her eyes wide with terror. Temple's head began to dizzy and his eyes glazed over. He looked at Losha helplessly…fading.

Pivoting on her heels, Palomei's massive body fell backward onto the boulders. Her skull hit hard with a discernible crack. She rolled face down into the pond, ten thousand yellow feathers from her cape matted together in a wet mass and spread across the water.

The people drew breath.

Losha heard the sound and turned to see what had happened. The sudden realization that both had fallen to some unknown assassin in the crowd finally hit her. Feeling vulnerable to another attack, she shielded Temple's body. "Breath slowly," she warned him. And then, again, she called forth her powers of protection and healing.

Owane, who had witnessed Temple drop to the ground first, saw Palomei fall. He bolted from the stone platform with some of the soldiers following in his wake. Palomei's remaining guards repositioned themselves into a wider arc, and drew a wall of protection around Losha, Temple, and the Queen.

"It was a poisoned dart," someone announced.

"Who shot it?" asked another.

Naffa doubled over so no one could see his actions as he loaded the last dart into the blowpipe. "You are next, witch!" he said beneath his breath, and took aim directly at Losha.

Illa stood up, craning her neck over the shields to search the crowd with her eyes. "Naffa!" she called out. "Naffa! I know it was you!" she called again. "Do not do this!"

Naffa lowered the blowpipe.

Illa spoke again. "Naffa! Please stop! You would be killing another of the true Teachers!"

Naffa lowered his head again to hide, but the others spotted him in the crowd.

"Naffa, listen," she called out again. "Temple and Losha had nothing to do with ambushing us, or drowning me. I heard the Queen plan the attack. The Teachers knew nothing about it!'

"You have been bewitched!" Naffa yelled back. "He blew his breath into you. You are now his!"

"This is my fault," Mik-lon told Arma. He grabbed his spear and bolted to his feet.

Mik-lon and three soldiers moved swiftly toward the boy. Naffa swung around and aimed his blowgun at them one at a time. The men stopped.

"Temple brought me back to life!" Illa shouted. "Can you not see that?"

"The boy has killed Temple Fox," someone yelled.

"Kill her!" Naffa shouted. "All of you! Kill Losha! Do it now!" he screamed, his veins popping out from his neck.

The guards tightened their formation to shield Temple and Losha.

Naffa was encircled now, and his eyes flickered frantically from Mik-lon to the three soldiers. He turned around sharply, then behind him quickly, his nerves coming apart, his sense of helplessness taking him over.

I am surrounded!... But I killed the Wizard! I KILLED HIM!!

He pointed to Losha. "KILL HER!" he said again, commanding, pleading.

When no one responded, Naffa stood very still. From his waistband he pulled the black glass bottle, which contained the antidote, and held it up for all to see. Mik-lon and the soldiers, who pressed down on him, slowed their pace, curious as to what the bottle might contain.

"Here is the antidote to the poison!" he shouted.

He ripped out the stopper with his teeth, tipped the bottle and drained its contents onto the ground. He tossed the bottle to the side.

"Naffa! No!" Illa cried.

Then Naffa slid the dart from the mouth of the blowpipe and held the dart between his fingers. He looked at the sharp point for a mute second and then into Illa's eyes. "I am sorry," he said. He rammed the dart into his stomach.

Illa squeezed through the wall of defense. She ran to him as he collapsed to his knees. "Nooo!" she screamed.

But it was too late. Naffa fell onto his back, his eyes taking on a distant cast. He looked up at the evening sky, the purple and crimson hues growing vibrant, sounds in the caldera falling flat and muted. He saw Illa's face appear above his own. She was crying, and others struggled to pull her back. There was nothing but the sky above him, but he noticed that one cloud grew bright with intensity as if the sun had suddenly reappeared in all its glory at dusk. And in the cloud he saw an indistinct face slowly taking shape. The face drew closer, crisper, and Naffa's entire field of vision was filled with Temple Fox's placid image.

Temple gazed down at the boy with loving eyes. He offered Naffa his hand.

Not knowing why, Naffa stretched out his arm and clasped Temple's hand. And at once the boy was filled with the warmth of total acceptance and a profound, ineffable peace.

"Come, lad," Temple said. "I will guide you home."

Temple helped Naffa to his feet and, and the boy found his spirit lifted effortlessly into the air far above the crowd.

Naffa watched as the crowd beneath him grew smaller, and the two hovered together in what felt like the eternal depths of black space. Temple pointed, and a curious tunnel made of a nacreous light appeared. Beyond it was a dark void.

Together the two floated inside the tunnel and watched as its walls changed into an array of swirling rainbow colors that rotated softly. And beyond the void, a scintillating light of purity beckoned Naffa.

"Go through the void into the light," Temple said, coaxing the boy along.

"And you?" the boy offered.

"I have other matters to attend to," Temple said.

And with that simple declaration, Temple released Naffa's hand, and the boy floated slowly through the tunnel, drawn by the Light of God…into the Heart of God.

The crowd watched as Naffa's eyes rolled back into his head and then simply closed.

Illa doubled over on the ground crying, until others pried her off Naffa's body and lifted her to her feet. She stumbled blindly over to where Losha held Temple in a loving embrace. "I am sorry," she sobbed. "He was the True Teacher…as you are. I…I know that now."

Losha looked onto the girl's sorrowful face with calm. "Do not speak of Temple Fox in past tense," she whispered.

"What can I do?" Illa pleaded.

"Tani would know, but she is not here." Losha paused in thought. "I do not know what kind of poison he used. Quick! Go to the spot where your friend dumped out the antidote and find the empty bottle."

Illa ran to the spot where Naffa still lay on the ground, found the obsidian bottle, and raced back.

Kulo and Cranik gathered around Losha as she sniffed the empty bottle, then dipped her fingertip into it. She touched her finger to her tongue.

"Get me some sapodilla seeds. Grind the seeds and make a paste for me. Be quick!" she said to Illa, and the girl bolted off.

Losha looked up at Kulo. "Elder Kulo, pick someone you trust to find some indigofera pulchra, and make a root paste of it with neem oil. When you have the paste, infuse it with healing energy. Then bring it to me."

"Could that possibly help?" Cranik asked.

"He should have died by now. I will try all means to bring him back."

"Anything I can do?" he asked.

"Pray. We all must pray for him now."

All but Ikus' few Rebel friends gathered together until they formed a great circle around Losha and Temple. And without being told what to do, they dropped to their knees before the Divine couple and pressed their palms together in prayer, weaving a web of energy and an unbreakable bond. And together they sang and prayed, becoming clear conduits of pure love and compassion.

Owane and some guards pulled Palomei from the pond and dragged her heavy body onto a flat boulder. Owane noticed the dart protruding through a tangle of his wife's necklaces directly into her heart. He plucked it out and handed it to one of the soldiers.

"Such a tiny thing," he whispered hoarsely, and then began to sob. "Does no one mourn her!" he howled.

His plea drew the attention of a few soldiers and Elder Kulo. They strode over to the old man and stood in respectful silence as Owane cradled Palomei's massive head.

Temple's spirit moved into action. He drifted over to where Palomei's spirit stood brooding over her own body.

Is that me? she asked, staring down at the huge mound of flesh that was her physical body.

No, Temple answered. *This is you. Your spirit is who you really are.*

Palomei's spirit looked over at the glowing god-man. She held her hand out in front of her, noticing the same luminosity.

It's time to go, he said quietly.

Barely a whisper escaped from her lips. *I know,* she said. Her words came out painfully, slowly. *I have failed.* She winced, but her gaze held steadfast to the electric blue in Temple's eyes. A wave of compassion fell over her. *I have drawn the poison dart...to myself. That is what you would teach me, is that not so? I have failed myself.*

You have learned. And there's no judgment on how you have learned, Temple said.

Palomei was drawn deeper into Temple's eyes and understanding. *You must go now,* he said. *There are others waiting for you.*

A glimmer formed in the distance and drew closer. All at once Palomei was surrounded by heartfelt warmth. Out of the radiance stepped several figures, two of which were much taller than the rest.

Mother? Palomei whispered.

One of the towering figures moved forward, her ruddy cheeks taking on a glow of their own, her long red hair blazing with a fiery brilliance, her powerful build exuding strength and wisdom. She embraced Palomei, and Palomei fell into her arms like a long lost child.

I missed you! Palomei cried.

We have been with you all along. In a sense we never left, but tried to guide you from where we reside.

And where is that? Palomei asked, looking up at her Mother lovingly with new curiosity.

Just a breath away, she answered. *We have always guided you, but you were not always listening.*

I think I made a horrible mess of things, Palomei confessed.

You played an important role. See the results, her Mother said. *Look at the Rebels now.*

Palomei looked at the crowd surrounding Losha and Temple's slumped body. All but Ikus' group was deep in prayer.

Temple is dead, Palomei whispered.

No, her Mother said. *There is no such thing as death. You will understand soon enough. But you see most of the Rebels? They are united now. And now you will be reunited with us again.*

The other colossal figure stepped forward out of the wavering light. Its shape coalesced into that of an older woman even taller than Palomei's mother, her jaw and brow thick, her hulking body stately, but rugged in form.

Grandmother! Palomei breathed the word with awe and stepped forward and embraced the old woman around the waist. And as she hugged her she saw two diminutive forms step forward. *Father! Grandfather!* She released her hold on her Grandmother and ran up to them with pure joy and embraced them both. Behind them she beheld the figures of her Mother's other Husbands.

If you all are here…then… Palomei stopped short.

Her family moved aside like a curtain parting, and a shorter, slender young woman with flashing red hair and broad smile stepped forward.

Shaza! Palomei called out and the two walked up to each other and collapsed into each other's arms. *Oh, my precious Daughter! How I missed you! How I grieved for you every day!*

I was never gone, Mother. I was always by your side.

I felt you, Palomei whispered. *I should have listened.*

It is time to go now, Shaza announced.

The family of giants gathered together, forming a circle around Palomei. And in a blink of an eye…they all were gone!

★　　★　　★　　★　　★　　★

The wet bees that clung to Palomei's crown of blossoms suddenly rose in the air in a maddening swarm.

Temple's spirit gazed down where Owane sat with Palomei's huge head resting in his lap as he affectionately stroked her fleshy cheek.

Owane lifted his head to watch the bees spiral into the air.

Temple opened his heart and cast a beam of calming energy into the heart of the older man.

Owane whispered, "Temple? Is that you?"

"It's me," he answered in Owane's mind.

"She is gone," he said quietly.

"I know."

"Is she all right?"

"She has been reunited with her family. They will take good care of her."

Owane nodded that he understood. "And what about you?" he asked.

"I guess it's my time now," was his only answer.

Just as Owane's strange conversation started to draw the attention of the guards, he heard the crowd suddenly gasp in unison. Shouts of joy echoed throughout the caldera, and Owane sighed deeply with relief.

Temple Fox was alive!

CHAPTER SIXTY-FOUR

THE KEY

THE KEY
*"The mystery lies
in the visible key
unlocking an invisible lock.
Quite the paradox."*

Elo Tivloc, popular Makolese poet
The Makolese Scroll on
The Return of the Ka and the Mending of the Su #64

When Great Grandfather Okon spied the two giant fins dip beneath the waves, his boat suddenly lost momentum. Coasting toward a wall of fog so thick he couldn't distinguish between sea and sky, he found himself blinded, isolated…lost.

Draped in fine mist, the tiny droplets began to run down his forehead, cheeks, and chest, leaving him hot and clammy. "I am close," Okon said to himself. "I can feel it."

The old man sat motionless, his body slack, mind at rest, and spirit long acquiesced to the will of the Gods. The boat drifted slowly now, yielding to the rhythm of the rolling gray waves and the breath of a gentler wind. Suddenly, the soft sea breeze died as if a great door had shut and the waves played themselves out in torpid time. His boat sat bobbing in the surf.

"Tahneyah, the Wind, holds its breath," he said aloud in the silence. And he went deeper into himself, releasing the last of his little will to the greater will of the Gods.

Accepting the unfathomable depths of the unknown, the old man stood up in the slowly rocking boat and threw his arms out to his sides in a gesture of complete surrender.

An unnatural stillness enveloped Okon, and the hairs on his arms stood erect, causing his skin to tingle. The silence thickened and became the muted drone of nothingness, and the prickling that crept all over his flesh grew sharp and painful. He steadied himself and raised his hands at shoulder height, palms outward to test the energy field.

"Intact," he whispered.

Just as Tani and I suspected. The Barik Limits is as strong as it has ever been, so strong that I can almost feel the presence of a physical wall. But it is not impenetrable. I have the key.

Fixed in his memory for over fifty years, Great Grandfather Okon prepared the ancient song prayer in his mind again – a song he had learned in secret in the old Makolese tongue from the Eldest of the Eldest before him, down through the centuries, until this auspicious moment. Although the most senior of Elders had learned the ancient song, none ever truly imagined they would actually ever sing the prayer. Even Okon had thought the song would never be sung, not for another five hundred years or more. After all, it was only to be sung once…but only after the dreams had come. But he had been wrong. The dreams did come…repeatedly…and he was the one chosen for what would be regarded as the most dangerous and misunderstood act in all of Makolese history.

It is time, he thought.

Okon filled his lungs in one deep, powerful breath and his song poured forth from the most innermost part of his soul in all its ineffable beauty.

All at once the still air began to vibrate to his bittersweet melody, and flashes of light appeared in the heavy fog in horizontal bands of orange and red. Okon began to breathe in the rhythm he had learned from his predecessor, matching the cadence of the bright pulsations.

The surface of the sea moved like thick cream being stirred in a huge pot.

Minor energy fluctuations beat the air like wings, and Okon wondered if these oscillations might be the weaknesses in the Barik Limits, which allowed ships from Outsiders to enter Makolese waters, but kept the Makolese bound within. A gate controlled by the Gods? Or were the curious fluctuations fortifying the Limits?

The brilliant flashes died as quickly as Okon's mind questioned the sources.

"I have gone too much into my rational mind. There is no need to analyze. I need to be out of my mind completely," he said in self-reprimand.

Okon pulled the ceremonial gris from its sheath and began to sing his prayer again, this time with more focus and more power. The flashes reappeared, and the magic crystal began to glow in his hand, pulsating to a rhythm matching the tempo of his breath and the streaks of light.

The air all around him began to flash like a stroboscopic lamp.

Okon steadied himself as the waters started to toss, until what little of the ocean he could see in the fog was roiling. Suddenly, the boat lurched sharply leeward to the port side. Before Okon could catch himself, he was thrown to the bottom. He cried out in pain, but held on firmly to the gris.

The boat rotated counterclockwise in place, leaving Okon dazed and dizzied with no frame of reference. Six distinct horizontal bands of red and green lights formed atop one another through the impenetrable fog, appearing as streaks as Okon whirled round and round. They began to pulsate rapidly, and his heart fluttered.

He witnessed a broken bar of light as he rotated. Above this, a long solid bar, two broken bars, another solid bar, and then another broken one, each stacked one above the other. The streaks turned from red and green to gold, while the top three bars changed order and glistened brighter.

The fog broke apart into millions of tiny tight spirals that swirled and danced in midair. The eldest of the Elders suddenly sensed the Barik Limits open and a force pull him forward.

CHAPTER SIXTY-FIVE

ILLA'S LAST SAY

*"The Divine may have used me to restore your
sight, old friend,
but I can see you are still blind."*

Elder Kulo Kempok
The Makolese Scroll on
The Return of the Ka and the Mending of the Su #65

"He is breathing again!" Illa exclaimed.

"Tai. If he was meant to die he would have been dead by now," Losha announced quietly to all nearby who could hear. "Right now he is in a coma and is not totally back yet. It will take sometime for the poison to be drawn out of him completely and for his fever to break."

"Can I do anything?" Kulo asked.

"Find two red garnets," Losha said.

Kulo looked at Losha, puzzled.

"We will press them to his ears. It will help rouse him from the coma," she said.

Kulo hurried off and Cranik stepped forward. "What do we do?" Cranik asked.

"Continue to pray for all those who lost their lives," Losha said. She looked up at the others with the divine light of compassion shining through her dark eyes. "But do not speak their names except for Temple Fox," she whispered, knowing the dead sometimes lingered with the living when their names were spoken.

★   ★   ★   ★   ★   ★

As the evening settled into darkness, the mournful sound everyone anticipated filled the caldera. Conches were blown, drums beaten, and the message they conveyed resounded beyond the bowl where the bones of Lord Tagheetu rested. News could be heard throughout the Queen's compound nearby, to all the villages that skirted the shore, to the more distant Shaman's compound, and out to sea where the night fishermen hunted. And as the message was repeated, all on the isle of Makol knew that the Queen was dead, Temple had been mortally wounded, and the Rebels had been subdued.

Throughout the night former Rebels and soldiers sat in a silent vigil, praying in shifts. As the swollen moon cast bold light over the crowd and the stars burned brighter, those who grew drowsy laid down to rest.

All but the followers of Ikus, who were the only true Rebels now, slept. They made a fire and posted their own guards. Circled tightly together far from the reformed Rebels, they never allowed the few daggers concealed beneath their clothing to leave their clutches. Bending their heads close to listen to Elder Ikus, their new leader, they talked quietly into the night, frightened and confused, angry and embittered.

Nomuk plucked at his matted hair. Flecks of dirt and dried blood fell into the air and mingled with the rising smoke. "The Queen is dead and we all know who will take her place," he said.

All heads nodded.

"You can be sure that Losha will become Queen," Ikus said, his deep, grainy voice strained to make a whisper. "It was the plan all along."

"And what will become of us?" Shobiyohe asked, his wounded arm wrapped in a rough bloodied cloth.

"No one has moved against us so far," Nomuk said, scratching his scalp.

Sounds of footsteps drew close. One of their guards intercepted the intruder with his dagger held out. "Who is there?"

"Put your gris away, Koteki," Kulo said, recognizing the voice. "We are unarmed. It is I, Elder Kulo, and Illa."

"You have a lot of nerve coming over here," Koteki said.

Ikus squinted up through the firelight as Kulo and Illa were escorted closer to the campfire. "Traitors are not welcome. Go back to your Wizards and your dead Queen!"

"We have come to talk," Kulo started.

"There will be no more talk," Ikus said.

"Did you come to say good-bye to old friends?" Shobiyohe said. "We will probably be dead by morning."

"Shut up, Shobiyohe!" Koteki said.

"I see no friends before me," Ikus stated flatly to Kulo. "All I see are impressionable idiots and traitors!"

"There will be no more killing," Kulo replied, deflecting the remark. "Owane says he will give you a choice. You can stay here on the island if you do not make trouble, or you will be exiled to one of the outer islands. Besides, there are only" – he counted the faces around the circle – "twelve of you left who are Unbelievers."

Nomuk spoke, his face tightened with anger. "Oh, so Owane is making all the decisions now, and not your new Queen and her White Wizard Consort?"

Kulo noted the sarcasm and brushed it aside. "We have come to tell you he is allowing you to live."

Illa leaned forward. "And I came to tell you that Losha and Temple were not aware of Queen Palomei's plans to entrap and threaten you if you did not proclaim to be Believers. I heard it with my own ears."

"And how did you come about hearing such a plan?" Ikus asked. "Why would the Queen tell you – a child?"

"I crawled through the fresh water canal from the northwestern side of the Queen's compound so I could warn the Queen about Losha and Temple working together."

"You were warning Palomei that we had two Wizards on our hands?"

"Tai. Only now I know the truth. Unlike you, I have the courage to admit I was wrong."

"Why not just leave and go back to your villages?" Kulo added. "You cannot change things now. What has been done is done. Just go in peace."

"Peace!" Ikus threw a stick into the fire with vehemence. "There will never be peace with such lies… such vile witchery and sorcery ruling the land!" He grunted and looked up into Kulo's face in the firelight. "You reef worm. You were always dim-witted. You have never had an original thought in your life."

Kulo pulled his slumped shoulders back. "The Divine may have used me to restore your sight, old friend, but I can see you are still blind. Do what you wish, Ikus. We have brought our message." He turned around and lumbered away back into the darkness with Illa.

"Did you really die?" Nomuk called out to Illa. "Or was that some sort of performance?"

Illa turned around and stood with her hands squarely planted on her thin hips in youthful defiance. "Did it look like a performance?" she spat out.

"Then you really did drown?"

"Tai, I did drown. And Temple Fox really did bring me back to life."

Koteki pointed his dagger at her. "Think he can bring you back to life now?"

"We will hear no more of your stories," Ikus barked. "Live with your misperceptions and dangerous delusions. Go!" he said with a wave of his hand.

"And you can live with your 'dangerous delusions,' Elder," Illa said, then turned on her heels to join Kulo.

When the veil of darkness swallowed the two, and only a glimmer of their forms could be seen receding in the moonlight, Nomuk's voice rang out if only to get the last word. "Praise to the boy, Naffa, our hero!"

A sandal came hurtling through the darkness and struck Nomuk squarely on the nose. He grunted softly, rubbed his sore nose, then tossed the sandal into the fire.

Illa had the last say.

CHAPTER SIXTY-SIX

THE WARNING

"Not everything is solved by violence."

Losha Ninti
The Makolese Scroll on
The Return of the Ka and the Mending of the Su #66

The dawn was swollen with heat and humidity. The makeshift campsite that held soldiers, reformed Rebels, and Ikus' small band of Unbelievers, quietly buzzed in the morning with whispers and prayers. The smell of cassava baking in fire pits and pu-erh tea clung to the moist air. Elders Kulo and Cranik stayed with Owane inside the Great Round House while many sat in meditation, praying for the god-man to regain consciousness.

Losha and Winyon sat by Temple's side near the pond of the stone skirting that surrounded the Great Round House. A wide berth of space for privacy was given them as Temple lay in a coma, the poison still lingering in his veins. Losha mopped his brow and quietly sang her healing prayers.

The rising sun, bold as a large gold coin, suspended in a turquoise sky. When its first rays crept over the edge of the caldera, filling the great bowl of earth with a golden light, the polished dome of the Great Round House shone with a blinding brilliance.

The sunlight reflected from the pond hit Temple's eyelids, and he opened one eye, then the other. "They're coming," he whispered in English so weakly that that no one heard him.

Losha gazed down at him, stunned with delight that he had finally awakened to full consciousness. She glanced over at Winyon, who was beaming.

"Temple," she said, with a profound sense of relief. "You are back!"

"I'm parched," he managed to say.

Losha dipped a gourd into the pond and placed the gourd to his lips.

Temple's lips were still numb from the poison and he sipped a little to see if he was able to swallow. He swallowed hard, but couldn't feel the water slide down his throat. She moved the gourd away as he came up for air. "More," he begged, and she tilted the container. He gulped the water down until it was empty.

"Everyone prayed for you," she said. "It was a supremely beautiful and genuine act on their part."

Temple grinned back, weak and slightly more alert. "I know. Thank them for me."

"Can you wiggle your toes?"

Temple grimaced with the effort, but his toes didn't move. "I can't feel anything. It's like I don't have a body."

Losha felt his head again. "You are still paralyzed. And you still have a fever."

His countenance changed when he spoke, his tone more serious, his voice faltering. "They're coming soon…Maybe…It all depends."

The two woman leaned in closer. "Who is coming?" Losha asked.

"The Arab dhows," he whispered feebly in English. "Forty of them."

Losha jerked her head back. "But you predicted they would come in three months! And it has only been one month since you fell from the sky!"

"I saw them when I was out of my body." He wiped the crusty debris from his eyes, but couldn't feel his fingers or his face. He gestured for more water. "Sorry I took so long…getting back." He drank more water and wiped his chin with a numb trembling hand, but felt neither his hand or the water dribbling down his chin. "I needed to do a bit of traveling," he said breathlessly. "You will be able to see the dhows appear over the horizon three days from now…at dawn when the Chumban Mati, or Kissing Sun, is parting from its own reflection. Of course it all depends on where the people are in their consciousness…and what they desire collectively."

"But you predicted…"

"I know what I said." His voice wavered. "But it was based on probability. Something happened between the time I predicted it…and now."

"The Queen's death? Your being struck down?"

"I don't know exactly. But I feel it has something to do with Great Grandfather Okon. I saw him in a long boat being towed, I might add, by two great white sharks."

Winyon's mouth parted, and the two women looked at each other as if someone had just thrown cold water over them.

Losha paused in deep thought. "That is his power animal."

"What does that mean? What do you think happened?" he whispered hoarsely.

"Where? Where did you see the Great Grandfather? In what direction?" Losha asked.

"North of Makol…far past the tiny coral isle…where Winyon was kept as an exile."

"And he was alone?" Losha asked.

Temple raised himself up on wobbly elbows, the action now drawing the attention of others around them. "Tai…I mean…except for the sharks. So what does this mean?"

"I do not know," Losha answered. She looked to Winyon.

"I do not know either." Winyon shrugged.

Losha thought for a moment. "Tani must know. She has been spending time with the Great Grandfather at the Queen's compound."

"I am surprised she has not come here by now," Winyon stated, her face suddenly flushed with dread. "She should have come when she heard the conches and drums."

"You have voiced my same concerns," Losha said. "Can you go find Elder Tani at the Queen's compound and tell her what Temple just said, then come back here?"

"Tai! Tai!" Winyon said, bolting to her feet. She looked down at Temple with raw fear. "But first we must act quickly! We must blow the conches and warn the people! And we must organize all warriors, guards, and able-bodied people with weapons at the shoreline! Bi kana lo! Tiv told me that the new airboat had been destroyed! And now all the lightning spears have been used up!"

Losha looked over her shoulder at the crowd. "Please stop," she said.

Winyon shook her head violently. "What we need to do first is gather all women, children, the old, and the ill, and get them inside Hollow Mountain. They need to take food for themselves and an offering to the Spirit of the Mountain and the Mountain Gods. Then the rest of us must stand and fight!"

The people couldn't hear the words of the conversation, but noted the panicked tone in Winyon's voice. They began to murmur to each other excitedly.

Losha whispered to the glaring figure. "I do not know how to explain what I am sensing, but please just do what I ask you to, and go find Elder Tani."

Winyon's eyes grew harder. "I will not!" she argued. "We need to defend ourselves! We are not cowards! We must stand and fight!"

Losha rose to her feet and stepped up to Winyon boldly, unintimidated.

The older woman grew rigid, her face burning, her temper smoking.

Losha looked over her shoulder again at a throng of people heading her way, then back at the older woman. "Winyon, please listen. I am not your enemy. Fear is your enemy." She glanced over her shoulder again. "Can you please keep them away so we can talk?"

Winyon walked briskly over to the crowd and held her arms out to block the encroaching crowd. "Please, give us space…and privacy!"

Too weak to keep himself propped up, Temple eased himself down again. He reached out for Losha, but his arm fell to his side. "I'm about as useful as a chocolate teapot."

"A what?"

"I can't help anyone when I'm like this, my love. I will do what I can while I'm out of my body."

"You are going back into a coma? But if you do not get water you could die!"

"You don't understand. While I'm out of my body I am so free. When I'm out of my body I can see and understand things better…like this place."

Losha leaned closer. "What do you mean?"

"This island is like a human body with numerous vortexes of energy swirling through it. Did you ever notice that this crater, for instance, is in the exact center of the island? I mistakeningly thought this crater was a caldera from an old volcano."

Losha cocked her head down and her bushy hair fell into her eyes. "Is it not?"

"It's the second highest feature on the island, excluding Hollow Mountain. There is something odd but wonderful about this place. It holds a powerful energy that I can feel more keenly when I'm out of my body. It feels like the very heart of Makol. And the stone dome…" He tilted his head toward the Great Round House. "Didn't you see how it repelled that lightning spear I had deflected?"

"No, I was busy spinning to deflect the next spear. So what are you saying? If this is not the collapsed mouth of an old volcano, then what is it?"

"It's an impact crater from a very large meteorite. This place has been hit by substantial meteorites, not once, but three times."

Losha raised an eyebrow. "Three times! In the same spot? That cannot be by accident, but by purposeful intent. It is true this is the place where iron is found for forging metals. No doubt Mefakani used those meteoritic metals to forge his super weapons."

"Beneath the short grasses inside this bowl of earth is pulverized quartz sand, a magnifier of energy. And the Great Round House rests dead center over three evenly spaced underground springs that form a perfect star pattern. It's a tremendous place of power and is where the spring bubbles up from beneath the dome. This bowl, in fact, acts as a collector of immense cosmic energies. And with the Great Round House in its exact center, the dome functions as a kind of lens that receives and then radiates energy out in a smooth, rounded direction."

Losha noticed that some of the crowd had bowed with respect and had backed away. Winyon would be heading back soon. "So what does this all mean?"she asked anxiously.

"It's a natural amphitheater that collects and magnifies energy, and sends whatever energy is created here outward in an even radiating pattern. And it is very, *very* old. Left by the Gods, I imagine."

"We know it as 'The Place Tagheetu Rested.'"

"You can actually see faint markings that have been carved into the stone platform skirting the dome, but the markings have been eroded by time and are very faint. You can really only see them from above, when the sun is at an angle."

"So how does this information help us now?"

"I don't quite know yet until I get out of my body to do some more exploring."

"But, Temple, you must show the people you are alive! It gives them hope. It gives them heart."

"They have you," he said. "I promise I will return back to my body from time to time, if only to see your bright, shining face." He smiled as he closed his eyes and lay silent.

"Temple. Temple!" She shook him, but he didn't respond. She checked his pulse. "Thank the Goddess Hianna he is still breathing."

Winyon walked back to Losha where she was bent over Temple. Winyon's veins protruded from her neck, her anger not assuaged, but mounting, and she stared down at the man-god. "What has happened?" she asked, with a resurgence of alarm.

"He has gone back into a coma."

"Bi kana!"

Losha looked up at Winyon, trying to hide her worry, but not wearing it well. "It is all right. It was his choice to do so until his body heals completely. Believe me, his consciousness is quite active right now."

"Slavers," Winyon muttered. "At least he came back in time to warn us."

"I know you are upset, but please listen."

Winyon crossed her arms over her bare chest. "I am listening," she said, holding a slight edge of thorniness in her tone.

"Please understand that there is nothing Temple can do about this situation in his present state. He can, however, assist us while he is out of his body. I can also help. But more importantly, the people must help. The time for lone heroes and saviors is over. Or have you forgotten the prophecy? 'One without the other is empty. Power multiplies tenfold and then again tenfold, again and again…' Everyone has to take a part in this."

Winyon unfolded her arms and stared into Losha's eyes. "I never understood that part of the prophecy, until now. Then we all play a part. We leave it in your hands to organize this?" she asked.

Losha nodded. "Please do not tell the others about the Arab Slavers until I have more guidance…and a plan."

Winyon's gaze hardened. "What will you do?"

"I do not know what will be expected of me just yet. I only ask you to find Elder Tani. Speak to her and find out what Okon is doing. Then return here. Tell her to come as quickly as she can."

"But…how will you…?"

"I would never tell the Gods how to solve this problem," Losha interrupted. "I will find a quieter place to pray and ask the Gods for help." She tucked her bushy hair behind her ears and gazed down at Temple, who still lay unresponsive. "I will go as soon as I can find someone to tend to him."

"I will get Pao-ta to care for him before I go to find Elder Tani." Winyon bowed and turned to leave.

"Thank you, Winyon. Flying would be faster!" she called out.

As Winyon hurried away Losha heard her mumble "We are doomed" beneath her breath, loud enough to be heard.

Losha withdrew into herself as she watched Winyon search for enough space to make her change, and a crowd gathered around to watch her spin.

"What will I do if I fail?" Losha asked of herself.

"You won't fail. I believe in you," she heard inside her head, knowing the voice was Temple's.

"Still, I might." She stared down lovingly at Temple's body, so still and yet so full of the lifeforce.

"Let's just take one thing at a time, shall we?" Temple advised. *"Say nothing to Owane, and Elders Kulo and Cranik, until you fly to the northeast where the sands are black."*

"Black Beach Cove?"

"There is someone who awaits you there. They will help you. Let other things we have to do unfold in time."

Losha straightened her head and looked squarely at Temple's calm and placid face. "Tai, but it is time we have so little of," she whispered.

Losha walked in front of the Great Round House and bowed steeply to the people. "I must go now and pray to the gods in private," Losha announced. "I ask you all to pray for Temple and the well-being of our people until I return."

Without further explanation she took a deep breath, and without faltering, she sang her invocation. Astonishment filled the people's eyes as she twirled into a blur, flashes of white light bouncing from her, creating a harmonic resonance all around her. And as she spun faster she illuminated the bowl of the crater and the great dome, until there was a burst of light. When the light dimmed a magnificent wild swan stood before them, points of radiance sparkling from the tips of her white feathers. She tossed her head proudly and issued a cry. And then the beautiful Swan spiraled above the green crater and flew out of view.

CHAPTER SIXTY-SEVEN

THE SCROLL

"We have no Queen now. What will we do?
And what will I do if I can no longer serve you?"

Maome, Queen Palomei's personal servant
The Makolese Scroll on
The Return of the Ka and the Mending of the Su #67

Winyon flew to the Queen's compound seeking Elder Tani in the place Losha had last seen her. She circled around and around, fluttering in and out of windows, down corridors, whizzing past everyone, flying largely unnoticed. But she could not find the Elder. She finally found the lodges that housed Palomei's Husbands and flew through the closest window.

Jalok stepped back in fright as a thin whirlwind formed in the middle of the tall pavilion, flashing from iridescent green to luminous gold to rich purple, and back to green again. A form took shape inside. Jalok lurched back, knocking his writing table over and spilling his ink jar. And the form coalesced into a thin woman with long silvery hair fanned out in all directions, until she spun to a stop.

Winyon shook her head to stop the room from spinning. When she saw Jalok, she bowed steeply.

"I apologize for the intrusion…especially at a time like this," she said, panting. "I am profoundly sorry to hear about the death of our Queen."

"Who...who are you?" he asked. He touched the gris by his side.

Winyon eyed the dagger. "I am Winyon, widow of Captain Kneller, and former exile, who has been exonerated by the Queen."

"Tai, I remember now. And Temple Fox? How is he?"

"He returned to full consciousness, but went back into a coma."

"I am sorry to hear such news." Jalok took a step closer. "I have sent runners to gather more news, but since you are here… There was no mention of Owane. Do you know if he survived?"

"Tai, he is alive."

"We will depend on him now, for we have no Queen to lead us," Jalok said.

"I beg your forgiveness, Jalok, but right now I am looking for Elder Tani."

Jalok ran a hand over his sweaty scalp. "We have not seen her or Great Grandfather Okon. Both are missing. We have searched everywhere to tell them the news about Palomei…" He cut himself short. "We have heard that she was killed by a poisoned dart. Is it true?"

"Tai, it is true. And the assassin, a young boy, has died by his own hand…in the same manner."

Jalok looked down and shook his head. "I am not surprised it has come to this – all this fighting among our own people. And Palomei's brutality…" He stopped again, his voice falling into a mixture of dispair and grief. "Now the old ones are missing."

"The Great Grandfather has been seen in a boat tethered to two great whites…heading north," she started.

Jalok raised his head in shock. "But why?"

"That is what we are trying to find out from Elder Tani. Perhaps he has offered himself as a sacrifice…to stop the fighting. Do you have any idea where she might be?" she asked.

"If I did, she would have been found by now." He looked up into Winyon's sympathetic eyes. "Naturally, we are frantic with worry."

"I am faster when I fly. I can search for you. If I find her I promise I will return and let you know what has happened."

"Thank you," Jalok said. He paused for a second and gave her a slight bow. "I am glad your name has been restored to honor and you have returned to the mainland."

Winyon smiled. She crossed her arms and gave an even steeper bow. Without another word she moved to the center of the room and began her invocation to the Spirit of Tahnah-henah. The pavilion was aglow with her magic.

When she had flown out the window Jalok picked up his writing table and absentmindedly blotted up the spilled ink with a discarded silk he had found. The faint hint of perfume with the heavy odor of sweat filled his nostrils, and he stopped to examine the silk.

"Palomei," he whispered.

$$\star \quad \star \quad \star \quad \star \quad \star \quad \star$$

Maome sat at the Queen's dressing table, too numb to feel anything. She caressed Palomei's silk skirt that was draped over her shoulder, resting her gaze on the queen bee in the design. She stared at herself in the obsidian mirror and mindlessly fingered one of Palomei's bone-and-pearl necklaces that had a megalodon's tooth the size of a large man's hand attached at its center. "Oh, my Most Beloved Palomei," she muttered to herself. "We have no Queen now. What will we do? And what will I do if I can no longer serve you?"

Suddenly, the necklace broke apart, and the bones and pearl beads clattered to the floor and rolled in all directions. Maome chased them to every corner of the chamber and scooped them up into a pile. She stared at them mutely, bent down and plucked the mammoth shark's tooth from the pile. She hesitated for a guilty second, then swiftly tucked the tooth and a single pearl beneath her sash. Her eyes flickered with panic when her finger brushed against a barkcloth scroll.

"Bi kana! The scrolls!" Having remembered the four scrolls she had been given by Palomei, she marched on swift feet to Jalok's lodge where she knew Palomei's Husbands would be gathered together in mourning.

She found them in Jalok's lodge congregated together. Sensing the dark veil of grief and shock she had penetrated, she bowed steeply, barely able to hold back her tears. The scroll addressed with the names of Palomei's four Royal Husbands rested in her sweaty palm, the other three scrolls still hidden beneath her sash.

"I beg your forgiveness," she said.

Jalok lifted his head. "You have more news for us, Maome?"

She nodded and handed Jalok the scroll. She bowed again and left crying.

"It is Palomei's personal seal," he said. The others crowded around him.

Tauhans began to weep before the seal was even broken.

Jalok's eyes flickered over the brushed script. "Bi kana lo!" he exclaimed.

CHAPTER SIXTY-EIGHT

ON DOLPHIN BAY

"Pray. But do not tell the Gods how to do their business. Pray for the most harmonious outcome to manifest in perfection with grace, ease, compassion, mercy, and love. Then thank the God for our precious lives."

Elder Tani
The Makolese Scroll on
The Return of the Ka and the Mending of the Su #68

The sun was riding high and bright in the late morning sky by the time Winyon found Elder Tani. She spotted the old woman rocking in her boat in the rising tides off Dolphin Bay, the boat still anchored in the center above the ancient Sea Bells.

Winyon circled around Tani's head to draw her attention.

The old woman shielded her eyes from the harsh sun. "I see you found me."

Winyon shot straight up into the air, then dived, tightening her spiraling flight as she flew faster and faster, her wings fluttering into a blur of colorful light. She landed in a burst of rainbow light, missing her target and landing in the ocean.

When Winyon surfaced with a sputter Tani reached down and offered her gnarled hand.

"Are you all right?" Winyon panted.

"Tai," is all Tani said. She helped lift Winyon into the boat.

"Sorry, my aim was off," Winyon said.

A gummy frown creased Tani's face, her eyes distant, morose. "I have heard the conches blown. Palomei is dead. Temple was wounded, but has survived," the old Healer said.

"Tai. And you and the Great Grandfather have been missing! Why did you not come to Olonopo Crater when you heard the news? The Royal Husbands are frantic! We know where Okon is. We just do not understand why." She looked the Elder dead in the eye.

Tani raised her thin eyebrows and shrugged her bony shoulders. "We could not tell anyone," she confessed.

Winyon stared at her, puzzled, her brows furrowed. "Tell anyone what? What did he do, Elder Tani?"

Tani pointed her chin in the direction of the northern sea and remained silent.

"This is no time to keep secrets," Winyon pressed. "When Temple regained consciousness he said he had seen the Great Grandfather in his long boat being pulled by two great whites."

Tani nodded with what looked like approval. "So that is how he got there. Last I saw him through the magic of the Sea Bells, his sail was torn and his boom was broken."

Winyon threw a crop of her wet hair over her shoulder. "And then Temple reported seeing an armada of dhows, creeping over the horizon. They are less then three days away!"

Tani gasped. She squeezed her eyes shut and let her head dropped. She nodded as if she knew.

"Did you know about this?"

Tani opened her eyes. "I knew there would be risks. But now that you bring me this terrible news...I know Okon succeeded."

"Succeeded at what?"

"He breached the Barik Limits," she whispered.

"He what?"

"He..."

"I heard what you said!"

"But in his attempt to open the ancient portal he must have folded time...shortened its length by mistake."

"But WHY?"

Tani looked squarely at Winyon knowing she would be misunderstood. "He cut the portal open because he was told to."

"By WHO? Demons!" Winyon's face flushed red.

"We both have had recurring dreams."

"He did this on the guidance of a dream?!" The veins popped out on Winyon's neck. "He is defying the gods! It is not even possible to do such a thing! We have been kept inside the Barik Limits for thousands of years."

"Tai. And now we will be able to leave. We will have that choice now," Tani said quietly. "It is time to join the larger world."

"But why NOW?" Winyon shouted. "It brings the Slavers right to our shores!"

Tani dropped her head again, her lips pulled into a chevron. She avoided Winyon's angry stare. "We did not really know what would happen. He did what he did because he was told to."

"And you helped him? Why did you not stop him?"

"Because I had the dreams too," is all the old woman said.

"But it makes no sense! We will all be killed or enslaved!' She gave Tani a sharp look. "You know that better than most."

"Tai, I do," she said in a grave tone. "But listen, child. No one can second guess the gods. Nothing is as it seems anymore."

"Tani, we have less than three days to prepare ourselves for a major catastrophic invasion!"

Tani wiped a tear from the slits of her eyes. "Tai. That is all we have."

Winyon struck her fist on the gunwale, which vibrated through the wooden ribs of the boat. "I do not understand! And what has become of the Great Grandfather? Was he in his right mind when he made this stupid decision?"

Tani nodded slowly.

Noticing Tani's tears, Winyon softened her tone to a whisper. "Will he return?"

"Probably not," Tani said quietly.

Winyon grabbed a thick strand of wet hair to wring it out, but yanked on it instead as if to rip it from her scalp. "First Palomei is murdered. Then Temple gets struck down by a poisonous dart and returns to us too weak to do anything. There is only Losha now. But what do *we* do?"

Tani took hold of Winyon's fist and pried it open slowly. "Pray. But do not tell the gods how to do their business. Pray for the most harmonious outcome to manifest in perfection with grace, ease, compassion, mercy, and love. Then thank the gods for our precious lives."

CHAPTER SIXTY-NINE

BLACK BEACH COVE

"Please know that you are not alone. We are all here to help you. Right now your gratitude to your people is the only gift we want. We will bring this gift to the Source of All, knowing that to know your people is to know the Source. Loving your people draws you closer to the Source, for it is the Source of All who created your people out of love."

The Voice of Spirit
The Makolese Scroll on
The Return of the Ka and the Mending of the Su #69

Losha soared above the northeastern coastline of the island to a stretch of black sand where Mefakani had once drawn his dark magic. From the air she spotted a clear level area encircled by mammoth acrocomia palms and sensed a powerful energy emanating from the ground. She spiraled down. When she touched the black sand, she dragged her webbed foot in a circle to mark a sacred space to make her change.

The giant acrocomias blurred through her brain until she came to a stop.

Disappointed that no one was waiting for her, she remained silent and still, taking in the presence of all the trees, bushes, and the dark sand beneath her feet. This was a place where she often found refuge as a child, its peacefulness inviting and throbbing with the lifeforce. She ran her hand across the bulbous trunks of several acrocomias and placed an offering of coconut meat in the center of the circle she had drawn. Losha thanked them for their presence.

"Is anyone here?" she called out. She waited several minutes, but there was no answer. A dread took her over. "Please, be my witness," she whispered to the life all around her, tears beginning to fill her eyes. "The island is in danger! Temple Fox has been wounded, and I must stop an armada of invaders! But I am afraid. I do not know what to do!" The weight of responsibility made her pulse quicken as panic took a stranglehold on her, and her breathing came in shallow gulps. The burden became too much for her and she doubled over on the black sand and began to cry.

There was light touch in the center of her brow which Losha at first ignored. A breeze, a strand of hair, maybe an insect? But the touch grew more pronounced and she felt as if the entire space was hugging her.

"Losha," an inaudible, but perceivable voice called out.

Losha lifted her head.

The touch increased in pressure between her eyes, and Losha was certain a pair of hands had been placed onto her shoulders. She turned her head slightly. No one there.

"Temple?" She breathed the word. There was no answer. "Mother?" She was surprised by her own question.

"No. I am your father. Your mother and I are always sending our love and support to you."

"My father? Then you are dead as well!" she said, suddenly horrified.

"I am very much alive in physical form."

"But you could not have possibly known my mother bore me. You do not even know I am alive!"

"I do know about you. I have seen you over the years in my dreams, and have sensed you when I am deep in prayer and meditation as I am now."

"I did not know this," she whispered.

"I know you need help right now," he said, softly, inside Losha's mind.

"Tai, I do," she said, her terror rising again. "An armada of forty Arab dhows is heading our way! Temple has been poisoned by a blow dart, and I am responsible to protect the people and the entire island!"

"You are not alone," her Father said calmly. *"All of the gods and the spirits hear your plea. And as you so wisely said to that older woman with long silver hair, everyone will participate in the outcome."*

"Will you guide me? What do I do?"

"Seek the Source of All. The Source does not guide. Guidance implies there is a right way and wrong way. The Source can share only perfect knowledge."

"Then I seek the Source and beg It to please share Its perfect knowledge with me."

There was a span of silence, and Losha felt a keen lightness fill her head. When the voice in her head spoke again the quality of the energy had transformed into something more expansive and inclusive, as if a collective of voices called out to her, the vibration harmonious and singular.

"We must ask you, do you come out of fear of death by the Invaders? Or do you come out of love for your people?"

Losha drew back into herself, feeling somewhat transparent and ashamed. Recognizing her anxiety, she took three deep breaths to center herself, and a deeper calm engulfed her. "I am sorry," she confessed. "I did come fearing for everyone…and fearing I would fail the people."

"Please understand that the destruction, or the enslavement, of the physical body is a projection of the mind. The body is truly the ally of the ego. The false mask you wear will always use the body to conspire against the mind. Know this truth. You are a child of God. Only that is real."

"I understand, and yet it is so easy to believe we are primarily our body, especially when there are other lives crying out to you," she explained.

"The body is only a symbol of what you believe you are. As you well know, the mind can heal the body, and yet the body can never heal the mind. The mind is always stronger than the body."

"I will remember this," she said. "Thank you."

"Know that you are not solely responsible for everyone else's lives. They will have to be responsible for what they believe, just as you must be responsible for what you believe.

"Please know that you are not alone. We are all here to help you. Right now your gratitude to your people is the only gift we want. We will bring this gift to the Source of All, knowing that to know your people is to know the Source. Loving your people draws you closer to the Source, for it is the Source of All who created your people out of love."

Losha drew in a deep breath. "But that feels too simple. Right now it all feels so big to me. I feel so... so small and helpless."

"It seems our trust in you is greater than your trust in yourself or in us at this moment."

"No, no, no!" she said. "I did not mean that. I do trust you!"

"All miracles are a natural expression of love. What you ask of yourself is no harder than the other miracles you have performed already. We are here to help you understand that."

Losha wiped the tears from her face.

"Like Temple Fox, you have fulfilled the prophecy. We are proud of you. Do not be afraid. You can do this. We have watched you and know your heart. Simply pray from your heart. Pray with conviction."

"But after everyone finds out about the Slavers, they will pray as well. I fear they will want a different outcome."

"Acknowledge that they are willing to lay down their lives for your people. Love them. Simply love them. And appreciate them. For appreciation is an equal gift given to all."

"I will…I do. Thank you. Thank you all."

She felt the quality of the vibration shift and the unique touch of her father's hands on her shoulders again.

"You will intuitvely know what to do. I will be in contact with you later. I love you, my precious daughter."

New tears fell from her eyes. Her heart full, she felt her father's energy lift from her shoulders. She stood up with more confidence and looked around her, knowing she was not alone and was helped by a multitude of spirits. "Thank you, Father," she whispered. "Thank you all."

When she felt ready, she began her prayer of thanks, and a deep potency rose from the dark sands into her feet, her loins, her belly, and her heart. It coursed up her spine like a snake formed of undulating light, until it slithered from her radiant heart up into her throat, her mouth, and rose into her forehead where the space between her brow began to glow a luminous indigo blue. It pulsated there with a rapid rhythm, until it shot higher, rocketing beyond the crown of her head in a shower bursting with brilliant white and violet light.

All at once an energy that felt like warm oil with the sublime quality of pure light descended through the top of Losha's head and cascaded through her energy field, out the bottom of her feet deep into the sandy earth. All of her darkest doubts and fears washed from her mind, and she stood like a tree connected to earth and sky. She basked in a bubble of love that continued to expand beyond the limits of the island, far out to the surrounding sea.

She turned in each cardinal direction as she prayed, starting with where the sun rises.

"I thank the Ancient Spirits of the East for appreciating the Makol people and helping us to unfold our true destiny. I thank the Ancient Spirits of the South for loving our people and connecting us all to our divine purpose. I thank the Ancient Spirits of the West for respecting us all and helping us release the false mask we wear. Thank you for continually rebirthing us. I thank the Ancient Spirits of the North, and all the Ancestors, for loving us, and appreciating us, and showing us the way by acting as a mirror for us. Thank you for joining me in my prayers. Thank you for your wisdom."

Losha dropped to her knees and grabbed a handful of black sand. "I thank the beloved Mother, and the Spirit of Makol Island for loving us." She let the grains of sand sift through her fingers, sensing the connection and the exchange of love.

She rose to her feet and held her arms high, her head tilted back to address the sky. "I thank you, Father Sky, Grandmother Moon, People of the Stars Islands in the vast sea of Heaven, and the Source of All Creation." Finally, she bowed her head and touched her heart. "I thank all Life, the Spirit Which Moves In All Things, the Divine Goddess within me. Thank you for loving the people of Makol as I do."

Losha held her breath, and the air around her seemed to pause as she waited for something – anything – as a sign that her prayer had been heard. And while she waited, she delighted in the warm sand beneath her feet, the sunshine on her chocolate brown skin, the soft breeze that began to stir, caressing her face. The salwood, their branches upraised in praise, swayed in the breeze like sky worshippers, their limbs creaking and clattering as if etching mystical signs in the lapis air. Even the rustle of palm leaves sounded like a shaman's rattle, and she smiled to herself as the forest danced in rhythmic devotion to the Earth and the great ocean of atmosphere.

A deep sound reverberated beneath the breath of the wind. Losha thought she heard the ground groan. The wind kicked in harder, and her bushy hair blew around her head haphazardly. A sudden crack of thunder caused the air to quiver, and she sensed something pressing into her that was forceful...almost violent. She turned around in a circle to see the tamarind bend, the sapodilla drop their fruit, and the ground begin to shake.

Her prayer had, indeed, been heard.

CHAPTER SEVENTY

THE GREAT ROUND HOUSE

"War is unnecessary."

Losha Ninti
The Makolese Scroll on
The Return of the Ka and the Mending of the Su #70

Temple lay on a bed of ferns by the pond beneath the stone skirting shielded from the heat. Pao-ta was dabbing his forehead with cool water when she spotted Losha stepping out of a ball of light and a swirling cloud of white swan down.

Losha walking briskly up to her. "Thank you for taking care of Temple," she said with a respectful nod.

"His fever has broken," Pao-ta said. She looked away for a self-conscious second. "So many feel terrible about what has happened. My friends feel so guilty for not recognizing Temple Fox as the true Teacher when he first arrived. Me too," she confessed, her head tilted slightly to hide her guilt.

Losha gently turned Pao-ta's face around with her fingertips and looked into the older woman's moist eyes. "Then you must tell them to forgive themselves. And tell them to be in gratitude for all that they are, for they were created with Divine perfection. Now that they have changed their perceptions about Temple, please tell them it is about time they changed their perceptions about themselves, and appreciate who they really are. We were all born equal."

Pao-ta's head bobbed in understanding. Then, out of the corner of her eye, Losha saw Temple stir. She bent close to his face and spoke in English, for his ears only.

"Temple, I am back from Black Cove Beach," she whispered. "It would be wonderful if you came back as well. And, yes, I met my father, who seems to be as adept as you at soul traveling and communicating through the mind. I would dearly love for you to return to your body now so we could get some fluids into you. We need to talk."

"It's all so amazing, Losha! The tunnels beneath the Earth! The stormy red eye on Jupiter close up! And you should see what's happening on Ganymede!"

"Temple! Why are you traveling the solar system? You should be focusing on what is happening here. Get back into your body! Now!" Losha demanded.

Temple spoke again inside Losha's mind. *"My little pigeon, we have plenty of time. You must remain optimistic and keep your frequency up."*

"That is easy for you to say." Losha looked over at Pao-ta heavy with concern. "If he does not snap out of the coma, have him moved inside the Great Round House beside Palomei's body."

"Wait!" Temple pleaded. His eyes fluttered open. "Your wish is my command."

"Ah, he is awake!" Pao-ta drew back with surprise. "Would you like some privacy?"

"Tai. Thank you, Pao-ta. And please tell the others what I told you."

Pao-ta got up, bowed, and left to warn the people to keep away from the two Teachers. As they gathered around her she also conveying Losha's message.

Temple rubbed the sleep from his eyes, then touched his ear where he had been cut, noticing sensation had returned to his body. "Losha, why am I wearing earrings?" he asked.

"We put red garnets in your ears to bring you back from your coma."

"Garnets? First a skirt and now this," he huffed. "Never mind. How many people do you think can fit inside the crater?"

Losha let out a grunt of annoyance. "Are we playing games now? Why did it take you so long to return?"

"Oh, come on, my little pigeon. I was only gone a minute or two."

"No, you were not," she insisted. "And stop calling me 'pigeon'. I am the Swan, and you have been gone all morning!"

"Blimey! Where I was there is no time," he explained. "Now, back to my question."

"There is no time for games. How do you feel?"

He ran a tongue thick with mucous over his teeth. "I'd feel better with some water." He grabbed the container himself and slugged down the entire contents.

"Well, I see you are moving better. And your fever has broken as well." She took the container and refilled it, then handed it back to Temple. "To answer your silly question, I would say the crater holds about five thousand people or more."

Temple threw the last bit of water over his head and rubbed it into his oily scalp. "And what is the population of Makol?"

Losha let out a little snort. "About five thousand or more. I see a plan forming."

"And after your morning adventure, I sense you know exactly what to do?"

Losha leaned forward and kissed Temple fully on his lips. "Temple, we are not going to war. We are going to have a grand celebration of life – a great ceremony of appreciation for our lives and all beings."

Temple smiled, savoring the kiss. "And that energy of pure joy will be magnified in this sacred place and radiate out into the far reaches of Heaven."

"And also out to sea where the Slavers are. The vibration of greed and hatred cannot withstand the vibration of love and joy. It could actually drive the Slavers mad!"

"But how will the people feel when they find out that the Slavers are coming? Do we tell them? Or do we wait until the ships appear over the horizon?"

"It is time that the coconut shell gets separated from the meat."

"Huh?"

"Quickly now! Get yourself well, hydrate and eat. I will meet you on the platform after I return from speaking with the First Advisor." She rose to leave.

"I wouldn't miss this for all the tea in China," he said, grinning.

She smiled down at him. "It will be a grand celebration! And we will dance together in divine union."

"Dance?"

"Why, of course," she said, her voice drifting away as she scurried toward the stairs to the Great Round House.

"But, Losha, I don't know how to dance! Looo-shaaa!!"

Losha approached Nijaga, who guarded the entrance to where the First Advisor had spent the night in silent vigil inside the coolness of the Great Round House. She gave him a polite nod. He opened the door. She entered quietly, and he closed the door behind her. When her eyes adjusted to the dark chamber lit by oil jars, she spotted the assassin's body draped in a rough barkcloth near the entrance, his body attracting a cluster of flies. The dome was filled with an annoying buzz.

Queen Palomei was laid out in front of the empty obsidian throne on the raised dais, her body resting on a bed of uruku moss to ward off insects. Her wet yellow feather cape had been draped over her massive body, leaving her round face exposed. Owane sat by the Martriarch's side, his shoulders stooped and rounded, heavy with grief. He rose to his feet and bowed when he saw Losha approach.

She bowed in return and placed her hand on the old man's shoulder. "I am so sorry it came to this."

Owane wiped a tear from the corner of his eye. "She was like a daughter to me, you understand. Not really a wife."

"I understand."

"And Temple? How is he doing?" he asked.

"His fever has broken, and he is completely out of the coma now. He is even moving around," she reassured him. "But I have come bearing other important news."

"And I have important news as well." Owane handed Losha a scroll sealed with Palomei's wax emblem. "While you were gone a runner came to tell us that the Royal Husbands are on their way here. They will retrieve Palomei's body and place it in the Si Te Cah's burial cave in the foothills of Hollow Mountain.

"The runner also brought me a scroll bearing Palomei's personal seal and the scroll you are holding now that bears Temple's and your names. I beg your forgiveness. I know it is against protocol, but I took it in your absence so that I may give it to you now. All the Royal Husbands have received scrolls as well. Judging from what mine says, I think you will find yours interesting."

Losha broke the seal and uncurled the parchment, her eyes racing over the script. She gasped. "I am to become Queen?"

"It seems Temple's prophecy about Queen Palomei having an heir has come true after all," he said. "Only the heir is not from her bloodline as we mistakeningly believed. Losha Ninti, I honor you and pledge my allegiance to you as the Mother of our people." He bowed steeply and with great reverence.

Losha rolled up the scroll. "Then as the new Queen I ask that all islanders come to Olonopo Crater immediately."

Owane bolted upright.

"I need to address everyone at once. We will prepare a celebration of Palomei's life immediately, and announce to the people that I am now their Queen. But we must act swiftly."

"And why is that?"

"The Arab Slavers are two and a half days away."

It was as if the wind had been knocked out of Owane. He plopped himself down on the floor cushion dwarfed by the immense size of the obsidian throne. "And so we are to be invaded at last," he said wearily, his eyes puffy and dark. "But Temple prophesied this would happen two moons from now!"

"This has something to do with the Great Grandfather," she said. "He was seen in a boat near the Barik Limits being towed by two great whites. I have sent someone to find Elder Tani to see if she knows what has happened."

"It is hard to believe we have come to this," Owane said, his voice full of defeat. "As far as the Great Grandfather is concerned, I do not know what he is up to unless he somehow knew the Slavers would come early and set sail to petition the Gods for help. Naturally, we must move all women, children, the old, and the ill to the mountain immediately!" The First Advisor stared up at Losha with pleading eyes. "Can you help us assemble all our able-bodied people so we can fight the Slavers?"

"Temple and I have discussed this at length," Losha said. "Assembling people to fight the Slavers will not be necessary. In order for me to take the throne we must first fold up the last scroll on Palomei's life so that a new scroll may be written. We will celebrate her life by gathering the entire population for a grand celebration of life in this sacred of all places. Then the Royal Husbands can carry Palomei's body to the Cave of Giants in the foothills."

Owane stepped forward and bowed. "I beg your forgiveness, Losha. I know you are one of the great Teachers…and…and now our Queen, but you give us little time to prepare for war."

Losha explained in depth what Temple and she had discussed about the power of energetic actions taken while in complete focus and concentration, using the ancient chants, the sound of drums, and movement in dance while in harmony and complete union with all the elements and Spirits. She offered details about the unique vibrations the Olonopo Crater and the Great Round House held and how they could affect the entire island and beyond by such a celebration.

Owane began to pace nervously, his restless footsteps creating an annoying rhythmic beat and eddy of sound that echoed with the rising noise of the flies.

"It was what the Makolese were born to do," she concluded. "It is time for them to use their innate power to raise their own vibration, and heal the island from further invasions."

Owane stopped to gaze at Palomei, who appeared uncharacteristically serene. Flies circled around her chubby face. "Bi kano lo. Nijaga! Would you please take that boy's body out of here?" he snapped, and his voice echoed in the round chamber, repeating the demand.

The Head Guard heard Owane yelling, opened the door, and stepped inside.

Owane gestured to the small heap on the floor that once held the spirit of the boy, Naffa. "Move him out of here!" he shouted.

Nijaga dragged Naffa's body out the entrance and closed the door.

Owane turned to Losha again. "And so you command that we…?" he started to ask.

"I do not command anything," she said. "To command is to believe we are unequal to each other. When, in fact, we are all equal."

"But…you are now Queen…and one of the Teachers."

"To teach implies a lack when truly there is no lack, for the knowledge I carry is accessible to all."

Owane exhaled loudly and shook his head in exasperation. "All I know is how to obey."

"That is not true," Losha said. "You were First Advisor to Palomei's mother. And you ruled the people after she was murdered, until Palomei was old enough to make her own decisions. You taught Palomei how to rule. Were it not for you, Owane, the last of the Si Te Cah rulers would not have been as merciful as she was. I stand here in appreciation of your courage, your administrative skills, and your wisdom."

Owane ran a hand over his balding scalp and nodded. "So, are you saying I have a say in this? We all do?"

"I ask that we send out the call for the people to assemble here along with the message that I am their new Queen. What I have to say must be said to all," she said.

Owane's eyes loomed larger. "Might we have a shorter celebration for Palomei and to announce you are now Queen, and still have our Warriors waiting at the shore?"

"Like I said before, we must close one scroll before we open another. I will go and find a drummer."

Owane looked askance at Losha, avoiding eye contact with her. "Well, then…I will meet with the Royal Husbands when they arrive." He bowed to her and headed out the Great Round House. When he got to the door he turned sharply to address the new Queen. "Do we tell the people about the Slavers coming?" he asked, his brow furrowed.

"If we do not forewarn them, then they may bypass their fears and raise their vibration to the level you say they are capable of. On the other hand, if we do not tell them, we will be caught unprepared for war. It could be suicide."

"I will tell them once the people have assembled," she said. "Events will unfold as they will. But as I said before, war is unnecessary."

Owane gave Losha a questioning look, then a quick nod, and hurried out of the dome with a cloud of flies following him.

★　　★　　★　　★　　★　　★

Owane's breath quickened as he combed the crowd with his eyes, until they landed on Elders Cranik and Kulo. He lumbered down the stone stairs, the latest news bearing hard upon him.

"Elders!" he called out. He grabbed Kulo and Cranik by their forearms, pushing them into the shadows beneath the stone platform far from Temple's ears. The news spilled from his lips in rapid whispers.

Kulo was all smiles. "Losha is the new Queen. That is wonderful!"

"You do not understand," Owane explained, his voice low and dangerous. "While she insists we celebrate all life, forty Arab dhows will be heading to our shores!"

Elder Cranik jerked backward as if he had just been stung by a bee. Kulo caught his arm and pulled him forward. Both listened intently while Owane told them about Great Grandfather Okon and his exploits on the sea far north of Makol, and about the power that lay within Olonopo Crater. Cranik sucked on his long yellow teeth and plucked at his bushy eyebrows nervously as he took in the news.

Kulo stayed calm and focused. "And Losha told you this and still wants a celebration?" he asked.

Owane nodded.

"Then we follow her. She and Temple know better than we," he said.

Owane's voice sounded as if it had been chiseled from granite. It was rough, sharp, sarcastic, and almost accusatory. "Naturally, good Elder, I advised her to order all women, children, the old, and the infirm to hurry to Hollow Mountain immediately. And all warriors should be called to the shore."

"That would be wise, First Advisor," Cranik said. He stole a quick glance at Kulo beneath his heavy brow.

Kulo took a cautious step away from the two and held up his hands to buffer further words. "I think you doubt the Teachers. I do not, and will not be apart of anything you might try to do to sabotage Losha's efforts to unite the people. Good day to you, First Advisor." He nodded to Owane and walked away.

Cranik stared into Owane's rigid face. "What are we going to do?" he asked.

"Well, I am not going to waste all my time planning a celebration." He lowered his voice. "Losha may be one of the great Teachers, but she knows nothing about ruling as a Queen. I am going to find Commander Boran and tell him to gather all warriors and Palace Guards."

Owane scurried off, leaving Cranik standing looking dumbfounded and out of place.

★　　★　　★　　★　　★　　★

Not wanting to draw attention to himself, Kulo slipped silently through the crowd so that he could seek out Ikus and his ragged band. He spotted the renegades gathering to leave. Koteki blocked his view of their leader with his massive frame.

"You are leaving?" Kulo asked.

"You said we could leave if we did not make trouble," Koteki said.

Kulo stared up at Koteki. "You might want to know what is going on first."

"Let him come," Ikus called out, his voice rougher than the night before. "He is as harmless as a sea slug."

Koteki stepped aside and Kulo walked up to Ikus.

"You might like to know that we are under attack," Kulo said to Ikus.

Ikus hurled his words like a spear. "Of course we are, you sack of wormy whale grease. Are you just realizing that now!" Ikus rose, his bony frame wobbling a bit. Nomuk steadied the Elder with his hands. Ikus looked up at Kulo, his obvious vulnerablity humiliating.

"We are not being attacked by the two Teachers as you have imagined," Kulo said.

"Oh, stop with this talk about the Teachers!" Ikus spat back. "Say your piece, then leave us alone."

"Forty Arab dhows will be here in less than three days," Kulo said.

Ikus' mouth parted.

"Please stay," Kulo said.

Ikus' countenance grew grim, angry. "And you believe this falsehood?"

"I do. The Teachers have asked us to stay inside the crater."

Ikus looked at his men, then back at Kulo. "This is some kind of trick!"

"Will you stay?" Kulo asked, not taking his eyes off of Ikus.

Koteki answered instead. "If this is true, we will go and fight!"

Ikus looked at Koteki with approval, then stared at Kulo with narrowing eyes.

Kulo stepped forward to engage Ikus closer. All of Ikus' band moved closer in unison, until their leader held up his hand. He motioned to them to step away.

Ikus felt Kulo's imposing height tower over him, and a curious strength exuded from Kulo that he had never noticed before. His knees began to buckle, but he stood his ground. He pointed his dagger at Kulo. "Temple Fox has drawn the Slavers to our shores," Ikus said. "You heard, Koteki. We go to the beaches to fight!"

If Ikus' grainy voice was bombastic and full of fire, Kulo's voice was long past any smoldering anger and ash, the energy of his utterance stirring in the air between them into something Ikus couldn't identify. It started taking form – rounded, flowing, and enduring.

Kulo's voice was direct and full of love. "My dear old friend, you are ninety years old. Are you really going to fight? With what? Your words? Your gris?" He looked down at the dagger by Ikus' side.

The fire in Ikus started to burn out as if he had just been dowsed with water.

"If you go, I will lose my best friend," Kulo said, his voice heavy with sadness.

"Everyone, leave me!" Ikus ordered. His men looked at each other in astonishment, then stepped further away to give the two men privacy.

"This is not who you really are," Kulo whispered.

"But it is what I have become," Ikus whispered back, sadness falling into the cracks of his voice.

"Do you wish to play another role?"

"What do you mean?"

"I believe we may have lost the Great Grandfather."

Ikus' eyes widened in shock, the power taken out of him completely now. He cocked his head, perplexed, his eyes hardening with distress at the news.

"He was seen in his long boat, heading toward the Barik Limits. His boat was being towed by two great whites." Kulo waited for a response.

Ikus stared up at Kulo, startled, all barriers dissolved, for this was the talk for Elders only. "Then it is he who has brought this crisis upon our heads? He must have been given the signal by the Gods…to open the Barik Limits with the key."

"Open the Barik Limits? With the key? What key?"

"A special gris made of quartz crystal given to our Ancestors from the Gods long ago."

"Then you knew about this thing?" Kulo asked.

"I am senior to you. I know things you do not. Only the Eldest of the Elders knows that someday one of us would be called upon to open the Barik Limits." His eyes took on a distant cast. "I had always imagined it would be a woman. Okon must have been called."

"Tani is the second oldest. She must have known this as well. She has been missing," Kulo said. "So, you see why we need you?"

Ikus looked up.

"We need all Elders," Kulo whispered, "to keep the people united. To teach the children. They all need us…more than ever now."

Ikus looked away. "What future do we have if the Slavers come?" His voice was hoarse and dry.

Kulo pressed gently, but firmly. "If you want to preserve our culture, then choose to stay alive first. You can do so little by waving that little thing." He eyed the Elder's dagger. "Yours would be a senseless death. But you can do so much more by staying alive to share your knowledge and your wisdom with the Elder Council, and the young ones. You hold our history. Who among us will be there to pass down the old songs and prayers?"

"There are other Elders," Ikus offered.

"But none like you, my friend."

Ikus engaged Kulo's eyes. "But you do not even think I am a wise old man. You do not believe as I do."

"Tai, you offer a different view. But you lived it. What kind of people are we if we are not forgiving and accepting of others who do not view the world the same way? And we are not a true people if we do not maintain our history. And you are living and breathing it. In fact, you are making history!"

"I am," Ikus whispered. "I held fast to my beliefs. I never budged."

Kulo smiled with his eyes. "Well, a little," he said. "You thought Mefakani was the True Teacher."

The smirk on Ikus' face was tinged with guilt. "Well, maybe I did for a minute or two."

"If I do not have you around anymore, who will I argue with? Cranik? He is too stupid."

Ikus laughed at that.

Just then the drums and conches sounded, calling the people to assemble at Olonopo Crater. The conches announced a new Queen had been chosen by Palomei, and the new Queen was one of the Prophets and Teachers, Losha Ninti.

Cheers filled the crater.

The Rebels cursed and spit on the ground. Ikus looked up at Kulo with a deep scowl. "Well, you got what you wanted. Now the Wizard's woman is Queen!"

"You should stay here where it is safer," Kulo insisted.

Ikus lowered his head in thought and raised a thin eyebrow. "Tai. Maybe I should stay and fight on the same front I have been fighting with all along."

"Exactly." Kulo nodded and grinned.

Ikus jerked his head up. "You say the false Prophets want us to stay inside Olonopo? Are they going to fight the armada for us?"

Needing to avoid the question, Kulo bent down and whispered into Ikus' ear, while his men watched from a distance, stirring with agitation. "You need to keep both Losha and Temple in your sights. Right? So you need to stay right where you are and not make any trouble. Temple Fox can do little. The poison has rendered him helpless." Kulo nudged the old man a bit harder. "Ikus, we will still need an Elders Council no matter what happens to us all. Will you not stay here and agree to make no more trouble?"

Ikus stared at his old friend for a mute second, then clasped Kulo by the hand. They grabbed each other and embraced.

"My men now know about the invasion. They will decide on their own what they want to do," Ikus said.

"I beg you, please tell them to say nothing to anyone else. Losha plans on telling the people about the Slavers in her own way," Kulo said. "I will see you later…here." He pointed at the green grass at his feet.

"Tai, I will stay, but I doubt you will see them." He tilted his head toward the men who were now mumbling to each other.

"We all make our own choices," Kulo said.

CHAPTER SEVENTY-ONE

THE ORCHID

"It would be a momentous occasion if we all could take a shortcut in becoming more consciously awake, and deal with this matter with as much ease, grace, and peaceful mind as possible. It is what the Makolese are destined to do."

Losha Ninti
The Makolese Scroll on
The Return of the Ka and the Mending of the Su #71

As before, villagers all over the island stopped their work to listen to the message the drums and conches repeated again and again in rapid succession. Fishing nets were pulled out of the water as men returned to shore. Baskets of fruit were left abandoned by women's feet as they gathered to confer with other women. Food baking in fire pits was left unattended. Excited children ran amuck.

"The news has spread everywhere!" one woman said excitedly. "You heard that the old prophecy has been fulfilled by two people? Not only do we have Temple Fox, but we also have the Queen's own Interpreter, Losha Ninti." She clapped her hands together. "And now…Losha is Queen!"

Another older woman joined the small gathering of women. "The gods show us favor on this momentous day," she said. "And now with Palomei's death, my husband's murder has been avenged." She sucked in her breath. When she let it out, she began to shake, and the women all drew closer to console her.

"Tai, there will be no more Makolese Queens from the Si Te Cah Clan engorged on human flesh. That redheaded barbarian is dead!"

★　★　★　★　★　★

Soon food and flowers were gathered in abundance. Sha was poured into lengths of bamboo and hoisted on the backs of men and women. And the people moved like a steady river up the wide, winding stone stairs leading to Olonopo Crater, while the most adventurous climbed the steep hill with food, drink, and babies tethered to their backs.

Hidden in the shadows, a minority of Unbelievers drew together in small groups to shelter themselves from the eyes of their neighbors. As agreed upon, the Unbelievers either continued with their chores, or stayed in their huts.

★　　★　　★　　★　　★　　★

Not wishing to engage in any arguments, Arma kept her head down when Ikus' men passed by. After they passed, she searched for Mik-lon in the crowd, and rushed over to him.

"I just heard the strangest thing," she whispered to Mik-lon. "I just overheard one of Ikus' men mumbling something about an invasion…on the eastern shore."

Mik-lon's face tightened. "Slavers?"

"I do not know, but I will go and find out if any of this is true," she said.

Arma wound her way through the throng of people beneath the stone plinth where Losha and Temple were being swallowed by the crowd with guards forcing them back.

"Queen Losha Ninti," she said, her voice raised above the others. "Is there something you are not telling us?"

Sensing Arma was a natural born leader, Losha signaled the guard to allow Arma through the crowd and to push the others back.

"What is your name?" she asked, motioning the bold woman to join them.

"Arma," she answered.

"Arma, do you trust me?" Losha asked.

"Implicitly."

"Good. It would be in your best interest, and the interest of our people, if all our people gathered inside Olonopo Crater."

"But I just heard that invaders…"

Losha nodded her head, coaxing Arma closer. "I plan on telling everyone what is happening, but as fate would have it, I see a rumor is already floating in the breeze."

"Is it true?" Arma asked.

"It is true, and I will tell the people, but not before I can get as many as I can inside the crater."

Arma's brows knit together, causing her forehead to wrinkle. She felt suddenly old. "But would it not be better to have those who cannot defend themselves shelter in the caves of Hollow Mountain? The rest of us can fight."

"It would be a momentous occasion if we all could take a shortcut in becoming more consciously awake, and deal with this matter with as much ease, grace, and peaceful mind as possible. It is what the Makolese are destined to do."

Arma's wrinkles deepened.

Losha looked into Arma with unfocused eyes. "You have not had your Ka restored?"

"How did you know? It is true. I…I have not. There was a mix-up when…"

Losha placed a finger in the center of Arma's chest. A powerful tingling sensation filled Arma and radiated down her arms, into her belly and womb, then down through her feet. Arma began to swoon.

Losha removed her finger and cupped Arma's face in her hands. "You are so beautiful," she said.

Arma looked into Losha's large brown eyes, rendering her speechless.

"You have an orchid bulb," Losha said delighted. "Two of them."

"Why, yes. How did you know?"

"May I have one?" Losha asked.

"Of course," Arma said. She dug into her sash and pulled out one of the tiny bulbs. Losha plucked it up and placed it squarely in Arma's palm. She closed her hands around Arma's hand, and a distinct energy filled her palm. All at once Arma felt a stirring in her hand.

"Open it," Losha said.

Arma opened her palm. Before her astonished eyes she witnessed the bulb shiver and burst its fragile skin. Tender green tendrils began to sprout. A spindly shoot shot upward, until a leaf popped out, and then a bud. Before another minute had passed a delicate purple orchid blossom rested inside Arma's palm.

"Everyone has a choice to love all life…or fear death," Losha said. "Please understand you cannot focus on both at the same time. Chosing love, however, is so much more beautiful, and is far more fun. Now go and make your choice. And if you choose life, perhaps you can help organize our people so they move more swiftly to the crater in a safe and orderly fashion."

Dumbfounded, Arma bowed to Losha, then ambled away mindless of the people who crowded around her, asking what had happened between her and the Teacher.

Arma returned to where Mik-lon was waiting for her. She held the tiny purple orchid cradled gently in her palm. She placed it behind her ear and grinned.

"So what did she say?" he asked.

"It is not what she said, but how she showed me what she meant." She looked up into Mik-lon's forest green eyes.

"Meaning?"

She whispered, "We will dance tonight, even though those Arab dhows that Temple Fox predicted are coming."

Mik-lon appeared as if his eyebrows caught on fire. "Then we must call all the soldiers together quickly and prepare for battle!"

"Shhh!" she said. "But that is not what Losha and Temple Fox want us to do. Like the message said when the drums were beaten and the conches were blown. The entire population must come to the crater so Losha can address us. She plans on telling them on her own terms."

"No, Arma. We must go and prepare to fight!"

"Mik-lon, stop. I beg you. Do not go to fight!"

"Arma, I am a trained warrior. I have been taught by our own High Shaman and have passed all his tests. It is what I was born to do! Who am I if I do not fight?" he complained.

"I know. But I am asking you to trust the Teachers and do as they ask."

He bore down on her with a hard gaze and a harsh whisper. "How can someone not defend their own people? I am no coward!"

"I know that," she said. "But I do not wish to see you harmed in any way. You could die."

He pointed to the mountain. "I could have died on that mountain before as a renegade and Unbeliever."

"But you are not the same man now," she said, patting him on his broad chest. "You *are* a Believer! I beg you to please trust the Teachers' guidance and do not go to fight! I love you!" The words slipped out, and Arma touched her lips as if they had betrayed her secret.

"You love me?" he asked, his eyes growing sharper and brighter.

She bit her lip and nodded.

He drew close to her, so close they could feel each other's heat…and breath. "I…I feel the same way," he confessed. He looked deeply into her large copper-colored eyes. "In truth, you are the woman I have been waiting for all my life. Your strength, your beauty, your…your boldness. I admire everything about you."

Arma broke out in a wide smile, her teeth gleaming, her eyes dancing.

He stepped closer and hugged her, and she fell into his embrace. And there they stood basking in their newly found love, until Arma pulled away, holding him by his muscular forearms. "So, will this mighty warrior I see before me now help me to organize the people so they may safely journey to this sacred place?"

His eyes smiled. "And if I do not?"

She folded her arms over her breasts and looked away. "There will be no kisses for you…ever," she quipped.

"It is against my warrior nature," he started to say.

Arma twisted her face in disapproval, grabbed Mik-lon, and playfully wrestled him to the ground. They rolled around until she pinned his arms by his side.

"A warrior sometimes needs to learn surrender," she said, straddling him. "Trust me."

He looked up at her with a grin. "Then I must surrender. But not before you surrender first!" He quickly rolled her over and held her arms over her head. "Give up?" he asked.

"I give up!"

"Good." Mik-lon lowered himself down on her and kissed her gently just as Pao-ta waddled by.

"Are we making babies here, or are we going to help the babies and their mothers get inside this crater?" Pao-ta asked.

Arma and Mik-lon turned their heads in Pao-ta's direction and burst out laughing, all fear from them vanished by the lure of love and the power of human passion.

CHAPTER SEVENTY-TWO

THE WIDOWERS

*"We will make certain it all ends on the
beaches...one way or the other."*

Owane, First Advisor, and Queen Palomei's First Husband
The Makolese Scroll on
The Return of the Ka and the Mending of the Su #72

Dressed in their finest white silk wraparounds trimmed with golden thread, and bound with the yellow feathered waistband that marked their widowhood, the Royal Husbands wound their way down the wide stone stair into the crater.

Second Husband, Jalok, appeared preoccupied and remote as he carried a brazier of burning incense. Kuhil, his bulk hidden behind a bundle of white flowers, was grim and gray, while Tauhans, who carried a white kala wing, wiped his face from sweat and tears from time to time. The young Loa'a cradled the sacred channak bowl in both hands, his mouth slightly creased with an unapologetic smirk. And as the procession slowly descended the stairs, the Royal Husbands' personal servants followed a few paces behind.

Maome, who led the servants, was swathed in a length of white silk. She carried a box of funerary supplies filled with ointment jars, combs, long lengths of silk, and Palomei's most sacred jewelry, knowing this would be the last task she would do for her beloved queen.

Owane jostled through the crowd and sprinted halfway up the stairs to greet the husbands when he stopped short to catch his breath.

Jalok gave the signal for the procession to stop, leaving the husbands perched on the stone stairs waiting for Owane.

The First Husband bowed to the four husbands. They bowed in turn.

Jalok was first in line and called out his ceremonial greeting. "Owane, Principal Consort."

"Jalok, Second Husband." Owane panted as he climbed the last few steps.

"We heard the drums. Did you receive your scroll from Palomei?" Jalok asked.

"Tai, but we are in trouble. Deep trouble."

With heads inclined they listened to the news about the approaching armada.

Maome kept her eyes cast down, pretending not to listen.

"We must get to one of the drummers and tell them to beat out a warning about the Slavers," Loa'a said.

"I tried," Owane said, "but the drummer thought I was trying to usurp Losha's orders. He said that now that Palomei is dead he would take orders only from the new Queen."

"Should we leave now?" Tauhans asked. "We could go to Hollow Mountain without Palomei's body."

"Tauhans, you coward! We stay and fight!" Loa'a said. He gaped at Tauhans in silent reprimand.

"We cannot go back now," Jalok said. "There are crowds of people pressing behind us."

"Then we stay?" Kuhil asked.

"Let us wait until after the funeral," Owane advised. "Maybe Losha will have seen reason by then. If she has not come to her senses we will carry Palomei's body out of Olonopo as planned. I still intend to honor her."

Jalok's voice fell tight and small, his words barely above a whisper. "But how do we warn the others?"

Owane leaned closer. "I have organized a short funeral. After we carry Palomei through the jungle to the river's edge, let us find some conches and drums and send out a warning call to the people on our own. When the people hear our call they will leave Olonopo Crater and gather on the beaches to fight."

"And then what?" Kuhil asked.

"I will not abandon Palomei," Owane said. "When we get to the Ananba River we can place her body in a boat and proceed to the Cave of Giants to put her soul to rest as dictated by the traditions of the Si Te Cah Clan. It will take us a full day, but it will also take the people that long to return to the beaches. We can join them by morning."

Loa'a looked up behind him at the perimeter of the crater. "Olonopo Crater is a fortress in itself." His voice turned sharp. "But only if the Slavers do not find this place. Perhaps the Elders, the women, and the children can stay here."

Owane nodded. "Tai. Losha did say it was safe here."

Tauhans blotted the sweat that streamed down his face. "Unless the Slavers have killed or enslaved us. What if they find the Queen's compound is empty and climb Olonopo? The people left behind will be like a school of trapped threadfin."

"We will make certain it all ends on the beaches," Owane said, "one way or the other."

The others nodded in agreement and together descended the stairs in stoic silence.

CHAPTER SEVENTY-THREE

THE SERVANT LEADER

"Now is the time we will dream a new dream together."

Losha Ninti
The Makolese Scroll on
The Return of the Ka and the Mending of the Su #73

Hand in hand, Losha and Temple climbed the stairs to the stone platform. Temple, fully recovered, stood by her right side along with the First Advisor and Elder Tani. Palomei's other husbands stood on Losha's left side rigid and tense, their hands folded in front of them, their eyes cast down. Nijaga, Kulo and Cranik remained behind them to the side.

Losha pulled Tani aside. "Now that we have you back, Winyon is missing. Have you seen her?"

Tani shook her head.

"Or Tiv, Jabal, or his friend, O'Juma?"

"Tiv is helping some of the children. The crater is packed with people," Tani said, scanning the crowd. "Jabal and O'Juma are bound to be in here somewhere."

Losha gave Tani a shallow nod. Her heart began to ache as her eyes wandered over the faces of all the anxious people. She leaned over and whispered into Temple's ear, "Are we doing the right thing?"

"There's no right or wrong in this, love," Temple said. "It's going to play out in its own way. After all, we live on a planet of calamity."

Losha let out a little groan. "Tai, calamity was there when we all came screaming into the world, and will be there at the end when we are placed in our funeral boats with all the flowers, fruits, flies, and flames."

Temple squeezed her hand. "This world was never designed to be fair. We'll do the best we can."

When the crowd hushed in anticipation, a single conch was blown. Owane raised his arms to signal he wished to speak. He sang a prayer to invoke the Ancestors, and giving thanks for their lives, and that of Palomei. Then he issued an apology. "I regret that Great Grandfather, Okon is not with us today. He…he has taken ill." It was the best excuse.

The people mumbled their regrets. And those surrounding he Great Round House bowed their heads out of respect.

Owane spoke with complete candor about the history of Palomei's early reign, emphasizing she was no more than a frightened child when she first took the throne. As he added stories about her more hilarious mistakes as a child queen, he even evoked the crowd's laughter. He highlighted her accomplishments in trade, her battles won with the Spanish, the Arabs, and the Dutch, and her efforts to preserve the prophecy and history scrolls in keeping with Makolese traditions. Never mentioning his own role in her development, Owane underscored Palomei's compassion as a loving mother, and her kindness and fairness in all matters both complex and risky, but excluded any mention of her temper or brutality.

Although Owane did mention the raising of pigs for food for the delight of the Royals, he never once mentioned the horrible acts for which leaders of the Si Te Cah Clan were notorious. Even though Palomei had been the last of her kind, she had tasted human flesh once as a young woman, mostly out of curiosity, and a desire to draw closer to the clan she would never know. Seeing how her followers reacted to the abomination, she forbid her own daughter or any future progeny from such savagery, knowing this new action would win many hearts throughout Makol.

The last thing Owane brought to light was Queen Palomei's complete acceptance of Temple Fox when he first fell from the sky, and later Losha's acceptance as one of the prophesied Teachers.

"Before we sing our final farewell to our most beloved Queen, I will repeat the good news," he shouted. He held up the scroll for all to see. "Before Queen Palomei died she bequeathed the throne to another. Losha Ninti, who has fulfilled the ancient prophecy along with Temple Fox, will now rule as our new Queen."

A barrage of encouraging shouts were heard and the atmosphere lifted into conviviality and joy. When Losha stepped forward to speak, the people hushed and lowered their heads to the ground.

She shouted so all could hear. "Before I agree to be your new Queen, I must ask you all, do you feel I should take on this great honor and enormous responsibilty?"

The accolades were multiple, and an unanimous storm of cheers filled Olonopo Crater.

Ikus kept his head down, hoping no one would notice him.

"Then I accept Queenship!" She smiled and bowed low.

There were shouts of praise for the new Queen, and the air was abuzz with excitement.

Tani stepped up behind Losha with a white bundle in her arms. She smiled from ear to ear. The old woman unfurled her load, and a robe made of swan feathers fell open to the delighted gasps of the crowd. Tani rose on her tiptoes and draped the garment around Losha's shoulders, bowed, and stepped backward.

Owane moved forward and placed Palomei's pearly scepter in Losha's hands. He bowed slightly and stepped behind the new Queen, then nodded to Tani. The old woman came forward and handed the First Advisor a crown of blossoms. Owane held the wreath up high, intoning the blessing of the Ancestors, and placed it onto Losha's head. He bowed and moved back to his place on the platform.

Losha gave a regal nod to them, then turned to face the crowd again. "Thank you for your trust in me," she said, her voice cracking slightly. "I hope to serve you well. As your new Queen, and the second to fulfill the ancient prophecy, I want you to know that there will be no more Masters on Makol. Here ends all hereditary queens in the future. All queens after me will be selected by only women in the Elder Council. Myself, and all queens after me, will no longer be dictators, but will be servants of the people. And all other leaders will be servants as well with the people's welfare foremost in their hearts, minds, and actions.

"I, Queen Losha Ninti, also vow to act as a spiritual mentor to the people, and will add a provision in our laws for my removal from the throne if I am found lacking by you all."

She looked to Owane. "We are beholden to both Queen Palomei and her First Advisor, Owane, for so wisely expanding and reenvigorating the Elder Council. It is my intention to improve upon that process. I, Queen Losha Ninti, declare that two new councils will be formed. In addition to the Queen's Council, and Elders' Council, we will establish the People's Council first by elections, and in years to come, the Children's Council, for the new souls who will be born when the Su is mended will be very advanced. Although the Children's Council will not have the power to create laws, they will want and need to be heard by us. Each of the first three councils," she declared, "will from this day forth be equal in power. "

One woman turned to another whom she knew to be an Unbeliever. "That should change your mind," she said. "What Queen would share in her power?"

The other woman remained silent.

The first woman spoke again. "And Losha Ninti is intelligent as well. She is a scholar of the History Scrolls, and has knowledge of many languages."

Losha's voice rang throughout the crater. "Our people have lived under centuries of a monarchy with only two small councils advising. We know little about what a democracy entails. It is true that a totalitarian government is less complicated and easier to run. But it represents humanity's infancy where people are told how to behave. Democracy is more advanced and harder to manage. Democracy is elegant, requiring more finesse, skill, and hard work. It is like a rare jewel that constantly needs to be refaceted and polished so it casts more and more light into the world. Its implementation is a delicate operation that will require our patience.

"With this new form of government it is my hope that we will collectively have a say in governing ourselves. My hope is that we will grow a peaceful heart, knowing our inner selves will eventually reflect in our outer world.

"As for now, we will bring closure to Queen Palomei's life and her reign by celebrating her life. Let the Ancestors hear our prayer." Losha sang a well-known Makolese chant: "Aum Gam Gana-pata-ye Namah. Aum shrim hrim klim glaum gam gana-pata-ye vara varada sarva janamme va-shaman-aya svaha." The people joined in and the sound cleansed them, lifting their spirits higher.

Losha felt the energy change as she sang another song she composed on the spot, a song of celebration and good-byes to souls departed who gathered in the clouds that swept overhead. And no one breathed a word when she made no mention of Lord Tagheetu and the swamps. They listen enraptured by the poetry of the words, and the rising and falling of her sweet falsetto voice.

While she sang, the bells clanged and the conches were blown again, this time with a mournful tune, and all the Royal Husbands and three guards carried Palomei's body out of the Great Round House on a carrier constructed from thick bamboo.

Maome padded alongside the body making last-minute adjustments to the white silk that covered the giantess's corpse. On tiptoe she rearranged the garland of purple gardenias draped around Palomei's massive head. When she had finished, Maome fell in step behind the solemn procession. They moved solemnly down the stone staircase, across the short coarse grass in the sandy crater. When the procession started up the steep staircase, Maome stopped. With tears in her eyes she gave Palomei one last bow, and the body was carried to the top of the stairs. Then the heavy burden was lifted up and over Olonopo Crater, and the people lowered their heads in respect while Losha sang a song for Palomei's safe journey, not to the Lord Tagheetu's swamp, but to the other world of light and pure love.

At the crater's rim Losha sang the last verse of farewell to Palomei in so melodious a voice that the people wept for its simple beauty, even though many had hated the former Queen.

The new Queen looked out over the crowd of eager faces. "Each of you are made of the Divine Light of God." Her voice echoed throughout the crater. "You are pure consciousness. You were born with your eyes open, but chose to close them in pursuit of an empty play…an empty dream on a circuitous path that inevitably leads you back to God. We will not invite or chase after the delusions that hold us in fear any longer…not even the fear of inevitable death…for there is no such thing as death.

"Now is the time we will dream a new dream together. Now is the time we celebrate writing a new scroll for the Makolese people." She held her arms up high. "We are about to have the most magnificent feast and joyous dance the Makolese have ever known!" she said, excitedly. "I ask that you concentrate on who you really are, and return to the root of your own Divine being, which is pure consciousness. Focus on the glorious being you are. The Creator and you are not separate. You are an immaculate, immortal being – an exquisite expression of Goddess or God.

"So, let us set the intention to celebrate not death, uncertainty, or fear, but all life and love, using the power of self-forgiveness, a deep appreciation for all life, and your love for self and all others. We owe it to our Ancestors. We owe it to our future children. For we carry both the past and the future within us. I ask you now to fall in love with the island again like never before. Fall in love with all life. We thank The Spirit Which Moves In All Things, and all the Gods and all the Ancestors. We thank the pulsing consciousnesss of every grain of sand, every blade of grass, every fish, cloud, bird, raindrop, and breeze. We fill ourselves with the appreciation for every river and waterfall, the Sun, the Moon, our sacred mountain, and ourselves.

"I ask that you perform this grand ceremony with joy and harmony in union with all that is, and to keep your minds focused with concentration on love, beauty, and the utmost gratitude for our precious island and our lives. For you are the clean, clear quartz that embraces the light. You are the ruby in granite, the emerald in stone, the spark in the unblinking eye of God. You are the light. Will you all dance with me this day and night?"

The people began to shout that they understood and would follow.

"Thank you for your bravery and open-heartedness. The Ancestors give us strength. Unified and strong we wake up together."

She paused and caught Temple's eye. "In order to perform my duties as your new Queen I wish to draw a deeper happiness and joy to myself in order to assist my people in their deeper joy. As you all know, as your new Queen and servant to you all, I must also choose a husband."

Temple blinked at Losha as if he had just been hit between the eyes. He smiled nervously at the crowd. He leaned toward Losha and whispered, "Are you about to propose to me? Isn't it supposed to be the other way around?"

Losha held up her hand, acknowledging the interruption, and a few giggles rose from the crowd. "Only a Makolese woman can make such a proposal. I am not only a Makolese woman, I am a Makolese queen. This is how it is done," she whispered back, then grinned apologetically at the crowd.

She turned toward Temple again and peered into his sky-blue eyes. She took his hands in hers. "Will you, Temple Fox, be my First Husband and Principal Consort?" she asked, beaming.

The smile on Temple's face dropped like the belly of a fat Victorian woman who unbuckled her corset. "*First* Husband?"

"Tai, I must marry four more husbands to maintain continuity and custom."

Temple shook his head like a wet dog.

A wave of laughter rippled through the crater.

"Just say 'Tai,'" she said, then kissed him long and passionately.

After he came up for air he shouted. "Tai. Tai! I accept! I ACCEPT!"

The laughter grew louder and everyone broke out in song. And the couple stood arm in arm surrounded by a blanket of love and joy in which the people wrapped them. After the people sang their song of goodwill, they started clapping rhythmically, calling for the couple to dance.

Temple pulled Losha closer and spoke out of the side of his mouth. "When do we tell them about the armada? "

"I cannot break them out of their joy right now," she whispered.

Ikus, frail but determined, edged his thin frame through the crowd and positioned himself several yards in front of the podium. "And when were you going to tell us about the armada of forty Arab dhows bearing down on us?" he yelled.

Temple inclined his head toward Losha, his words meant for her ears only. "Calamity just stomped forward like an angry stepchild. Right on Divine time."

Losha gazed down at Ikus. "It is true," she said.

A collective gasp was heard from several people in front. And the great bowl of earth filled with a thundercloud of commotion as an expansive wave of terror rippled through the crowd like a brushfire.

"That does not change who we are," Losha said to Ikus.

"Are we cowards?" he asked.

"We must be ready and fight them!" someone called out and others nodded in agreement.

"Problems are never solved by violence," Losha said. "I cannot tell you what to do, but Temple and I strongly agree that there will be no need to fight. Instead, everyone on the island will celebrate by…"

"Celebrate!" Ikus shouted. "While we are being invaded by Slavers!"

"That is insane!" a voice rang out from the back of the crowd.

Losha's voice was calm, forthright and bold. "People, now is not a time to merely petition the the Spirits and the Gods for help, but to move into a state of union with the Creator. It is your birthright. You have your Kas now! Use the power of intention with your words, thoughts, song, and dance. Use this power the Gods have gifted you, along with your imagination, to create such a magnificent harmonic energetic field of resonance that no Slavers will even find us!"

"Dream a new dream! Raise the vibration and frequency of the island so that only beauty finds beauty. Have the passion and faith to do this so that we live fearless lives. By doing this we love ourselves. By doing this we love and honor each other. Life is a precious gift. And freewill is a gift from the Gods. Use your gifts! It is your destiny!"

Ikus' voice reverberated across the crater. "TEMPLE FOX AND LOSHA NINTI ARE COWARDS!"

Everyone turned their heads toward the old man. The Elder stepped forward and shouted again. "Temple Fox and Losha Ninti are committing us to suicide! Dance away and be cowards if you want to, but I will die to protect our people!"

The rickety old man took another audacious step forward and pointed at the new queen. "You and that White Wizard call yourselves human gods, but what you really want is to distract us while the Slavers come to take our children!" He turned to face the people. "It is this White Wizard and his woman who has corrupted you! It is his people who are speeding to our shores now! SLAVERS!" he screamed.

Tani shuffled forward and stared at Ikus. She spat on the stone platform. "One maggot spoils the whole pot!"

"Then remove the maggot!" someone shouted from the crowd.

"Tai! Why are you even here if you are not a Believer?" another questioned Ikus.

Kulo tilted his head toward Temple, Losha, and Tani, his face as flushed as a red tide. "This is my fault. Owane told me about the invaders. I told Ikus and convinced him to stay. I thought he would be safer."

Cranik grabbed Kulo's arm. "Then you fear this as I do?" Cranik asked.

"Tai, I do," Kulo admitted.

"I believe in you and Temple Fox!" a man called out.

Losha acknowledged the man with a nod. "Tai, and I believe in you. The question remains, do you believe in yourselves to raise the vibration of this island?"

"I will listen to no more nonsense. It is every man for himself," a man hollered back.

"Tai, I have my Ka!" another shouted. "I have the power now and do not fear death!" He held his spear up high. "This will soon bite Arab flesh!"

Cranik caught the sight of the simple spear and its head chipped from common rock. "Forty ships!" he murmured. "It will be a massacre!"

A thunder of voices called out in protest. Losha sensed she was losing ground and struggled to remain anchored and calm.

She shouted over them. "Listen people, the infinite God lies within us all. Sow the seeds of love and harmony…or sow the seeds of fear and chaos. But know this. You can only choose one or the other. Decide for yourselves what you want to happen here."

"Then you will not order us stay?" a voice called out.

"It is an individual decision. I am giving you some seeds here, but it is up to you to plant them, and allow them to take root.

"Please listen!" Losha continued over the storm of voices. "Temple and I choose the path of least resistance. We choose to celebrate all life throughout the night. I cannot stop you, or blame you if you choose to do something different, but I ask you to stay with us, unified together. United together we are stronger. Most of you possess your Kas now. We only ask that you harm no one. Use your Ka along with your imagination, but use it, knowing what you do will be out of gratitude for our lives, out of love, and out of self-forgiveness."

"What do we have to forgive? Bringing the Slavers to our shore?" someone asked, her voice laced with sarcasm.

"Oh, so now it is our fault the Slavers are coming?" Ikus shouted back at Losha.

Losha raised her hand so they would listen. "In the greater reality there is nothing to forgive. But in the physical world, our outer world reflects what is inside of us," she explained. "In our recent past we have been caught up by a collective, consensual delusion created by the Si Te Cah Clan, who feared that someday our people would upsurp their power and leadership. The giants were brutal because they feared us, but they also projected those fears onto Outsiders.

"I cannot tell you what to do, but share with you what Temple and I have decided to do. I only ask that you deliberate with great care. Choose love or choose fear. You cannot choose both. Use your Kas. Use your imagination."

Maome, who was still rooted at the foot of the staircase, squinted at Losha in the distance. "Why does she keep saying that?" she asked a bystander.

The bystander shook her head. "I am frightened," is all the woman said.

Maome looked over at the woman and saw the terror in her eyes. At that moment Maome came to her own decision. Without anyone noticing, with nimble feet, she dashed up the stair.

Losha made her final declaration. "Those who choose to celebrate life and love, please join us in a grand celebration here in Olonopo Crater. The few who can hold the new dream with the highest vibration know who you are. Please join Temple and I inside the Great Round House. All others…I beg you to stay and pray with us inside the crater."

There was a collective pause, but a heartbeat later there was a great churning of moving bodies as half of the Makolese population swarmed toward the stone steps and steep slopes that would lead them out of Olonopo Crater.

The Teachers stood in silence for over an hour listening to the pleas of women who clutched their babies and kissed their husbands good-bye. They witnessed families ripped apart, fist fights, and shouting...weeping...sorrow, and stubborn refusals.

Losha rested her face against Temple's stubbled cheek. "It begins," she whispered.

"Just remember, little pigeon, there's light behind the darkest clouds. Stay hopeful."

There were only the occasional cries of children shaking the bowl of the crater when an hour later the remaining devotees settled down, their faces pointed upward at Losha in the emotional spectrum of strained anticipation, grief, remorse, or quietude.

Losha bowed to them. When she rose she began another chant unknown to even herself. The words fell from her lips effortlessly, and the song flowed like a river, each vowel wrapped in a hypnotic resonance. And as she sang in spectral tones no one had ever heard before, the Makolese people sang along in layered overtones, and a pale magenta and violet sheen glazed the air inside and above the arena, surrounding the bowl of earth in a bubble of purity and love.

And while the ancient name of God – All That Is, The Spirit Which Moves In All Things, And Is All Things – was chanted in the old Mother tongue late into the day, no hunger was known, no thirst was suffered, nor fear felt as deeply, for the purity of the sound fed and nourished the people.

The people remained transfixed and transformed, and profound serenity fell over everyone…even Ikus who had hidden behind a scrub bush.

The chant had a sublime way of flowing, cleansing, honoring everything good that the people were, until in little eddies of sound it curled like wisps of incense and subsided into sacred silence. The song ended with the people sitting deep in meditation in timeless stillness.

When the sun had rolled over the western lip of the crater, and the heat-pounded air had cooled, campfires were quietly lit, and the smell of jasmine and pu-erh tea filled the air still suffused with the prayerful song. Losha suggested food and drink be served. With the resonance of love having broken all barriers of doubt and fear hours before, the people feasted in peace, until the drums beat, and the people slowly stirred into dancing.

"Care to dance?" Losha asked, offering her hand to Temple.

Temple leaned against Losha's shoulder. "Some are still grieving."

"As they should," Losha said. "Allow them the time to go through what they need to go through. We will celebrate their loved ones' lives. Meanwhile – " She pressed Temple's hand. "Would you like to dance with me?"

His words stumbled. "I…I really don't know how."

"Just follow me," she said. Her torso and hips swayed with the beat in slow sinuous movements, her eyes never leaving his.

Temple let out a little yelp. "I don't mean to be such a wanker, but just watching you makes my plums stony, and I'm afraid my willie will go stonkin' wonkers. This bloody skirt I'm wearing is…you know…It doesn't exactly hide the family jewels."

"You are most peculiar. I do not know half of what you just said, but you must dance with me. You are to be my First Husband."

"Oh, sure. One among four others."

"Do you not feel the joy of the people? My joy?" She cocked her head, and her full lips pulled into a smile.

"I sure as hell do right down to my coin purse and tallywacker. That's what I've been trying to tell you."

"Then follow the music."

Temple made a few awkward attempts to stomp his feet to the beat of the drums. Losha grabbed his hips and twisted them sharply to the left then to the right, which sent the people into waves of laughter.

"Okay. Okay," he said. "Don't damage the toolbox. I get the idea." He undulated in imitation of her movement, then pulled her hips to his as if he was competing in collegiate sculling. When the people saw the rowing motion they laughed again and mimicked Temple's movements with exaggeration.

On that memorable night a new dance was born, and a new dream was dreamed.

CHAPTER SEVENTY-FOUR

THE HUSBANDS

"How much more do you want me to endure?"

Owane, First Advisor and Queen Palomei's First Husband
The Makolese Scroll on
The Return of the Ka and the Mending of the Su #74

The Widowers shielded their eyes from the glare of the morning light when they emerged from the Cave of Giants. With no further delay, they hiked down the foothills, and made their way over to the boats that lay in wait. From there they rowed up the Ananba River, until they disembarked where the quickest trail would lead them to the eastern shore.

When they arrived at the shore by mid-morning, the beaches were congested with men and woman sharpening wooden pikes, sparring with scimitars and long knives, and throwing spears at makeshift targets made from bundles of sawgrass.

The new Commander, Boran, and his new First Man, Sumuro, were organizing the people when a call rang out.

Owane climbed the steps of the Common House to address the crowd. "Thank you, good people. Now we will do what Queen Palomei would have done. WE WILL FIGHT!" he shouted.

The crowd cheered and waved their weapons.

"Has anyone seen the armada yet?" someone asked.

Owane found the voice in the crowd. "It has been predicted they will come over the horizon by tomorrow morning. I will climb back to the rim of Olonopo Crater. When I see them, I will send out the warning call."

"What about us?" Tauhans asked, eyeing all the other Royal Husbands.

"You can stay and fight…or join the women, children, and the cowards inside Olonopo Crater."

"I do not believe the Teachers are cowards, Owane," Jalok said sharply.

"Neither do I," Tauhans offered. "But what do we do? We have not been trained in the art of war. We cannot fight."

Owane's voice tightened. "And yet, every able-bodied man and woman are here right now prepared to lay down their life for us."

"Then why are you going back to the crater?" Lao'a asked. "Tell one of the guards to scout for ships. They can blow the warning call."

"Who can I trust but myself," Owane said, glaring at Lao'a. "Am I not still the First Advisor? I wish to speak to the Teachers. I would like to hear any strategies they have formed against the armada in our absence."

A young man crept forward and gave a sheepish bow. "I beg your forgiveness, First Advisor, but the new Queen asked that we stay inside Olonopo Crater, insisting there was no need for war. She celebrated life throughout the night. She gave us a choice to stay or leave. As you can see, many have come…even the old ones."

Owane stiffened. "I will go and speak to the Queen myself." He pointed to Tauhans. "You have no skill or stomach for war. You come with me." He motioned for Commander Boran to follow him as well.

"Saving yourself, Owane?" Loa'a called out. "Let Tauhans go, but order Nijaga to send out the warning when the ships come. Stay with us and add your blood to Makolese sand, or forever be marked as a coward."

With the speed of a crocodile snatching its prey, the older man lunged at Lao'a and grabbed him by the throat. "Do I look like a coward? Were you even alive during the massacre? How much more do you want me to endure?" He pushed Lao'a so hard the young widower toppled to the ground. "I need to consult with Commander Boran at a better vantage point on Olonopo, you idiot! From there we will direct the battle."

Lao'a rose and brushed the sand off his skirt. He gave Owane an apologetic bow.

Owane grunted, grabbed Tauhans' arm, and turned, on his heels.

Boran sprinted by Owane's side with Tauhans trailing behind them. Owane spoke to the Commander without turning his head. "Make certain the other three are far from the shore doing something that will not endanger them. They were, after all, the Palomei's Royal Husbands."

"I understand," the Commander said. He spied Sumuro jogging his way and waved him over. "Place the Royal Husbands in the rear," he ordered.

"Yes, Commander," Sumuro said, as he matched their stride. "But first, I need to speak with you. It is an urgent matter. I have just received word from a fisherman who was checking his boat early this morning beyond the northeastern peninsula."

Sensing the news was important the three stopped to listen.

"Hours before dawn he noticed several fishing boats were missing. He said he saw a dozen or more boats heading out to sea…to engage the enemy, I assume."

"I ordered no boats into the ocean!" Owane's tone was gruff. He nodded for Tauhans to continue back to the crater without him. Tauhans broke into a run. "Did you?" he asked the Commander.

The Commander shook his head.

Sumuro spoke again. "He said it was too dark to tell, but he thought they might be children who…"

Owane's eyes widened. "Children!" he said in alarm. "But all the children are in the crater!"

"There were maybe a hundred of them. He said it was dark, and they were so far away that it was hard to make out just how many."

"Quick!" Owane ordered. "Alert the blowers. Tell them to send out a call, 'All boats return NOW'!"

Sumuro sent out the orders to the blowers, and the message was blasted in the air out over the island and beyond.

Owane and Boran raced across the open beach toward the jungle that would lead to the crater.

CHAPTER SEVENTY-FIVE

OWANE

*"I believe that the events in our world manifest
before us according to the attention we give them.
If you keep judging, criticizing, and fearing
something…then you will give energy to whatever
it is you are judging, criticizing, and fearing."*

Temple Fox
The Makolese Scroll on
The Return of the Ka and the Mending of the Su #75

Owane was poised on a vantage promontory on top of the crater rim with Temple and Tauhans by his side. The gold trim of his barkcloth wrap gleamed and flapped in the building breeze as he braced himself with a walking stick with one arm, and held an obsidian magnifier to one eye with the other. He shook his head and handed the magnifier back to Temple. "Look again," he insisted. He pointed out to sea.

"You don't believe me, do you?" Temple said.

"Well, I am not crazy," Owane said, his face reddening. "Commander Boran sees them!"

"You're not crazy," the Teacher said reassuringly. "That's why I've sent for the child." He gestured behind him to Elder Kulo, who promptly escorted Losha's niece, Galana, onto the gusty terrace of rock.

Temple smiled down at the child. He handed Galana the magnifier. "Galana," he said, "look out there and tell us what you see."

The bright-eyed girl put the magnifier to her eye. She found the scallop of shoreline first, then lifted the scope to search the great expanse of water far in the distance. "I see masses of people gathered on the shore, and a school of dolphins over there." She pointed to the southeast out near Dolphin Cove. She scanned the horizon to the north.

Owane's eyes strained. "Do you see anything on the horizon to the northeast?" he asked curtly.

"Fishing boats...many of them." Galana looked up at the First Advisor, feeling she might have disappointed him. She peered up at Temple with concern.

"Now, let Tauhans try." Galana handed Tauhans the magnifier. He looked far out to sea.

"Why, I see ships!" he shouted. "Arab dhows! Sound the conches!"

"Do you see any smaller boats?" he asked Tauhans.

Tauhans looked again and spied a blur of dark spots far to the northeast dwarfed by the ships behind them. "I cannot make them out clearly. Looks like some of our fishing boats heading to shore. It better be *our* people in them!"

Owane turned to the Commander to give the signal call. Everyone held their breath as the panicked sound of the conch wailed.

"Tell the first and second group to receive our boats. If they are filled with Slavers then that means they took the children. Tell our people to attack without mercy!"

The conch cried out in different pitches with a series of short and long blasts in code.

Owane addressed Temple again, his face blistered with fury. "How is it that Tauhans can see the ships? Commander Boran and myself can see them, and yet you and the child cannot?"

"Owane, this is your chance for revenge," Temple said. "This is what Palomei and your people always dreamed about. War."

"Please answer the question," he insisted.

"That's the point! Don't you see it?" Temple said. "What you see before you out there is what you've always wanted. It's been your greatest desire."

"Then why is it that Galana could not see them?"

"She is young. Her mind is pure," Temple stated.

"And mine is not?" Tauhans said, his voice edged with indignation.

"Your mind," Temple explained, "has been filled with fearful stories...hollow fantasies."

Owane ran his hand over his face. "What is the point in all of this?" he demanded.

"The armada is real for you," Temple answered plainly, "but not for Galana, or the people down inside the crater. You and Queen Palomei have feared the Slavers so thoroughly that you've drawn them to your shore.

"Remember the exorcism I performed to remove Amron from Galana's energy field? The same principle applies to her. She was probably so terrified with all the talk of her Uncle becoming a demon that she may have inadvertently opened herself up to possession. At the very least, she was vulnerable to possession by her own Uncle because she knew him well and loved him."

"That is ridiculous," Owane complained. "You prophesised the Arabs coming yourself!"

Temple remembered what the Voice had said through him a month before. "Prediction is based on probability," he explained. "You see, you and the people have fantasized about a war like this for so long that chances are it had to happen. I believe that the events in our world manifest before us according to the attention we give them. If you keep judging, criticizing, and fearing something...then you'll give energy to whatever it is you're judging, criticizing, and fearing.

"You must admit, Owane, not all of the ships that have come here over the years were slave ships. Many were merely trade ships, and many innocent traders were murdered."

Truth resonated in the air and Owane tightened his grip on his walking stick.

"Losha and I have thought about this a great deal," Temple said. "As the giants who ruled the island died off, and became increasingly outnumbered by islanders, they became paranoid that they would lose their power to rule over the Makolese. Believing Palomei's own people would never usurp her, the Slavers invading the island became her projection, her fear of losing Queenship. You see, Owane, by projecting, you blame. And when you blame, you disconnect and disown your own projection. In the end, everyone must be responsible for what they believe," Temple said.

His voice softened. "After this is over, when the Su is mended, the new children won't hold such dark beliefs or dark projections. They'll know better how to love, not completely at first, but they'll be better able to love, and draw love back to themselves. That's the way it was always designed to be. And that, First Advisor, is a prophecy."

There was a moment of tense reflection, and Owane looked back out to sea. He threw the Teacher a disturbing look. "How many people do you think will be able to see the armada as I do?" he asked.

"The majority inside Olonopo will not see them, particularly those who are inside the Great Round House. We've asked that only those whose minds are focused with utmost concentration on love, beauty, joy, and harmony to join us there. They sit in deep meditation for the appreciation of all life...even the lives of the Slavers. They have actually changed their reality." He lowered his gaze to the beaches below. "But everyone down there will see them."

"You said you would help us to defeat our enemies – our fears," Owane said.

"This past month I've given you some of the tools." He paused. "But it could take anywhere from mere seconds to many lifetimes to grasp the teaching fully."

Owane gave a sullen nod. He walked a few paces away to the edge of the cliff and stared out to sea again at the approaching fishing boats and larger dhows.

Temple thanked Galana and Tauhans, who both bowed and left. Signaling to Boran with a flick of his head, the Commander stepped away so Temple could address Owane again…alone.

"There's no right or wrong in what you decide, Respected Advisor," Temple said sympathetically. "The people ultimately decide their own fate. Will we war with hatred? Or will we love ourselves enough that we can entrust our lives to the Divine...even if our physical safety is not guaranteed?"

The old man heavied a sigh of such weight that he paused to inhale. He spoke over his shoulder at the Teacher. "It is a dangerous gamble, this trusting in the Unknown."

"Who better to trust in?"

Owane muttered over his shoulder with his eyes to the far horizon. "Theories. All theories." He paused. "And so," he said, turning toward to Temple, "these are the great powers you spoke of a moon ago? Love and trust?"

"Tai. It's love and appreciation of self, and all things, and that total trust in the Divine that absorbs and purifies the fear, neutralizing and disarming the enemy." Temple ran a hand through his beard in thought. "I must say, however, that it doesn't always work as we expect it to. It depends on the person's level of understanding, and their ability to place all matters in and through the heart to be purified. And it also matters what lessons a person has yet to learn."

"So…you will not help us fight? You will still stay?" Owane asked.

"My place is with the people…here," Temple said.

"Then go," Owane said a bit too sharply.

"And you?"

Owane stared down at his feet as if he were lost. "It is my duty to stay with my people."

"Your people are also inside the crater," Temple said, sensing Owane was conflicted. "We need leaders to carry on after this is all over."

Owane fought back the rising grief, and the futilty of the situation. "I will not abandon the others."

Temple took a firm hold of Owane's shoulders and hugged him good-bye. "The Gods are with you always," he said, then bowed.

"Good-bye, Temple Fox."

When Temple had left, Owane waved the Commander over. "Send out calls of strategy as you see fit, Boran," he whispered, his voice having lost its power. "I will join the others soon."

★　　★　　★　　★　　★　　★

Owane waited until the conches were blown again, and ambled over to a pile of rocky spurs that ran along the basin's inner rim. He stared down through the violet haze into the crater where the people sat in meditation in a series of large concentric circles that formed around the great dome. At the edge of the circumference the children played. He watched Temple, a mere smudge in the distance, descend the stairs, cross the basin, and climb the facing stairs that led into the Great Round House.

"First Advisor!" Boran called out. The Commander looked out to sea with the magnifier still glued to his eye.

Owane turned his head. "What is it?"

"Around the bend of the far northeastern peninsula…our fishing boats are close to shore now." He swung the magnifier higher back to the horizon. "And I see fire…on the horizon. Two of the dhows are on fire…" He paused, searching with his scope. "Two more dhows have torn masts and… Bi kana lo!"

Owane strode over to the Commander. He ripped the magnifer from Boran's grip and found the blazing ships with his narrowed vision. "The ship with the torn mast is out of control," he muttered in concentration. "It just rammed another. And another dhow is turning to head back out to sea!" He lowered the magnifier and grinned. "Bi kana, we are winning!"

"I beg your forgiveness, First Advisor." Boran recaptured the magnifier and aimed his eye at the slim finger of land where he had seen the fishing boats. "Fry me or eat me raw!" he exclaimed.

"What is it? Please tell me the children have returned? Tell me they have returned safely!"

"Those are NOT *children*!"

"Bi kano lo! Slavers?"

"NO! They are violet howlers! Boat loads of them!"

"What? We have been saved by an army of MONKEYS! Monkeys cannot sail boats!"

"I assume they are enchanted," Boran announced. He swung his eyeglass back to the horizon. "Six dhows have been disabled, one flees, but the remainder advance." He moved his eye back to the distant shore. "The howlers are landing, and are running over the spine of the peninsula at top speed and…" He squinted harder. "They are not heading back to the jungle. They are heading for the foothills."

"The foothills? But why?"

Boran shook his head.

"Boran, stay here and direct the troops. Bi kana lo, if monkeys can fight…so can I!" Owane drew his scimitar from its scabbard and lumbered over to the stone stairs that would lead him to the beaches. He felt numb…forgotten…suddenly old.

He paused at the cliff edge that dropped to the stone stairs and closed his eyes. "I know what I promised you, Palomei," he murmured under his breath. "I will do as you would have done. I will go and fight." His eyes rimmed with moisture. His voice became a mere whisper. "I will join you soon, my Most Beloved."

Just as he made his way to the top of the landing, a strong updraft pushed him back nearly knocking Owane off his feet. He lowered his head, held up his walking stick and sword, and leaned at a sharp diagonal to approach the stairs again. Again a powerful wind drove him back so hard that this time he dropped his sword. He struggled to rise, using his stick, but another stronger wind attacked him from above and battered him to the ground.

"Bi kana lo!" he cried.

The wind answered back with a shriek, then died down to a soft haunting moan. Just when Owane thought the wind had played itself out, a buzzing noise stirred above his head. Using his stick, he pushed himself to his feet, his heart palpitating madly. Daring to look up, he shielded his eyes from the sun.

A swarm of bees encircled him. In a sudden surprise maneuver, they dived to drive him away from the stairs, forcing him along the Olonopo's spine toward the set of stairs that would direct him down inside the crater.

Owane batted at the bees with his stick to no effect. The bees stung him repeatedly, until he dropped his stick, his arms and hands swelling sharp with pain. His arms flailed in the air. "Palomei, I know it is you! Why are you doing this to me? I need to go! I need to do this!" he cried.

Bees stung his face, others on his legs. He doubled over to protect himself from the swarm, but the bees covered his back, stinging him unmercifully. He shuffled forward, until his foot dropped to the first stair tread that steered him down into the crater. "You cannot dictate to me from the dead!" he shouted. He stumbled forward, and his other foot dropped to the next tread, then onto another...and another.

Slowly a sweet energy that emanated from the crater enveloped the old man, and the bees ceased their assault, and rose into the air.

Owane unfolded himself, his body covered with red welts. With swollen eyes, he glanced above his head cautiously. The pain gradually abated, and a light effervescent energy filled him, until he felt light-headed, almost giddy.

"All right! All right! You win!" he whispered, brushing the dead bees off himself. "I will go back! I promise!" he said breathlessly, and the bees circled around him once, then flew down toward the Great Round House.

CHAPTER SEVENTY-SIX

TIDES OF CHANGE

*"Many have lived through an incredible
experience while hungry,
but no one should retell their story on an empty
stomach."*

Temple Fox
The Makolese Scroll on
The Return of the Ka and the Mending of the Su #76

"Monkeys?" Mason asked, disbelieving. "I thought the old tale of the army of violet howlers was merely an embellishment added to entertain children."

"It was every bit as real an event as all the rest of the story."

The Scribe looked at Temple askance. "Are you sure you're not pulling my leg?"

"Would I pull the leg of a man with a bad knee?" he grinned. "I have a sweet tooth, and am feeling a mite peckish. Got any biscuits?"

Mason jerked his head around, his fingers poised above the lighted tablet that rested in his lap. He looked at Temple incredulously. "No, I do not. So, what happened after that?"

Temple let out an exaggerated huff of disapppointment. "Boran watched from a distance, but even the people on the beaches eventually saw that two of the Arab dhows were burning. Witnesses who had magnifiers reported that one purple howler, wearing a string of pearls, led the army of monkeys up into the foothills."

"That's fantastic."

"We imagine some of the Slavers got spooked. But more than thirty dhows were still pressing onward to the shore. That's when it all came apart."

Mason tilted his head and waited.

"Bugger! How do you expect me to finish this story when I'm famished?" Temple's stomach let out a loud liquidy growl. He pointed to his abdomen. "See!"

"How about a granola seed bar? You're part bird. You should like that."

"Don't be cheeky. I'm not a bloody pigeon. I could use some bangers and mash right about now."

"Well, I don't have any."

"Bollocks. You may not have the mash, but you have exactly eight potatoes in that storage bin right over there, and a half-eaten one you've masticated to oblivion in your cooler." He gestured with a nod of his head.

"Exactly eight, huh?" Maśon rose with a groan and limped over to a wooden bin. He opened the lid and emptied the contents one at a time while he counted eight fat red-skinned potatoes. He growled at Temple with mock anger.

"Mind if I nick all eight?"

"Do I have a choice?"

"Of course you do, boy. Look, I'll leave the half-eaten one for you."

"Gee, thanks." Maśon stood motionless waiting for Temple to make a move.

Temple wagged his finger in the air. "Well, stop dithering. Peel and cook them up for me before I pass out."

"What? Too lazy to mumble incantations over an empty plate?"

"Actually, my good friend, I feel you have been sitting too long. Cooking will give you a much-needed break."

"You're like the grandfather I never knew," Maśon said, smiling. "I should disown you."

Maśon peeled the potatoes and stored the skins in a cloth sack. "How was it possible for a monkey to lead an army?" he asked over his shoulder. "I mean, they didn't even have weapons."

"Didn't they? Don't you think a humongous megalodon tooth makes a good cutting tool...good for cutting sailcloth?"

Maśon spun around with the paring knife in his hand. A moment of quiet thought wrinkled his brow. "Wait a minute. Maome took Palomei's megalodon tooth from the necklace she broke."

Temple cocked his head and gave a sly grin, egging Maśon on.

"Pearls," Maśon muttered. "Maome also stole one of Palomei's pearls. But it was a purple howler that..."

Temple's grin widened.

Maśon threw his hands up. "Maome trained the monkeys?"

Temple shook his head. "Close, but no banana."

Maśon's face creased with concentration. "Maome *was* the howler?"

"Bingo! You get a free Ford stallion and a gallon of gas." Temple reached into the cooler and snatched up the half-eaten potato before Maśon could complain. "Seems she was quite inspired by Losha when she first saw Losha spin in the Queen's chamber. After Maome had her Ka attached she tried to spin on her own. She had many more failures than I did, of course, but she practiced privately over and over again, until she taught herself to spin. Like Winyon, she was a natural. That's how truly amazing the Makolese are. A gifted race." Temple took a bite out of the leftover spud.

Maśon plopped the last potato into the pot of water. "How do you know this?"

"She left a scroll detailing her misadventures," Temple said with his mouth full. "A confessional really. She wrote it before she left for battle just as Palomei would have done. Seems she made a deal with the other violet howlers on the island, promising the Su would be mended if they helped the humans win the war. What she didn't explained was why she started stealing Palomei's jewelry?"

"You have theories, of course."

Temple leaned over Maśon's shoulder with a smile, watching the water boil. "She wanted to be a part of Palomei. She wanted a piece of her like many people do with the rich and famous. Kind of like wanting a strand of Elvis' hair or Jody Foster's sweat socks."

Maśon screwed up his face.

"I do have a pair of Jodi Foster's sweat socks, matter of fact."

"You do?"

"Not really. I just lied." He grinned, and swallowed the last of Maśon' potato.

"So, if the army of howlers didn't deter the entire armada, what did?"

The hearts of the people inside Olonopo joined with one intention, one purpose, and the energy inside the crater swelled into a fearsome vortex that spun above the dome of the Great Round House in violet hues. And when it reached its peak of potency…

Like the suffering patient spread across a chiropractor's examining table, who suddenly snatches his breath after his spine is realigned with a crack, an underwater ridge that ran along the eastern sea floor...shifted.

And the sea drew in its frightful breath.

Loud screams from the violet howlers echoed through the jungles at the foothills of Hollow Mountain. Mice ran and chickens danced in the air, flapping their wings. Pigs rioted inside their pens, and snakes, lizards, and insects slithered upward into trees. And every palm on the beach shook its leafy head in one sweeping wave as the Spirit of Tahneyah joined forces.

Somewhere beneath the ocean floor, where a tectonic plate had buckled, the waves began to rise into a muscular surge of raw power. And then the waves began to roll, gathering force, speeding to the shore like a runaway freight train.

From high on the plateau rim of Olonopo, Boran watched as the dhows in the distance suddenly rose in the swell, tossing haphazardly. And the ocean in front of his people recoiled, leaving a far expanse of wet beach exposed.

There was a terrible calmness before the words were shouted.

"TSUNAMI! RUUUN!"

The conches were blown with the same two words repeated in code, until the blower tossed the shell aside, and hung over the rim, bellowing the same phrase in his own booming voice.

A hot wave ran through Loa'a's body. He yelled for the other husbands to hurry as the three raced through the jungle path thick with liana vine. Loa'a's legs pumped so fast the others lagged behind him. Kuhil tripped, and fell on a root of a strangler fig, and let out a deep grunt. Loa'a stopped, and ran back. He grabbed Kuhil's arm and yanked the older man to his feet, then dragged him down the trail. By the time the base of the crater came into view a multitude of bodies jockeyed for a way to squeeze up the stone staircase.

Loa'a jerked Kuhil away from the stairs to the steep slopes, and they scrambled on all fours up the sides, shouting for Jalok to hurry. But Jalok had stopped to help a woman who had fallen and was limping.

"GO!" Jalok shouted to the others.

The roar of rushing water strangled the air of all sound except for the creak and crashing of trees, and the screams behind them.

Kuhil kept slipping and sliding backward. Loa'a stopped and lowered his chest against the sheer incline offering his back to Kuhil. "Climb on!" he shouted. Kuhil grabbed Loa'a around the shoulders, and wrapped his legs around Loa'a's waist. The young man clambered upward, his hands and knees tearing on the sharp rock.

An explosion shook the trees, and desperate screams punctured the air. Kuhil glanced over his shoulder and saw Jalok and the lame woman trying to outrun a roiling wall of mud. He witnessed them disappear beneath the wave, all but Jalok's hand reaching upward into the air. The outstretched hand was carried in the currents around the basin to the north, and then disappeared. It was the last he saw of Jalok.

Kuhil braced himself for the impact. "Hurry!" he shouted, kicking his feet against Loa'a's sides.

The force of broken timber against Kuhil's back was so strong, the air was crushed out of him. He lost his grip on Loa'a and fell like a limp rag into the morass. Loa'a was smashed against the crater wall, his head thrust into the mud, his hand clawing the slippery slope. In the rising wave he felt Kuhil's weight fall from him, and a tangle of soft human limbs and sharp branches scrape against his frame, ripping his flesh, confusing his senses. He swallowed a mouthful of mud as his foot found something to brace against. He sprang upward out of the water, gasping for breath. But the sloshing wave and debris pummeled him again, and he tumbled beneath the mud without any way to control his movements. Just as easily as he had been forced beneath the mud, the wave jostled him upward, and spit him out. He choked on mud and air, found a firm handhold on something he could only identify as barbed and solid, and began pulling himself upward again, using only his hands to lift him.

Bodies pressed against the base of the crater mangled with broken trees. Bodies torn and naked. Bodies so caked in mud, sand, and blood their identities were lost.

Loa'a craned his neck upward toward the lip of the crater and open sky. Men attached to ropes decended like huge brown spiders. Excited cries urged survivors to either hang on or keep climbing. And one by one arms were extended, ropes tied around the survivors, and the rescuers hauled up their catches.

Loa'a clung to the muddy wall and kept his focus on the clear blue sky and white fluffy clouds coasting placidly overhead. A far-off peace overlaid the screams and cries. A thinner, clearer air and calm hazed over the stench of brackish water below.

Loa'a's hand began to slip, and the drifting clouds were quickly forgotten. His heartbeat became ragged, his breathing desperate. He forced himself to hold on tighter to wait his turn.

Soon he felt arms and a tugging at his body. And his torso grated against the side of Olonopo as he was pulled upward. He remained dazed, numb, his nerves having collided into a mass of rawness like the heaping, jangled quagmire below him.

CHAPTER SEVENTY-SEVEN

BROKEN LIGHT AND SHADOW PLAYS

*"What we find manifested is the consequence of
our thoughts and prayers. In spite of the powers
you think Losha and I possess, this has been a
collective consensual process, for we are all
equal."*

Temple Fox
The Makolese Scroll on
The Return of the Ka and the Mending of the Su #77

Three days had passed in horror from the shock of all the destruction
and death, but also wonderment for the courage and strength shown by
the Makolese people. For Losha and Temple, walking the top
perimeter of the Olonopo was a grim reminder of the power of thought
in a polarized world designed for catastrophe, a challenge to rise up to
compassion and understanding. Wounded survivors were still laid out
side by side, their broken limbs and injuries bound, their caretakers
speaking in quiet, encouraging tones. Most sat despondent, grieving,
shocked.

Losha and Temple spotted Tani and Winyon binding the wounds
of a young woman, when the injured woman stretched her arm out,
and called to Losha.

Leaving Temple, Losha strode over to the woman whose face was
swollen and blackened with bruises. She grabbed Losha's hand. "You
are our Queen. You should have made us stay. You should have used
the soldiers to drive us back."

Speechless, Losha squeezed the suffering woman's hand, and
nodded to her. She looked over at Tani, who glanced back with
guarded eyes, her lips pulled into a chevron, her eyes swollen with
fatigue and grief. Losha nodded again and backed away.

Seeing Losha's distress, Winyon stepped back to join her.

"Are you all right?" she asked.

Ignoring the question, Losha asked Winyon if anyone had seen Jabal and O'Juma yet.

"Sadly, no. But I will spin and search again today," Winyon said. She gave a shallow bow, then left.

Losha stood rigid. Temple moved closer and put his arm around her. "Are you okay?" Losha shrugged off the question with a sullen nod. He leaned near and whispered. "One of the guards said he saw large orange orbs rise out of Hollow Mountain and skip across the ocean last night. That's the third night in a row he's seen them." He handed her the obsidian magnifier.

"Do you have any idea what this means?" Losha asked.

"I have my suspicions. The creatures in the mountain are very curious."

"You mean the Mountain Gods," she said in a corrective tone.

Temple could feel his nerves on edge. "No, I meant creatures. I never really had the chance to tell you about my experience with them. They've been kidnapping your people."

Losha's jaw tightened. "I cannot possibly focus on that right now." She pulled away from him as a Scribe approached. Losha handed the Scribe the magnifier, and from the rim of the crater, Temple, Losha, and the Scribe took turns looking far out over the island. Trees had been ripped from their roots, shattered like matchsticks on the soggy earth. Unrecovered body parts still lay broken in tangled heaps of debris. Limp bodies, dead bodies, hung from trees. Hundreds of people were still combing the wreckage for the living. And Losha and Temple stood in deadly silence just as they had done three days before.

The Scribe winced in horror. Losha caught the look. "Our goal is to restore and preserve," Losha said bravely.

"Restore?" the Scribe said bitterly. "Preserve? You mean after we have destroyed. Is that not what you meant to say?"

The divinity shone sharply, confidently through the Swan's eyes, yet brimmed with human tears. "Yes, there was violence and destruction. What we did inside the crater was designed as an act of love, for the purposeful good, to preserve what is good to create a new vision of the world. Whatever has occurred has been in accordance with the prayers of all the people."

The Scribe's eyes narrowed with perplexity. "I do not understand."

Temple intervened. "It was done in concert with the will of our own desires. Whatever we find below today will be the results of both our fears and our love for the people and this island. For what we find manifested is the consequence of our thoughts and prayers. In spite of the powers you think Losha and I possess, this has been a collective consensual process, for we are all equal."

The Scribe shook her head in dismay. "Did you know this would happen?" She started scribbling with her brush on a scrap of mulberry paper.

"We did not," Losha answered. "We were told only to lay our appreciation for our people on the altar before the gods. Temple and I had a strong sense we would not have to engage in war. We chose to trust in the Divine."

The Scribe's brows knit together. She nodded, then wandered away without another word.

Losha flicked an eye of concern at Temple. "We should go out again to search for more survivors," she whispered.

The Scribe looked up in wonder as the two Teachers sang and spun themselves into whirlwinds of white light, then rose in their bird forms and flew off together. They circled once around the crater, the debris from broken trees piled together in huge mounds, creating twisted hillocks scattered against the sides of Olonopo. They headed east over the lower stretches of land laid waste, like some forgotten corpse with nearly a tree or plant to cover its stripped skin. They spotted no more survivors.

Losha tipped her wings and the two headed west, north of Olonopo, to the Queen's compound along the Ananba River that had swollen into a massive waterway. In the distance, on a rise of land, sat the mammoth stone compound, its outer fortress wall still intact, and its interior filled with islanders helping the wounded. The two circled around and around, but saw nothing moving but the breeze that stirred surviving trees.

Temple gave out a signal cry and the two headed toward the mountain. A thermal breeze lifted them high enough to spy the northeastern side of Hollow Mountain where shattered fishing boats were crushed on top of each other in heaps. They soared further north where the sea met walls of rock. The tsunami had chiseled huge basalt slabs from the cliff faces, leaving craggy turrets and battlements behind, the ocean littered with megalithic rubble.

From the mountain, the Owl and the Swan soared in a figure eight formation over what remained of the southeastern beaches. Nothing remained of Tani's old hut, but the central pillar of stone with the old Grandmother banyan tree still standing, surrounded by mounds of broken bamboo stalks.

Losha let out several grunts, and the two looped around and headed further inland.

The Common House, and the huts from all four villages had been torn from their foundations and pushed into ruinous heaps that rested hundreds of yards from their original sites. Rescuers pulled out dead bodies, while greedy seagulls and birds of prey circled round to pick off pieces from the new carrion.

Temple let out an alarming shriek.

Losha coasted closer to the Owl to signify she shared his horror, then circled around once. Without knowing why, Temple watched as Losha soared in the opposite direction to Black Beach Cove, and flapped his wings hard to catch up to her.

When they made it back to the far northeast of the island, they dipped low over what had once been jungle rising to brushy knolls, now stripped of their vegetation. Beyond, standing bare in the wet wind, a new hill had been formed from an avalanche of mud. It blocked their vision so they sailed over it.

Losha cried out when she spied a ring of black sand holding back a dam of seawater. Whole stands of uprooted acrocomia palms floated in the new lake like corpses.

Temple tilted his wings to descend, but noticed Losha's flying had become erratic. He banked around to chase after her as she circled around the new dam once, then sailed to find more solid land.

Everywhere Losha looked the beaches had been washed into the sea, and the coast was scalloped with new coves. The two flew lower still. Strewn below were broken pilings from vanished huts, piers, and the bones of men, and beams of dhows and dugouts twisted like loose teeth in a dead man's jaw.

Losha was the first to draw a circle on the beach and change into her woman-form.

Temple spotted the lone figure sitting on the broken boom of a dhow mast, recognizing it was the woman who sat there, and not the goddess or queen. He landed in front of her on the sandy loam, his eyes locked onto a stalk of broken bone – possibly human, he couldn't tell – standing upright on the sea-swept beach.

"The Scribe was right," Losha muttered, still gazing downward at the bone as Temple completed his transformation. "Everything is destroyed."

Temple spoke softly, trying to justify the destruction he saw all around, now that he had seen it close up yet again. "But it had to happen."

Her tone was sharp. "Did it? Explain that to the wives whose husbands lay before me now in tatters." There was a burning in her breast. "Explain it to their children." Her voice cracked.

Temple climbed up to the broken boom and sat down by her side. He encircled her in his arms.

"Great Gods and Goddesses, I never wanted this. I did not want violence," she cried.

Mindful of Losha's pain, he held her gently. "This violence was not your fault. There's no fault in this, my little pigeon. Believe me. They made their own choices."

Losha's head snapped up. "They chose to die?"

"Losha, they are all heroes. They chose to sacrifice their lives for their people. Please just honor them."

"But they never had to die. The storm dealt with the Slavers. But our people sacrificed their lives for nothing." Losha looked at her lover with swollen eyes and his heart began to break. Temple couldn't hold his tears back any longer, and the two wept together in each other's arms, until time passed and the sun rolled overhead.

"The storm was an answer to our prayers…but at such a price," she finally said with a sniffle. "Now all is wiped clean and we can rebuild on a new foundation."

Temple dried his face with his large hands. He stood very still for a long moment. "You know...there's something in all of this." He paused, his mind moving somewhere beyond his immediate surroundings. "It reminds me of something that happened in English history when a huge Spanish armada was about to invade England. They were defeated by a storm. If it wasn't for that storm England would have suffered under the Inquisition." His gaze grew softer. "This will happen again...only on a much grander scale...when we're on the brink of a global invasion by the shadows of our own creation. The entire planet," he said in a breathy whisper.

"Another prophecy?" she asked, her voice as quiet as his.

"The most important one."

"When?" she asked.

"In our lifetime...if we live to be as old as Tani."

Losha pulled her bushy hair off her face. "But some of the destruction can be avoided. I feel it in my soul. But it will take masses of people worldwide to first change what is in their hearts and minds."

"It'll be their hardest lesson. But they bloody well will have to try or..." He looked at her with the kind of intensity that could kindle into panic. "Or the whole universe will fall into peril."

His eyes dimmed with a sudden weariness as he thought about the destruction before him, and the even greater destruction he was certain he foresaw in the future. "Aren't you tired of this endless drama? Especially the conflict and pain we instigate in others?"

"You mean, even if it is their unconscious choice to be experiencing it?" she asked.

"Yes. And yet I know humanity often draws what they don't want for themselves so they can know and appreciate what they do want." He breathed a heavy sigh. "Find me something, *something* beautiful to light my eyes on to give me a reason to go on. Just one thing, please."

Losha lifted his hand and kissed it, and he felt a warm tingle fill his being. Undramatic and simple as the gesture was, the beach took on a sudden diffused glow that blinded him for a second. When his vision cleared, he saw that the ship beams had disappeared. Gone were the splintered bone and the rubble that had been tossed in heaps on the battered cove. In its place was a new island, a garden of great beauty filled with tropical flowers and fruit trees laden with their luscious bounty. A warm breeze carried the sweet scent of jungle blossoms. He smiled knowingly with new tears in his eyes, then laughed out loud. "Gazing upon your beautiful face would've been enough for me, magical woman."

No sooner had he spoken these words and the vision before him vanished in a flash.

"Well, you didn't need to be so abrupt about it," he snorted, knowing he had just learned yet another valuable lesson about the power of thought.

"You did it, not me, you silly god-man." Losha laughed even louder, and the two felt the joy of mutual discovery and understanding.

Temple eyed the torn beach once more, the ideal having vanished. He felt a rugged kind of peace and saw beauty for things that had been wiped cleaned and primed for new beginnings, when above their heads he heard a thrumming sound.

A tiny ruby-throated hummingbird danced around their heads.

Losha looked up in wonder. "Winyon?"

The bird hovered in front of Losha's face. It pivoted in midair over to Temple, then darted off.

Winyon returned fluttering her wings madly. She rocketed off again, until she stopped abruptly, hovering, as if she was waiting for them.

"Do you want us to follow?" Losha asked.

The bird responded by flying circles around Losha's head, then shot up into the sky again. Losha and Temple sang their invocations to change rapidly into their bird forms to chase Winyon. When they had caught up, Winyon was headed for the southern coast.

Losha trumpeted loudly. Below she spied what once was the Snake River. The landscape was dotted by leaf-stripped cypress, their tops sticking out of the sea. Tagheetu's swamp, Mefakani's holy ground, had been transformed into ocean bottom, and all traces of the Shaman's compound had been swept away. In its place were tidal mud flats, Makol's new contour to the south.

Little remained of the southern coast except higher ground, and the places where the mangroves proved the hardiest by trapping sediment among their roots.

Winyon dropped lower, and Losha and Temple descended rapidly.

Temple let out a piercing shriek when he spotted two figures, one standing on the rock roof of the great library, waving frantically. It was O'Juma! The other figure lay on the roof beside him. It was Jabal!

CHAPTER SEVENTY-EIGHT

HEROES

"What kind of life would we have without the history of our past and our prophecies to guide us into the future?"

O'Juma, the Lesser Apprentice
The Makolese Scroll on
The Return of the Ka and the Mending of the Su #78

The island was shrouded in a pall of smoke, even after three weeks had passed since the last funeral pyre had been lit. Funeral pyres had been used before, after other tsunamis hit the island. They proved to be the most expedient way to deal with so many corpses since few boats were left undamaged for any proper funeral rite. Now throngs of people meandered on the beach from one pile of rubble to another, salvaging what they could, and burning what little was left.

Loa'a, whose face was still slightly bruised and swollen, labored by Owane's side. They had put the finishing touches on a staircase that led up to the newly built Common House when they spotted O'Juma in the distance. Both abandoned their work and gave the boy a steep bow.

O'Juma nodded and returned the gesture. He lifted an armful of splintered wood and sauntered back to a small campfire where a private meeting was being held with Temple, Losha, Winyon, Elder Tani, and Jabal huddled close in conversation.

Tani's forehead drew into a maze of wrinkles. "Not one body from the Slavers was ever found? " she asked.

"Several of the guards and many others saw large spheres of light come from the mountain at night. I saw them too," Temple said.

"Many of our own people have not been found. Surely they were lost to the sea forever, but perhaps..." Tani cut her comment short when O'Juma dropped his load to the ground. They smiled at him, gesturing for him to join them. "Does E-lon-e' know?"

"Tai," Losha said. "She is greatly disturbed by this, too."

Jabal began to feed the debris into the fire just as the Administrator arrived.

Losha studied Temple as his eyes roamed from E-lon-e''s dark eyes to her breasts, hidden beneath her silk dress, and back to her ravishing face which was framed by her hair loosely tied back.

Tani detected the slightest hint of a smirk on Losha's face when the Administrator bowed to Temple first, then to Losha, and everyone else at the campfire, one by one.

Everyone stared as E-lon-e' smoothed out her silk dress with a graceful sweep of her hand. She sat in the circle, pulling her legs to the side.

"I find it remarkable that you manage to remain so tidy when everyone else is such a mess," Losha stated, as she pulled back her wild tangle of bushy hair self-consciously. She watched Temple's eyes wander up and down E-lon-e''s torso again, and rolled her eyes at Tani. The old woman winked back.

Forgetting the Administrator was a vegetarian, Losha placed a steaming fillet of rock cod onto a woven mat and handed it to E-lon-e'.

"I am fasting," she said politely, declining the offer with a slight wave of her hand. "Again, please accept my apologies for taking so long to have a proper meeting with you all."

"Understandable under the circumstances," Losha said as her untamable hair fell into her eyes.

E-lon-e''s eyes flickered back and forth between the two boys in front of her, settling her final gaze onto Jabal. "I heard about your illness and injuries. I am happy you are well enough to finally meet with me. And so your illness was the reason you did not come to Olonopo Crater?" E-lon-e' asked Jabal.

Jabal nodded. "My fever had finally broken, and my ribs were healing well thanks to the kumbabs O'Juma had made for me." He grinned at his companion. "Imagine such healing skill from a Lesser Apprentice?"

O'Juma looked askance at Jabal. "Tai, but if Elder Tani had not told me to return to the Shaman's compound, you would have surely died, my friend."

"So, Elder Tani, and this 'Lesser' Apprentice, you so mistakeningly call him, saved your life," E-lon-e' said with arched eyebrows.

Jabal let out a hardy laugh. "I am humbled," he said. He lowered his head to pay homage to Tani first, and then, his lover, O'Juma. He addressed the Administrator again. "When we heard the call to gather inside Olonopo Crater, O'Juma told Tiv and the others to take as much medicine as they could carry to the Great Round House. I was still too ill to be moved. Later, when we heard the conches blown, warning us about the tsunami, O'Juma had to carry me. We made it as far as the libraries. The water rose too fast, so he carried me to the roof of the History Library, where we became trapped. O'Juma did what he had to. I could not even help him."

The Administrator peered at O'Juma, perplexed. "All nine hundred Prophecy Scrolls?" she asked.

A subtle smile crept across O'Juma face. "Tai, and all of the History Scroll as well."

"But there are thousands of those. You saved them all from the flood and risked your life!"

O'Juma gave a modest nod. "What kind of life would we have without the history of our past and our prophecies to guide us into the future?"

"But how did you manage to do this?" E-lon-e' asked.

"All I did was divert the water. The libraries sit on top of a huge cavern," he explained. "It is taboo to go down there, and has been blocked by stone for as long as I can remember."

"Tai, a long, long time," Tani nodded.

"The water rose steadily," he said. "I knew the libraries would soon be destroyed. I noticed that a tree had grown from the pile of boulders that blocked the entrance to the cavern. There must have been a gap between the tree and the boulder because I saw water siphoning off below. The floodwaters started to sluice the soil away beneath that tree and some boulders, and the ground began to crumble. I jumped onto the tree and rocked it back and forth, until it toppled over, loosening the soil so the boulders would dislodge on their own." He grinned. "With the help of the gods and a little muscle, the boulders fell free and pulled other rocks with it. A huge opening appeared, and floodwaters poured into the cavern. The height of the floodwaters lowered just enough to keep them away from any of our precious scrolls."

"I know that whole area is honeycombed with caverns just like Hollow Mountain," Temple said. "That cavern must be absolutely enormous."

"Everyone cannot thank you enough," E-lon-e' said, and she bowed from where she sat.

"Believe me, what I did pales in comparison to something of even greater importance," O'Juma said. He turned to his companion. "Go ahead, Jabal. Tell them."

Every eye turned back to Jabal.

"Tai, everything seems to happen for a reason," Jabal said. "The week before, when I was deep within the tunnels that led to the Mother Stone, I had an unfortunate encounter with a very large and hideous cave spider."

"Tai, I remember," Winyon said. She ran her hand down the length of her silver hair, remembering the sticky webs that had once gotten tangled in her feathers. "I had gotten caught in its web. Jabal saved my life by eating the spider!"

E-lon-e' leaned closer.

"Small lizards my size can barely handle their poison. I did manage to regurgitate quite a lot of it. But when I spun back into my human form, I had no chance of digesting all of the toxins. Not only had my wounds become infected from falling off the bamboo bridge, but I was on the verge of death from the spider's venom. That is when the Mother Stone spoke to me."

E-lon-e' tilted her head to one side. "Do you think you were hallucinating from the poison?"

Jabal shook his head. "I am a Shaman's Apprentice. I can tell the difference."

"What did she say, Jabal?"

"The Mother Stone told me that after Temple and Losha mend the Su, they must go to the cavern that lies beneath the library which holds the history scrolls. A passageway there will lead them to the Mother Stone." He looked at the two Teachers. "She wishes to meet with the two of you."

E-lon-e' clasped her hands together in delight. "Then it was fortuitous that O'Juma opened the entrance to that cavern below the libraries. Providence moves in."

"Tai," Losha said. "The Mother Stone must have known the tsunami was coming days before it happened, and would wipe out the Shaman's compound, and the only known passageways that lead to her." Her face turned grim. "I only wish I had known about the tsunami ahead of time." She glanced at Temple.

"Stop blaming yourself," he said softly. "Obviously, we weren't meant to know."

"Now the passageway is completely under water," Jabal said. "The Mother Stone must have known what would happen or she would not have warned me of the dangers of passing through the cavern. After that, I must have passed out.”

“What kind of danger?” E-lon-e' asked.

Jabal shrugged. “I have no idea.”

Sensing the vibration around Tani had spasmed like a wounded bird, Losha turned to Tani. “Tani, do you know anything about this?”

Tani visibly shivered. “That is where the Nagawa people once dwelled.”

“Who in the bloody blazes is the Nagawa People?” Temple asked.

“The same clan Naweze Ka-Seipa came from.”

A dark cloud fell over Temple as if he had been covered by the smoke of a funeral pyre. He coughed to recover from the news. “My past life has come back to haunt me once again. Naweze Ka-Seipa was the one who made people worship me as Gadji by going through Lord Tagheetu, using himself as a power broker.” He scratched his beard in thought. “The entrance to the cavern above the libraries may be open now, but it’s flooded,” he pointed out.

“But that is no problem for a water bird like me,” Losha chimed in.

“True. And I can see well in the dark,” Temple added.

“Then we will go,” she insisted.

“There was something else the Mother Stone told me,” Jabal continued.

Losha and Temple cocked their heads in his direction.

“The Mother Stone said the Su must be mended when the moon ripens three times from now.”

A reverent silence fell over everyone, and the energy quickly lifted to one of hope and pure joy.

Losha pursed her lips, her eye aimed at Temple.

Temple grinned back with mock annoyance. “So, I am being conned into doing that mumbo-jumbo ritual dance the creatures in the mountain taught me, aren’t I?”

“You mean the Mountain Gods,” she said, smirking at Temple. She took a handful of her untamable hair and tossed it over her bare shoulder. “There is great power in the dance, as you know.”

He smiled back with a twinkle in his eyes. “Well, I’ve already had my first dance lesson.” He leaned over and kissed Losha tenderly. “I guess I just committed myself to staying on Makol and to being your Husband.”

“First Husband,” she corrected with a mischievous grin. “I still have to pick four more.”

“How could I forget.” He sighed with a wince.

Everyone laughed. And the couple sat together for quite awhile surrounded by their closest friends, savoring the island of calm in which they were enveloped, in spite of their surroundings...and particularly because of it.

CHAPTER SEVENTY-NINE

THE MENDING OF THE SU

NEW WATERS

Circumvent the new pond
clockwise three times
and you will hear
the bullfrogs return,
giving their throaty call,
beating the time out
with measured grunts.
See the cloak of time
slip from the mirrored surface,
quivering slightly
with the breath of change?
Like the last exhalation,
new breezes rush in
clean as the first breath
of morning air,
clearing the moist opal fog
of forgetfulness,
spiraling softly,
embracing the trees
that hold up the stars
as the stars hold up the trees.
Roots reaching the Source,
drinking Her in freely.
And the big black Snake,
snapping saplings in its wake
winds through the forest,

stopping to rest
and test the curve of new space
at the water's edge
before it curls 'round the pond of stars
head to tail,
to hold the next illusion.

Elo Tivluk, popular Makolese poet
The Makolese Scroll on
The Return of the Ka and the Mending of the Su #79

Losha lay naked and at ease in the torn moonlit glade. Tani, Winyon, and E-lon-e' rubbed the last of the scented oil into her dark skin, making it shine. Joking and laughing, they lifted their Queen to her feet, and wrapped her in her wedding skirt woven from fine white silk, bejeweled with shells, pearls, and feathers. They hung a wreath of pink flowers around her neck. There was a rise of giggles when out of the darkness Jabal appeared on all fours, head held down in supplication.

Before Losha could issue a gentle rebuke, Jabal raised his head. His tone was somber. "Forgive me, Most Respected. I do not come to disturb the great Swan. May I have a word with you?"

Losha nodded.

Jabal's voice grew even more grave as he stood up. "I have searched high and low for a suitable orchid for you, and yet no blossom has survived the tsunami except for this single bulb." He held it up between his forefinger and thumb. "I got it from Arma. She said you might remember her."

Jabal's youthful disappointment was quickly dismantled with Losha's warm smile. She held out her hand, and Jabal placed the tiny bulb in her palm. She closed her eyes, and went into a distant, open space inside herself. The air around her dark brown skin cast off a shimmering glow, and in her open palm the bulb began to quiver. In moments, tiny green leaves burst their tender casing, and tendrils appeared. She placed her other hand over the shoot and the glow around her intensified, illuminating the broken glade.

When night had once again reclaimed the new Queen, and Jabal's vision had readjusted to the moonlight, she stood before him with a pink orchid blossom in her hand.

"Thank you," she whispered dreamily. She tucked the blossom into her pink sash. As she moved to leave, she caught the boy crouched in a half-bow. "Greater things you will do than this small thing I have just done," she said. "And when you do – remember this, Jabal. What is sometimes bewildering is that the ability to connect with the Divine is not exclusive to the gifted, and yet it is often the gifted who must deliver this message first. The ideal is for everyone to become 'The Chosen.' We become awakened first, and then we help to wake the others. You see we are all equal. We are all gods in human embodiments. So, honor me, but resist placing yourself above or below others, Jabal. It is not the Way."

"I will remember, Most Respected," he whispered. Seeing that the Swan had entered a trance, Jabal bowed, then raced back into the black forest.

On a bleak and barren hill that rose beside the clearing, the only soul not participating in the ritual mending moved her brush quickly across the fine barkpaper, recording all that she was witnessing.

The Scribe watched with a keen eye as Losha moved through the tattered jungle into the ritual circle, the air filled with scented oil, wood smoke, and the mystical music of flute and drum. Brightly colored beads and swan feathers were braided into the Queen's hair, and her hips swayed with the grace of a swaying palm. Her silk skirt, sewn with the plumes of white swans, strands of cowrie shells, and pearls, invoked air and ocean, rattling and clinking with the music. Her torso undulated sinuously, mimicking the movement of water birds and ocean waves as she circled to the left of the central fire. And while she performed the ancient dance, Jabal, Tiv, and Winyon beat out a quicker rhythm on hollowed logs to make ready for Losha's groom.

It was Losha and Temple's marriage day, the day the Su would be mended.

Although she was in a light trance of her own, Tani recalled how the islanders had made pilgrimages to the Hollow Mountain to pray for their own fertility, and for the success of the great dance to restore the barren island. But no one, except Tani and Temple, retained any slices of memory of the Mountain God's tiny probing fingers, or the cold hard laboratory tables.

Now the old Healer, and the Scribe, watched as twelve chosen women circled around their new Queen with the beat of the drums growing louder. They rolled their sensual hips in unison, deepening their own trances. Beyond them, a circle of twelve men, naked and proud, feet imitating the blood-filled beat, moved in a counter-clockwise circle around the twelve women and their Queen.

Surrounding them all in hugh concentric circles danced the people. And at the far reaches of the vast ritual circle, musicians played drums, flutes, delicate chimes, bells, shrill whistles, and enormous gongs. As they played, tiny orbs of light appeared above their heads.

Behind the musicians, hidden in the shadows of battered trees, swayed a multitude of violet howlers…with one notable howler rocking to the rhythm. She wore a strand of pearls.

Temple entered the circle deep in trance. His clean-shaven face was marked with the spiral from Losha's clan. All he wore were owl feathers in his braided hair, the heavy scent of musk, and a loincloth made from a large leaf. Temple's foot movements matched the heartbeat of the Earth, and his arms undulated with the motion of the Wind, becoming the Wind. And the rhythm of the drums quickened as the musicians played with their eyes rolled back, focusing only on the Divine.

The groom slipped into the ring of musicians and made them all his partner for a round, knowing well that the tiny spheres of light that spiraled about each of them now were the Nature Spirits of the jungle, who joined the sacred dance. And the Spirits moved with joy, knowing that the people's restored Ka would once again connect each with the other.

Temple advanced, his movements flowing. He danced in perfect synchronization to the beating of the men's hearts in the inner circle, attuned to the Spirit Which Moves In All Things. He danced with the men until he knew them, knew their pulse and their purpose. And then he danced on, weaving his way in and out through the circle of women, moving against the tide of their clockwise motion as they danced ever faster around their new Queen. And when his energies had mingled with every soul, forming a tightly woven web of light, he joined his shining bride.

For the first time in twelve thousand seasons, the Su wedding song was invoked in the ancient tongue. Losha's rich voice rang out and she sang sweetly as she swayed.

"My vulva is full of eagerness like the young moon.

My untilled land lies fallow.

Who will plow my vulva, my high field, my wet ground?

And who will fish the waters of my womb?"

"I will," sang Temple, the deep timbre of his voice resonating in the thick air. "I will bring you honey."

"You will water my womb," she sang in response. "You are the honey that sweetens my breast."

Losha took the orchid blossom from her sash, and tucked it behind Temple's ear while he sang:

"My Best Beloved Swan, Hianna,
your breath is the scent of blossoms
carried by the eastern breeze.
Your hair is the windblown jungle.
Your breasts, the twin peaked mountain.
Your womb - the sea.
Let honey flow from me to you
to sweeten your own.
And let the fish pour forth from you,
and I will drink and eat."

Losha took Temple's hands and placed them on her hips.

"Make yourself thick and sweet, Gadji.
And I will quiver and shine for you.
I will pour forth the sweetest honey into your hungry mouth.
I will let an abundance of fish swim in your tangled hair,
so you may catch them at your leisure.
And the jungle will overflow with abundance
and make the people glad."

At a signal beat from O'Juma, those in the inner circles who were still deeply entranced broke from their circles, and paired off with one another into couples.

Tani watched carefully, her own trance still intact. She noticed the quiet flickering of lights from the Nature Spirits, and smiled when each of the women chose her male partner. Aching to participate in the ritual, but knowing she couldn't, she reminisced about old Okon and his tender embrace, how he cooed back with pleasure. She smiled.

Temple's body pulsated with heat and the rhythm of the beat as he sang the last of his song.

"I will serve you and the people
and the Spirits of All Life.
In Queenship, I am your Advisor.
In Council, I am your Advocate.
In Love, I am your Consort.
In all Conflict, I am your Shield."

Losha sank to the ground next to the central fire, and pulled her lover down with her. The women followed suit with their partners. And there the new Queen and her First Husband sat entwined in sacred embrace, face to face with their legs wrapped around each other, eyes cast only on the light within the other. And their vital Ka energies spiraled up their spines and out through their hearts, becoming one with the other.

★　　★　　★　　★　　★　　★

The Scribe paused. The wet fertile voice of thunder drummed overhead. Her hands shook as she dipped her brush into her ink pot. The ink pot tipped over onto the ground, and it began to rain. The script ran and smeared in the fine mizzle, causing the Scribe to fuss and fumble until she picked up her ink pot and brush again. But try as she might she was not allowed to record the sight before her.

The wedding couple levitated a foot off the ground, legs still wrapped around each other in tantric splendor, eyes gazing deeply into the eyes of the other, minds lost in the Divine.

A warm pulsating wave fell over the Scribe and electrified all her cells. She understood what it was; knew the balm for the aching soul; the keys to her prison rattling against the cage of her heart.

Feel It. Know It, it seemed to whisper to her.

The brush dropped from her stopped hand, and along with it her thoughts lay pooled in a heap before her like her script. And like the others, the Scribe and the world became one in love.

The man-god…consort…the cosmic recruit, and the goddess-woman…renegade bride, and queen, lifted higher through the spark and drizzle. A wave of white light rippled out across the island, and the air became a field of diamonds. Buds suddenly burst on limbs, new life unfolded into green leaf, and the jungle teemed with the vibrancy of bird song and fresh rain. And the couple's bodies burned brighter still as their spirits rose like twin stars into the Heavens, and vanished into the night.

EPILOGUE

CHAPTER EIGHTY

THE POET

THE SINGER
"Radiant messenger of sacred song,
you have become the Wind.
I hear your songs
cradled in the swaying boughs
of the mighty pine,
high in the hill
and mountain country,
sweeping the valleys
like a hand of hope.
We feel them
tugging at us
like a needy child
begging to be noticed.

Thank you
for keeping your light bright
as we dream our dream awake."

Elo-Tivluc, popular Makolese poet
The Makolese Scroll on
The Return of the Ka and the Mending of the Su #80

Maśon bowed over the writing table on his lap, his legs uncomfortably crossed. He put the tablet aside, and pressed his hands together prayerfully. "Bravo!"

Temple got up and took an exaggerated bow.

"A great ending for the second book," Maśon said. "Thank you, Temple. I will end this scroll right here." He hit the save command on his glowing tablet, and started to tidy up the sheaves of barkcloth that surrounded him on the ground when he stopped to stare into the fire.

"You okay?" Temple asked.

Maśon frowned. "There are a lot of loose ends. I have a thousand questions. I don't know why, but one tugs at me the most. What happened to Tiv?"

"Oh, Tiv. Well… I thought you knew his story better than me."

Maśon raised his eyebrows in surprise. "Me?"

"Why yes," Temple said.

"I haven't a clue."

"Okay then." Temple tossed another log into the woodstove and settled back on his chair. He gestured for Maśon to grab either his tablet, or his ink brush, and a fresh piece of barkcloth.

"When Tiv was heading to the crater with baskets filled with medicines, he encountered a girl along the trail. She shared his load, and they talked for awhile. Although his words came out awkwardly, he realized the more he conversed, the better he could think and speak.

"Once Tiv and the girl made it to Olonopo, he spent time with her. She helped him dispense some remedies. They got to know each other pretty well."

"And they fell in love," Maśon interrupted with a smirk.

"Exactly." Temple smiled. "Tiv had found his first girlfriend."

Maśon nodded back unimpressed. "And the girl found her first boyfriend."

"Yes. Tiv found Galana, and Galana found Tiv."

Maśon dropped his brush, smearing everything he had just written, and looked up at Temple in shock.

Temple cocked his head. "You didn't know?"

Maśon's cupped his mouth in shock. "Galana was my Grandmother."

"But of course she was," Temple said.

Maśon puffed out his cheek, his head reeling. "Tiv was my Grandfather?"

"You didn't know that as a boy his nickname was 'Tiv'?"

Maśon shook his head, stunned.

"You knew you were a direct descendant to Makol's finest singer and mystic poet, Elo-Tivluk."

"Well, of course I did. It was my Grandfather's writings that got me interested in writing your biography in the first place."

"And you knew your Grandmother, Galana, became a well-known healer and scribe. What you might not have known is that her skills as a healer and her great patience helped Tiv to heal more completely. But you never knew Elo-Tivluk was Tiv?"

"I thought Tiv was just an imbecile."

Temple gave the Scribe a penetrating mischievous look that could melt stone. "Now you know otherwise. And now you have just learned that nothing...*nothing* in this world is incurable."

Mason narrowed his eyes on Temple. "Wait a minute! You knew all along that I didn't know!"

Temple's grin widened into a broad toothy smile. He shrugged his shoulders. "Maybe I did. Maybe I didn't. Do you believe anything can be healed now?"

Mason fidgeted on the ground, reluctant to admit what he now understood. "Yes! YES!"

Without a hint of warning, Temple bolted to his feet, collected his cape, and threw it around him as he ran to the door. "Quick! Get up! We need to leave immediately!" He opened the door, rushed out, and slammed the door behind him before Mason had a chance to move.

Mason sat immobilized for a second. When he came to his senses, he leaped up and ran to the door. He jerked the door open and raced outside. The cold air slapped him hard, and his cheeks turned pink. The woods were laden with a fresh mantle of pristine snow. He looked around him in all directions. There were no footprints in the snow. He sprinted around the perimeter of his hut, but there were no signs of Temple. He stood silent and still, watching his breath swirl in the air in cloudy patches.

Mason wandered back inside the cabin and sat down on his warm blanket. It was then that he noticed the pain in his left knee had completely vanished. His eyes filled with tears. "Fooled again. Wherever you are, Temple Fox, thank you. Thank you, dear friend."

Mason wasn't sure, but he thought he heard the faint sound of laughter.

*** END OF BOOK II ***

AUTHOR'S NOTE

The pages of "Book One: The Education of Temple Fox," have long since yellowed during the writing of "Book Two," and most of "Book Three." Earning a living selling rocks, minerals, and fossils almost feels like an interruption in my quest to finish the series. In "The Return of the Ka and the Mending of the Su" I went to places I didn't want to go to. Tackling issues, like how to prevent civil war, almost tackled me, but made me play them out in my mind to find real, energetic solutions.

There is always the itch to entertain. But on deeper levels I yearn to serve a greater purpose by stimulating thought and possibly action in others that will serve a higher good. I pray I have accomplished this.

Patricia S. Christy
September 27, 2016

★　　★　　★　　★　　★　　★

PATRICIA S. CHRISTY was born in Baltimore, Maryland with a silver spoon in her mouth, which tarnished beyond recognition by age six, and was hocked for rent money by age twenty-one. At age fifteen she began to *wake up*. It was from that point on that she knowingly interacted with those in the invisible realms. It would be accurate to say that she is a resident on this Earthly plane, but also resides in other places beyond fractured, focused Time. Call her a traveler, but one whose passport has been temporarily confiscated.

CHRISTY lives with her partner and two cats in Black Mountain, North Carolina.